Praise for *Josiah's Treasure*

"*A wonderful historical romance! Nancy Herriman is a talented author.*"

–4 STARS, RT BOOK REVIEWS

"*From her stunning 1830s London debut* Irish Healer *to her haunting new San Francisco historical* Josiah's Treasure, *Nancy Herriman is quickly establishing herself as a name to watch—and devour—in Christian fiction.*"

–JULIE LESSMAN, AUTHOR OF THE DAUGHTERS OF BOSTON SERIES AND THE WINDS OF CHANGE SERIES

"*Vividly drawn. . . .* Josiah's Treasure *is an engaging and lively tale, populated with layered characters, blossoming romance and a suspenseful air, confirming Herriman's talent with the written word. Romance readers rejoice!*"

–RELZ REVIEWZ

"*A sweet story about finding love in unlikely places.*"

–CBA RETAILERS + RESOURCES

Previous praise for Nancy Herriman's *The Irish Healer*

"Vivid characters, tender romance and enduring themes . . . a perfect read."

–Margaret Brownley, *New York Times* best-selling author

"The Irish Healer *is a wonderful debut novel. . . . I'll be watching for more books from Herriman."*

–Robin Lee Hatcher, best-selling and award-winning author

"Debut author Herriman . . . knows how to engage readers to win their hearts."

–4 stars, RT Book Reviews

"A lovely period tale of personal transformation and abiding love."

–USA Today Book Blog Review

"The Irish Healer *holds plenty of promise of an enduring career for the talented Nancy Herriman."*

–Relz Reviewz

NANCY HERRIMAN

Published by Worthy Publishing, a division of Worthy Media, Inc., 134 Franklin Road, Suite 200, Brentwood, Tennessee 37027.

Helping people experience the heart of God

eBook available at worthypublishing.com

Audio distributed through Brilliance Audio; visit brillianceaudio.com

Library of Congress Control Number: 2012956460

Scripture quotations marked (KJV) are taken from the King James Version.

For foreign and subsidiary rights, contact Riggins International Services Inc.; rigginsrights.com

Published in association with Natasha Kern Literary Agency.

ISBN: 978-1-61795-479-6 (trade paper)

Cover Design: Kent Jenson, Knail, LLC; knail.com

Cover Photo of Woman: Steve Gardner, PixelWorks Studios; shootpw.com

Interior Design and Typesetting: Cindy Kiple

Printed in the United States of America

13 14 15 16 17 QGFF 8 7 6 5 4 3 2 1

To the nurses at COHA–

you were a blessing to me at a time of great need.

This book is dedicated to you all.

Lay not up for yourselves treasures upon earth, where moth and rust doth corrupt, and where thieves break through and steal: but lay up for yourselves treasures in heaven . . . for where your treasure is, there will your heart be also.

—Matthew 6:19–21 (KJV)

San Francisco, California
June 1882

"IN THIS TOWN, SARAH JANE, *a man's worth is calculated in dollars and cents. Measured by what he has to show for himself . . .*"

Sarah Whittier clasped her hat against the stiff summer wind and stared up at the four-story building on Montgomery Street, the soaring stone facade and row upon row of arched windows impressive, daunting. Worth a great deal of dollars and cents—a concrete manifestation of Josiah Cady's oft-repeated saying. Sarah refused, however, to be intimidated by the carved limestone and the windows reflecting the fog-laced California sky. Even though, before Josiah left her a house and a chance, she had once been worth not much more than a plugged nickel.

Sarah sucked in a breath, as deep as her corset would allow, and returned her gaze to the real estate agency's front door, housed smack-dab in the middle of the courses of gleaming stone. This morning marked the third time she'd come by. Mr. Pomroy would be unhappy to see her again, but she had to secure the lease on the Sansome Street storefront. It was the perfect space for her design studio, and she had promised the girls she would get that lease no matter what. For them, she would work until she dropped and defy the most stubborn man she'd met in California. Opening the shop so each of the girls could have a real chance at a decent future had become her mission. Her sole purpose: to take care of them. They were her family now, after the one she'd been born into had tossed her onto the street.

Mistakes—her terrible mistakes—had proven awfully hard to forgive.

"You goin' in?" A man from the adjacent business, an insurance agency, had come on to the sidewalk to smirk at her. "Or you just gonna stand there and stare at the front door?"

Sarah gave him a tight-lipped smile. "I am going in." *Not that it is any of your business what I do.*

His smirk broadened. "I've found applying your hand to the doorknob helps."

"Thanks ever so much."

The glass in the door rattled when she closed it firmly behind her, drawing a scowl from one of the clerks occupying the front office of Pomroy Real Estate Associates.

"Miss Whittier." He squinted, his long nose crinkling. "Come to see Mr. Pomroy again?"

The low hum of male voices swelled and chair casters squealed as the men turned to stare, abandoning any pretense of working. Cigarettes smoldered forgotten in fingers; fountain pens halted mid-sentence; ledger pages ceased being flipped. The sandy-blond fellow perched on a stool near the tall windows—if she continued to come here daily, she'd probably learn his name and everyone else's—elbowed the man seated at his left. They guffawed loud enough for Sarah to hear. She ignored them.

"I have an eleven o'clock appointment," she said.

The clerk with the long nose consulted the logbook atop his desk. "Somehow, you do."

"Miss Whittier." Ambrose Pomroy's voice boomed. He strode through the crowded real estate office, weaving his way between the cluttered desks arrayed like rows of produce wagons at a country market, jostling for prime space. "Here you are once more."

He made her arrival sound like a visitation of the plague.

"I've secured a loan from Mr. Theodore Samuelson. For five hundred dollars." She showed him the note from Lottie's father that had delivered the news. Charlotte Samuelson—excellent business partner, better friend—had come through as promised. "And more importantly, I finally have a buyer interested in the property in Placerville that Josiah left to me. It will provide plenty of cash to cover my business expenses for several months."

Mr. Pomroy inspected the letter and then folded his arms. He had the air of a man who was used to assessing, and right then he was assessing her. "You have been hard at work."

"You said you needed me to provide proof that my studio will have a sound footing, and I have."

"What you should have done, Miss Whittier, is obtain a partner with experience managing a business." Mr. Pomroy punctuated his statement with an arch of his graying right eyebrow. "That store space is a valuable piece of property. I want the right tenant."

"I *am* the right tenant."

"You are a *potential* tenant. Whether or not you are the *right* tenant remains to be determined."

"Mr. Pomroy," she said, fixing him with the steely gaze she had taught herself after hours practicing in front of a mirror, "you seem to be under the impression I am going to leave this office today without a rental contract. Well, I can tell you this time I—"

He didn't wait for the rest of Sarah's sentence. Mr. Pomroy turned on his heel and marched back the way he'd come. Sarah set her chin and chased after him, her half boots tattooing a beat on the polished oak floor.

"Mr. Pomroy," she called, clutching at the skirts of her striped amber twill dress to keep from tripping on the hem, "you must listen to me."

He serpentined between stools and trash cans and an errant filing cabinet, the tail of his frock coat flapping against his legs. "I have listened."

"I am not going to give up today. I promise you."

A clerk sniggered openly as Sarah passed, affirming that she looked ridiculous, pursuing Mr. Pomroy like a street urchin.

"Turner, back to work," Mr. Pomroy snapped at the man. "We are trying to make money here, not offer commentary on our clients."

Sarah's bustle brushed against the side of a desk, scattering papers and causing another of Mr. Pomroy's employees to grumble a complaint about women and their proper place. "Might we discuss this matter in private?" she asked. *Might we sit down?*

"A private discussion will not reduce my concerns about your business venture." He paused in an aisle and leaned close to emphasize his point, near enough that she could smell the lemon-clove astringency of mouthwash on his breath. "A custom artwork studio run by immigrant women? What do illiterate seamstresses and coarse factory girls know about operating a lithograph press or coloring photographs, balancing the books?"

"As I explained yesterday, they will know everything they need to know by the time I have finished training them. They all possess the necessary talent or else I wouldn't have taken them on. I'm satisfied we'll be successful."

"Be honest with yourself, Miss Whittier," he said bluntly. "Your enterprise is more of a charity than a business. If you are so keen to have a job, then teach young ladies—ones able to pay a fee—how to paint. A more genteel and respectable occupation than this folly."

"Mr. Samuelson and the others"—she wished there were more than one or two "others" but she wouldn't mention that now—"who have offered to support my shop don't seem to think my artwork studio is a charity."

"I would not be so certain about their opinions, if I were you."

He started walking again, leaving the open floor area to stride down a hallway.

Sarah sprinted after him. "My girls need the good jobs this shop will provide them, Mr. Pomroy," she persisted as sweat collected beneath her collar. "I can't let them down."

"Your girls are street savvy. They will survive. Their kind do."

Sarah halted. *Survive? Would they? Would I have survived, if it weren't for Josiah?* She'd come frighteningly close to paying a terrible price for her misdeeds and had far more in common with her girls than Mr. Pomroy need ever know. If he ever did find out . . . a shudder rolled across Sarah's shoulders.

"I want those girls to do more than survive. I want them to thrive," she said to his retreating back. "I don't know how you can be so indifferent to Josiah's wishes. You know he wanted this for me. You told him before he died that you would help."

"Josiah Cady was too sentimental."

The offhand criticism bit, sharp as a wasp sting. "Is that what you've been thinking all along? All these days I've been coming here, urging you to lease me that storefront, you've been thinking Josiah was simply overly sentimental? I thought you were his friend."

He stopped and faced her. Red blotched his neck above his collar.

"It is precisely because we were friends that I am working so hard—unsuccessfully—to convince you to see sense, Miss Whittier, despite what I may or may not have said to Josiah," he answered. "If those men do not come through with their offers of money and your shop fails, think how that will crush those girls of yours. Young women to whom you've promised a great deal. Are you willing to bear their disappointment and upset?"

He was right; they would be crushed and might blame her. She wouldn't let it happen, though.

"There's no need to worry, because I will not permit the shop to fail." Sarah closed the gap between them and peered into his face. He had to understand. He had to see. "I don't care what you said about Josiah—he wasn't being sentimental when he encouraged me. He was shrewd and you know it."

"You are very determined."

"If I intend to be a success, I have to be."

"Which is why Josiah Cady took to you like a tick to a dog, Miss Whittier." He softened the assessment with a hasty smile that twitched his mustache.

A spark of hope flickered. "Take a chance with me, Mr. Pomroy. Six months. Lease me the space for six months, and I will prove to you my shop is a viable business."

She saw the retreat in his eyes. Her hope bloomed into a flame. He was going to concede; she was going to win.

Sighing, Mr. Pomroy opened the nearest door. His personal office sat hushed in the dim morning sunlight, exhaling the scent of cigars and leather chairs, beeswax polish. "The paperwork is on the desk. Allow me to fill in the necessary details and the shop is yours. For six months."

The strain she had lived with for weeks, and longer, released from Sarah's shoulders like a watch spring uncoiling. "Thank you. You won't regret your decision."

Sarah swept past her new landlord. After he modified the rental agreement to include her name and the length of the lease, she signed both copies, folding one carefully and tucking it into her reticule.

"Here is the first month's rent," she said, handing him the money. Eighty-five dollars. An unimaginable sum not so many years ago.

"You will have a one-week grace period for a missed rental payment, with a fifteen-percent penalty fee. Miss that payment and you will be evicted from the premises," Mr. Pomroy said, kneeing aside his rolling chair so he could access the center desk drawer. He glanced at her. "You do trust these girls you've hired, correct? They are not going to do anything to, shall we say, cast you or your business in a bad light?"

"They may have made bad choices in their pasts, Mr. Pomroy, but I assure you, that is behind them."

"Good, because after the last disgraceful tenant we had in that space, my partners and I would prefer not to discover the name of a client in the newspapers again."

"You will not have any trouble from us." She extended a gloved hand, palm up. She was thankful it didn't shake. However, she had practiced forgetting her transgressions far longer than she'd practiced her steely-eyed gaze. "So if everything is in order, might I have the keys to the shop?"

"I believe so." He slid open the drawer and slipped his copy of the paperwork inside. From the same drawer, he extracted two sets of iron keys.

"Front door. Alley door," he said, identifying each key with a flick of his forefinger. "The next rent payment is due on the twenty-fifth."

He dropped the keys into her hand. They were heavy and reassuringly solid, and she closed her fingers tightly around them. "You will see my check on the twenty-fourth. Good morning, Mr. Pomroy. And thank you again."

"Prove me wrong to worry, Miss Whittier."

"I shall," she answered.

Sarah rushed out of the office, past the prying stares of Mr. Pomroy's clerks, down the narrow hallway. Grinning, she burst through the front door of the building, into the din of Montgomery Street. She had done it. She had persisted and won.

You always believed I would, Josiah. Even when I didn't believe it myself.

While pedestrians rushed by, Sarah gripped her reticule tightly and breathed in the energy of the city. Inhaled the aromas she so strongly associated with San Francisco—the iodine tang of the bay and the metallic sharpness of factory smoke and steam engines, the acrid reek of horse manure and construction dust. The sweet spiciness of food intermingling with the lye from laundries in the Chinese quarter two blocks distant. The warm yeastiness of a bakery.

She stepped back as a flock of tourists scuttled up the sidewalk, bound for the sights of Chinatown with a policeman as guard, eager to peep at vivid red joss houses and opium dens. If he took them farther north, they could venture into the saloons of the Barbary Coast, jangling with piano music and drunken laughter. Sarah watched them disappear around the corner and wondered if they felt the city's vibrancy too. If they could sense its limitless possibilities, where people from every walk of life scraped and struggled to be better than they were before they arrived. To become someone new, just like she had done.

"Miss Sarah!" Minnie Tobin hurried along the asphaltum sidewalk, her faded gray dress kicking wide, brown curls bouncing beneath her straw bonnet. "Have you done it?"

"Minnie, how did you manage to get here?" She was the first young woman Sarah had plucked from the streets, the ragged daughter of a drunken grocer, a girl with a cheerful disposition, enviable spunk, and a gift for painting. Her father had plans to marry her off to his brutish best friend, consigning her to a life not much better than slavery. But not if Sarah had anything to say about it. "Your father allowed you to leave the grocery early?"

"I snuck out." Minnie's grin dimpled her cheeks. "I had to know if we'd got the shop. I couldn't concentrate on stacking tins of meat, knowing you were down here today, fighting for us."

"Here is your answer." Sarah held out the two sets of keys and jingled them. "We have the shop."

"Oh, thank goodness!" Minnie leaped into Sarah's arms and hugged her tight, knocking her hat askew. "That's wonderful!"

"It is wonderful, and an incredible relief." Sarah extricated herself from Minnie's grasp and dropped the keys into her reticule. "What do you say . . . chocolate macaroons from Engelberg's Bakery as a treat?"

"It'll have to be quick, if I'm to make it back to the grocery before my pa returns from his lunch. Don't want him to find me gone." Minnie's voice conveyed her dread.

"Then quick it shall be."

Buoyant, Sarah planted one hand atop her hat, clutched Minnie's arm with the other, and strutted down Montgomery.

"Miss Charlotte will be pleased about the shop," Minnie said as they paused at the intersection, waiting for a cable car to collect its passengers and make the turn, clearing the roadway.

"Lottie never doubted I would be able to convince Mr. Pomroy to lease us the space." But then Lottie had endless faith, far more than Sarah could ever claim. Enough to convince her father to invest in the shop against his lawyer's wary nature.

"I never doubted, either, Miss Sarah," said Minnie, her nut-brown eyes full of trust.

Sarah's heart constricted. *I will never let these girls down. Not a one.* "Thank you."

"'Welcome, miss," Minnie replied with a dimpled smile. "What's next?"

"Tomorrow I plan to go to the storefront and make a list of any necessary repairs." A lengthy list already existed in her head, but she had been too superstitious to commit it to paper. "Then I'll make down payments on the equipment we need—first and foremost the lithograph press—take you and the others to see the space, and begin tidying and organizing. In a week, the first of our supplies should arrive. We can start to move in then."

"That's so exciting, I think I'm gonna burst!"

"Please don't, because I need you whole," Sarah teased.

The cable car clanged up the road, and they hurried across the cobbles.

"I predict Whittier and Company Custom Design Studio will be a roaring success," Minnie proclaimed with a dramatic wave of her forefinger. "Because if anyone can do it, you can, Miss Sarah."

"If anyone can do it, *we* can." Sarah squeezed the girl's arm. "Remember that."

Minnie giggled and Sarah joined in, the sound of their carefree laughter snatched by the breeze swirling along the street, carried off with the fog lifting into the blue, blue skies. Their spirits lighter than a bubble floating.

And hopefully not, thought Sarah with a shiver, *just as fragile*.

Two

"ACCORDING TO THE CITY DIRECTORY," the hotel clerk spread his fingers across the pages of the book and pointed, the freckles dotting the backs of his hands looking like splashes of orange paint, "he's listed as having an address on Jones Street, sir."

Daniel squinted at the entry, upside-down from his vantage point across the waist-high desk. There he was. After all the months Daniel had searched, he'd finally located the man. In a San Francisco directory, owned by every hotel in the city, plain as could be.

"This directory's over a year old, though. We haven't received the latest, so I can't guarantee the address is still current," the clerk added, apologetic for any shortcomings exhibited by the Occidental Hotel. "Might have moved on by now. Folks around here come and go like ants on a hill."

"It'll do for a start."

Slowly, Daniel spun the directory on the smooth walnut surface until the entry was right-side up. He traced the print with his thumb as if the contact of his skin on paper would verify the reality of what his eyes saw. The noises of the hotel—the chatter of guests lounging on the plump furniture, the tinkle of the piano meant to entertain them, the rattle of the elevator arriving on the ground floor—became a distant buzz. All Daniel noticed, his entire concentration, was focused on two words. *Josiah Cady*, in wavy typeset. He was still alive. Daniel had started to wonder.

I've found you at last, Josiah. Dear old Pa. The scoundrel who had gone to strike it rich in the gold fields never to return or ever send a dime home, leaving his family without the proper means to survive. Daniel felt heat surge, and he curled his fist atop the open book. He had found him, just as Daniel had promised his mother on her deathbed he would, had promised his sisters. An answer to a prayer, if he ever prayed. Which he didn't. Not any longer.

"You've come a long way to unearth the fellow," observed the clerk, filling the dead silence. He glanced at Daniel's fist then shot a nervous look at his fellow clerk, helping another guest at the far end of the main reception desk. "All the way from Chicago, eh?"

Daniel uncurled his hand and willed himself to relax. He would save his anger for when he met Josiah face-to-face. "Yep."

The clerk exhaled his tension and smiled. "One of the fellows who work the dining room says the train can get here from Illinois in just five days. Is that so, Mr. Cady?"

"I can't tell you, because I didn't come directly." No, he'd been traveling since October, poking through every godforsaken mining town between here and the Rocky Mountains, across windswept wastelands and craggy snowcapped mountains, searching for traces of the man who had been more in love with gold than with his family. "Where is this address on Jones Street?"

The clerk released a low whistle. "Up Nob Hill, sir. One of the best parts of town," he explained when he realized Daniel didn't recognize the name.

"Folks are rich up there, then."

"Lots of them sure are. Real estate investors, businessmen . . . gold speculators. Wish I'd had the nerve to go mining." A wistful look crossed his boyish features. "Why? The fellow owe you money?"

"In a manner of speaking." Thirty thousand dollars, based on Josiah's final telegram. His father's take of the profits from the small gold-mining company he and a partner had run. Daniel kept the telegram, faded and deeply creased, in the inner pocket of his coat. Read it over and over again, a reminder of what Josiah owed Daniel and his sisters back in Chicago. Cold, hard cash. Enough to set himself up in business and build that fine house he had promised to Lily and Marguerite. Because, the Lord knew, he and his sisters weren't looking for a father's love anymore. "How do I get to Jones Street from here?"

"Go north two blocks and catch the California Street cable car. That's your best bet. Only costs a nickel and the views up there are first-rate. You can see right across the Golden Gate, you can! I take my sweetheart on the Clay Street cable line all the—"

"Is it far?" Daniel interrupted the man's enthusiastic praises.

He shook his head. "Five, ten minutes at most, Mr. Cady."

"Good."

Without being asked, the clerk scribbled Josiah's address on a scrap of paper and handed it to Daniel. Tucking the note in his pocket, Daniel headed downstairs and out of the hotel. At the street corner, he had a clear view of the city cloaking the sandy hills until every square inch seemed to be covered by pavement and buildings. Up there, among the jumble of dusty streets and bay-windowed houses, church spires, and telegraph poles, Josiah lived in comfort and security. Oblivious to the surprise he was about to receive.

Daniel secured his hat on his head and stepped off the curb. Five, ten minutes at most to get to Josiah. Not long, but long enough for Daniel to decide exactly what he intended to say to him.

"I forgive you, Father" was not on the list.

"I did it, Mrs. McGinnis," Sarah announced to the empty entry hall, her voice echoing off the curving staircase. Out of habit, she brushed fingertips across the solitary painting hanging above the demilune table tucked against the wall. A painting she'd done of her family farm, a watercolor almost as wispy as her memories of the place, the gilt frame rubbing bare down to the wood where she touched it all the time. "Mrs. McGinnis!"

Rufus, their orange tabby, jumped down from the padded chair that was his observation post on the second-floor landing, his claws tapping rapidly across the floor. Sarah stripped off her gloves and threw her hat onto the table. It bounced against the floral wallpaper along with her discarded reticule, the keys inside releasing a satisfying clink. "Mrs. McGinnis?" Sarah peered at the empty dining room, the darkened front parlor to her right.

The housekeeper, wiping her hands on her apron, bustled through the kitchen doorway at the far end of the dining room.

"There you are," said Sarah.

"*Wheesht*, lass, stop screeching, I heard you," Mrs. McGinnis chided, shaking her head. A strand of brown hair escaped from the tidy bun at the base of her neck. "And where else would I be at this hour? Gone for a stroll?"

Sarah smiled, patting her hair and finding more than a few strands of her own unwound. She jabbed hairpins home. "It *is* a beautiful day."

"And *nae* time for someone like me to enjoy it."

Sarah clasped the other woman's fingers. They were gritty with flour, strong as bands of iron, chapped from lye. Warmth and support and fortitude all wrapped up in the hands of a servant.

"I did it," Sarah repeated. "I have the keys to the storefront and a six-month lease. On my terms."

The other woman's answering grin, the light in her sea-blue eyes, was infectious. When she smiled, she was so pretty that Sarah wondered, yet again, why she had never remarried after becoming a widow. Wondered why she had spent the last six years tending first to a crotchety old prospector and now to Sarah.

Mrs. McGinnis enfolded Sarah within her arms. She smelled of vanilla and Castile soap. "I knew you would, lass."

"I must have been the only one who doubted."

"You need more faith."

Sarah made no comment; they'd had this conversation before and she did not need to reply.

"Mr. Pomroy was difficult, but I think he just wanted to challenge me to make certain I was resolute." She dropped onto the chair against the wall and wiggled out of her half boots, freeing her aching feet. For Mr. Pomroy she had bothered to purchase new ones, as if the sight of buff Dongola leather might have swayed his faltering opinion of her worth. Dollars and cents. A plugged nickel. "I had macaroons with Minnie and then stopped by the storefront on the way back home. The shop is going to need some work to get into shape, but the girls and I can do it. The space should be ready in a couple of weeks."

"So quickly?"

"We have to open the shop as soon as possible and bring in income. Mr. Samuelson's loan and the proceeds from the sale of Josiah's land in Placerville won't pay the bills forever." Sarah massaged the cramps in her toes and looked askance at her boots. She wouldn't be buying shoes from that store again. "I can't wait to show the girls. Cora will love to paint in that second-floor room. The light is perfect for even the most detailed work. And of course there's a nice area for the lithograph press, and there is even a small corner room for Emma to work on the accounts that is well lit by gas lamps. It's nearly a miracle to have secured the space at such an excellent price."

Mrs. McGinnis rested a hand on her shoulder. "Mr. Josiah would be proud of you."

"Yes." The aching twist she felt in her heart was a constant companion. "He would."

The housekeeper dropped a kiss to the crown of Sarah's head and stepped back. "Change out of that frock afair Miss Charlotte arrives with Anne and Emma for instruction this afternoon. You don't want paint on yer best outfit."

"Lottie . . . I almost forgot." After a final rub of her toes, Sarah stood. "First, I'd like to spend a minute with Josiah, though. Then I'll go change."

In her stockinged feet, she entered the parlor just off the entry hall. Rufus slunk down the stairs and followed her inside.

The shades had been pulled against the noonday light, and the room lay dim and quiet. All these months later the sweetness of Josiah's cigar still lingered, clinging to the drapes and the Turkish rug covering the mahogany parlor table, as unwilling to relinquish the memory of him as she was. Sarah had always tried to shoo Josiah off to his upstairs library to smoke, but he loved to sit in his overstuffed red velvet chair by the bay window and critique the neighborhood happenings. Nobody could convince Josiah to do anything other than what he set his mind to.

Sarah trailed a hand over the lace-trimmed antimacassar spread across the back of the chair, the indent of Josiah's weight still visible in the nap of the velvet seat cushion, and felt salty tears rise in her throat.

"I didn't want this house and that bit of property, Josiah, if it meant I had to lose you." The dearest friend she'd had. A replacement for the parents, the family she'd lost.

If he were alive, he might laugh his gruff laugh at her sentimentality. Right before pain shot through his green eyes. The sight of it, though, would be gone as quick as the spark of a lightning bug, ephemeral. As if the pain had never truly existed.

Sarah crossed the thick carpet, plush against her toes, to the corner of the parlor where an easel held a painting draped in black crape. She flapped the fabric over the top of the frame. It was the first work he had commissioned from her, a portrait of him seated in his favorite white wicker chair out in the garden. One leg was thrust forward, a cigar clamped in his left hand and a sly, all-knowing smile tilting his mouth beneath his thick, graying mustache. In the portrait, Sarah had been careful to erase the most obvious signs of Josiah's ill health, highlighting the details of the garden instead. The little fountain bubbled at his back and his roses bloomed all around in dense profusion, a halo of vermilion and gold and salmon. A marble statue of a chubby cherub perched on its pedestal to Josiah's right, an ironic counterpoint of innocence, he'd claimed, to all the wickedness in his soul.

He'd bought an elaborately carved walnut easel for the portrait and set it in the most prominent location in the parlor, in the far corner where it was easily spotted by folks entering the room. He would grin at the painting and tell anyone who cared to listen that Sarah had painted it right after she'd arrived in San Francisco. He would insist that she had been the quickest portrait artist he'd ever met and that, for a reasonable fee, she could paint their portraits too. Sarah would find herself blushing from head to toe as their visitors smiled politely and ignored Josiah's hint. They were there to smoke his excellent cigars and to eat Mrs. McGinnis's delectable meals, not to commission a painting from a young woman who had an irritating tendency to speak her mind and whose past had never been explained to everybody's liking.

"I signed the rental agreement for the shop this morning, Josiah," she said to the portrait, while Rufus slithered between the easel's legs, making it wobble. His bent tail, broken in a skirmish that had occurred before she'd rescued him, slapped against her skirt hem. Sarah pulled a handkerchief from the pocket of her skirt and swiped dust from the frame. "I think Mr. Pomroy is of the common opinion that I'm foolish for wanting to help the girls, but I won't let his opinion or anyone else's stop me. It's going to happen, Josiah, just as you said it would."

She returned the handkerchief to her pocket. It was silly to talk to the painting, but she always felt comforted when she did.

The doorbell sounded in the hallway. Restoring the black crape over the painting, Sarah looked over her shoulder and smiled, expecting to hear Mrs. McGinnis's footsteps coming from the kitchen to answer the bell.

Lottie and the girls were very early.

"They're here already, Rufus."

They would be so pleased with Sarah's good news.

Daniel frowned. It seemed no one intended to answer the doorbell, but the house hadn't been abandoned. The steps were clean and the greenery in the front garden maintained. The cut leaded glass in the double door was spotless, and he could've sworn he'd seen movement in the hallway beyond it.

He took a step back from the front door and stared up at the house's facade. Ornate didn't begin to describe the carved frames surrounding each window or the scrollwork flourishes atop the columns supporting the porch roof. At the cornice, brackets curved like the unfurling leaves of a fiddleneck fern and were painted an eye-catching peach shade in contrast to the pale cream of the wood exterior. There were more splashes of peach paint to highlight a detail here, the dentil design there. And only a blind man could miss the massive bay windows projecting from each floor, plus two on the left side of the house, sunlight sparkling off the glass.

"You did make a profit off gold, Josiah." Anger rose in Daniel's throat. "Although I expected a grander house than this."

Which made Daniel question where the rest of the money had gone. Undoubtedly into a fat bank account someplace.

Next door, a middle-aged woman peered through her shutters at him. When he didn't smile a greeting, she let the wood slats drop back into place. Her house was even more ornate than Josiah's and a floor taller. Up and down the length of Jones Street stood the signs of San Francisco prosperity, a jumble of turrets and bay windows. A recently erected church, its granite stones solid and sturdy compared to the wood houses surrounding it, towered on a distant corner. Hammers pounded on an adjacent street, another home under construction. Every structure teetered on the edge of vertigo-inducing hills, clinging to the soil as if one false move would send them tumbling into the choppy waters of the bay.

The neighbor's front door opened and a Chinese boy stepped onto the porch. Daniel had seen dozens of Chinese immigrants in San Francisco, but the sight of another managed to astonish him again.

The boy, who looked to be in his early teen years, stared at Daniel. His piercing eyes were dark as two bits of coal and his hair was the glossy blue-black of a crow's wing. He looked a bit like a bird, watchful and waiting.

"Hullo," Daniel called across the gap of twenty feet. "Do you know if anyone is home here?"

The Chinese boy folded his arms across his thigh-length tunic and didn't answer.

"This is the Cady house, correct?" Daniel asked. Maybe the lad didn't speak English. That would make him a pretty useless servant, though.

"Yes," the boy finally said.

Daniel nodded and pressed the bell again. Someone had to answer the door eventually, and he'd stand here forever until they did, if it were required.

The handle of the rightmost door jiggled and then opened. A woman a few years younger than him—twenty-one or two, if he tried to guess—with mahogany hair and eyes the color of chocolate, stood in the doorway. A servant, he supposed, though her brown-striped dress was of a better material than he'd seen most servants wear and her corseted back was as straight as the tortured spine of a society miss. She was missing shoes, however. Strange.

"Yes?" She appeared confused, as if she'd been expecting someone else.

"I am looking for my father."

A crinkle formed between her brows. She was actually rather pretty, and her gaze, shrewd. It had taken in the worn cuffs of his coat, the scuffed toe of his left boot, the dirt he could no longer clean from his trouser legs. The search for Josiah had taken longer and been more arduous than Daniel had expected, and he wasn't one to stop for a new suit of clothes simply to make an impression on his father. As a result, he looked like a beggar. Which, by some folks' definition, he precisely was.

"You have the wrong house," she declared.

"Not according to that boy over there." Daniel thrust his foot forward to prevent her from closing the door, which she looked ready to do any second. "I'd like it if you'd let me in so I don't have to wait for him out here on the porch. And don't worry; you won't get in trouble with him. Just tell him I was being difficult."

The corner of one eye twitched, the sole indication his comment hadn't been well received. "I am not a servant worried about getting in trouble with anyone. I own this house."

He hadn't expected that. "He's already skipped town . . ."

Her gaze softened. Had he sounded that crestfallen? "I don't know who it is you are searching for, but if you need help, the Unitarian church on Geary Street runs a benevolent society—"

"I don't need a benevolent society," Daniel snapped. "I need to know where to contact my father."

"Miss Whittier," the middle-aged matron next door, who had come onto her front porch to stare along with her servant, called across. "Do you need any assistance there?"

"No, Mrs. Brentwood, I'm fine," Miss Whittier answered, her attention hastily returning to Daniel. "I suggest you seek out the mission, sir. I also suggest you remove your foot so that I might shut my front door without damaging it."

"Not until you answer my question."

"You haven't asked a question. You've made a statement that you are searching for your father, whom I have assured you is not here."

"Perhaps if I gave you my name, you'll understand. I'm Daniel Cady. Josiah's son." Daniel swept his hat from his head. "And I've come to claim my money."

Three

IF HE HAD ANNOUNCED HE WAS THE KING of England, Sarah could not have been more stunned. "That can't be the truth."

One dark eyebrow rose above eyes the hue of forest depths or winter's pine. Eyes that were vaguely familiar. *Daniel.* That's what he had said his Christian name was. Sarah didn't recall if Josiah had ever mentioned the names of his children. He had hardly ever spoken of them, so she didn't think he had.

"Which isn't the truth—that I've come for the money or that I'm Josiah's son?" he asked in his concise Midwestern accent.

"It's impossible." Sarah searched his face, hunting for similarities beyond an eye color that anyone could possess. His hair was trimmed more closely than most men she knew chose to wear theirs, as if he hadn't the time to bother with whatever was currently fashionable, and his jaw was clean-shaven and free of the thick sideburns that made some men look like stuffed chipmunks. But where Josiah's face and eyes had been kind, this man's were hard as glass. And where Josiah's smile had been ready, never far from his mouth, Daniel Cady looked as if he had never smiled in his life. He and Josiah were about the same size, if she envisioned Josiah as a man in his prime, and when the fellow lifted his eyebrow and tilted his head just slightly to one side, like he was doing now, there was an echo of the man who often looked at her the same way. But an echo did not make him Josiah's son any more than the copies she painted at art exhibitions were originals. "You can't be his son."

He emitted a sound halfway between a laugh and a choke. "I promise you, I am."

"You can't be, because Josiah's son is dead."

His fingers crushed the brim of his hat. Somewhat battered, the dark brown porkpie didn't look as though it could long withstand the pressure. "Is that what he told you? Well, you shouldn't believe a word Josiah Cady speaks. They're all lies."

"You really need to leave." Off to her right, Sarah noticed Mrs. Brentwood's servant descending the steps to the street. Ah Mong was only a teenage boy and could hardly protect her if this man decided to become dangerous, a fact that wouldn't stop him from trying. *Thank goodness*. "There's nothing for you here."

She pushed the door against the toe of his boot. It didn't budge.

"Here. Wait. I should show you this." He fished around in the pocket of his coat, dusty from traveling, and pulled out a yellowing telegram. "Proof of my identity, if that's what you need in order to tell me where Josiah is living now. It's the telegram he sent my family when his gold mine turned a profit in '75."

The date brought a rush of memories. Eighteen seventy-five was the year Sarah had first met Josiah at her uncle's house in Los Angeles. She was fifteen and reluctantly permitted to join the adults at supper. *A special occasion to welcome your uncle's partner to California*, Aunt Eugenie had lectured, *so you had best behave*. Aunt Eugenie's heavy lids had revealed her doubts Sarah possessed any inkling of refined manners. Back then, Josiah was a grizzled middle-aged man who laughed loudly and smoked a great quantity of cigars, filling the dining room with his outsized personality. Suffering and misery, mistakes and penance, were still ahead for the both of them.

"Let me see that telegram." Sarah snatched the piece of paper dangling from Daniel Cady's hand. The message had certainly come from Josiah—she recognized the bluster of his words, even in clipped telegram prose, and the news it contained. The year 1875 was also when he and her uncle had made good in the Black Hills, although not as much as Josiah had told his family.

She looked at the man standing in her doorway. Daniel Cady must think she was stupid if he believed an old telegram was any sort of proof. "All this proves is that you obtained a telegram Josiah sent to his family in Chicago. Hardly a birth certificate or a baptismal record."

The sapphire blue of Ah Mong's thigh-length tunic caught her attention. Coming quickly to check on her, the boy had reached the middle landing on the steps leading to her house. "Miss Sarah?"

"I'm all right. This gentleman is leaving." Sarah folded the telegram and handed it to him. "Aren't you."

It wasn't a question, and a muscle along Daniel's jaw ticked. "Not until you tell me how to reach Josiah."

"You can't reach Josiah." Sarah felt her nostrils flare as she gulped in air. "Because he passed away earlier this year. After a long illness."

He reached for the door frame's support. Fleetingly, his gaze registered his hurt. She doubted he realized how clearly she could see it. "You could have told me . . ." He gripped the wood, his knuckles turning white.

"I am sorry." Her hand hovered, ready to comfort him. Sarah dropped it to her side. "I am. That was careless of me to just blurt it out."

He straightened and dragged shaking fingers through his thick, black hair. "Let me come inside, Miss Whittier."

"There really isn't any reason for you to come in."

"I need to sit down. For just a minute."

Sarah let her hand slip off the door. She was going to trust him, an utter stranger whose green eyes reminded her of Josiah's. Her willingness went beyond any resemblance to Josiah; it was her weakness, taking in stray cats and girls whose need flickered like a flame in the dark, or a man whose tailor-made suit had been worn past its respectable worth. She couldn't help them all, tabbies with crooked tails, young women with bruises and tarnished reputations. She certainly shouldn't pity him, a man who might or might not be telling the truth.

But she did.

Sarah nodded at Ah Mong, waiting patiently. "Ah Mong, would you come into the house and help Mrs. McGinnis prepare some tea for my visitor?" She raised her voice. "Mrs. Brentwood, I hope you don't mind if I borrow Ah Mong for a short while."

Her neighbor scowled at the man blocking access to Sarah's front door. "Most certainly. Keep him as long as you need." Meaning as long as Daniel Cady took up space in Sarah's parlor, recovering.

"Thank you." Sarah eased the door open. "Come inside, Mr. Cady."

"You've decided to believe I'm who I say I am?"

"I have decided I don't know what else to call you."

He nodded and stepped into the hallway, trailing the citrus tang of lime shaving lotion. Ah Mong glared menacingly as he darted by Daniel, which prompted another lift of an eyebrow.

"Is it common to have Chinese working in the house?" he asked, stopping in the center of the entry hall, noting the boy's hasty disappearance into the kitchen.

"It is in San Francisco."

"An interesting place." He slid the brim of his hat through his fingers as he examined his surroundings. Standing there, in the shadowed light of the hallway, he did look like Josiah. Just a bit. Enough to force her to reconsider what Josiah had told her about his past.

Daniel scanned the paneled woodwork and the heavy wallpaper above it, her watercolor of the farm and the crystal chandelier suspended over the curving staircase, the patterned carpet climbing the treads, seemed even to make note of the polish on the floor. And her pair of discarded boots. Sarah flushed and curled her stockinged toes beneath the hem of her dress.

"Very nice." His tone was admiring, possessive, and the first tingling of alarm shuddered down Sarah's spine. If she hadn't been so stunned by his announcement on her doorstep, so bemused by her impulsive urge to aid him, she would have realized earlier what his arrival meant to her. And to the girls.

"If you still need to sit, we should go into the parlor, Mr. Cady," she said, corralling her galloping nerves. If he really was Josiah's son, alive and breathing, this house and all its contents, the property in Placerville, the deed to a spent mine in Grass Valley she'd rather forget about, even her dwindling bank account could be claimed by him. His very existence could topple her dreams like a nudge to a procession of dominoes.

I will not let that happen.

"Mrs. McGinnis will serve us tea in there, and then you can leave."

Sarah crossed the entry hall, careful to give him a wide berth. Rufus had returned from wherever he'd been hiding to trot ahead of Sarah, his bent tail held proudly aloft.

"How long have you lived here?" Daniel asked, his scrutiny of the house's interior continuing as he strolled into the parlor. Rufus, the traitor, happily rubbed against his leg.

"Nearly four years, ever since I left Arizona to work as Josiah's nurse-companion," she answered with seamless effort, thankful he was more engrossed in the room's crown molding than in searching for truth in her eyes. Few people knew she was actually from Los Angeles, a place she wanted to forget more than that mine in Grass Valley. "He and my uncle were friends, and I was glad to tend to him. My aunt and uncle, whom I'd been living with since my own family passed away, were even gladder to be rid of the expense of caring for me." Though not for the reason most people assumed when she made that statement.

"You didn't return to your relations after he died."

"I love this city, and I have found a satisfying life here."

"As an unmarried woman alone?"

"I'm not the only one in San Francisco in that situation."

Sarah pulled open the shutters of the bay window, sunlight slitting the crimson and cobalt Brussels carpet. Outside, the robust figure of Mrs. Brentwood patrolled the sidewalk. She paused occasionally to rise on her toes and study the windows of the house. The gossip that a strange man—Mrs. Brentwood would undoubtedly embellish the story by mentioning he was good-looking in a dark and dangerous sort of way—had visited the unconventional Miss Whittier would be all over Nob Hill by nightfall.

Sarah set her back to the window. Daniel Cady had moved on to examine a series of watercolors she'd painted, scenes of Golden Gate Park and the beach near Seal Rocks, that hung above the ultramarine brocade settee. Ignored, Rufus had stalked off. "These are quite good."

"They're mine."

He glanced over at her. "You're a painter?"

"You don't have to sound so astonished, Mr. Cady. There are many professional female painters in San Francisco. At Josiah's suggestion, I started selling my landscapes right after I came here, though I prefer to work in miniature." Why she had explained her preferences to him, she couldn't fathom. "I intend to open an art studio to showcase my work and the work of my students. Also something that Josiah encouraged."

"You were fond of him." He sounded as though he couldn't comprehend such an emotion.

"He was the kindest man I've ever known." The one miracle God had granted her in a life filled with loss and regret. "He not only employed me, but he gave me a home when I had nowhere else to go. Josiah believed in me and cared for me like a father. Cared more than any of my blood relations ever did."

Sarah hadn't meant to tell him that, either, but acrimony was a difficult sentiment to shed. She had proven an utter disappointment to Aunt Eugenie. Her aunt had taken in an orphaned niece, a surrogate for the children she'd never borne, and believed rigid discipline and harsh punishment were adequate substitutes for love.

Daniel's hat resumed its circuit through his fingers. "He cared about you, did he?"

"Absolutely."

"Maybe he's not the same Josiah Cady."

Sarah's pulse tripped. If only that were true. "You should sit, Mr. Cady."

"Actually, I don't think I will." He crossed the room, joined her in the center of it. "I want to tell you about the Josiah Cady I knew."

"He never spoke much about his past."

The corner of his mouth twitched. "Small wonder."

He folded his arms and stared down at her. "Nine years ago he took off to pan for gold, ending up in the Black Hills, bound and determined to become a wealthy man. Not the first time he had abandoned his children and my mother in order to scratch that particular itch. He prospected in the Sierra in 1850 before they married and went to Colorado in '61. Stayed with us for a while after he returned from there." He was still looking at Sarah, but his focus had gone someplace else entirely. "When he went to the Black Hills, though, he never came back. Never even contacted us again. The scandal just about killed my mother. *Did* kill my mother." Daniel's gaze sharpened. "Nice, caring fellow."

Sarah wished she had complete faith that Daniel Cady was misleading her. But Josiah, for all his kindness, had always kept secrets.

Just as she had.

"Josiah told me that his wife and children perished during an influenza epidemic. Their deaths were the reason he moved to

San Francisco and never returned to Chicago." That's what he'd told her and she had believed him. She had to; she wouldn't permit Josiah to be so horribly flawed. All the same, she felt queasy. "He loved them dearly and settled here to distract himself from his loss."

Daniel appeared unmoved. "That's a nice tale."

"Listen, Mr. Cady," she responded, "you've told me an interesting and sad story, but it still doesn't prove you're who you say you are."

He tipped his head to one side, understanding lighting his eyes. "You've inherited this place, haven't you? That's why you're so interested in getting me to prove who I am. My existence means you could lose this house."

Rufus meowed and leaped onto the table at her side, bumping his head against her elbow, sensing her anxiety. "I am the owner as far as the probate judge is concerned. I'm not the only one who would need more conclusive proof of your identity than an interesting story."

"What else did Josiah leave you?"

You can't have it. "He spent a lot of his wealth on this house. There is some property northeast of here, in Placerville, but much of the rest, I spent on doctors and specialists."

His eyebrow rose again, just like Josiah's might have with the same skeptical expression. "And on setting up an art studio?"

Anger flared, burning her cheeks. She should never have let him step foot in the house. Pity him. What had she been thinking? "Anyone could come here and claim to be Josiah's long-lost son, eager to snatch up an inheritance. Thousands of people in this town are looking to make a quick dollar by any means possible."

"Including you, Miss Whittier?"

"You have overstayed your welcome, Mr. Cady." Sarah swept out of the parlor and yanked open the front door.

Daniel strolled across the entry hall. "I'll get that proof. You'd better prepare yourself. Packing might be a good place to start."

He tapped his hat onto his head. "Farewell, Miss Whittier. For now."

The second he crossed the threshold, Sarah banged shut the door, clattering glass for the second time today. She collapsed against the doorframe, the smell of his lime shaving lotion lingering in the air, taunting her.

"Miss Sarah, here's the tea . . . what's happened?" The tea service clinked as Mrs. McGinnis clasped the japanned tray tight to her chest.

"Before Lottie and the girls get here, Mrs. McGinnis, I need you to tell me all you know about Josiah's life before he came to San Francisco."

"Now, didn't he tell you all his stories, over and over, Miss Sarah?"

Sarah peered through the leaded-glass door insert at the wavy image of Daniel's receding shape. "Apparently not."

Daniel tugged his coat about him as a chilly wind whipped up the hill. It was just as cold as the sound of Miss Sarah Whittier's voice. He had overstayed his welcome?

Quite the contrary, Miss Whittier.

He paused to secure his collar around his neck, taking in the scenery, the sunlight reflecting off the bay in the distance. A poet might claim the light glinted like a hundred diamonds scattered upon a sheet of sapphire silk to tangle in the masts of the ships bobbing upon the water. What a view. It would be the sort of location Josiah would choose: the top of a hill, the brilliant blue heavens overhead, and the wealth of San Francisco sprouting around him like goldenrods in the verge.

This should have been for Grace and Lily and Marguerite, not for some opportunistic young woman whose hair smelled of roses. Daniel's mother and sisters were the ones who had suffered the most from the scandal after it had become clear Josiah had abandoned them. Grace had endured the humiliation and her father's endless taunts, defending Josiah until the end, loving her husband more than he deserved. They moved out of Hunt House, Daniel working at any job he could find to make ends meet, living for the day he could hunt down Josiah and reclaim their money. Enough money to give his sisters the future Daniel had promised without him having to beg Grandfather Hunt for help. He'd rather crawl through hot coals than ask that man for a penny.

Well, the day for reparation had finally come, and Miss Whittier was not going to stop him. Even if her keen eyes had seen the hurt he worked so hard to conceal. The teenage boy's heartache he'd spent years attempting to forget.

Stepping off the curb along California Street, Daniel hailed the street car driver to halt, paid his nickel, and climbed aboard, tipping his hat to a young woman in a tattered bonnet and threadbare cloak. Not everyone in San Francisco was rich.

At the end of the line, he disembarked and headed down Montgomery. The doorman of the Occidental Hotel nodded a greeting and pulled open the door. Daniel retrieved his room key from the reception desk clerk.

"A profitable day, sir?" the fellow asked, his hair a shock of orange as conspicuous as his freckles.

"Let's say it was a surprising day." Daniel set his hat upon the desk. "I'd like to send a telegram to my attorney in Chicago concerning a legal matter and another to my sisters."

"I can attend to that, sir."

The clerk extracted a stack of Western Union telegraph forms from one of the many cubbyholes beneath the desk and handed Daniel a pen. First, Daniel composed a note to his attorney asking him to obtain proof of Daniel's identity and to contact a lawyer in San Francisco. Then he bent to telling Lily and Marguerite the most important news of all. They were only ten; how would they take it? Having no memory of their father, they'd probably take it a lot better than he had.

Dear ones,
Found house in SF. J has died. A young woman claims to have inherited estate. Have contacted lawyer. Will return when settled.
D.

Daniel stared at what he'd written. *J has died.* Three words, eight letters summarizing a bitter fact. His searching had come to an end, but it didn't feel like closure. A grave stood between Daniel and the chance to seal the wound Josiah had left on his heart.

The clerk cleared his throat. Daniel suspected he'd been trying to gain his attention for some time. "Is that all, Mr. Cady?"

"That's it." He wouldn't waste money on a telegram to the Hunts; they could learn of Josiah's death on their own. "Here are the addresses, and put the charge on my bill."

The clerk took the information and the forms. "I'll have the operator send your messages at once."

Daniel watched the boy hurry off to a back room. He probably shouldn't have mentioned Miss Whittier to his sisters because they really didn't need to know about her. He would handle that woman on his own.

At least, he thought as he picked up his hat, he hoped he could.

"NOW WHAT DO I DO?" Every muscle in Sarah's body felt taut, and the edge of the chair dug a groove through her skirt, petticoats, and chemise right into her legs. A trickle of sweat followed the groove. "Where does this leave me?"

Interrupted before he'd left for his downtown office that morning, Mr. Samuelson propped his elbows on his desk and steepled his fingers beneath his chin. A successful lawyer, his balding head made him look older than he was, and his permanently peaked eyebrows, continually surprised. Or alarmed. An attribute, he asserted, that knocked his courtroom opponents off their guard. But his gaze was as steady as the prow of a boat slicing through calm water. He had that in common with Lottie. Who, at the moment, was seated in the chair at Sarah's side and clenching her fingers in the lap of her perfect peach confection of a dress.

"Papa, please answer Sarah and do not stare enigmatically." Lottie glanced at Sarah. If Sarah had to pick which parent her friend favored, the choice was easy—Mrs. Samuelson. Like her mother, Charlotte McElvey Samuelson was enviably lovely, her hair a riot of blonde spirals, and her face the heart shape sighed over in poems and popular songs. But the winsome exterior hid a resolute spirit, as if satin bows and lace hankies had been wrapped around an iron beam. "Can you not see how anxious she is?"

A twitch of annoyance crossed Mr. Samuelson's face. It was

out of character for Lottie, ever considerate, ever respectful, to badger her father. She must be just as worried as Sarah.

"Charlotte, your mother needs to do a better job teaching you patience. Remember, 'the patient in spirit is better than the proud in spirit.'"

"I am sorry, but ever since Sarah told me her news . . ." Lottie rested her hand atop Sarah's, gripping the chair's arm. Her palm was cold. "It is utterly unfair."

"Just tell me what you think about my situation, Mr. Samuelson," said Sarah.

His fingers separated and spread flat across the desktop. He didn't smile. Sarah appreciated that he wouldn't bother to blunt his opinion with false optimism. "Probate law is not my specialty, but I am aware of another case where a child, presumed deceased and therefore not mentioned in the will, returned and was able to claim his share of the inheritance." He considered her for a moment longer. "If this fellow can prove his identity, then he will likely be found to be the rightful beneficiary of Josiah Cady's estate. He and his sisters equally."

"You're telling me they have the right to come and take my inheritance from me?"

"They certainly have the right to challenge the probate, Miss Whittier. I also must tell you that, if a challenge is granted, access to your assets will be limited until probate is settled."

"I won't be allowed to spend the money Josiah left me? Or use the proceeds from the sale of his property?" Her resolve was crumbling like a sand castle being consumed by the tidal flow.

"I would advise against spending any more than the bare minimum in the chance the judge decrees you must reimburse Mr. Daniel Cady the full sum," he answered solemnly. "Presuming a challenge to the terms of the will is granted and a new probate hearing agreed upon, that is."

"How could this man possibly be Mr. Cady's son, though?" Lottie asked, unwilling to believe.

"Miss Whittier?" her father asked.

"I don't know." A lengthy conversation with Mrs. McGinnis—and an hour spent poking through Josiah's papers—had shed no fresh light on Josiah's past. And no light at all on the man claiming to be his abandoned son. "He might be."

"I suggest we proceed as if he is," Mr. Samuelson answered.

Lottie squeezed, pinching Sarah's hand against the chair arm. "Will Sarah be left with nothing?"

"Josiah intended for her to inherit, so the judge will have to take his wishes into consideration. He may allow Miss Whittier to keep all the money she has in the bank, for instance."

"That is enough to manage for several months, Sarah," said Lottie. "We should be established before that runs out."

"I hope so, Lottie."

"I said 'may,' Charlotte. No guarantees." Mr. Samuelson's nostrils flared as he drew in a long breath and contemplated Sarah. "If you want to know what to do next, Miss Whittier, I recommend you convince the judge you are deserving and worthy of every penny he might let you keep. Though usually fair, John Doran can be a hard man when he's in his courtroom."

"You will not give up on me, will you, Mr. Samuelson?"

He steepled his fingers again, examining her over their tips. She had revealed too much in that question. "Why should I?"

Because I am not so very worthy? "If I can't make use of what Josiah left me," Sarah said, instead of the thoughts uppermost in her mind, "then your loan and the money my other backers have offered are all I have to pay the bills. Won't you and the others think it's unwise to support the studio if it's in jeopardy?"

"No one will retract their offer simply because this Daniel Cady fellow has shown up in San Francisco, Sarah." Lottie was adamant. *Bless her.*

Mr. Samuelson leaned across his desk. His peaked eyebrows didn't make him look surprised or alarmed right then, but rather intensely serious. "Miss Whittier, I didn't give you that loan for five hundred dollars because I have money to spare and nowhere better to invest. I have always trusted you to do what was right."

But what about Mr. *Pomroy?* she wanted to ask. Or Mr. Winston, the banker who had been reluctant at first to support a woman's ambitions, yet he planned to donate funds anyway?

Sarah patted Lottie's hand, easing its grip on her arm, and nodded calmly. "I thank you for your trust, Mr. Samuelson. I hope the others continue to believe in me like you do." She wished more fervently that she'd gotten all of those pledges committed to paper, instead of mere promises made over tea and coffee and sandwiches.

Mr. Samuelson smiled, a quiver of movement across his mouth, and reached for his pocket watch; their time was up. "Do not worry, Miss Whittier. We'll find a way for your shop to survive, even if Mr. Cady has the terms of Josiah's will overturned. Have confidence."

Lottie rose and went around the side of the desk to deposit a kiss upon his cheek. "Thank you, Papa."

Sarah thanked him also and left the study with Lottie. "I suspected he'd tell me Daniel Cady and his sisters would get everything."

Lottie closed the door behind them. The hallway was quiet and empty, the sounds of the house readying for lunch a distant rustle of noise. "Papa did not say exactly that."

"But it's what I expect. Given the 'hard' Judge Doran." Sarah sighed. "I do hope our backers continue to stick by us. We'll manage if they do."

"Of course they will." Lottie rubbed a hand down Sarah's arm. "Do not be downhearted."

"I'm not," she insisted. "But I do honestly wish I had never, ever opened that front door yesterday and let Daniel Cady in my house."

"Keeping the door closed would not change the fact that he exists."

"But it would have delayed my knowing it!"

Lottie laughed, a reassuring sound, and together they strolled to the front of the house. The Samuelsons' maid, Bridget, had anticipated their arrival and had gathered Sarah's cloak and hat. Well dressed and well fed, Bridget had the comfortable demeanor of a young woman who knew she'd landed square on her feet. Unlike the immigrant girls Sarah sought to help. Had to help.

"Thank you, Bridget," said Lottie, dismissing the young Irish girl, who bobbed politely and hurried off. "Perhaps Mr. Cady will change his mind about wanting all of Josiah's estate and be generous," she suggested once they were alone again.

Sarah couldn't imagine a more unlikely outcome. "Not him. I think he needs the money to go along with the abundance of vengefulness he already possesses. His coat was a little threadbare."

"Well." Lottie's pale eyebrows perked. "If he does need money, maybe we can buy him off."

The shocking suggestion made Sarah grin. "Never in a million years, Charlotte Samuelson, did I imagine you would suggest we bribe someone." She shook her head. "I don't have the sort of funds to buy him off. Not when he stands to gain thousands of dollars from Josiah's estate."

"You never know, Sarah. Perhaps a few hundred dollars will be sufficient."

Would it? It might be worth a try. "Perhaps. I do have some money coming to me from two paintings I put up for sale . . ." Money she had intended for repairs at the shop that were proving to be more expensive than her budget had allocated; she'd also been hoping that any money left over from the sale would allow her to buy each of the girls a second new dress to go with the ones she'd already ordered. The dresses would have to wait and the repairs as well, unless she could sell more of her work and soon. Or wrangle another loan from someone. "The sale of those paintings isn't going to get me an amount anywhere near a few hundred dollars, though."

"We have to at least try. We must hold on to the shop. It is too important to the girls." Lottie's gaze held Sarah's. "It is too important to you."

Only Lottie knew the full story of Edouard and her past; she would understand what Sarah hoped to achieve with the girls and the shop and why.

The studio was more than important to her.

It was *everything* to her.

"Don't worry, Lottie. I don't plan to let go of that shop, no matter what Daniel Cady intends."

"A fresh Imperial, sir?" The server working the Occidental's lounging room, another skinny boy with a frizz of orange-red hair and a profusion of freckles, nodded at the glass at Daniel's elbow. It sat three-quarters full of the sugared lemon-water concoction. Daniel had been too busy contemplating a mahogany-haired painter who answered the door in stockinged feet to remember to drink it.

"No. Thank you," he said.

The server bent to clear it away.

"Are you new to San Francisco?" he asked the boy before he continued on his rounds.

The server gave his other customers a cursory glance. The ground-floor room was busy that afternoon, full of tourists eyeing the pedestrians passing the large plate-glass windows, their voices echoing off the marble floor, competing with the click of billiard balls from the rear parlor. Despite the crowd, the boy seemed inclined to stand and talk with Daniel. After he'd paid last evening's waiter for information on Josiah—three dollars, as much as the daily hotel charge—Daniel would guess every server in the hotel would be content to chat with him, whoever waited for them.

"Moved here last spring, sir. Come from Kentucky. I'm the first one in my family to go anywhere more'n twenty miles beyond Washington County." The boy's broad grin revealed a gap where a tooth once resided.

"Too new to know anything about a Josiah Cady, then, I suppose." Daniel didn't expect the boy to have heard of Josiah—the fellow last night hadn't either—but Daniel was always hopeful. The more he knew about Josiah's dealings in San Francisco, the better Daniel could assess the extent of his father's assets. In case Miss Whittier opted to be less than truthful about them. The first task for the San Francisco lawyer, right after the man examined Josiah's will, would be to review his father's bank accounts and real estate dealings. "Or a Sarah Whittier, for that matter. When they arrived in San Francisco. How much they might be worth. Any gossip at all."

"Never heard of 'em. But Cook was born here," he said, making the fact sound like a miraculous achievement.

"And Cook might know if, oh, there were stories about Josiah Cady arriving here with a lot of money or maybe gold from his mining operation. Gold or money he might have hidden somewhere. To avoid taxes." Or to avoid paying his family what they'd been promised.

The server's eyes widened. "I've heard about stuff like that happenin'."

"I take it you'd be willing to ask Cook what he has heard."

He nodded and licked his lips as Daniel reached for his money clip. "A dollar now. Two more if you bring me useful information."

Another three-dollar investment toward his ultimate goal to obtain Josiah's assets. Even if it meant taking the property away from Sarah Whittier.

"I'll get right on that, sir." The greenback disappeared into a deep pocket in the boy's pants. "And my name's Red, in case you're needin' to talk with me again."

He trotted away. Daniel leaned into the seat cushion and

stretched out his legs. Felt a twinge of guilt. *Don't be stupid, Daniel. Don't feel sorry for her.*

Don't care.

"Fifty dollars?"

Sarah blinked at the proprietor of Grant's Emporium as if he had sprouted a third eye to go along with the pair staring at her from behind wire-rimmed spectacles.

"That's what I said, Miss Whittier," he replied, flattening his hands on the counter that stood between them.

He'd sold her two best landscapes for only fifty dollars. The amount was a travesty. However, the San Francisco Art Association only took work on consignment and would never agree to buy paintings outright. She'd needed the money quickly in order to cover the cost of the studio repairs, forcing her to rely on Mr. Grant's dubious ability to sell high-quality artwork. She needed even more money now.

"Fifty dollars," she repeated, feeling a rush of panic. Hardly enough to buy off Mr. Daniel Cady, whose arrival in town had thrown more than just her budget into disarray. Lottie's suggestion was sounding sillier by the minute.

Sarah brushed her fingers across the brooch pinned to her waist and rejected the impulse to pawn it. She never would. Not the miniature of the *Rêve d'Or* roses, the petals a blush of salmon-tinged gold, the color her mother loved so much. It was the first ivory miniature she had successfully painted and so full of memories that Sarah could feel the weight of them whenever she touched its surface. Not even for the girls would she part with the brooch.

"That is less than what you told me your customer was willing to spend, Mr. Grant. These paintings are worth far more than twenty-five dollars apiece." Edouard had claimed Sarah had a rare gift, a true talent as an artist. He had lied to her so much, she should reconsider whether his flattery had been a lie as well. Mr. Cady had seemed genuinely impressed, however, and he had no reason whatsoever to lie to her.

"Miss Whittier." The proprietor's lips settled into a grim line as he extracted a handkerchief from his inner coat pocket, removed his spectacles, and took to cleaning them. He regarded her myopically. "I do not recall giving you any particular sales figure. After all, this is not a fine arts gallery. This is a decorative arts emporium."

Restoring his spectacles to the bridge of his nose, he waved a hand at the room, crowded with overstuffed chairs, tables, and glass cases to display his goods. A colorful collection of Japanese plant pots filled one corner. Figurines—including numerous scaled-down copies of the *Venus de Milo*—dotted every surface alongside blue and pink glass vases, fancy silver frames to hold photographs, and paper knives in mother-of-pearl and silver and carved ivory. On the walls hung Mandarin fans, though there would be better and more authentic to be found in Chinatown, and popular prints and copies of famous paintings, tags declaring their prices hanging from their gilt-edged corners. The bric-a-brac and decorations of the aspiring classes, but few original pieces of artwork and certainly no watercolors of the quality she produced. And though that was the case, Mr. Grant had assured her that he could sell her paintings for more than twenty-five apiece, even if today he had conveniently forgotten the sum.

Sarah sighed. Any amount was better than none.

"Thank you, Mr. Grant." Nodding politely, she folded the fifty dollars and put the money in her reticule. "I'm grateful you sold them for me at all. Perhaps you would consider another?"

From off the floor at her feet, she retrieved the paper-wrapped painting of the Seal Rocks that Daniel had admired in the parlor and laid it on the counter.

Mr. Grant exhaled and peered at her through his spectacles, his eyes distorted by the glass. "How much do you want for this one?"

Sarah fixed a calm smile on her face. "I would like thirty-five. It's one of my best pieces and a very popular subject." Enough to pay for the repairs, but not enough to also buy dresses for the girls. Those would simply have to wait.

Mr. Grant shook his head. "Miss Whittier—"

"Don't say no. You did sell my others quickly, and this will sell too. I'm confident." She pushed the watercolor closer to him.

"You know, it's not as though Leland Stanford is going to stroll in here any day soon looking for the next great landscape painting to hang in his parlor. Although I wouldn't mind at all if he or his missus did."

"I don't need Leland Stanford to buy it. Just someone who wants to appear as rich and influential. I'm sure you know a few folks in town who fit that description."

Rubbing his knuckles against his jaw, his glance moved between her and the painting. "You've worn me down, Miss Whittier." He undid the string holding the paper closed and peered inside. "Very nice. I'll put it in my front window and hope one of the Stock Exchange Board members strolls by and takes to it."

"I would appreciate that. Good day."

Before he changed his mind—or uttered any more quips—Sarah turned and left the shop, heading south on Kearny. She didn't have far to go to reach her destination. Mrs. McGinnis had shown her the newspaper when Sarah had returned from Lottie's, Daniel Cady's name a prominent mention among recent arrivals in San Francisco. He was staying at the Occidental, one of the finest hotels in the city.

The proper place for a man who must believe he was soon going to claim a sizable chunk of money.

Having nowhere better to go that afternoon, Daniel still had his legs stretched out and his fingers intertwined atop his waist when she walked through the ground-floor doors. Reflexively, he sat up straight. Unexpectedly, he realized he was pleased to see her. It had been a lonely eight months, searching for Josiah. He missed sociable conversation. Even with a woman who didn't look like she'd come for a chat.

He watched her make her way through the room. She wore a blue walking outfit so lacking in ornamentation, she made the other women in the lounging area look like peacocks, with their towering feathers and cascading flounces and sweeps of pearls. The vast majority of the female occupants of the room took one look and dismissed her as irrelevant, trivial. The men looked a little longer, until they decided she was no great beauty and the street scenes beyond the windows were more interesting. To dismiss her was to overlook her greatest attribute—a spine made of steel. Who was she? If he were a betting man, he'd lay odds she was not some uncultured girl from a rough Arizona town. Sarah Whittier spoke with intelligence, could paint with exceptional skill, and carried herself with authority. She had either quickly learned how to ape her betters or was not exactly who she claimed to be.

"Miss Whittier," Daniel called out and stood. She noticed and crossed to where he waited. "I didn't expect a visit. Yesterday, you left me with the impression you'd had quite enough of me."

"'Misery acquaints a man with strange bedfellows,'" she replied.

Shakespeare. *Well, there's another surprise*. "Are you in misery?"

"That rather depends on you, Mr. Cady."

She swept past him, trailing the scent of rose water, and settled onto the chair across the table from his. Daniel understood why Josiah had taken to her. She might not be arrestingly lovely, but with her even features and a habit of looking people in the face, she was more appealing than most women Daniel knew.

Sarah placed her reticule on the table but forgot to remove her crocheted gloves. Nervous, then. Rightly so.

"To what do I owe the pleasure?" he asked, retaking his seat.

Undoubtedly she was there to beg him to part with enough of Josiah's money so she could make her way until she found employment. He might be willing to give her a small amount—say, thirty or forty dollars. Any more would make him a sucker for a pretty face. As bad as Josiah.

"The Occidental is a first-rate hotel, Mr. Cady. Better than where I thought you might be staying." Her gaze slipped to the cuffs of his shirt. Looking for signs of wear, he supposed. "But in spite of appearances, I'd guess you are used to fine accommodations, since you're the grandson of Addison Hunt of Chicago and your arrival in town warrants a mention in today's *Daily Alta*. An announcement that saved me from having to hunt all over the city for you."

So that was how she had found him. "I am indeed related to Addison Hunt." Somehow. It was a mystery to Daniel how a man so cruel could've sired a daughter as gentle and loving as Grace Hunt Cady.

"What does he do?"

"He's a railroad tycoon."

"Then you can afford a room here, after all." She tilted her head, showing off the curve of her neck above the lace trimming her collar. "Or maybe you're counting on that inheritance to pay your bills."

"I have enough money to pay my way, Miss Whittier, and the Occidental has affordable rooms, believe it or not." A small reward after months of dusty boardinghouses and seedy rented lodgings. Besides, when he'd arrived in San Francisco he hadn't been planning on staying long. "I hate to disappoint you by not occupying one of the hotel's luxury suites, but my grandfather is the tycoon, not me."

Sarah peered at him. Once again, he experienced the unsettling feeling she could read his thoughts. See the bitterness in his heart. "In that case, Mr. Cady, perhaps you will accept my offer."

She retrieved a handful of bills from within her reticule, piquing his curiosity. What was she up to?

Miss Whittier laid the money on the table. "Fifty dollars, for now. Five hundred as soon as it's available."

"A BRIBE?"

Daniel Cady stared at the folded bills as if she'd just laid a pile of rancid fish on the table. Sarah swallowed, her tongue sticking to the dry roof of her mouth. She would really enjoy one of those lemonades the waiter was carrying past on a silver tray. It was hardly the right time to stop and order one, as if she were at the Occidental on a friendly social visit.

"Not a bribe, Mr. Cady," she replied, trying not to notice how hard his eyes had gone. When he'd first called to her, he'd almost seemed glad to see her. Not any longer. "A settlement against Josiah's estate. Fifty now with five hundred to follow."

He pushed the bills toward her, knocking a few onto the floor. "Five hundred dollars won't satisfy me, Miss Whittier, when I stand to inherit property worth thousands. I don't know what makes you think I would be happy to take a dime less."

Sarah scrambled to retrieve the fifty dollars, the stays of her corset jabbing her ribs. "I was thinking you might not ever prove you're actually Josiah's son and would be happy with the money." *And go away*.

"Oh, I'll prove I'm his son, Miss Whittier. Whether he wanted to admit it or not. And I'll get that estate."

Sarah shoved the money into her reticule, snagging her glove on the teeth of a hair comb stored inside. "Is that all you care about, Mr. Cady? Getting hold of Josiah's money?"

Her raised voice drew censorious glances from two women seated on a nearby sofa, who fell to whispering.

"I'm not the only one here who wants Josiah's money." His eyes were growing harder and darker by the second. "Isn't it your plan to use the proceeds from his estate to open some art studio to display the inferior creations of self-deluded society girls?"

"My students aren't society girls." She yanked the ribbons of her reticule. "They're poor immigrant women who desperately need the work I intend to provide them."

"A charity," he scoffed.

Sarah scowled at him. "Is there something wrong with wanting to help those less fortunate?"

"I didn't figure you to be the type who would throw good money after bad."

"Mr. Cady, you can't have failed to notice all the factories in San Francisco. Their smokestacks nearly crowd the skyline in some parts of the city. In some of those factories, women labor at menial tasks, barely able to make a living. Some resort to other means to support themselves and their families." He seemed a well-traveled man of the world; she didn't have to fill in the details for him about what those means were. "I want better for them, or those few I can assist who have some talent for art. Anything better than a life on the street or in some filthy and dangerous factory."

"And you believe your studio is the solution," he replied, his tone too flat to decipher.

"I had one particular ability when I came to San Francisco. I am an artist and reasonably talented. And I know how to teach others to sketch and execute designs." "*Such talent, ma mie. Mon trésor.*" Sarah shook off the memory and focused on Daniel, looking skeptical. "My partner, Miss Charlotte Samuelson, and I have been selecting needy girls with demonstrated skill and training them to become first-class artists. We will specialize in chromolithography and colored photographs. Actually, any custom artwork someone might desire. Those less artistic will run the press and work with the customers. In addition to the lessons in technique I give, Lottie teaches them grammar and arithmetic, if they're not already proficient."

"Setting up a business is an expensive proposition, Miss Whittier."

"I do have financial supporters who believe in my cause." She realized her mistake the instant his gaze flickered.

Daniel leaned into the padded back of the lounge room chair. "Doesn't seem to me like you need Josiah's inheritance, then. Seems like you've got matters under control."

Sarah balled her hands into fists, the fine crochet stitching of her gloves preventing her fingernails from digging into her skin. He was a dreadful man. Arrogant. Selfish. Smug. He would never be generous with her or the girls. She felt lost and she hated it.

"What are *your* intentions for Josiah's estate?" The two women seated near them rose and huffed off, likely tired of listening to her argue with Daniel. "As the grandson of a railroad tycoon, perhaps you've discovered a pressing need to build a mansion or purchase a yacht. Or perhaps to impress an heiress?"

He didn't even flinch in response to her sarcasm. "I think I already explained I'm not the tycoon. But if you must know, I intend to start an import business and build a decent house for my two sisters with the money. We've been living in a cramped three-room apartment for too long and they deserve better."

Her pulse was thrumming so intensely in her head it began to ache. She could just imagine what sort of house the grandson of a railroad tycoon thought would be decent enough. Probably one that would be a lot larger than the house on Nob Hill. "Ball gowns and tickets to the opera can be so expensive."

"They are ten, Miss Whittier, and don't need ball gowns." Daniel pulled in his feet, preparing to stand. "I commend your noble goals, but I'm rather certain the probate court will rule that my sisters and I are the lawful heirs to Josiah's estate. I'm not going to apologize for that fact. Your bribes won't change my mind about pursuing the case and neither will your attempts to make me feel guilty."

Remorseful, she gripped his hand to stop him before he could rise. "I want you to see the shop. See what I intend to do."

"You're wasting your time."

She very likely was. "My future and the futures of four girls are on the line, Mr. Cady. Everything we've dreamed of. Let me decide if I'm wasting my time or not."

Daniel's irritation had eased by the time they had gone a block. He'd been insulted by her attempt to buy him off and angered by her implication that the promises he'd made to Lily and Marguerite were a less worthy use of Josiah's money than her plans, but the walk in the refreshing afternoon air had cleared his head and let him think. Miss Whittier was merely fighting for her cause. He would do the same in her shoes. He *was* doing the same, fighting to win his proper inheritance. For his sisters' sake. For the vow he'd made to his mother on her deathbed.

The woman marching along the sidewalk beside him hadn't said a word since she'd stalked out of the Occidental, Daniel in her wake. Sarah's face was as stern as a schoolmarm's, the ribbons of her hat fluttering beneath her chin. She couldn't possibly hope she would convince him that her shop would detach him from his . . . from Josiah's money. But then, Sarah Whittier wasn't like any other woman he'd ever met. Maybe she did.

And maybe she would.

Sarah looked over and caught him staring. "Debating how to tell me you don't want to see my shop after all, Mr. Cady?"

"No, Miss Whittier, that's not what I'm thinking about in the least."

"I won't ask you to elaborate," she retorted.

Spunky and determined. Could be a dangerous combination in a woman.

He almost smiled at the thought as they hurried across the street, dodging a draft horse with a shopboy astride its broad flanks, his feet barely reaching the stirrups. Going the other direction, a wagon carrying what looked to be freshly arrived Chinese trundled up the road, each of the men—and many boys—perched atop a canvas bag probably filled with their belongings, their eyes downcast and shoulders slumped. *Interesting place*.

Sarah reached the curb before Daniel, evading his attempt to take her elbow to assist her onto the sidewalk. Typical for her, he decided.

Sarah stopped at an empty corner storefront and pulled open the beaded reticule suspended from her wrist. "Here we are."

She turned a key in the lock and stepped through the doorway ahead of him, the shop bell jingling over their heads and the musty smell of unused space swirling in the air. "Don't lean against anything. I only received the keys yesterday and haven't had a chance to clean."

"The dirt doesn't bother me."

"It does, however, bother *me*," she replied, sounding impatient that he didn't understand that she would want everything to be perfect.

Removing his hat, Daniel wandered through the rooms, his footsteps breaking a trail through the dust coating the scarred wood floor. Lined on two sides with large windows, the store comprised a medium-sized space walled off in the corner to form a separate set of offices. An iron staircase against the separating wall punched through the ceiling, leading to the upper floor. Given the location—at the center of the city's commercial district—and the size, the shop had to have come with a hefty price tag. But he already could see why she'd selected it—the space was perfect.

While he wandered, Sarah explained her plans in a carrying voice. How the main floor would be used to display samples and would be where they'd interact with customers. That design work and painting would take place upstairs, where the windows were large and airy. That the gas-lit room right behind him was for a girl named Emma's business office.

"The lithography area will be located against the back wall," she was saying. "The stones are heavy to move and have to be near the press, so it's critical to have a large ground-floor workspace. Also, there's a sink and plumbing available for washing away etching solutions and inks, along with these wonderful windows to work by."

The more she talked, the stronger and more confident she sounded.

Daniel fiddled with his hat brim and observed her, took in the gratified smile curving her lips, the assured sweep of her arms as she gestured to point out this or that. She was too young to comprehend all that might go wrong in spite of her best intentions. Naive about the world. If her donors withdrew their financial support, the loss of the store would be a terrible blow. With no one he could see to pick her back up.

The guilty spasm in his gut that had taken hold in the Occidental's lounge tweaked harder and forced him to look away.

"Whoever rented this storefront before left in a hurry," he observed, having to say something, anything other than what was on his mind.

"A milliner." Out of the corner of his eye, he could see that her gaze followed his, scrutinizing the countertops and display shelving tacked to the walls, grime darkening their surfaces. Pausing where a table edge had rubbed a hole in the striped pale green wallpaper and been left unrepaired. Noting the water stain on the ceiling. "I don't know what happened with her."

She sounded bothered by the fact. Maybe she was worried that if the space had failed the milliner, it might fail her too. Not totally naive.

"I hope you won't be unsuccessful like she was, Miss Whittier," he said before he could put two thoughts together as to why he felt the need to reassure her.

An amused look crossed her face. "You can't suddenly be on my side, Mr. Cady."

Daniel crushed his hat brim before he admitted that as well. Miss Whittier was intelligent and determined, strong willed and pretty enough . . . commendable attributes, but ones he couldn't afford to admire. He had to remember that she was not to be trusted until his lawyer had finished reviewing the particulars of Josiah's estate. Not if he wanted to keep a cool head around her.

Not if he wanted to keep himself from caring.

"I came here to fetch what Josiah owed me and my sisters," he said plainly, truthfully, "not to ruin a young woman's future."

"You might succeed in doing both."

He slapped his hat against his thigh, fanning an eddy of dust across the floor. "Listen, I'm not out to hurt you. But I can't go back on the promises I've made, any more than you can go back on yours. You believe your girls need you. My sisters need me."

"Do you honestly think we can fulfill both our promises, Mr. Cady?"

"You have your backers," he pointed out.

"Anxious men whose charitable impulses read well in the newspaper but don't always hold up under pressure." She wasn't naive in the least.

Daniel stilled the nervous motion of his hands. Pretty young women like Sarah shouldn't be so cynical or worldly-wise. They should be sheltered and supported, what he'd spent half a lifetime doing for his sisters, trying to keep them from suffering the worst of the damage Josiah had caused. He didn't have to learn much about Sarah Whittier to realize that, even though she'd worked for Josiah in that comfortable house, she'd had to scrape and claw to be where she was today. Just like he had, making them two of a kind. An uncomfortable recognition.

"What do you want from me?" he asked.

"I didn't bring you here to impress you with my empty shop and its filthy floors." She pulled in a long breath. "I brought you here because, if you succeed in gaining Josiah's estate, I want you to invest in the studio. I would pay you back, with interest."

"I can't do that." Even if he wanted to help Sarah Whittier, for the sake of Lily's and Marguerite's futures, he couldn't.

Sarah gave him a withering look and retrieved her reticule from the countertop where she'd left it. Apparently she had let herself hope for more from him.

"You were right." Her eyes were deep brown, the color of cocoa or polished walnut. Lovely even when dull with disillusionment. "I did waste my time."

Soon, me boy, soon you'll be rich.

The tip of his cigar flared orange as he inhaled. A curl of blue smoke writhed above his head, dashed away on the wind, and he shifted his foot to let the ashes fall to the plank sidewalk. Frank thought, with an upward contortion of his lips—which no one who knew him would ever call a smile—that it would be funny if the wood caught fire and burned down the entire block. All these rich folks in their fancy houses, the glass of their bay windows blinking like diamonds in the setting sun, the fancy flowers, bright as rubies and sapphires, in their gardens scrabbling to take root in the sand, showing off like they're better than everyone. Pretending, just because they were lucky and struck gold—or figured out how to swindle the ones who'd struck gold—that the twirls of their carved wood doorways and banisters made them superior. Made them forget that they'd been grubbing in dirt once, sprouting blisters on blisters, patching old clothes and stuffing newspapers inside their shirts to stay warm when the fog clung like soot on a chimney stack.

Well, he'd be lucky too. And then he'd build himself a house right next to theirs on Nob Hill. Show them all what it meant to be rich. Just like he'd always planned.

Frank watched through the window as the light in the kitchen flared and held. The cook was at work starting a late dinner, for her and that Whittier woman who owned that house too big for just the two of them. How preciously sweet that old man Cady had left her everything, according to what his woman had found out. Frank chuckled. He knew men like Cady. When it came time to meet their Maker, they suddenly turned as generous as a saint.

Well, she could keep the house. He just wanted the gold, thank you very much. And he wasn't alone. When that reporter had come around the saloon that evening, asking questions about Cady, he'd set off a frenzy of speculation. Frank had supplied a few answers to the fellow—wasn't a problem at all, not when the reporter was handing out silver coins like they were going out of fashion—told him about Cady's mine in the Black Hills, but Frank wasn't going to tell the reporter more. Not if the stories were true. He was here for the main chance, because if there was gold for the getting, he was the man to get it.

Shifting his hips on the stone steps of the unfinished house across the way, he dragged on the cigar, a final puff that filled his lungs, and felt satisfaction in his bones. It'd been worth roughing up Manuel for one of these Havanas. When he was rich, he'd buy himself as many as he wanted. Dozens. By the box. By the case. He felt so good, he grinned at the Chinese boy hurrying along the street with a sack of cleaned laundry slung over his shoulder. The boy, slitted black eyes judging pretty fast, wisely trotted to the other side of the road, steering clear. Maybe he'd get himself a Chinese servant boy when he was rich. And an Irish girl to do the cleaning. Yep, that sounded good.

Soon. The next time the Whittier woman was outta the house along with the servant, he'd find that gold. The nuggets old Josiah Cady had stored away in a hidey-hole. If it took more than one visit . . . Frank chuckled again. Visit. Like he was an invited guest. If it took more than one visit to find the gold, he didn't care. And if he had to rough up the Whittier woman because she wouldn't oblige him, he didn't care about that, either.

He dropped the cigar on the planks and stood.

Soon, me boy, soon you'll be rich.

"It did not go well yesterday afternoon, did it?" Lottie's polished ivory leather boots stepped into Sarah's view, peeping beyond the ruffled hem of her draped rose-pink skirts. Only Lottie could wear light-colored shoes in San Francisco and keep them pristine. "Sarah?"

Sarah looked up from the worktable. Her friend's pale eyes, the sort of startlingly clear blue that appeared bottomless, fathomless, hooked Sarah's with the tenacity of a fishing barb.

"Emma is waiting for further instruction, Lottie," Sarah said, pointing her pencil at the young German woman seated at the corner desk. Hearing her name, she lifted her head. Her full, smooth face masked a fierce pride that permitted no one to get close, no one to learn the details of her hardscrabble childhood. It didn't conceal her keen mind.

"Emma is working the balance sheet examples I gave her," Lottie responded. "She will be busy for the next few minutes, at least. Please tell me exactly what happened yesterday."

"During lessons is not the time to discuss this." Sarah returned her attention to the girl at her side. "Remember, Anne, when you draw the master for a chromolithograph, keep the lines distinct so that when we make our transfer copies for each color, you won't get confused."

The girl, her tall back bent over the table set beneath the window of the second-floor study Sarah had converted into a workroom, frowned with concentration. Beneath her pen, the outlines of a palm tree and oaks near a pond came to life, filling in with her imagination the details the photograph Sarah had provided did not contain. Anne had a natural gift for sketching landscapes. Her talent would go to waste plying a needle as a seamstress, which was how she earned a scant living.

Sarah's gaze flitted over the girl's profile. The bright sunlight streaming through the window lit Anne's face. A fresh bruise bloomed on her chin. She had tried to turn away from the blow, this time. Sarah wondered how many other bruises were hidden beneath her high collars and long sleeves. Emma's life might be hardscrabble, but at least she didn't arrive at lessons with her face purpling from a man's fist.

Sarah's fingers wavered, wanting to brush away the strand of chestnut hair fallen across the bruise. She had touched Anne only once, when the girl had first come to work for her. A quick hug that had caused her to flinch like she'd been doused with scalding water. Sarah had never touched Anne again.

She returned her gaze to Anne's careful sketching. "That's it. Lovely."

"Sarah, you need to tell me." Lottie leaned over as far as her corset and her heavy bustle permitted. She stared Sarah in the face. "What did Mr. Cady say?"

Anne's thin, dark eyebrows scrunched. "Mr. Cady?"

Sarah shot an admonishing glance at Lottie before responding. She hadn't planned on telling the girls about Daniel until absolutely necessary. If he turned out to be a swindler—an unlikely possibility, but she had to hope—they would never learn of him at all. "A man who claims he's a relative of Mr. Josiah recently arrived in town. He came all the way from Chicago."

"What does he want, Miss Sarah?" Emma asked from across the room.

This house, my inheritance . . . "He simply wanted to visit Josiah, Emma. He was unaware he had passed away. That's all."

Emma exchanged a look with Anne. "A man does not make a long train ride from Chicago, Miss Sarah, simply for a visit," said Emma. "He looks for something else, I think."

Setting down her pencil, Sarah regarded the girls in turn. "I will handle Mr. Cady, girls. Please don't speak to the others about this. You need to concentrate on your studies and our preparations for the studio, that's all. Don't worry."

"Why might we worry?" Anne asked.

Sarah frowned; she'd made a poor choice of words. "Anne, you can begin coloring the master sketch. You've drawn enough detail to give a good sense of the landscape. Lottie, I need to speak with you in the garden."

Sarah removed her apron and swept out of the room, frightening Rufus from his favorite chair on the landing.

"So it did go badly," Lottie stated, pulling her skirts upward to keep from stumbling as she dashed down the stairs behind Sarah.

Sarah strode through the dining room, Rufus trotting behind, straight out the rear door past the kitchen and down into the garden. She breathed in the sweetness of the roses, enjoyed the sunlight warming her face, listened to the burble of the fountain. *For just a moment, let there be peace . . .*

Any peace she would feel would be an illusion, though. An illusion she could ill afford to lose herself in.

"He didn't accept the bribe. He threw the money back at me, in fact." Sarah hugged her arms around her waist and watched Rufus weave between the legs of the wicker garden chairs, his bent tail slapping against the stretchers. "He boldly proclaimed he would definitely prove he was Josiah's son. And then, foolish me, I thought to take him to the shop. I wanted to show him what we intend to do. Maybe even convince him to invest in our business. As if my plans could melt that glacial heart of his."

"I do not believe you have known him long enough to assess the condition of his heart, Sarah," Lottie replied with a small, sly smile.

"Oh, Lottie, don't tease. Not at a time like this." Scooping up Rufus, Sarah took to pacing along the tiny gravel path. After Josiah's passing, she had paced endlessly, wearing a track in the parlor carpet, which Mrs. McGinnis had spent hours repairing with a hot iron and a coarse coconut-fiber brush. "What am I to do now?"

"I will not suggest you plead or beg him to be generous. I know that is not like you."

"We'll have to find more donors. It's obvious." But if she lost the house and the Placerville property, would anyone be willing to provide enough money to cover all her expenses? The question made her brain churn like a paddlewheel on a riverboat. "And I'll have to sell more paintings. Beyond that, I can't think of what else to do. And before you say 'pray'—"

"Sarah," Lottie interrupted, her tone chastising but her expression kind. "We simply must trust in God's mercy."

Trust in the God who had let her father die and then her mother and siblings perish in a summer storm, blown away on the wind? The God who had deposited her in the home of a bitter aunt who didn't know what it meant to love? The same God who had brought Edouard Marchand into her life, the man who had nearly led her to ruin?

Sarah curled her fingers through Rufus's fur and looked away, stared at the roses basking in the sunshine, let the tabby's purr rumble through her arms. And she said the words burning in her heart that would make Lottie cross. "God sent Daniel Cady here. If He intended to be merciful, the man never would have found me."

"You cannot know what His plans are for you. But I believe you are not meant to fail now, so near to realizing your dream. Our dream."

"Let's hope Daniel Cady pays attention to God's merciful plans." *Because I do not trust them.*

The rear door slammed open and Minnie burst through,

bounding down the steps into the garden. "Miss Sarah, I've found another girl."

"Minnie Tobin," Lottie chided. She squeezed Sarah's arm before wagging a teasing finger at the girl. "How many times have you been told to make a more ladylike entrance?"

Minnie flushed. "Sorry, miss, but Mrs. McGinnis said you were both out here and I wanted Miss Sarah to know about Phoebe right away." Minnie turned to Sarah. Lottie was her partner, but it would be Sarah's decision if they took on another girl. How they could afford to, given Daniel, she had no idea.

"Phoebe, that's her name," Minnie continued, sensing Sarah's uncertainty and sounding a tad frantic. "Pretty, isn't it? Says she's French. She's a dress and cloak-maker alongside my sister. My sister says her needlework is first-rate, and she has embroidered designs of her own creation on some of their customers' collars. Best yet, she's good at talking with folks and pretty. She might make a smart shopgirl. But her ma died not long ago and she has huge debts to pay because of the doctor bills, and she's thinking of working the streets in the Barbary."

Sarah's fingers must have pinched Rufus's skin, because the cat mewled a protest.

"Not there," Lottie whispered.

Sarah tried to catch her breath. She could not let anyone make a choice to work the alleyways of the Barbary. Daniel Cady and the threat he posed would have to be set aside. Because there was another girl for them to help. Another homeless cat with a broken tail.

"Will you help her?" Minnie asked. "Emma's already said she can take her in."

Lottie nodded. Sarah handed Rufus to her. "Tell Emma to get ready for her, Minnie. We'll meet her at her boardinghouse in an hour. With Phoebe."

"I expect, if the documents are as described, we should have no problem presenting your case, Mr. Cady. They will make a very solid set of evidence as to your identity in addition to this telegram from your father." Mr. Sinclair darted a hasty smile, white teeth flashing beneath his ample mustache as he ran a trimmed fingernail across the crease in the telegram and returned it to Daniel. He had the round face and belly of a man who indulged his tastes and eyes that glittered with conceit. A heavy dosing of his citrusy Farina cologne permeated the closed room, causing Daniel to question Sinclair's ability to smell. At the lawyer's back, a tall window framed a scene of the turreted bank building across the street, a pompous view of a pompous property. Appropriate for a pompous man. "My review of the will revealed the omission of your name and that of your sisters—Mr. Josiah Cady was very thorough in his claim that you were deceased—so I will be so bold as to say the judge shall declare you the proper beneficiaries of the estate. Without demonstrated intent to leave no bequest, probate rules in favor of children."

"I'm happy to hear it." Daniel tucked the telegram into his inner coat pocket and reclined into the curved arms of the office chair. He didn't have to like the view or the lawyer. He merely had to pay the man for his services and be done with him. "How much do you think my sisters and I will receive?"

"Once all the properties are sold and all taxes and fees are settled, I would say around twenty thousand total."

"That's all?" Much less than the thirty thousand his father had bragged he was worth. Leave it to Josiah to exaggerate his value. Or to do an exceptional job of hiding his riches.

"Twenty thousand is no small change, Mr. Cady." Sinclair tucked a thumb into his silk waistcoat pocket. "Enough to fund your business venture and build that house you were telling me about, with money to spare. There might have been more, if the mining claim your father staked in Grass Valley hadn't turned out to be a bust."

A failed investment. Josiah had been a fool to the end. "Is it possible my father could have placed some of his proceeds in a secret account somewhere? Or bought property we don't know about?"

The lawyer shrugged, his heavy gold watch chain winking with the movement. "If he did, he probably took that information to his grave. Unless he let Miss Whittier know its whereabouts. Your father seems to have been awfully fond of her. I always find it peculiar when a man leaves money to a single young woman who isn't a relation."

Daniel let the innuendo pass; Miss Whittier had claimed Josiah was like a father to her and Daniel believed her. "Could you look into it? As you can see in that telegram, Josiah claimed to have made more money off his gold strike, and I wouldn't put it past him to have hidden some away if he did."

"I might be able to uncover additional assets." He examined Daniel. "For an extra fee."

"I'll pay it."

"Good. Very good." Another smile, all white-teethed smugness. "For her sake, I hope Miss Whittier has been aboveboard on reporting all known assets. Any deception will not sit well with Judge Doran. As it is, she'll see her share of the inheritance severely curtailed."

"How much might she get?" Enough to support that shop of hers? He hadn't calculated how much her expenses might be or asked how much money her supporters were going to supply. He'd presumed the funds would be enough; he hadn't wanted to learn otherwise. "She has a business she's trying to fund."

"A business? Really? Are you certain it's legitimate?"

Daniel's jaw tightened. "It seems legitimate to me." If that shop wasn't, it was a pretty elaborate hoax.

Sinclair shrugged. "Let's just say it's best for us to be on our guard when it comes to dealing with Miss Whittier."

"How much might she get after probate's settled?" he repeated.

"Judge Doran will make some provision; several hundred

dollars, maybe even a thousand. More than she probably had when she came to this town, but not much to men like you or me, right, Mr. Cady?" Sinclair chuckled. "After all—and I quote the Roman who first said it—'money alone sets all the world in motion.'"

A quote Daniel's grandfather would have appreciated. An opinion, he had to admit, he'd started to share.

"I can recommend the name of an excellent real estate agent for the auction of the house once you obtain ownership," Sinclair continued.

"I'm sure you can," Daniel said. That was his plan—sell the house, get his money, and go back to Chicago where he belonged.

Sinclair slipped a card from his coat pocket and flipped it to its blank side. He produced a pencil from the same pocket and wrote down a name. "Contact my friend at this office. If you hire me as your attorney to represent you, you wouldn't even need to remain in town to see the transaction through. I could handle everything for you and send the proceeds to Chicago."

He made it sound so simple. So painless. But it wouldn't be painless for Sarah Whittier. Daniel wondered where she would go. Back to her relatives in Arizona, possibly, even though she claimed to love San Francisco. She must have friends in town who would take her in if she wanted to stay. Where she ended up really wasn't his concern. And neither was whatever would happen to her needy girls and her shop. If he kept that in mind, he would be fine.

Daniel slipped the card from Sinclair's fingers and stood. "Let me know what you find out about Josiah's assets."

"Absolutely, Mr. Cady."

Before the man could rise to see him off, Daniel strode across the Turkish rug covering the office floor and stomped down the stairs and out onto the street. He sucked in the San Francisco air, wanting to clear his lungs of Sinclair's citrus-spice cologne and the stale smell of greed. But he couldn't, and he had a feeling the stench would cling to him a very long time.

There were worse places in San Francisco than the streets near the wharves. Worse neighborhoods, where prostitutes and opium dens and gambling houses coexisted, impoverished immigrants crammed tight into dilapidated quarters, and excrement mingled with rainwater to form a soupy, disgusting mix on the cobblestones. But not by much. If it weren't the middle of the day, Sarah would never dare come here.

She stood in the doorway to Phoebe's apartment and took shallow breaths. The bay breezes wafted the sour stink of a nearby tallow factory through the one window, and her stomach rolled. She wouldn't be there much longer, though. The girl was eager to quit her dank and gloomy room, and she was hastily rounding up her few belongings with Minnie's help. Minnie chattered incessantly, untroubled by the surroundings, happy to have another girl at the shop. A new member of their family.

More delicately boned and frail-seeming than Sarah had visualized, Phoebe met Sarah's first criteria by looking her directly in the face and proclaiming she would work harder than anyone. Phoebe had been quick to recognize her best opportunity to flee the life she was living. Her mother's passing had left her alone—no siblings, no relations to tend to or be tended by. Sarah understood how it felt to be adrift in the world, as untethered as a cottonwood seed. A lesson Sarah herself had learned more thoroughly than she had ever anticipated she might. She had tried to cling, nonetheless—to Aunt Eugenie, who had resented her; to Edouard, who had betrayed her; to Josiah, who had perished. Each loss harder than the last. Would she be forced to leave San Francisco, too, in order to start over once again? Find a new situation to cling to? She hoped not.

Phoebe finished bundling a spare bodice and stockings, hair

comb, and a collection of embroidery needles inside her winter shawl and strode to the front door. About the same amount of possessions as Sarah had taken away from Los Angeles. Funny how one's life could be reduced to the number of objects one could carry in her arms.

"Do you need to leave a message for your landlord or perhaps make a final payment?"

"I have not paid him for a month." The girl's nonchalance surprised Sarah. "He will be happy to see the back side of me."

"So long as he doesn't fetch the police on you," she said.

"The police? They think my landlord is worthless too. They will not bother." Phoebe smiled at her. Sarah was ridiculously glad to see the girl had all her teeth. Clean, white ones that shone against her plump, pink lips. "*Merci*, miss. There has never been anyone to care about me. Never."

The slip of French brought Sarah up short, a harsh reminder of Edouard, and she was more abrupt with Phoebe than she intended. "I want to help you and can. That's all there is to it."

"That is not all. There have been other women at the dress-making shop who come and pretend they want to help. They bring flowers and such, as if a bouquet would make life better, smile and pat our hair like we are stupid children, when all we want is decent work and respect. They shame us. But you do not shame me."

Tears burned the back of Sarah's throat. This . . . *this* was why she had to do all she could for her girls. This need to be free of shame. This need to have a decent life full of promise and second chances. She recognized Phoebe's feelings because she'd shared them the moment Josiah had taken her in, no questions asked, no explanation needed as to why she was on his doorstep or what she'd done that had brought her there.

"Work hard and there will be no need to thank me and no need to ever feel shame again." Sarah smiled away the tears. "You're one of us now, and I will take care of you."

Minnie grinned over Phoebe's shoulder. Sarah had said the same to her. To Cora and Anne and Emma as well. "That's exactly right. You're part of our little family, Phoebe."

Phoebe's eyes sparkled. Maybe with grateful tears. "Family? I have not had one in so long, I forget what that is!"

Oh, oh. Sarah's breath caught. "I will take care of you," she repeated.

Seven

"WHAT DO YOU THINK?" Sarah asked Lottie, standing next to her in the shop the next morning and also taking a break from her chores.

With an embroidered linen handkerchief, Lottie blotted the sweat glistening along her hairline. "Of Phoebe? Or the shop?"

"Both, of course."

Lottie's gaze tracked Phoebe as the French girl followed Cora Gallagher around, her skirts hitched into her waistband, rough boots peeping beneath the heavy twill. Compared to Cora, with her large frame and shock of luscious auburn hair, Phoebe was petite and delicate. But the two girls seemed to have hit it off, if the fact that their giggles were growing louder and louder was any indication.

"She is the most curious mixture of French charm and American resilience," Lottie answered after a peal of laughter rang out, echoing in the space, and Phoebe slapped Cora playfully with a rag. Lottie tucked her handkerchief in the sleeve of her dress—a printed cotton that came the closest to a work dress Sarah had ever seen her in but would be a fine Sunday frock to most women—and smiled. "I rather like her."

Sarah did too.

"And what about the shop?" She waved impatiently at the space, already a thousand times cleaner than when she'd brought Daniel there. They had stripped the ruined wallpaper and scrubbed the display shelves, which were ready for fresh coats of paint, and the oak floor nearly gleamed gold in the morning sunlight. The shop had become more a diamond in the rough than what earlier could have passed for a chunk of dirty granite. If Daniel Cady saw the space this morning . . . Sarah released a frustrated sigh. He would still be unwilling to invest. "A location on Market Street, close to all the stores, would have brought in more customers."

"Someday we will get there. But for now, this is ideal." Lottie bent to dip a washing cloth in the bucket of soapy water sitting beneath the front window. Wringing it out, she glanced up. "I wanted to surprise you with this later, but Mr. Halliday has committed a sum of money for the shop. After no small amount of cajoling and being stuffed with Cook's excellent berry tarts yesterday afternoon, I confess. And I will soon approach Mrs. Linforth about becoming a customer. She has that new house she needs to decorate, and a series of Anne's lithographs would be perfect in her parlor. I might even be able to convince her to host a supper and a showing of our art in support of our cause. If we get enough customers and backers," she continued, leaning close so the girls couldn't hear, "we will not need to worry about Mr. Daniel Cady and his claims on the estate. We are very close, as it is."

"That's wonderful!" *We will succeed despite you, Daniel Cady.*

"And why you have me as a partner, Miss Whittier."

"There is none better, Miss Samuelson."

Cora caught Sarah's attention as she swayed behind the main counter, sweeping a rag across the surface, a popular Irish melody on her lips.

"If we don't get the girls to concentrate on their tasks, it won't be Daniel Cady that stands in the way of this business opening." She raised her voice. "Cora, you've missed some spots. I don't know if dancing and cleaning go well together."

Cora grinned and winked at Phoebe. "Ah, but they do for

me!" she said with a flourish of the rag, sending a billow of dust twirling in the air.

"Well, don't teach Phoebe any bad habits," Sarah teased.

"She is not, miss," Phoebe answered, her faint French accent distorting the vowels, tugging painfully at Sarah's heart.

If she'd realized the girl would remind her of Edouard every time she opened her mouth . . . "I certainly hope not. Don't forget to mop the back room too."

"We won't," the girls answered in unison.

Sarah took up the broom and retrieved her dustpan to work a pile of soot and old dirt into the center of the room. It was good to hear Cora and Phoebe so happy, so full of life. She shouldn't begrudge them any joy, when outside of this shop they had so little. Sarah started humming along to Cora's tune.

"Cora, what is that you are singing?" Lottie asked as she scrubbed smudges from the front window.

"Just a tune my pa is fond of. It's called 'Finigan's Wake.' It goes like this, Miss Charlotte." Cora cleared her throat while Phoebe stood aside, a delighted look on her face.

"Tim Finigan lived in Walker Street,
a gentleman Irish mighty odd
He'd a beautiful brogue, so rich and sweet,
and to rise in the world he carried the hod

But, you see, he'd a sort of a tippling way,
with a love for the liquor poor Tim was born
To help him through his way each day,
he'd a drop of the craythur' every morn."

Sarah paused in her sweeping and noticed that Lottie's washing cloth had ceased its circles on the windowpane.

Cora grinned, possibly taking the silence as approval, and continued:

"Whack, hurrah! Blood and 'ounds! Ye soul ye

Welt the flure, yer trotters shake
Isn't it the truth I tould ye?
Lots of fun at Finigan's Wake!

One morning Tim was rather full,
His head felt heavy, which made him shake;
He fell from the ladder and broke his skull,
So they carried him home his corpse to wake."

Lottie's brow furrowed and she looked over her shoulder to stare at Cora.

Sarah fought a smile. "Cora, that's probably enough."

"It just gets funnier from here, Miss Sarah. You have to hear." Right then, the shop bell jingled. Cora proceeded with the rest of the verse, hitting the notes with gusto.

"They rolled him up in a clean white sheet,
And laid him out upon a bed
With fourteen candles at his feet
And a barrel of whiskey at his head—"

Cora abruptly halted, her eyes gone wide. Sarah glanced toward the door to see who'd entered the shop.

Oh dear.

"Am I interrupting a party?" asked Daniel, slipping his hat from his head, taking in the scene.

Two young women, dressed in coarse-cloth work gowns and heavy shoes, gaped at him from behind the store's counter. The one who'd been singing nudged the petite, dark-haired one and then, astonishingly, winked at him. If these were examples of Miss Whittier's employees, he didn't hold out much hope for the shop.

There were employees, though, and that he was glad to see. He'd let Sinclair's concerns trouble him unnecessarily. Drive him to come here this morning and prove to himself that Sarah was, at least, not lying about this.

"We were . . . we . . ." Sarah was stuttering, her cheeks pinked. He thought anew that she might not be conventionally beautiful, but she was pretty enough. She would be prettier, though, if her mouth weren't hanging open.

She glanced at the blonde woman at her side, looking for support. With her elaborately coifed hair and tailored dress, the woman didn't look as though she belonged in a dusty storefront, a dripping washing rag in her hand and a stained apron tied around her severely corseted waist. Her pale eyes narrowed, assessing Daniel, questioning who he was. Apparently Sarah wasn't going to enlighten her just yet.

"We were enjoying a song while we cleaned the shop," Sarah finally said. "Music helps the work go more quickly, don't you agree?"

Daniel propped up an eyebrow. "Interesting song choice." An Irish drinking song. Her girls certainly weren't bored society misses.

"Yes, well . . ." Sarah huffed, aware of the poor impression the song and her girls, who had stopped gaping and moved on to whispering together, had made. Crisply, she set aside her broom and stripped off her apron. "What brings you to our studio this morning?"

"Sarah, you might want to introduce us," the woman next to her interrupted.

"Oh. Certainly," she answered, though the snap of her brown eyes suggested she would much rather march Daniel right back out of the shop.

She addressed the girls. "Cora Gallagher, Phoebe Morel, this is Mr. Daniel Cady."

Stepping forward, he could see them more clearly. They were both pretty, youth filling their cheeks, but he wondered how long it would be before hard work eroded the unlined skin.

Cora batted her eyelids. "Minnie told me about you. You're Mr. Josiah's relative."

Relative. Not *son*. Sarah must not want her girls to know exactly who he was, information that might present a host of embarrassing questions. Such as why Sarah had inherited the house and not him. He'd let it go. For the moment. "That's me."

"And this is my business partner, Miss Charlotte Samuelson." Sarah indicated the woman at her side.

"Very pleased to meet you, Mr. Cady," Miss Samuelson replied softly and politely, her fingers squeezing his with the acceptable amount of strength. "Sarah has told me so much about you."

He could just imagine.

"Are you only visitin', Mr. Cady, or have you come to stay in San Francisco?" Cora asked.

"Cora, it is impolite to ask his plans," corrected Sarah.

"Just visiting, Miss Gallagher," Daniel replied.

He scanned the shop, pausing where the most noticeable changes had occurred. There were a lot of improvements in a short time. Miss Whittier was serious about her business. *Thank God something's for real in this town*. "Much tidier, Miss Whittier. Not that the dirt bothered me."

"We have a long way to go." Sarah glanced down. She'd been twisting her hands around the handle of the broom as though she hoped to strangle it. She relaxed her grip.

"We intend to open in a week or so," said Miss Samuelson. "We have every confidence we shall be ready by then."

Trusting in those backers Sarah mentioned. Or that maybe he wouldn't get Josiah's will overturned. An awful lot of trust. "Looks like you shall, Miss Samuelson."

"What brings you by?" Sarah asked again.

Daniel strolled farther into the shop. "I was out for a walk. Nice day. Thought I'd see how things were going here. Glad to see you're hard at work." Very glad. But now he was back to worrying how she would support it.

"I told you my girls are diligent, as well as talented. This shop is their future. Right, Cora, Phoebe?"

Phoebe nodded. Cora took the opportunity to smile pertly at Daniel before responding to Sarah's comment. "Absolutely, Miss Sarah. We'd work our fingers to the bone for you."

"Hm." He suspected they would, the way they gazed adoringly at her, their personal savior.

"She's teaching us to paint and draw like the best artists in California," Cora continued, her hands gesturing with enthusiasm. "But none of us will ever be as good as she is."

"Thank you, Cora," said Sarah without a trace of arrogance, sounding humbled that some ill-educated immigrant girl thought the world of her.

Daniel swallowed, though the action didn't relieve the tension in his throat.

"I never did ask you how much the lease was on this place," he said. She had to have spent some of Josiah's money on the first month's rent and supplies. Maybe even wages to the girls. Money Daniel might never collect.

"Eighty-five a month." She lifted her chin, daring him to call her a spendthrift. "Rental property is expensive in San Francisco."

"Sarah negotiated an excellent deal," said Miss Samuelson, rising to her friend's defense.

But given what a probate judge was likely to award . . . "Several hundred dollars wouldn't go far," Daniel unintentionally murmured aloud, finishing his thought.

Miss Whittier's brows scrunched together. "'Several hundred dollars' . . . what are you talking about, Mr. Cady?"

He caught her gaze. He couldn't answer. She'd find out soon enough how fragile her dreams were. *Go back to Arizona*, he wanted to tell her. *Go back to your relatives and marry some banker or shopkeeper and stop wanting to help the downtrodden of San Francisco. Stop being as foolish as Josiah, who thought the world was better and more promising than it was.*

And don't make me be a villain.

"I should let you get back to your work, Miss Whittier." He tapped his hat onto his head. "Miss Samuelson, a pleasure. Ladies."

"What an interesting visit," said Lottie, climbing behind Sarah onto the open dummy car of the Stutter Street cable line. "I wonder what Mr. Cady really wanted."

"So do I." Sarah settled onto one of the outward-facing benches, where the views were unobstructed and the air was crisp and damp on her face, the evening's coming coolness tempering the sun's fading warmth. "I don't believe for a second he was merely out for a stroll and happened to decide to stop in for a visit. Those questions about the rent . . . he's trying to figure out if I'm squandering Josiah's money."

"That is your view, Sarah, but I have decided he has changed his mind about not supporting the shop and wanted to check on our progress." Lottie lifted her bustle out of the way to take a seat on the bench next to Sarah. With a ding, the cable car lurched forward.

"You are a dreamer, Lottie."

"I like to think the best, because he does not seem as bad as you suggested."

Sarah reclined against the seat back as best as her corset permitted. "Have you become an admirer of the stony-hearted Daniel Cady?"

"You are too harsh, Sarah," Lottie countered. "Consider his situation. He came searching for a father he believed abandoned him, only to find the man had passed away and left all he owned to a stranger. You would be out of sorts too. Give Mr. Cady time to grieve and adjust."

"I doubt time to grieve will turn him into a compassionate human being, Lottie. And for the life of me, I truly can't fathom why he bothered to come to the shop. I don't think it was because he's decided to support it. He probably did so for no other reason than to remind me of his presence in town." *Not that I would forget.* "He is absolutely annoying."

"And amazingly handsome." Lottie settled her hands atop her skirts and regarded Sarah. "A fact you neglected to mention."

"The man has come to take my inheritance. I'm not likely to forget his intentions and swoon over his handsome face like Cora and Phoebe."

"I do see the resemblance to his father. Though his eyes are much sadder."

"So do I," Sarah conceded. When it arrived, Daniel's proof of his identity would be superfluous. "I only wish the similarities went further than skin deep."

Lottie reached for the pole as the cable car bounced over a rough spot in the track. "I think they might, Sarah." Her voice was so steady despite the jarring of the cable car. "I really think they might."

Sarah clung to the nearest leather strap and wished Lottie were correct.

The cable car climbed the steady grade, the busy streets around Union Square giving way to quieter neighborhoods. Within minutes they reached Jones Street, where they would have to disembark. Sarah signaled to the conductor to stop. They hopped down to walk the steep ascent up Jones Street, Sarah regretting an overly ambitious lacing of her corset that morning that left her short of breath.

At a crest, they paused.

"My goodness," Lottie whispered. "I can never tire of this view. I am glad you asked me to come to your house to go over the shop books, though I hardly need much of a reason to come up here."

The prospect from the summit was stunning, the sun slanting low on the horizon to stretch long the shadows of the buildings blanketing the hills of the city, the evening fog beginning to creep up from the ocean to spread its fingers amid the dips and rises. Between houses, Sarah could see all the way down to the bustling hub of the city and the sparkling waters of the bay where the Oakland ferries trailed smoke from their stacks. A three-masted schooner, probably freshly arrived from China, was angling into one of the wharves. She twisted about, and off to the north she could see the blue-green of the Marin Headlands beyond the Golden Gate. If she were to paint the scene, she'd pick out cadmium and ochre, olives and sapphire blues, buffs and French gray.

Soon, it might all be Daniel Cady's view.

"I can see you fretting, Sarah." Lottie's touch upon the back of her hand was gentle. "Be of good courage."

"Perhaps I *should* swoon over Daniel Cady. Perhaps his hard heart would be softened if I fluttered and flirted. That might be more successful than a pitiful attempt to offer him money."

"I would never tell you not to try!"

Laughing—heavens, how grateful she was for Lottie—they strolled the remaining short distance to Sarah's house.

She noticed the commotion outside of it before Lottie did, and her bright spirits vanished. "Whatever—?"

Mrs. McGinnis was seated on the front steps with her head in her hands. Their neighbor, Mrs. Brentwood, paced the front porch, her mandarin orange dress as bright as a beacon light. A policeman had just climbed into his wagon parked at the curb and pulled away, a cluster of curious bystanders turning to watch him go, one of whom annoyingly looked like a newspaper reporter.

"It does not look good," said Lottie.

"No. It doesn't."

Sarah broke into a run, Lottie close on her heels.

Eight

"THANK GOODNESS YOU'RE FINALLY HERE, Miss Whittier." Mrs. Brentwood's eyes fairly bulged. "Oh, merciful heavens, the shock! Horrible!"

"What has happened?" Sarah sprinted up the remaining stairs to the porch. Lottie tripped over her skirts in her effort to keep up, catching herself before she fell. She reached for Sarah's arm to steady both of them.

"Miss Sarah." Mrs. McGinnis looked up when she heard Sarah's voice. Her face was pinched. "I've ne'er been so scared. I came back early from the shopping and was making tea in the kitchen, knowing you'd be home soon, when I heard a noise on the rear steps. Thought it might have been Rufus, though I kent he wasn't outside. I peeped through the door and saw an evil-looking man staring back at me!" She shuddered. "I've ne'er screamed so loud in me life. Rufus'll ne'er come out of hiding, wherever that daft cat's gone to."

Someone attempted to break in? Sarah dropped to the housekeeper's side, caught up one of her clammy hands. "You're all right, though? You're not hurt?"

"*Nae*, miss, not one bit. Though I wouldna have minded dinging that man over his head and showing him what hurt is!"

"Awful. Dreadful!" Mrs. Brentwood sucked in air in noisy, rasping breaths. With every inhalation, her bodice's brass buttons strained against the wool. "The neighborhood just isn't safe.

Up here. In broad daylight! You'd think. Terrifying. Ah Mong and his brother can take turns guarding, but will it be enough?"

"I doubt there is any need for them to guard the house, Mrs. Brentwood."

"There most certainly is!" she said, aghast. "You need to be protected. The police have promised to increase their patrols, but if they'd done their job, this wouldn't have happened in the first place! Horrible. Horrible."

The situation was horrible, but hysteria would not help them. "I appreciate your concern, but we should try to stay calm." Stay calm and think. But who would want to rob them? And why?

"This is unbelievable," said Lottie, her arms clasped around her waist.

"Unbelievable doesn't begin to describe it." Sarah took Mrs. McGinnis's elbow and helped her stand. "Let's go inside. Lottie, can you open the front door for us?"

Lottie did as asked and guided the housekeeper into the dining room, where Mrs. McGinnis collapsed onto one of the cane-bottom mahogany chairs.

"Good day, Mrs. Brentwood," said Sarah crisply. "I think we'll be all right from here." She shut the door before the woman could collect herself and stride into the dining room with them.

Lottie said in a bright voice, "I shall go fetch that tea," and hurried toward the kitchen.

Sarah pulled out the chair next to the housekeeper. The afternoon sun lit the olive-colored walls and dark sideboard but barely warmed the room. Or maybe it was just that Sarah was so chilled from worry that she couldn't feel its heat.

"So what was this man like? Was he menacing? Did he have a weapon?" Sarah asked Mrs. McGinnis, trembling anew over the thought that she might have been harmed.

The housekeeper shook her head. "*Nae* weapon that I could see. As to his appearance, he was a big, hairy, evil brute of a fellow. I'll ne'er forget him."

"I wonder why he thought he wouldn't be spotted by someone. I mean, the sun is hours from setting yet."

"Loony's why."

"He must not have cared if he was seen." Lottie, carrying the tea tray into the room, must have overheard Sarah's question. "Or perhaps he is a night laborer and daytime is the only time he has for housebreaking." Dispensing the steaming tea through the strainer, she set a cup in front of Sarah. It rattled against the saucer.

Sarah glanced at her friend. Lottie's face was as pale as the cream glaze on the cups. "Lottie, you don't have to stay. I'm too shaken to review the books today. It can wait."

"What if the intruder comes back?"

"With the police just here, he won't be back anytime soon."

"But he might return later," Lottie answered. Mrs. McGinnis let out a fretful groan.

"Do you intend to lie in wait for him?" Sarah asked, attempting to keep her tone light.

"I could borrow Papa's Colt and sit in the parlor . . ."

Sarah had to smile at that. "Your father would lock you in your bedroom first."

"I would not tell him I had taken the gun. Really, Sarah, I am hardly a noodle."

"Thank you, but there's no need for such drastic measures."

Mrs. McGinnis huffed. "If that house lot in back wasn't empty, we wouldna have this problem."

"Have you ever seen him before?" Lottie asked her.

"I canna be sure . . ." The housekeeper's face scrunched in concentration. "I think I'd remember a face that ugly."

"If he was intent on housebreaking, I can't fathom what he might have been after," said Sarah. If he was willing to scale the rear yard wall in the middle of the day, that item must be precious indeed. What had he thought was in the house worth risking such a daring attempt? "Unless the fellow fancies tall case clocks or silk-upholstered couches, there's nothing of worth to steal. Besides, he could hardly cart those off, midday, without one of our neighbors noticing." How Mrs. Brentwood, who always seemed to have her nose pressed to her window glass, didn't spot him before Mrs. McGinnis had was enough of a wonder. "And I certainly don't have any jewels or . . ." She was about to say "gold" when an unwelcome memory stopped her.

Sarah flushed hotly. She didn't want to remember what had happened that day, how Edouard had betrayed her. But it was too easy to recall the sight of her Uncle Henry's gold nuggets wrapped in a scrap of newspaper that had been shoved deep into Edouard's inner coat pocket. Her shock, her anger and sense of betrayal were as fresh today as they had been that summer afternoon four years ago.

"Sarah, what is it?" Lottie asked, bending toward her. "You look ill."

"It's nothing. Just the shock of what's happened today finally hitting me, I guess." Edouard and her own past stupidity were irrelevant when she had very real and current problems to tackle. "I just wish I knew what the man thought he'd find here."

Lottie appeared satisfied with her answer. "I do too. What do you think, Mrs. McGinnis?"

The housekeeper's face was pasty pale. "*Och*, who knows?" Hastily, she stood and collected the teapot to replenish the hot water.

Sipping the tea—brisk black Assam tea that didn't soothe like she wanted it to—Sarah watched her housekeeper depart down the short passageway into the kitchen. "This intruder has really shaken her. It's possible she's mistaken about what this man wanted, though. I'm betting he didn't intend to rob us but was looking for a handout and Mrs. McGinnis's screams scared him off." She liked that conclusion; it would enable her to sleep tonight.

"I had not considered that," said Lottie. "It makes a lot of sense. You should tell Mrs. McGinnis so she is less upset."

Sarah nodded.

Lottie's tea remained untouched on the table. She glanced at it and sighed. "I suppose I should go." She rested a hand on Sarah's arm, the weight reassuring. "Tell me you shall be fine."

"The police are on alert and Mrs. Brentwood is lending us two capable sentries. If this fellow plans to return, we've done what we can." Sarah lifted her brows. "However, I wonder if maybe *I* should borrow your father's Colt."

"Or you could ask Mr. Cady to stand guard." Mischief danced in Lottie's eyes. "If he is so interested in acquiring your inheritance, he has a personal stake in keeping it safe."

Sarah's pulse skipped. "I would never ask that man to stand guard over me."

Daniel closed the hotel room door behind him. Fingering the envelope from Western Union, he crossed to the room's window and threw back the curtain. He tore through the envelope flap and extracted the telegram. Another one from his Chicago lawyer. There had been a slight delay in obtaining proper legal documentation as to Daniel's paternity. His baptismal record had been lost in the '71 fire, but Daniel was not to worry. There were plenty of suitable witnesses to attest to Daniel's identity.

Daniel creased the telegram between his thumb and forefinger and glanced over at the tintype of his sisters, stiff in their light gowns, that he'd propped on the dressing table. For them, he had pursued this course. The proof would unfailingly come and Sinclair would have all he needed to proceed with the case. The wheels had been set into motion, ready to crush into oblivion a sizable portion of Miss Whittier's carefully constructed world.

Daniel was not to worry.

He flattened his palm against the windowpane and stared down. Far below, the late afternoon hubbub of Montgomery Street reverberated off the stone and brick buildings, a jumble of rattling carriage and wagon wheels, the warbling calls of street corner hucksters, the clip-clop of horses' hooves on jagged cobblestones. His grandfather would jingle his coins in his pocket, grin, and call them the sounds of commerce, growth, progress. "*Energy*," he would say, when he was still speaking to his only grandson, "*energy*."

Daniel could do with less energy and tumult right then. He longed for a bit of silence so he could put his thoughts in order. He wished he knew how to pray. Wished he still *believed* in prayer, but his belief had dwindled with each passing year until it had disappeared altogether, leaving not even a trace to mark where it might have once existed. His purpose had been so clear when he'd come to San Francisco, his mind focused on one cause, his feelings contained and controlled. It was all a jumble now.

He kept thinking of Sarah's girls and the adoring way they looked at her. Kept recalling Miss Samuelson's flinty determination and Sarah's stiff-necked confidence, daring him to tell her she was unwise to continue with her plans. He shouldn't have gone to the shop and recognized how serious her efforts were. Even though he still had more questions than answers about her, one thing was clear: Sarah's business was no lark, which is what Sinclair apparently believed. She, her partner, and her girls may or may not succeed, but they certainly didn't intend to fail.

Even if he succeeded in claiming Josiah's estate.

Josiah.

Daniel dropped his hand from the window, leaving an imprint on the glass. Every day he spent here, stuck in one spot for the first time in eight months, forced him to deal with his memories of the man. Sort through the consequences of what Josiah had done since he'd left Chicago, including stoke the ambitious fires of hope in a brown-eyed woman who was as lovely as a spring day when she blushed.

He shouldn't have gone to the shop. Because in seeking some final reparation from Josiah, Daniel could no longer avoid knowing how much he was going to hurt Sarah.

"Everything is set for this evening, Miss Whittier." Mrs. Brentwood wagged a finger at Sarah, seemingly oblivious to Sarah's dinner cooling on the small parlor table. True to her nature, Mrs. Brentwood hadn't been dissuaded by Sarah's attempt at privacy earlier that day. The woman's curiosity always won out. "I told Ah Mong to be extra sharp about watching your house."

"I appreciate your concern, Mrs. Brentwood." Sarah offered a tight smile. She had opened the door to the woman's persistent knocking before looking through the glass to check who it was, expecting that it might be Ah Mong himself asking after her or perhaps the police come back to check on them. She would be more careful next time. "But really, it isn't necessary—"

"'Be smart and keep your wits about you,' I said," Mrs. Brentwood interrupted. "But he has the oddest way of looking at a body that I can never tell if he's understood me or not." She leaned close to whisper, as if her Chinese servant had the ability to hear through the walls of Sarah's house. "That brother of his is even more peculiar."

"I don't know why you keep Ah Mong on if you're bothered by him, Mrs. Brentwood," Sarah said, her voice edged with irritation.

"Because he's so much cheaper than an Irish girl, of course!" Mrs. Brentwood's close-set eyes peered down the expanse of her lengthy nose. "Mr. Cady did teach you about household finances and such affairs, didn't he?"

"Yes, he did."

"He always was practical and most careful about expenditures." Her neighbor's gaze swept the room much as Daniel Cady's had, resting on the finest pieces of furniture, the rug on the floor, and the gilded mantel clock in particular. "Never profligate with his money. Procured items of taste, but never extravagant. In fact, rather a miser, if the stories about his treasure are—" Her hand flew to her mouth. "Oh, I am sorry, my dear. I spoke out of turn."

"'Treasure,' Mrs. Brentwood?"

Mrs. Brentwood waved her hands as though Sarah was an annoying insect she was attempting to sweep away. "Silliness. It's nothing, Miss Whittier. Truly. I told Robert I'd never breathe a word."

A sick feeling burrowed into Sarah's stomach. "You'll have to apologize to your husband, then, because you have."

"You won't tell him I told you, will you?" Her brow pinched, deepening the wrinkles across her forehead. "He would be upset. I wouldn't have even thought of that silly rumor if not for your unfortunate intruder earlier today. Please don't tell Robert."

"What treasure did Josiah supposedly possess that Mr. Brentwood doesn't want spoken of?" *And why had Josiah never mentioned such dreadful rumors?*

She dropped her voice again. "Gold, Miss Whittier. From the Black Hills."

Relieved, Sarah shook her head and smiled. "I know about that gold. It was his share from his mining operation, but Josiah always said he spent most of it on this house, and I know what was in his bank accounts. Believe me, the money he left behind is a nice sum but no treasure. And if he had hidden any cash or gold nuggets on this property, he would've told me."

"Ah, yes. He would have." Mrs. Brentwood nodded. "That's good to hear, because it's these sorts of rumors that encourage the criminal element."

The sick feeling returned. "You believe the story of a treasure is why someone was sneaking around my backyard and came onto the kitchen stairs?"

"Sadly, I do."

"But why today? This house has been here for years and no one has attempted to break in before. Undoubtedly the man was simply looking for a handout."

"A beggar? You can't be as naive as that, Miss Whittier." Mrs. Brentwood sniffed indignantly. "And as for why this creature might have chosen today to lurk about . . . well, I certainly don't claim to understand the workings of the criminal mind."

Sarah pressed her lips together. She had managed to convince herself that their intruder had been harmless, but Mrs. Brentwood had succeeded in resurrecting her worry.

"I am tired from all the excitement, Mrs. Brentwood. Thank you for telling Ah Mong to watch out for me, though; his vigilance is comforting."

Mrs. Brentwood appeared mollified and let Sarah show her to the door. "He has always watched out for you, my dear. Mr. Cady asked him to years ago, right about the time Josiah's health went into serious decline."

Sarah's heart contracted. *Heavens, Josiah, how can you still be caring for me from beyond the grave?* And what had she ever done to warrant such fatherly affection? Especially from a man who must have suspected how far from perfect, how far from deserving she'd been.

"My thanks, anyway."

Mrs. Brentwood dropped a dry kiss on Sarah's cheek. "If you require further peace of mind, you could always borrow my Remington vest pocket pistol."

"I'll keep one of the kitchen knives close at hand," she replied, only partly joking.

Sarah saw the woman out. Closing the door behind her, Sarah leaned against the wood and stared up the turn of the staircase. Rufus mewled from his post on the landing, returned to his spot after concluding the ruckus had settled down.

"Do you believe such silliness as a treasure, Rufus?"

He flicked his crooked tail—not much of an answer. Sarah released a breath. Where would Josiah have hidden valuables? She knew the combination to his wall safe, and there were only legal documents and some letters inside it. She could search his bedroom. It had been months since she'd last gone into it. Months since she'd looked through any of his personal possessions, and at the time, it had only been a cursory examination. She simply hadn't had the emotional strength to do more.

Sarah pushed away from the door with only a passing thought for the meal gone cold in the parlor. Because the time had come to do more than a superficial perusal.

After two hours of rummaging through Josiah's belongings, Sarah sighed and sat back on her heels. She had searched his wardrobe and discovered nothing but clothes. She'd hunted beneath the bed and only found boxes holding shoes. Now the contents of numerous drawers lay scattered on the bedroom rug, and not a single piece had anything to do with treasure. There were a couple of IOUs, a few folded bank notes, underclothes and socks and handkerchiefs, a nice pair of jet-and-gold cuff links and another set in silver, a tortoiseshell comb and brush. Several good cotton sleeping shirts. A quick ink sketch Sarah had done of Mrs. McGinnis dozing by the stove. That item had made Sarah stop her search and cry.

But nothing unusual. In fact, all the typical property of a man.

Sarah refolded everything and returned Josiah's things to the drawers.

"I should not have listened to Mrs. Brentwood, Josiah." Gently, she placed the shirts in the bottom drawer, smoothing them flat with her palm, the yellowing cotton soft under her skin. "All that woman does is collect gossip for redistribution later. I should know better than to listen to her silliness and let her worry me."

She held on to the sketch—Daniel Cady might eventually succeed in claiming the contents of Josiah's house, but her drawings were hers to keep—and slipped out of the room, quietly closing the door. It was time for Mrs. McGinnis to pack the contents; Sarah had held on to the memories long enough.

"HE'S GOT A TREASURE HIDDEN up there, Mr. Cady, sir." The reception lounge server's eyes shone at the prospect. That and the fact Daniel now owed him two more dollars for his information. "Just like you thought."

"A treasure?" Daniel glanced about the dining room. Restless, he'd gotten up early for breakfast, never really having gone to sleep. As a result, the room was mostly empty, the nearest other diners a good thirty feet distant. Out of earshot.

"Yep! Exactly!" The boy—Red was his name, if Daniel recalled correctly—flashed a grin. "Cook says you were right and there's stories on the street about your Mr. Josiah Cady and his treasure."

"You didn't promise Cook I'd give him money for telling you this, did you?" The man might be making up a story just to get some cash out of Daniel.

The server looked hurt. "Didn't have to. Cook was more'n happy to talk all about it."

Daniel tapped his fork, the tines clinking against the china plate. His suspicions—he'd been ready to dismiss them, frankly—might be true, after all. If these stories were right, Josiah *had* hidden valuables, which would explain where the rest of his money had gone. It would also make Miss Whittier a confirmed liar.

Disappointment weighed heavily. After yesterday's visit to the shop, he had begun to want to believe the best of her. He didn't want to be shown she was as bad as Josiah, full of dreams, willing to sacrifice others—and the truth—in order to attain them.

When will I learn?

"What sort of treasure?" Daniel asked, and popped a piece of bacon into his mouth. Too bad he couldn't really taste the meat anymore, because it had been good.

The lad looked left and right, bent down, and whispered, "Gold nuggets."

Nuggets. What else would it be? Daniel waved his empty fork at the boy, urging him to tell more.

"Might be better if I sat, Mr. Cady."

"Then sit."

After a grand smile at the other waiters in the room, Red scraped back the chair and sat. "A few days back—sorry I didn't tell you earlier, Mr. Cady, but I didn't have to work again 'til today—I went and talked to Cook like I said I would. He told [illegible] his cousin knows some fellow who worked on the Cady house last year. It seems Josiah Cady asked him to install a secret compartment."

"To hold the nuggets."

"Well, what else? 'Course!" He leaned over his elbows propped on the table. "Cook said any of the folks who got rich in the gold fields have 'em. For hiding their diggings or their money. Guess they don't trust banks or somethin'."

"Why wait until last year to have this compartment built? I would think, if he wanted to hide his diggings, he would've had it installed right away." He was thinking aloud and didn't expect the server to have an answer to his questions.

"Mebbe he was scared of being robbed all of a sudden. Been some trouble around Nob Hill these past coupla years. Or mebbe he knew he was gonna pass on and decided . . ." Spots of red blushed the waiter's neck. "Sorry to mention his passing, Mr. Cady. No disrespect meant."

"None taken." Daniel's head started to throb in rhythm to the beating of his heart. Hidden treasure. Josiah had to have told her about it. "How many folks know about Josiah Cady's stash of nuggets, do you think?"

"The fellow who did the work. Cook. His cousin." The man scrunched up his face. "And me. 'Course, you too."

And possibly the rest of San Francisco, once Daniel had begun to make inquiries. A story this good wouldn't take long to spread. "Did you learn anything about Sarah Whittier?"

"Not much asides from her showing up a few years back like a bolt outta the blue. But if you want me to keep askin' . . ." He waggled his brows suggestively.

"Thanks, but no." Daniel reached into his coat pocket for his coin purse. He tossed two Morgan silver dollars—the balance of the money he had promised the server—onto the table. The boy snatched up the coins as quickly as a toad lapping up a fly. "I'll figure out that mystery on my own."

"So you're Daniel Cady."

The housekeeper's gaze flicked over Daniel, leaping from head to toe and all points in between, then slowed to an unyielding halt upon his face. *Does she think I resemble Josiah? Would it bother me if she did?*

"Miss Whittier's out back painting with one of the lasses until they're set to go on their excursion."

Sarah was busy and Daniel nearly apologized for the interruption until he remembered the reason he was there. Any notion to be polite snuffed out. "I need to talk to her."

His tone didn't leave much doubt that he was not going to leave without doing so. Mrs. McGinnis harrumphed. "I suppose you can come through the kitchen."

"Thank you."

The kitchen was tidy, if cramped, certainly much smaller than the massive whitewashed kitchen at the Hunts' mansion. Efficient and clean, the space smelled of freshly baked cookies. The Hunt kitchen had never smelled of something as simple and unpretentious as cookies. Mrs. McGinnis pushed open the rear door and Daniel stepped through, into the green of a garden and the hush of a world set apart from the grime and dust of the street.

He paused on the porch. Her back to him, Sarah hadn't heard him arrive. She sat with the red-haired young woman from the shop—the one who enjoyed singing—their chairs facing the corner of the garden so the sun would be at their backs. An easel was propped before them, and just beyond, a fountain gurgled, as civilized a scene as any in the finest neighborhoods of Chicago. Roses and jasmine tumbled off the wall, scenting the air, and heavy-headed lilies crowded the wood fence. They had lilies at Hunt House, planted alongside a bed of marguerite daisies. His grandmother's gardener had planted them in honor of his sisters' births. Back when Hunts still tolerated Cadys. Before the scandal. Before the heartache.

Blast you, Josiah, for growing them here, as if you had spared a thought for the two little girls you'd left behind before they could talk well enough to call you back. As if you had cared.

Sarah shifted in her wicker chair to clean off her paintbrush and spotted him. "Mr. Cady?"

Cora peeked over her shoulder and grinned. "Good morning, Mr. Cady! Are you coming with us today?"

"He's not here for that, Cora," Sarah said, frowning at him. Daniel wondered if she'd figured out why he *was* there. She didn't let on, though. "Did you have more questions about the studio?"

"I need to talk to you." He twisted the brim of his hat in his hands and descended onto the gravel path that wound between beds of kitchen herbs and marigolds. He shot a glance at Cora. "In private."

"Can it wait a few minutes? I was just finishing my lesson with Cora. She's missed so many recently and the weather is so fine, I thought I'd take advantage of the opportunity."

She turned back to the easel and the half-finished painting without waiting for an answer.

"Cora is our best watercolorist. I expect her work to sell very well. We already have interested clients." Sarah swished the paintbrush in the cup of water, turning it an even murkier shade of gray. Drying the bristles on a cloth, she dipped into the dark orange paint and began applying shading. Her brush flowed across the paper with practiced ease, graceful as a dance. "See, Cora, this is the best way to accomplish shadows on leaves."

"It really can't wait, Miss Whittier," said Daniel.

Sarah tucked in her chin and lowered her brush. "Please go into the house, Cora. The others should be arriving soon, anyway. If you hurry, you might catch Mrs. McGinnis pulling fresh cookies from the oven."

Cora rose and strolled down the garden pathway, pausing at Daniel's side. "You should come to our picnic today, Mr. Cady. You'd have lots of fun."

"I was not invited to a picnic, Miss Gallagher."

"'Miss Gallagher'!" The girl giggled. "How high and mighty! You should call me Cora."

"Cora, please leave us," said Sarah.

Pouting, Cora dragged herself up the steps and into the house.

"She really is a very talented artist, even if her manners need polishing." Sarah dropped the brushes into the cup and covered the paint receptacles. She stripped off her coarse cotton apron and laid it on Cora's empty chair. Uncharacteristically uncomfortable looking, she picked at a fleck of blue paint on one of her knuckles. "I suppose you've come to let me know your identification has arrived, and the court date has been set."

"Not even the fastest express train could get my documents here already, Miss Whittier."

"That's true." Slowly, she stood and faced him. "Why are you here then? A casual stroll didn't bring you all the way to Nob Hill."

He ran the brim of his hat through his fingers. He'd wear down the nap if he continued the habit. "I'm here because I want you to tell me about Josiah's treasure."

She paled. "Not you too."

"So there is one." He suddenly felt sick. "I'll tell my lawyer you're willing to admit to hiding valuables. He'll inform Judge Doran—"

"There is *no* treasure, Mr. Cady," she said firmly.

"I have been told by a reputable source"—*a bit of a stretch*—"that a hidden compartment was installed in this house for the purpose of hiding gold nuggets."

"Do I look as though I've been enjoying a secret hoard of gold, Mr. Cady?" Sarah gestured at her dress, a bland green check that looked rehemmed and in worse shape than his travel-worn coat. "I own four outfits, not a one of which is remotely new. Mrs. McGinnis and I eat simply and entertain never. Every spare penny I have has gone into my girls and my business."

"Then explain the story I've heard."

"I can't." She lifted her chin. A strand of hair had come loose from the knot at her neck, and it trembled alongside her throat. "But it is just a rumor. If you don't believe me, go ahead and tell your lawyer to have someone tear this house apart from cellar to attic. He won't find a treasure because there isn't one. Furthermore, you may tell your 'reputable source' that Josiah installed a wall safe last fall to hold legal papers and some money after a spate of robberies in the neighborhood. Hardly a secret compartment or a hoard of gold."

Sarah Whittier was either a crack bluffer or telling the truth. "Before, you said, 'Not you too.' What did you mean by that?"

Sarah pinched her lips between her teeth. "A man attempted to break in to the house while I was at the shop yesterday. Fortunately, Mrs. McGinnis scared him off. My neighbor, who knew about this rumor, seems to think this fellow must have heard it also. I'm apparently the last person in San Francisco to know."

"Josiah might have decided not to tell you—"

"Josiah would have told me," she snapped.

"Did he tell you about me?"

She couldn't answer that and not condemn the man as a liar.

Sarah swallowed and regrouped. "I do find it rather strange that within a day of some man poking around my property, you've come looking for these rumored hidden nuggets too."

The waiters at the Occidental . . . maybe they'd done more blabbing than he'd paid them to do. "Rumors travel fast."

"I'll say, and I hope you don't have anything to do with the speed."

Daniel crushed the brim of his hat; he wasn't simply ruining the nap, he'd need to buy a new one soon. "Tell me about this man who tried to break in," he said, trying to silence an annoying voice in his head. What if the story really *was* just a rumor? What if he was ready to believe it simply because it fit his tarnished image of Josiah?

What if he was wrong?

Sarah gave a small shrug. "Mrs. McGinnis said he was a big, ugly brute. Which could describe a thousand men in this city. We've informed the police."

"Good." At least she'd be safe.

She tilted her head. "Are you worried more about the rumored gold nuggets or me, Mr. Cady?"

The back door flung open, saving him from uttering the "you" that leaped to his tongue.

"Minnie and Anne have arrived, Miss Sarah," Mrs. McGinnis announced. "And Miss Charlotte."

"Thank you." With one hand, Sarah lifted her skirts. The other, she clenched at her waist. "My girls and I have planned a picnic at Golden Gate Park. A treat for them and time for me to show you out. Unless you want to conduct a search of the house right at the moment."

He returned her unblinking regard. He didn't know who or

what to believe anymore. "No, Miss Whittier. I'm satisfied."

"Thank heavens."

She turned sharply on her heel. He moved to follow. Holding her head very erect, Sarah swept through the kitchen then into the passage that led into the dining room. From the direction of the front parlor, Daniel could hear excited female voices whispering. Her girls, likely gossiping about him.

Miss Samuelson intercepted them just as Sarah reached the front door. "Mr. Cady, I did not expect to see you today. Are you joining us?"

"Hardly, Lottie. He came to ask some questions and has gotten his answers." Sarah flung the door wide. "Have a good day, Mr. Cady."

"Just a second, Sarah," said Miss Samuelson. "I will see Mr. Cady out."

Leaving the door wide open, Sarah retreated into the parlor and drew shut the pocket doors. The murmur of voices on the other side rose into a crescendo.

Miss Samuelson smiled as though she didn't hear the noise. "You should come with us."

"To your picnic?"

"Do not sound so dumbfounded! Yes, our picnic. The weather is perfect and the park is lovely. Have you seen it? No, you have not. Before you leave town, you must. Why not today?"

Her smile was both gentle and firmly direct. His mother used to smile at him like that, right before she convinced him to do something he didn't want to do. "I'm pretty sure Miss Whittier wouldn't care for my company. Which makes me wonder what you're up to, Miss Samuelson."

She paused to consider him. "I shall be honest with you, Mr. Cady. I want to prove to Sarah you are not as bad as she thinks you are."

"I don't see how a picnic will prove that." *Because what if I am that bad?* "And I don't know why you want her to appreciate my fine character. Seems to me it's best we have nothing to do with each other outside of our legal dealings."

"That is not true at all," she insisted. "Come with us. Get to know Sarah better and meet the rest of the girls. Clearly you are interested in our business endeavor, or else you would not have come by to see the shop yesterday."

"So, all this persuasion isn't about Sarah getting to appreciate me. It's for me to appreciate her more. And your business." Daniel shook his head. "I'm sorry, Miss Samuelson, I don't need to hear or see any more, and I'm not going to be swayed to offer financial support. I made a promise to my sisters to claim our due from our father. As I've already explained to your partner."

Miss Samuelson lifted her chin. Her face was as sweet as an angel's; her eyes were as hard as an auction house clerk's. "Mr. Cady, do not disappoint me by revealing that you are a coward."

"I beg your pardon?"

"You heard me. I saw your interest yesterday. You could invest in worse causes than our business." Her pale brows crept up her forehead. "But you are not willing to pursue your interest and appreciation, which forces me to conclude you are afraid."

And here he'd thought Miss Whittier had the steel spine. It seemed they both did. "I don't like to be blunt with ladies, but I question that your business has a chance of succeeding, Miss Samuelson. You're counting on customers to give their work to a shop run exclusively by women. Former factory girls. Rough immigrant girls. You're being overly optimistic, if you ask me."

"'Offer the sacrifices of righteousness, and put your trust in the Lord.' Psalm four, Mr. Cady." Her voice was patient and confident. "I have faith we are pursuing a right cause, doing the best we can, and hopefully making a positive difference in the world. It is not an easy path, but it is the only one worth taking. What path are you taking?"

His gut knotted. He'd lived the past months with only one

relentless goal. Not the sort of path she had in mind, but the one he'd had to be on.

Daniel gave a crisp bow. "I have another engagement, Miss Samuelson. I must leave."

She stepped in front of him. "Sarah is too proud to beg, but I am not. Please go on this outing with us. Spend some time and get to know the girls better. They are not all as silly as Cora Gallagher."

"I hope not."

A smile flitted across her mouth. "You are judging based upon her surface characteristics and not attempting to understand what she is about at all. I expected more of you, Mr. Cady." Miss Samuelson laid her fingers upon his sleeve. "Please go with us. If our efforts continue to seem pointless and overly optimistic after today, I will not bother you again."

"I really am too busy . . ."

"Humor me." Her hand tightened on his arm. "Because something tells me you need to have a cause and a purpose as much as Sarah does. And maybe, just maybe, you will even find the balm to heal your wounds."

Ten

A BALM? There was no balm on earth that could heal the wounds on his soul.

Daniel almost said that, stepped right across the threshold of Josiah's house out into the dull morning light, and turned his back to Charlotte Samuelson and Sarah Whittier. Why care, when caring brought pain? Why pretend that when you gave, anything good was ever returned?

But he didn't say that. Through stupid curiosity if nothing else, he was already affixed to their cause like a butterfly on a pin.

"All right, Miss Samuelson. You have made your point." Daniel inclined his head in defeat. "You win."

She smiled, gently closed the front door, and went to the parlor, peering through. "Sarah, Mr. Cady has decided to go with us!"

The whispers came to an abrupt halt. Sarah turned in unison with the three others assembled in the room, her face paling to the color of whitewash.

"He *what?*" Sarah's voice was sharp enough to slice metal.

Miss Samuelson laughed lightly while the young women—Sarah's "girls," though not a one looked much younger than her—stared at Daniel. "I know. It is a wonderful surprise, is it not? He has yet to visit Golden Gate Park. I thought this the perfect opportunity and he agreed."

Sarah frowned first at her friend, then at Daniel. "Just perfect."

His hat made a circuit through his fingers. "I don't want to be any trouble. I'll just head on out—"

Miss Samuelson skittered sideways to block his departure. "You promised me, Mr. Cady," she said between barely parted lips.

"I don't recall making a promise, Miss Samuelson," he murmured in return.

"I do, and you are not backing down." She took his elbow and gestured to the girls. "Let me introduce you to the young ladies you have not yet met."

He let her lead him around the parlor. There was Minnie Tobin, a bright-eyed young woman who curtsied, which he didn't think necessary. Cora grinned at him. The remaining woman stood apart. Anne Cavendish was tall and thin with an intense and watchful manner. A fading purplish blotch shadowed the left side of her chin and a cool challenge stiffened the set of her shoulders. One brisk glance indicated what she thought of Daniel.

Sarah, still looking flustered, had turned her back to him. "Isn't Phoebe coming?" she asked the girl named Minnie.

"She's had to work extra hours at the cloak shop, Miss Sarah. And Emma couldn't get away from the shirt factory."

"What a pity. The picnic was Emma's idea."

"Maybe it would be more fun to go to Woodward's Gardens than Golden Gate Park, Miss Sarah," Cora offered, glancing at Daniel. "They've an aquarium there, Mr. Cady, and a zoo and acrobats and dancing bears."

"Mr. Cady is no more interested in Woodward's Gardens than I suspect he is in Golden Gate Park, Cora," interrupted Sarah.

Miss Samuelson's brow puckered. "Sarah, I do not think we should presume Mr. Cady is not interested."

Sarah pursed her lips. She looked ready to ask him directly but changed her mind. "It's time for us to go. Don't forget to bring your shawls, girls. It can be cold at the park."

Hardly any colder than her attitude, thought Daniel.

The girls gathered their belongings and trailed behind Sarah like dutiful ducklings. Miss Samuelson held out her arm for him to take. He obliged.

"A balm, Miss Samuelson?"

"Surely, Mr. Cady." She gave a pert grin. "You are smiling over them already."

Whatever was Lottie thinking by inviting Daniel Cady to come with us? Why did I not protest? He has only come to question me about Josiah and that rumor about the nuggets, no matter what Lottie claimed back at the house.

But more importantly, how long does he intend to stare at me?

Sarah gathered her shawl around her shoulders and handed the picnic basket to Minnie. The girl, her eyes lit like Fourth of July rockets, had spent the entire streetcar ride to Golden Gate Park engaged in querying her about Daniel—how long would he stay in the city? What did he do for a living? Had Sarah met him before he'd come to San Francisco? How exactly was he related to Mr. Josiah?

That question Sarah had especially evaded.

She couldn't blame Minnie or any of the girls for their curiosity. A Cady didn't simply pop into their lives without evoking interest. But did he have to stare? He had from the moment they'd climbed onto the Geary Street cable car to the point where they had descended onto the platform at the Park. Perhaps Daniel thought with his unrelenting gaze he might compel Sarah into a belated confession about that purported treasure. She suspected she'd spent some of the time chewing her bottom lip.

"Should we go to the pond, Miss Sarah?" Minnie asked, her cheeks pink with excitement.

"If that's what you girls want to do."

"That sounds like an excellent idea, Minnie," said Lottie, snapping open a fringed parasol.

"Then let's find a good spot before it gets too crowded." Minnie clutched Cora's arm and whispered into her ear. Immediately, the two of them dashed down the wooden planks of the arrival area and onto one of the gravel paths winding through the park. Anne followed like a solemn watchdog. Lottie settled the parasol on her shoulder and set off with them.

Sarah clung to the ends of her shawl as if the paisley-printed wool might shield her from Daniel's scrutiny. At the moment, though, he wasn't looking at her, instead making a slow appraisal of the park, which stretched fresh and green beneath the clearing skies. What *did* he want? Any normal person would avoid spending time with someone they thought a cheat and a liar. Perhaps he lived by the adage it was best to keep your friends close and your enemies closer.

Disturbed by her thoughts, she must have made some sort of noise, because his attention flicked to her. "Unhappy that I decided to join you today?"

"Did Lottie pay you off, Mr. Cady? Or did you think of a new line of questioning?" She risked a look at his face, at the hard edge of his jaw. Her directness didn't alarm him; other men might have recoiled. Or looked scornful. "Well, you won't find any of Josiah's wealth hidden among the sandy dunes or the shrubs of the park."

"I didn't expect to." He paused where the path met a broad gravel drive. "I'm here because your friend called me a coward."

"Lottie called you a coward?"

She expected a crisp "yes," but he didn't answer straightaway, watching her closely and leaving Sarah with a funny flutter in her stomach. If only she could figure him out.

If only she didn't want to try.

He looked down at her. In the bright morning light, his eyes were as green as the new growth of a balsam fir. "Maybe I'm actually listening to her advice not to rush to judgment."

"What of your sisters and your promises to them?"

A shadow crossed his face, a flicker of regret or self-reproach. "We should call a truce, Miss Whittier. You don't mention my sisters, and I won't mention the rumors about those nuggets. How's that?"

Sarah nodded. "All right." She stretched out her hand. When he clasped it, his skin was warm and his grip firm, his strong fingers encompassing hers. Her stomach fluttered again. "Truce. For today."

He released her hand. "We should probably catch up to the others. I want to enjoy this park I've been so encouraged to see."

Wrapping her shawl close, she stepped onto the road that curved between hedges and a stand of palm trees. A horse and rider passed them, the fellow tipping his hat to Sarah and Daniel. A warbler trilled in a nearby tree, the crisp scent of the ocean hung in the air, and scraps of azure sky winked between drifts of clouds. The dirt and noise of the city were left far behind. She would enjoy the tranquility, the beauty, if she weren't so aware of Daniel Cady at her side.

Sarah fetched around in her head for a safe—and distracting—topic.

"In the future, Golden Gate Park shall stretch all the way to the ocean, Mr. Cady." Many of the trees were small, the eucalyptus scraggly, the cypresses just beginning to grow thick and tall. In the distance, the tawny sand of dunes was still visible. But here, the grasses were lush and bushes covered the reclaimed hills. It was fine and the promise of what it one day would be, already evident. "The conservatory is completed and they recently finished a music stand meant for entertainments, but there are plans for so much more. They intend to erect an aviary and plant an arboretum. I've even heard they intend to place a herd of buffalo in a paddock for viewing."

"Did you ever accompany my father here, Miss Whittier?" Daniel asked, his voice tight, as they rushed across the carriage path in order to evade a buggy and its energetic driver.

The question surprised her; she didn't think he would want to talk about his father any more than he wanted to discuss his sisters.

"A couple of times, in the first few months I worked for him. He became too ill to make excursions after that."

"Was he in a great deal of pain in the end?"

She cast Daniel a glance. What could she say? Josiah had always been in pain, as much from the grief in his heart as the aches in his body. Would that he was still alive to ask why he'd left a family behind in Chicago, causing endless worlds of hurt for everyone. "Josiah had a good doctor."

"And a good nurse."

"Hardly. Most of my life has been spent learning my duties as a proper young lady who happened to be passable artist. I admit I dreamed that I'd move to Paris one day and paint with the greats." Alongside Edouard, living off love. *Foolish, foolish Sarah.*

"Instead your aunt and uncle sent you all the way from Arizona to San Francisco to tend my father." He paused. "You know, I don't remember Josiah ever telling us he had friends in Arizona."

He sounded more regretful of the lapse than suspicious, but Sarah felt a nervous prick of unease anyway.

"Didn't he?" Sarah asked lightly, trying to sound unconcerned. "An oversight, I guess."

She kept her hands from twisting anxiously in her skirt. Had Daniel put two and two together and figured out that her uncle wasn't merely one of Josiah's friends but was his old mining partner? Was he trying to trip her up and get her to admit that the partner had lived in Los Angeles and not someplace in Arizona, and that she was lying?

Sarah wished she could tell Daniel the truth. That her last name hadn't always been Whittier. That, when the future she'd planned with Edouard had turned to ashes, she'd found herself in San Francisco with the barest shred of dignity intact. She hadn't been able to return to Los Angeles after what she'd done. Despairing, she'd taken a room in a women's benevolent society house, living off charity. Until she had spotted Josiah's name in the local newspaper, embedded within an advertisement for a nurse-companion. And found a future.

Daniel was watching her closely. She must not have succeeded in sounding unconcerned.

"I've told you they were happy to send me here, and I have a greater dream to pursue because they did, Mr. Cady," she responded, and it was easy to sound fervent when what she said was the plain truth. "I have no regrets." Not about stepping off a train in San Francisco. Not about answering an advertisement for a nurse-companion or pursuing her dream of opening an art studio with women who needed someone to give them a second chance.

Her mistakes, however . . . she had plenty of regrets about those.

Daniel and Sarah cleared a break in the trees and the lawns stretched ahead of them. The girls were climbing a low rise across the way. Cora's bright red hair, coming unbound, flashed in a sudden burst of sun. A peal of laughter echoed across the swale.

"They seem happy," Daniel commented. "You have accomplished that much."

"The girls never turn down a chance for a day in the park and a free lunch," Sarah responded. "They deserve to be treated well for once without someone expecting something from them in return."

"Is that what's happened with Anne?" he asked, his gaze trained on the girl's reed-thin figure, a dark line of sober gray among the fresh green grass. The other girls had disappeared over the hillock, Lottie along with them. "Is she not living up to someone's expectations?"

"I never question Anne. I see the bruises and hope she'll explain, but what could I do if she did? I'm not her guardian. The police won't listen to me. Or her, for that matter." Sarah sighed out her frustration. "Anne lives with a man she claims is her brother, but none of us believes that's really the case. He's a brick mason and a rough character. My hopes are that, once she takes up her position at the shop, she'll save up enough money to leave him."

"If he lets her."

Sarah tugged her shawl tight. Maybe she was hoping for too much.

"Anne's story is the worst, but all the girls have a sad tale to tell. Minnie's family owns a grocery store and they treat her like a slave, working her all hours, threatening to marry her off to their drunk neighbor so they can buy up his building and expand their business. Only because I pay Minnie some money weekly do they let her attend art lessons. Cora is flighty and has already weathered a ruinous love affair. I hope to stop her from making that mistake again. She only has a father, and he can't keep her in hand." Sarah remembered the afternoon she'd found Cora, sobbing on a street corner, tossed out of her house and fearful she was pregnant. The latter condition hadn't come to pass and the former had been rectified. For now. "Phoebe was desperately close to working the streets. Emma, whom you haven't met, has never revealed but the barest scraps of her life. I don't dare press."

"It is commendable that you want to help them like you do," he said, his tone reluctantly admiring, as if he questioned his own willingness to sacrifice as much. "But I still think you are gambling on those girls, Miss Whittier."

"I'm not, because I don't believe in taking gambles, Mr. Cady. I believe in myself and my abilities and my cause. Lottie would say it's my calling from God."

"And what do you say?"

Sarah stared into the distance. When she'd been little, she had loved to go to church with her mother, sing the songs, and listen to the sermons. She had felt God everywhere, in the music of her mother's voice, in the twinkle of sunshine upon the farm's stream, the scent of fresh bread from the oven, the warmth of a June sun, the sight of a daffodil-colored butterfly. But when the tornado struck and dashed everything to rubble, the farmhouse turned to a tumbled pile of rust-red bricks, the barn and coop vanished from the earth, all the chickens gone, she couldn't feel Him anymore. Not without Mother singing to her. Not without little Jess's laughter or Caleb's silly jokes.

They had never found Jess's body after the tornado. Alongside the casket holding Sarah's brother, an empty one had been placed atop Mother's as if a plain wood box were an adequate substitute for a little girl, an adequate vessel to contain all the grief pouring from Sarah's heart.

And Sarah had been left clinging to Aunt Eugenie's ice-cold hand. She didn't feel God in her aunt's touch. Sarah felt anger and disappointment. She never discovered whether Aunt Eugenie's disappointment was aimed at Sarah or at Mother, a sister who had committed the almighty sin of pride to remain in Ohio after Father had died at Kennesaw Mountain, bent on running the farm on her own with only three young children to help.

It didn't much matter which of them had disappointed Aunt Eugenie. Sarah had reaped all the consequences of her dissatisfaction in duplicate, and Sarah never attempted to feel or see God in anything anymore.

"I would say, Mr. Cady, that my need to help them is part of my being, as fundamental as the urge to breathe. Where that need comes from is beside the point."

Daniel paused in the middle of the lawn. Beyond him, carriages rolled past, ladies holding tight to their hats, drivers beaming. In the distance, two children chased a squirrel up a tree. A world so pleasant and peaceful outside the turmoil in Sarah's heart.

"I'm sorry I can't help you," he said.

"We have a truce requiring me not to mention your sisters." *And your vow, which is somehow more important than mine.*

The edge of his jaw ticked. Amazingly, he didn't take off his hat and crush its brim.

"For years my family has struggled to hold on to a semblance of respectability, Miss Whittier. I could beg my grandfather for a job in his company and probably grow pretty wealthy, but I don't do well eating humble pie. Not when I have a chance to regain what Josiah took from us." His gaze narrowed. "And if you're waiting for me to forgive him for what he did, then you're going to be waiting until kingdom come."

Sarah's face flamed hot as a coal stove. "Heaven forbid I should stand in the way of your getting every penny of your blessed money, Mr. Cady."

"Sarah! Sarah!"

She turned toward the shouts. Lottie was running back up the hill toward them, skirts flying, parasol discarded. Sarah scanned the grounds beyond her. Where were the girls? No Cora, no Minnie. No Anne. Just Lottie, her face taut with alarm. Panic squeezed Sarah's throat.

"Sarah, it's Cora!" Lottie yelled. In her haste, she tripped and fell, her outstretched hands skidding across the grass.

"Lottie!" Sarah bundled her skirts and sprinted down the hill. She knelt at Lottie's side. "Are you all right?" Lottie's palms were bleeding through the torn lace of her gloves.

"It's Cora, not me. Ouch!" Lottie struggled to sit upright. Daniel dropped to the ground and caught her shoulders, holding on to her. "Anne lost track of Cora and Minnie for a few minutes, and when she finally found Minnie . . ." Lottie swallowed. "Minnie thinks Cora has fallen into the pond."

"She can't swim!" Sarah gasped, ripping her skirt hem as she jumped up and began running toward the water.

Eleven

SARAH RACED DOWN THE SHALLOW RISE that swept past a thicket of trees and bushes. Beyond lay the small pond. A duck squawked its upset as it flapped overhead, chased away by Minnie's frantic screeches.

"Miss Sarah! I . . . I don't know where she's gone!" The sodden hem of her dress clung to her ankles. At some point, she'd waded into the water. "She was teasing about falling in. I didn't believe she'd do it. I turned my back only a second!"

Sarah scanned the smooth water of the pond. Could Cora have vanished beneath its surface so quickly and leave not a trace?

"Did you hear a splash, in the one second you turned your back?"

Minnie's cheeks turned red as radishes, and she rocked on her feet. "Um . . . maybe it was more than a second and maybe I was a bit too far away. I didn't mean to be, Miss Sarah. But this gentleman came up and asked for directions—"

Tearing off her hat, Sarah dropped her shawl onto the ground. She reached beneath her skirt to untie her bustle and strip off her outer petticoat. Wet, they would weigh her down more than she could manage. She stepped out of them, a pile of metal caging and pristine white cotton on the sandy bank. Next, she pulled off her half boots. They were far too expensive to ruin with pond water.

Sarah waded into the water. She wasn't prepared for the shock of the bone-numbing cold against her legs. Her skirts floated around her, dragging her back with their weight. She couldn't see any movement in the pond, even as she trod nearer to the center, the water rising to her waist.

"Miss Sarah, you'll drown too!" Minnie scurried back and forth along the bank.

Maybe over here, where the bank dropped precipitously, the rocks slick. That might be a place where someone could slip and fall in. Sarah struggled through the water, trying to peer through the murky depths, her stockinged feet slipping on moss-covered rocks. Wait. Was that a body drifting at the bottom? Or a shadow?

Suddenly, Cora splashed to the surface, her arms churning. She gasped for air. "Help!"

"Cora, I'm coming!"

Cora's head disappeared beneath the water again, the water burbling in her wake. Sarah's heart pounded furiously. Her legs, her feet were numb, but she pushed ahead. She wished she'd spent more time swimming, back in the stream at their farm in Ohio. She might be better prepared to do what needed to be done.

Heavenly Father, help me.

She offered the prayer right before she felt her feet lose traction, her legs giving way beneath her, plunging her into the cold dark, water filling her nose and throat to choke her.

"What does she think she's doing?" Daniel's pulse raced as he skidded to a halt at Minnie's side, sending gravel flying.

The girl's hands clenched and unclenched. "She's gone in for Cora, Mr. Cady!"

"Can she swim?" Daniel yanked off his coat and neckcloth as Sarah waded farther into the water.

"I don't know, sir."

He was bending down to remove his shoes when he saw Sarah stumble, her head plunging underwater. Daniel pushed past Minnie and dove into the pond.

The water hit his face and body like a sheet of ice, nearly stopping his heart. He fought not to gasp and inhale water. *Stay calm.*

"Sarah!"

Sarah's head bobbed above the water, then her shoulders. *Thank God. Thank God.*

"I'm fine." She sputtered, spit water. "But Cora! She's out there."

He waded up to her. Her skin was tinged with blue, and she shook so hard he feared she would collapse.

"I'll get her." Daniel reached for Sarah's arm and jerked toward the shallows. When he felt her feet gain traction, he released her and shoved her unceremoniously in the direction of the shore. "Go. Go!"

He didn't stop to see if she'd obeyed but turned back, diving into the water. Clouds of churned-up sand and mud obscured his sight. Cora had to be close by. He'd seen the splash where she had momentarily surfaced, and it wasn't far. Daniel pressed on, swimming hard through the murk, pausing to search for her. A few feet ahead, Cora's head broke the surface again. She thrashed as her sodden skirts pulled her back under. He willed her to hold on. *Just hold on.*

Daniel sucked in a breath of air and lunged forward, reaching for her. Terrified, she flailed and he couldn't grab hold of her arm.

"Cora!" he shouted, hoping to break through her panic.

Legs wheeling beneath him, Daniel made another attempt. This time he succeeded and clamped on to her waist. With all his strength, he thrust against the water and dragged them both to the surface.

Her head popped free.

"Mr. Cady," she gasped through trembling lips, long strands

of copper-bright hair plastered to her pale face. She clung to his shirt.

"Hold on, Miss Gallagher. I've got you."

Daniel began to pull her backward, his strokes long and even. Soon, he felt rocky bottom beneath his feet. He gathered his legs under his body and stood, righting Cora. She sagged against him, choking, as he trudged through the water and laid her onto the shore.

"Cora!" Minnie flapped on the sandy bank like a frantic chicken.

"Minnie, get her a dry shawl," Sarah commanded, her arms clutched around her wet gown.

Daniel turned Cora on her side while Sarah tossed both her shawl and Minnie's over the girl's shivering body. Cora coughed up a trickle of pond water.

"Oh, Mr. Cady," she wheezed, "Miss Sarah. I'm sorry. I didn't mean to . . ."

Be such trouble? Daniel glanced up at Sarah. Her eyes didn't meet his.

"It's all right, Cora. You're safe now," she said stiffly.

Cora clung to Daniel's arm like she'd never let go. "The water was so cold."

"Quite a shock, wasn't it?" Daniel asked, moving her out of his grasp so she could adjust Minnie's shawl around her shoulder, already going dark from damp.

Cora gaped at the pond like it was a gentle rabbit that had sprung unexpected fangs. "Yep, it was."

"Merciful heavens, Cora." Miss Samuelson hobbled down the bank. She had returned with Anne. "You gave us a horrible fright."

"I'm sorry, Miss Charlotte." She fixed a smile on her face and tried to snuggle back into Daniel's arms. "But I am thankful for Mr. Cady here."

Daniel jumped up, grabbed his coat off the ground, and threw it over Sarah's shoulders. They shuddered beneath his hands. Minnie took his place, hiccuping between tears of relief.

"You are taking a gamble, Miss Whittier," he muttered, dragging the coat around her arms.

"I will not give up on them, Mr. Cady." Her chin rose, and she ducked out of his grasp. "No matter how reckless they are or how foolish you think I am."

"You could have drowned," he spat, angry with her for risking her life. How dare she? He ought to shake some sense into her. "What were you thinking? Do you even know how to swim?"

"Not well, but if you think I'd be more worried about myself than one of my girls, you don't understand me at all."

"You won't do them any good deceased."

A trail of water snaked down Sarah's forehead, into her fierce eyes, unheeded. "I won't do them any good destitute, either."

"Anne, help Cora, please," Miss Samuelson interrupted as she struggled to her feet. "Mr. Cady, you shall freeze. Please take the blanket we brought."

"No, he can have his coat back." Sarah handed it to him, and retrieved the blanket herself. She turned her back to him and bundled up her discarded clothes. "Come, everyone. We need to get Cora back to the house to dry off and then to a doctor."

Anne, stern as a crow, hoisted Cora upright. The girl let out a yelp of protest but agreed to be hauled up the hill and over the path, Minnie fussing alongside. Miss Samuelson, her parasol called into use as a cane, glanced back just once as they crossed the ridge above the pond. Shoulders squared, Sarah didn't look back at all.

Daniel's socks squelched as he shoved his frozen feet into his shoes. *I will not care. I will not care.*

He seized the forgotten picnic basket, secured his coat, shoved his hat on his head, and marched up the embankment.

I will not care.

If he said it often enough, he might actually believe it.

She was numb. Not just her skin, cold and prickled from the pond water. But numb inside too. *Maybe I am a fool. Maybe I am making a mistake with these girls.*

Sarah drew the picnic blanket tight about her arms and glanced over at Lottie, seated across from her in the carriage Daniel had hired to take them home. Her friend's brow puckered, just a trifle, and Sarah nodded. Again. Yes, she was fine. Yes, she would survive. And yes, she was humiliated over the entire episode. Lord help Cora if Sarah ever came to suspect the girl had fallen into that pond on purpose.

Satisfied with Sarah's response, Lottie looked away and returned to buffing Cora's arms and hands. Rather roughly, if Sarah considered the movements. Perhaps she was suspecting the girl too.

Thankfully, at least, Daniel had taken a seat outside and she didn't have to see the questions or recriminations in his eyes. It had been easy to be sharp with him when he'd challenged her efforts to rescue Cora. But now . . . *Don't be silly. You'd do nothing different now than then, no matter what Mr. Daniel Cady thinks.*

The carriage drew to a stop and Daniel appeared at the door. Sarah turned her face and stared at Anne, seated across from her. The girl's expression was as blank as an unmarked slate, but Sarah could read it and what it had to say. Men, even ones who acted heroically, were not to be trusted. Given Sarah's limited, but richly painful, experience with them, she might agree.

"Miss Samuelson." Daniel extended his hand and it crossed into Sarah's view. His coat was damp from his soaked shirt, and a bead of water dripped off his cuff and landed on her foot. "Are you departing here?"

"No, Mr. Cady. I will see the other girls home. But perhaps you can help Cora out of the carriage."

"Certainly," he replied obligingly, though Sarah suspected he'd had quite enough of the girl. All of her talk about Cora being talented and hardworking was invalidated by what might have been a bit of silliness gone horribly bad. She had banked her future on a willful girl like Cora Gallagher, and Daniel was right to question her sense.

"Cora, go on up to the house," she said. "Tell Mrs. McGinnis to give you my old gardening dress to change into, then I'll take you to the doctor's."

Cora nodded and quietly exited the carriage with Daniel's assistance.

"I shall see the two of you tomorrow at the shop. Ten o'clock sharp," Sarah said to Anne and Minnie. She gathered her bundle of underclothes into her arms. "Anne, please inform Phoebe and Emma. We have more cleaning to do."

They nodded, not comprehending how tenuous their futures and that of the art studio really were.

"Good." She would not give up her dream of the shop without a fight. Her backers had promised her enough funds to get through several months, and perhaps Daniel would fail to convince the probate judge to award him all of Josiah's estate. They might survive despite his vow.

Perhaps pigs could fly too.

Sarah grasped the edge of the carriage doorframe and pulled herself through the opening. Daniel waited at the foot of the folding steps. His expression revealed nothing.

"Miss Whittier," he said, offering assistance.

With a hasty shake of her head, Sarah refused. Boosting her heavy, soaked skirts, she climbed down unaided. She wouldn't have him think her helpless. Ever.

Daniel returned to the front of the carriage to retrieve the picnic basket. At the house, Ah Mong had rushed down the stairs to help Cora.

Sarah shut the carriage door with a firm click. Lottie lowered the window and leaned through.

"Will you join us tomorrow?" Sarah asked.

"I intend to. I shall not let this silly sore ankle stop me." She wrinkled her forehead. "Will you be all right?"

"Once I'm out of these clothes and have some hot tea, I'll be fine."

Lottie's warm fingers closed over Sarah's, resting on the window frame. "That is not what I meant."

Sarah shot a glance in Daniel's direction. He was paying the driver and far enough away to not overhear. "You shouldn't have invited him, Lottie. After today, I'm afraid we've only confirmed his opinion."

"Do not give up on him, Sarah."

"Oh, Lottie." She rose up on her toes and pressed a kiss to her friend's forehead. She wanted to have a faith as unshakable as Lottie's. If her friend had lived Sarah's life—had endured tragic loss, indifference, broken promises—her faith might not be so solid. Might be as fluid and evasive as rushing water slipping through one's fingers. "I wish I truly had your optimism and didn't merely pretend I did."

Lottie feigned shock. "Do not tell me you are not Miss Unflappable!"

"I won't. Tomorrow. At ten." She glanced over at Anne, sitting in shadow. "You can help me decide where to place the lithograph press. Does that sound good?"

"Yes, Miss Whittier."

"Do not forget Mrs. Linforth's supper party tomorrow evening," reminded Lottie. "She has made room in her parlor so her guests can view the samples of our artwork we plan to bring over."

"How could I forget?" Bone-tired as she was, a supper party and showing at the Linforths' sounded dreadful but critical for the financial support it could bring the shop.

Sarah retreated to the sidewalk. Daniel signaled for the driver to depart, and the carriage rolled off, Lottie's hand waving through the open window.

"You don't need to see me up to the house," Sarah said to him. Next door, Mrs. Brentwood had realized Daniel and Sarah were out on the street and had raised the blinds on her front room window. "I'll see that Cora gets to a doctor. Thank you."

Ah Mong arrived to fetch the untouched picnic basket from Daniel. The boy hurried off with it.

"I'm going to come by the shop tomorrow to check on how the two of you are doing," said Daniel.

Did he care? Did he truly care? *Stop asking those sorts of questions, Sarah.*

She squared her shoulders, a feeble gesture of courage when she was shivering. "There is no need for you to bother."

"I'm not quite as insensitive as you believe I am, Miss Whittier." He was shivering too, and his teeth chattered. "I'm also just as stubborn as you are."

"I already know that."

Sarah sprinted up the house stairs and away from his gaze before he could see the confusion sprouting in her head. She reached the front porch. Next door, Mrs. Brentwood's blinds snapped shut. The gossip would fly today about that outrageous Miss Whittier and her unladylike young women.

Mrs. McGinnis threw open the front door just as Sarah reached it.

"Miss Sarah! You too?" She glanced over Sarah's shoulder, toward the street. Sarah didn't turn to look; she didn't want to know if Daniel still waited on the curb.

With a tut, the housekeeper hustled Sarah inside.

"The trip to the park was a disaster, Mrs. McGinnis." Sarah headed for the kitchen, where she could deposit the damp blanket. Rufus, bent tail sweeping the air, offered up an amused-sounding mewl as he slunk around the kitchen doorframe and scampered out of Sarah's wet path.

"I've put that Cora upstairs in the spare room where she canna damage the furniture with her wet clothes. But what am I to do with you?" Mrs. McGinnis grabbed Sarah's wadded pile of underthings and released a frustrated huff. "How can it be every day now that you're having an accident or there's some other trouble? I'm starting to think we've a curse."

"Indeed, we do." Sarah unwound her hair, wrung it out over the sink. "And its name is Daniel Cady."

Daniel's entrance at the Occidental caused raised eyebrows and at least one upright matron to make a wide berth, scuttling across the far side of the downstairs lounge like a water strider scurrying clear of a pond ripple. Thankfully, he was no longer as wet as a pond ripple, but his one good shirt might never recover from the water muck.

"Mr. Cady!" A man's voice boomed across the space. Sinclair, his rotund belly leading him forward. "There you are. But what in . . . what happened to you?"

"I went for a swim in the pond at Golden Gate Park," Daniel replied flatly.

"Ah. Yes. Well." The lawyer's movement backward was meant to be subtle but failed. "I have news for you. Shall we sit? No. I suppose not."

"Let's stand aside where we're not in the way." Daniel strode toward an empty arrangement of chairs. One of the servers peered over nervously, probably fearful Daniel might attempt to sit and ruin the velvet covering. "Make it quick so I can get out of these clothes."

"Yes, well, I checked on any possible bank assets that Mr. Josiah Cady might not have reported and so far I've come up with nothing." He tucked a thumb into his waistcoat pocket and leaned against the nearest chair back. "I have contacted two banks near Placerville where he might have had accounts but have not heard."

"All right, so he didn't have any bank assets."

"None that we can locate. I have heard an interesting tale, however." Sinclair glanced around and lowered his voice. "A rumor about a stash of gold nuggets."

Daniel frowned. "I've heard that rumor too. Hidden somewhere, maybe in the house."

"Ah, so you do know the particulars."

"Miss Whittier denies them."

Sinclair held his hands in front of him, palms up, and shrugged. "But she would, wouldn't she?"

"She might because it's the truth."

"Mr. Cady, I hope you have not become charmed by the little lady. We can't afford to be taken in by a woman's wiles when she is an opponent in a court case."

"I am not being taken in." Daniel glared at the lawyer. "I am merely saying that she denies that Josiah had a hidden stash of nuggets and I choose to believe her."

"Might I remind you, Mr. Cady, you were the one who asked me to look into these matters? It is in your best interest to stay detached."

He knew that, but his heart no longer seemed to be paying attention to his head. "Is there other news?"

"Yes. Your Chicago attorney has notified my office that your documentation is on its way. Given that, I have taken the liberty of requesting a court date for our hearing. It shall be the Monday after Monday next. Nine days from today."

"Nine days." Nine days for Sarah to prepare her supporters—and her girls—for an unpleasant outcome. Not much time.

"As I said . . ." Sinclair tugged his waistcoat and stared down his nose. "If I obtain any more intelligence on Mr. Josiah Cady's assets, I will certainly inform you. Otherwise, I shall see you at the hearing. My secretary will inform you of the particulars of the court time and location. Good day."

He strutted off, the smell of his cologne clouding the air behind him, oblivious to Daniel's answering scowl.

Twelve

"I've brought you tea, lass," said Mrs. McGinnis, shouldering her way through the half-closed door of the workshop. "Doing some painting on one of your miniatures?"

"Trying to." Sarah shifted the board so that the last of the day's sunlight, streaming through the upstairs workshop's bay window, fell upon the ivory oval secured to it. She had been polishing the ivory's surface for a half hour and seemed to be working a groove into the bone rather than smoothing the grain so that the watercolors would evenly adhere. "I was hoping some work would quiet my nerves, but I can't seem to concentrate."

"*Och*, well," the housekeeper clucked. She set the tray on the edge of the worktable. "'Tis to be expected, given the day you've had. If Cora's blubberin' was to be understood, you fair near drowned in that pond!"

"I hardly came close to drowning, Mrs. McGinnis." But she could still taste the muddiness of the pond water, feel it filling her nose. Thank God for Daniel. Thank God for his firm grip closing around her arm, yanking her free of the murky depths, saving her.

And Daniel Cady, if she were honest with herself, was the reason she could not concentrate. Why her hand shook even though she wasn't cold any longer. Why her gaze kept wandering to the houses across the street, to tree branches moving in the breeze. Why her thoughts kept returning to the scent of his coat, the press of his hands on her shoulders, the look of concern in his eyes. What if he did care about her, just a little? He was not like Edouard, who had overflowed with extravagant flattery and giddying charm, had been full of politeness and solicitude, some of it actually genuine. Handsome and easy to fall in love with. Instead, Daniel Cady was brusque and distant, single-minded in the pursuit of his vow, steeped in an old anger Sarah couldn't repudiate. His heart a carefully locked box. The wrong man for any woman. Especially her.

"Too near for comfort, lass." Mrs. McGinnis shook her head and set out the tea things, the *ping* of silverware against china bringing Sarah back to the ivory beneath her hands.

Sarah tucked an errant strand of hair behind her ear and bent over it. With one last circular stroke of the pumice-filled muslin bag, the tooth of the ivory's surface was as good as she could make it, given her state of mind. She dipped her wide camel-hair brush in water and washed the ivory until every trace of pumice dust was gone. Tomorrow, the bone would dry in the sun and bleach while she was at the shop with the girls. When she returned home, she could paint. In the uppermost corner of the workbench waited a vase of *Rosa gallica* roses she'd gathered from the garden. Rufus curled against its base, basking in the sun, his fur a blaze of cinnamon. Sarah paused to tickle the spot between his ears, which caused his tail to flick testily.

Mrs. McGinnis clucked her tongue against her teeth. "That daft cat. *Aye* in the way."

Sarah smiled and laid out her brushes, the red sable for the broader strokes, the tiny black sable for the fine lines. The reds would have to be just right to capture the muted pink stripes of rose petals, the hints of coral transitioning to a burst of lemon yellow at the heart of the flowers. She selected the watercolors she would use. The carmine to mix with Indian yellow. Gamboge and cobalt to blend for the leaves. Umber and ultramarine for shading. Vermilion for brilliance.

A freshly filled teacup and plate of cookies appeared, prodded into Sarah's line of sight by Mrs. McGinnis. "Thank you," Sarah said.

"And you're welcome. The doctor's sent his bill 'round already, along with a note, by the way." She extracted a piece of paper from her apron pocket, and held it at arm's length. "He reminds us that Cora hasna suffered overmuch from her, um, adventure at the park, but she'd be best served by a day's solid rest." The note returned to Mrs. McGinnis's pocket. "Bah. The girl doesna need rest. She needs someone to clap some sense into her head. Impetuous child."

"She's young. She'll learn."

Mrs. McGinnis briefly pursed her lips. "You're more certain than I am, miss."

"Not really," she answered honestly.

The housekeeper chuckled and leaned over to examine the sketch Sarah had prepared on tracing paper. "You've another request for a miniature?"

"This is actually a birthday present for Lottie."

"I do think your paintings are precious as gems. What did Mr. Josiah used to call them?" She straightened to consider. "'Wee treasures,' it was. *Och aye*, that was it."

Little treasures.

Sarah tapped a fingernail against the edge of the teacup. "Mrs. McGinnis, I need to talk to you about something I heard. I didn't want to mention it, but I suppose I should."

"*Aye?*"

She looked up at the housekeeper. The woman had never concealed the truth from her. "Mrs. Brentwood told me yesterday," Sarah began, unhappy that Daniel's questioning had forced her to give merit to her neighbor's story, "that there are rumors Josiah hid some sort of treasure in this house."

Mrs. McGinnis tensed. "Any stories Mrs. Brentwood has to tell are just *blether*, miss. You shouldna listen to her." She toyed with the napkin she'd brought with the tea, creasing the fold even though it didn't require fixing. "Anybody who was a prospector was believed to have brought back nuggets from the hills and hidden them away, even though most certainly did not. Folks do like to talk, though, about the successful ones like Mr. Josiah. Stories spread. You ken how that happens."

"So you're saying the rumor is not true?" Sarah laid a hand upon the housekeeper's to still her nervous motion. "I don't care if there really is treasure or not, Mrs. McGinnis, but others believe the rumor and are spreading it. Even Daniel Cady has heard."

A fine web of wrinkles appeared on her forehead. "There's no treasure or any such nonsense."

The housekeeper believed there was, though. Sarah could tell by how zealously she evaded Sarah's scrutiny.

Josiah, how did I not know? I thought you told me everything.

Everything except the truth about Daniel and Lily and Marguerite. And now this.

"I think you have always been honest with me, Mrs. McGinnis," Sarah persisted. "Please tell me where Josiah's treasure is hidden. I believe I deserve to know."

"Now, miss, why do you want to ken about such *pish*?"

"Because we had an intruder who, I'm afraid, might return because he believes such *pish*."

"I should have told you." Mrs. McGinnis's shoulders drooped. "After that beast of a man came here . . . I should have told you but I didna want you to worry. Instead I've only gone and made it worse."

"So the stories are true?"

"I canna say, truth be told. Mr. Josiah was guarding something someplace, but I don't ken what and I don't ken where. Or if it's e'en in the house anymore."

"I searched Josiah's bedroom. There's nothing in there." But his room was just one small part of the house. She would not, however, resort to tearing up floorboards or peeling wallpaper in search of hidden compartments.

"This rumor's not worth you fretting over, Miss Sarah. The police will find our intruder and everything will be fine. Mark my words." Mrs. McGinnis nodded her certainty. "But thank heavens and all good sense you finally decided to borrow Mrs. Brentwood's Remington this morn. That and trust in the Lord will keep you safe."

"Where have you been?" Frank asked from the dark corner of the front room, hunger and stale beer rumbling in his gut. His woman was supposed to bring him some dinner, but her hands were empty, clenched tight around air.

She slowly closed the street door, then turned. "I've been busy today, but I'm here now, aren't I?"

He rubbed his fist with his other hand, the knuckles grinding into his opposing palm. She reminded him of his mother when she looked at him like that, full of disdain, pitying him. *You're a failure, lad. A failure.*

He'd show 'em both.

"Did you find out if she's gone tomorrow?" he asked.

She didn't answer right away, deciding to make him wait, tightening her shawl around her shoulders like she had all the time in the world. "She will be."

"You coulda answered me sooner, woman." His knuckles ground, round and round. "You were willin' enough to help me when I first came up with this plan. You ain't gone soft on me, have you?"

Her gaze flicked to his hands, but she was careful, oh so careful, not to show any fear. She was so good he should take her up to the Barbary Coast the next time he went and teach her how to play cards.

"For how long?" he barked.

"How long?"

"You know what I mean." Annie was being difficult and it

riled him. "How long will she be gone tomorrow? And will that woman who works for her be gone too? You coulda told me she'd shriek like a banshee."

"I don't know. She'll be gone awhile. All day, I think. And they both have plans in the evening."

Frank grinned. "Good, good. Like to hear that. Need to work quick before anyone else gets the idea to move in on my mark, after that reporter's pokin' around."

"You'll never get away with this," she said, her lips flattening into a narrow line.

"Why? You planning on telling someone?" He made certain she heard the threat in his voice.

She was scared then. "No! I'd never tell on you. Never say anything."

"Good. 'Cause I don't want to wonder about you." He reached out to stroke her hair, catching hold of a strand before she could recoil. "You and me are going to be rich, when I'm done. Set ourselves up in a fine house on that hill. Like we've always wanted. Right?"

She nodded. "Say you won't hurt her. She's a good woman. You don't need to hurt anyone. Never have."

Her eyes turned soft and misty. He was the only one who saw this side of her. The side that cared. For him.

The fight, the hate subsided. "I won't have to hurt her, now, will I? I'll sneak in on cat's toes and she'll never know. Look around, find the gold, and sneak back out. It'll be over in a flash. Just like that time up on Russian Hill. Stole that pretty silver from that fellow up there and none the wiser, right? Over in a flash."

Frank snapped his fingers and guffawed.

She smiled weakly and headed for the kitchen. "I'll make us some tea now. And then you can have your dinner."

"By the day after tomorrow, woman, we'll be able to have us a servant to do that for you."

He felt the anger return, sizzling like a rattlesnake's tail, when she didn't agree.

"Are you telling me there might be an item of value hidden in your house after all?" Lottie blinked at Sarah the next morning. "And that is what the intruder was after?"

"I'm saying there seem to be well-established rumors to that effect, but I just can't believe them." Sarah took her friend's arm and together they stepped off the curb at the intersection of Kearny and California. "Josiah wouldn't have kept that from me. Would he?"

Lottie's brow puckered. "I refuse to believe Mr. Cady would have misled you about anything, Sarah. He adored you like the most beloved daughter in the world."

"He never told me about Daniel and his sisters," Sarah pointed out.

"There has to be a reasonable explanation for that omission."

"If you can think of one, let me know." They hurried past a corner barker hawking the amazing curative properties of Glenn's Sulfur Soap—the man's patter good enough to draw a small crowd, even at this hour of the morning—and pushed up the road toward Sansome Street and the shop. "I just wish I could be sure there is no treasure."

"Worrying about that rumor does you no good, Sarah. You have far more important matters to concern you," Lottie said.

"Such as whether or not I should tell the girls that the shop could be in trouble?"

"That and the fact I might not be able to help as much as I hoped." She glanced sideways at Sarah. "Mama was not happy when I got home yesterday afternoon. She says I am spending too much time with the women we have employed, women who are rough-and-tumble and expected to cause the sort of trouble they have."

Sarah halted in the middle of the sidewalk, forcing a black-suited businessman in an enormous top hat to dodge the sudden obstacle she presented. "I can't run the studio without you."

"I did not say I would not help at all, Sarah. I merely said Mama wants me to spend more time at home. Entertaining." She sighed. "Letting her acquaintances assess me as bride material over coffee and cakes is actually what she intends. I cannot snare a husband if I am at our studio all day. In fact, she told Mrs. Linforth to cancel tonight's gathering because we are to attend a supper at the Lawsons'. They have an eligible son, it appears."

"No supper or showing at the Linforths'?" Sarah felt her plans tattering at the edges like shoddily woven muslin coming undone. "After I managed to convince myself how worthwhile it would be?"

"I am sorry. Mama is acting ridiculous."

"I need you and she knows that."

"The situation is only temporary." Another businessman muttered unhappily as he skirted them. Lottie gathered Sarah's arm in hers and encouraged her to move on. "Once Mama is over her pique about my little accident, she will change her mind about my involvement with the shop. You shall see. But for now, her sympathy for our cause has run a trifle thin."

"We had none of these troubles before Daniel Cady arrived in town. I can't wait until he goes back to Chicago." Taking his questions, and the confounding way he made her feel, two thousand miles away.

Lottie's sideways glance held a world of implications. "I wonder if he will go back."

"He most certainly will, Lottie. He has assured me repeatedly."

"I saw the way he looked at you after he had pulled you from the pond, Sarah. He was genuinely worried about you."

A blush heated Sarah's cheeks. She wouldn't respond to that sort of speculation; she'd wasted enough time herself wondering whether he was worried.

Therefore, she changed the subject. "Look," Sarah said when they caught sight of the storefront. "The girls are here already."

"Oh, Sarah."

"I am not going to talk about Daniel Cady and the way he may or may not look at me. You've said yourself I have other matters to concern me."

She surged ahead of Lottie, scanning the cluster of girls waiting outside the locked front door. Minnie had her nose pressed to the window glass, her hands cupping the sides of her face to see inside. Emma was talking with Phoebe near the curb. But Anne was nowhere in sight, and she was never late.

"Where is Anne? She said she'd be here today." Sarah searched the streets for any sign of the girl. "This isn't like her."

"Yesterday, when the carriage dropped Anne at her house . . ." Lottie paused on the word. Anne's ramshackle rooms tacked onto the side of a saloon like a wart on a knuckle barely qualified as a "house." "When she stepped down, I thought I heard her assure Minnie she would be here this morning. I do not understand why she is not."

"I don't either and that's what worries me."

"Perhaps she will show up later," Lottie said hopefully.

"Minnie, did Anne say she'd be late?" Sarah asked.

Minnie peered over from the shop window. "She didn't say much yesterday, Miss Sarah. She's been in a strange mood for the past couple of days, if you ask me." She waved at the shop door, an impatient flip of her fingers. "Can we go in and see? Cora told me how swell it is and I want to prove to myself it's real!"

Sarah fished the keys from her reticule, unable to shake the feeling that Anne was somehow in trouble.

"Let's go in. But keep an eye out for Anne, all right?" Unlocking the shop door, she ushered the girls inside. Before she followed them inside, Sarah peered down the road one more time, but no tall girl in a dark dress appeared.

Lottie patted her arm as she passed. "She shall be fine, Sarah. Anne Cavendish is as tough as they come."

"I know." Too tough. Too unwilling to let anyone know if she had problems. How could she help Anne if the girl hardly spoke to anyone?

Sarah removed her hat and gloves. "Minnie, there are brooms and dustpans in the rear room. Take them upstairs. That's where we'll be working today. Phoebe, take that bucket and draw some water for washing. Emma, can you throw open the blinds?"

The girls hustled to their assigned tasks, eager to start work and turn the page on a new phase of their lives. Sarah watched them, hoping against hope today's efforts weren't just more wasted energy. But she hadn't pursued financial backing like a bloodhound, and she hadn't promised Ambrose Pomroy she would succeed, simply to fold under the threat Daniel Cady posed.

Sarah claimed one of the brooms. Behind her, the blind slats rose up the window with a clatter.

"Miss Sarah," Emma called out, "there is a man on the sidewalk looking in the window."

Sarah turned to see. With a tight smile, Ambrose Pomroy tipped his hat and headed for the front door.

Emma looked over her shoulder. "Who is he?"

"Our landlord, and I wonder why he's here," said Sarah. She could come up with a number of reasons, none of them good.

Thirteen

"Mr. Cady! Mr. Cady!" A man in an ill-fitting suit sprang up from one of the lounge room chairs, setting it to teetering. Balding and as thickset as a boxer, he didn't look like someone Daniel wanted to be hailed by after yesterday's mishap at the park and the sleepless night that had followed. He kept reliving the sight of Sarah sinking beneath the water until the image was branded onto his brain. She might have drowned. All that pluck and intelligence and noble zeal gone in an instant. The idea had left him in no mood to talk to a stranger.

So Daniel kept moving, heading toward the front door.

"Mr. Cady." Grabbing up his felt derby, the man shoved aside two hotel guests angling for prime seats in front of the street window. Almost upending the cups of coffee they carried, he tossed off an apology and caught up to Daniel. "Mr. Cady, I'd like to talk to you."

"I'm busy and don't have time to talk to strangers." He didn't look like anyone Sinclair might send over. He was far too scruffy.

"Then if you're looking for an introduction, I'm Archibald Jackson." Shorter by a half foot, he grinned up at Daniel as if they were meant to be the best of friends. "I work for the *San Francisco Chronicle*."

"I definitely don't have time to talk to a reporter." Daniel started walking faster, past a group of men trailing aromatic cigarillo smoke in their wake. One caught Daniel's eye and smirked over the reporter, jogging to keep abreast of Daniel.

Archibald Jackson was either used to being smirked at or didn't much care, because he didn't slow down a beat. "If you don't talk to me, then I might not get the story straight, Mr. Cady. And you might not like that."

Daniel halted. "What story?"

"It's come to my attention that you're the long-lost son of Josiah Cady." He punctuated the statement with a crisp jerk of his head and another grin. He smiled too much. "Yes it has. I've got good friends in well-connected places, you see." His gaze darted about, as if one of those good friends might be standing nearby in the hotel lounge.

"So what if I am?"

The reporter pursed his lips and considered him. "Know anything about gold nuggets he might have brought with him to San Francisco?"

Daniel dug a heel into the thick pile of the Occidental's Turkish rugs and started walking again. "I've heard that rumor. I don't think it's worth wasting ink on, Mr. Jackson."

"Wait, wait, wait, Mr. Cady." He snagged Daniel's sleeve. "Just tell me if I've got this part right. That he made his find in the Black Hills. With a partner by the name of Thayer."

Had that been Josiah's partner's name? He couldn't recall one way or the other. "Maybe."

"Maybe yes or maybe no?" Jackson pressed.

"Listen, Mr. Jackson, I've got business to attend to and certainly don't have time to stand around and talk with you. So if you don't mind . . ." He didn't care if the man minded or not. He was headed out to see Sarah and it made no difference what this shiny-headed reporter thought.

"You'll be hearing from me again, Mr. Cady! I'm as hard to shake as a bulldog with a bone! Yesiree!" Jackson called after Daniel's retreating back as he strode through the door and onto the street. "And give my best to Miss Whittier!"

Daniel wouldn't give the fellow the satisfaction of reacting, but the question dogged him all the way to Sansome Street as to how Jackson had guessed where he was headed.

"What might we do for you today, Mr. Pomroy?" Sarah asked after she'd introduced the girls and sent them all out of the room. She suspected Minnie lurked just around the corner in the back room, eavesdropping. If Cora were here today instead of recuperating, she'd be right at Minnie's side.

He already knew Lottie socially through her parents and made polite inquiries into their health before returning his attention to Sarah. "I had business with another tenant down the street, Miss Whittier, and I thought I'd stop in to see how you were faring."

"It's our second day of work in the shop. We have a great deal to accomplish yet," Sarah supplied when she noticed his gaze slip past her to examine the pile of stripped wallpaper curled in the corner, the forlorn stain on the ceiling. "But we can manage. None of us is afraid of labor."

Lottie's hasty glance in Sarah's direction suggested she was wondering what Mr. Pomroy wanted also. "Our equipment and cabinets should be arriving in a few days. You will be able to see then, Mr. Pomroy, how the business will function much more clearly than is visible today. You will be pleased, I am certain."

His polite smile twitched his mustache. "I suspect I will, Miss Samuelson, but I've recently heard some news that has me concerned about this shop's future."

"What have you heard exactly?" Sarah asked, unhappily anticipating his response.

"That a Mr. Daniel Cady arrived in town a few days ago. A son Josiah never told me about. I presumed all his children were deceased, as he once told me." Mr. Pomroy looked disappointed in the friend he'd trusted.

"Josiah said the same to me." As expected, his visit was about Daniel. These days, her whole life seemed to revolve around him, the irksome center of a maelstrom. "I was just as surprised by his arrival as you are."

He regarded her soberly. "He's going to claim Josiah's assets, I gather."

Minnie didn't stifle her gasp quickly enough to keep Sarah from hearing it. "You know I have been promised sufficient funds to pay the rent per our agreement, Mr. Pomroy, if that's what you're concerned about. Granted, it won't be as easy to cover all my expenses as I'd originally planned, but you and your partners won't be affected by whatever Mr. Cady does." Had she been persuasive? Did Mr. Pomroy look convinced?

"Do your backers know about him?"

"I don't know if they've heard yet," Sarah answered, her forced optimism fading. Lottie moved to her side, a bastion of strength.

Mr. Pomroy's gaze softened with pity. "While I was learning about Mr. Daniel Cady's arrival in town, I also was informed that a hearing contesting Josiah's will has been set for the Monday after next in Judge Doran's chambers."

So soon. Daniel was moving fast. "I hadn't heard."

"I am sorry, then, to be the one to tell you."

"I don't intend to change my plans, Mr. Pomroy. My girls still need me, and the outcome of Mr. Cady's case has yet to be decided."

"I suppose we shall see what transpires. In the meantime, I'll try to allay my partners' concerns." He considered them both. "The rest is up to you two ladies."

Lottie smiled as serenely as the Madonna statue outside the neighborhood Catholic church. "You do not need to worry, Mr. Pomroy. The shop will be fine."

"I worry all the time, Miss Samuelson. It comes with the job." He tipped his hat and reached for the door. "Good day to you both."

Minnie shot through the doorway to the back room before the overhead bell could stop jingling. "Miss Sarah, is it true?" she asked breathlessly. "Is Mr. Cady going to take what Mr. Josiah left you?"

Sarah clutched Minnie's hands and peered at her and the other girls, who had joined her in the center of the room. Phoebe looked confused. Emma's body had gone rigid, as if readying herself for potential upheaval.

"I will not let him ruin anything for us. We will be fine. Our backers are still standing by us," she said, whether or not it remained true. "What's more, we'll soon have plenty of customers buying all your wonderful work."

"Absolutely, girls," Lottie reassured them. "Do not be concerned."

"And if I have to share a room with one of you because I lose the house . . ." Sarah's words snagged in her throat. The house. She didn't want to lose the house. Her home. "Then that is what I will do. Trust me. Everything will be all right."

"We know you'd sell the clothes off your back for us, Miss Sarah. We'll never doubt you." Minnie's eyes glinted. "But when it comes to Mr. Cady, I promise I'm going to have choice words for him when he stops by today!"

Daniel turned onto Sansome Street, his frown chasing off a bootblack on the corner looking for some business. The reporter had left him in a foul mood. What was he after? That story about Josiah's gold nuggets was becoming a bigger nuisance by the day. Already, a prowler had been poking around the house because of the rumor. Sarah could be in serious danger if Jackson insisted on spreading the tale.

I'm worried about her because she matters to me. I've let her get under my skin and matter to me . . .

Lost in thought, he almost collided with a young woman

standing in the middle of the sidewalk. Right across the street from Sarah's custom design studio.

Daniel tapped the brim of his hat. "Sorry. I didn't notice you standing there," he said, peering at her familiar face.

"It's all right." Her long fingers clutched a ragged shawl around her neck, close under her chin. "I shouldn't be here."

Daniel finally recognized her. He should have right away because of the bruises. A fresh purple one, on her jaw right above the edge of her shawl, joined the fading yellow bruise he'd noticed yesterday. "Miss Cavendish, is it? Anne Cavendish?"

She looked gaunt and tired. And frightened. "I need to be going, Mr. Cady. Don't tell Miss Whittier I was here. I shouldn't be. There would be questions and I can't explain. I thought I could, but I was wrong."

"If there's something the matter, she'll want to help you."

His comment seemed to alarm her more. "I know. Good day."

She rushed off, bumping into a man exiting the pianoforte maker's shop next door.

"Hey!" the man yelled, annoyed.

Daniel moved to follow her but stopped, letting her slip out of reach; Anne Cavendish wasn't the sort of woman who appreciated a man's interference. Within seconds, he lost sight of her.

"Shouldn't let women like that around here," the man from the shop muttered, brushing at his sleeve. "They should stay in their own neighborhoods with their own kind."

"She works across the street," Daniel snapped. "This is her neighborhood."

The man scoffed and strode off.

Riled by his attitude, Daniel waited for a horsecar to pass and dashed across the roadway. He turned the studio's door handle and stepped inside, the bell alerting Sarah, who was alone in the main room and had been sweeping.

"Mr. Cady." It was sort of a greeting, but with the span of Sarah's work dress stretched tight across her plank-flat shoulders, taut as the upright column of her neck, and a broom gripped in her hands like a weapon, he couldn't be certain.

"Good morning to you as well, Miss Whittier," he answered, just as stiffly.

She seemed to perceive the abruptness of her attitude, although she was usually abrupt with him. "We've had a visit from my landlord, Mr. Pomroy," she explained. "He came here to talk about you."

"Ah."

"He's worried I won't be able to pay my rent, now that you've mysteriously come back from the dead to claim Josiah's estate." She considered him as she leaned against the broom. "Mr. Pomroy didn't know about you either, Mr. Cady, and he was one of Josiah's closest friends in this town."

"Just goes to prove what it meant to be a friend of Josiah." *Not much*.

Sarah returned to sweeping, the whisk of bristles against planking punctuating her words. "Apparently so."

Miss Samuelson appeared from a back room, a girl Daniel hadn't met before on her heels. "I thought I heard your voice, Mr. Cady. Sarah said you would stop in today."

Her words were polite but her typically friendly manner was absent. The girl with her stared at him like he was a mangy dog accidentally let in the front door.

"This is Mr. Cady?" The hint of a rough German accent had the effect of enhancing the scorn in the young woman's voice.

"Yes, Emma," Miss Samuelson confirmed. "Emma Schulte, meet Mr. Daniel Cady."

Footsteps sounded on the stairs that led to the upper floor. Minnie clattered down them, her skirts bunched high in her fists, torn stockings showing underneath.

"Mr. Cady, it's you." She grabbed the end of the railing and flung herself off the last step to land not far from where he stood. "You aren't taking everything away from Miss Sarah, are you?

Say you're not."

So that's what Pomroy had come to say. A blunt—and accurate—statement that cast Daniel in the worst light possible. It wouldn't matter to Minnie or the others that he had a right to Miss Sarah's "everything."

"He won't say that, Minnie, so don't ask him," said Sarah, her tone as frigid as the wind off a frozen Lake Michigan. She stabbed the floor with her broom and a bristle snapped.

"He might." Minnie turned hopefully to him. He couldn't say anything that would make matters right, so he said nothing at all.

"Minnie, Emma, I think you girls have work to do," Miss Samuelson reminded them.

"C'mon, Emma. Let's go help Phoebe." She trudged off, taking Emma with her to the back of the shop.

Silence stretched. In the rear room, a heavy object scraped across the floor and women's voices grumbled. The sudden clang of a horsecar bell from out on the street was startling against the dead quiet of the shop.

"I don't mean to keep you long." Daniel curled his fingers around his hat brim, loosening them before they closed completely. "I'm glad to see you appear to be fully recovered, Miss Whittier. And Miss Samuelson, I hope your ankle's not hurting you too much."

Sarah lifted her chin. "I'm doing perfectly fine."

"Thank you for asking after us, Mr. Cady. We heard from the doctor this morning that Cora is doing well also," said Miss Samuelson. "But he insisted that she continue to rest for the remainder of the day. She should be back with us tomorrow. Thankfully, because we need her help. We are somewhat shorthanded."

"I ran into one of your other employees outside the shop a few minutes ago," he said, just now remembering his encounter with Anne. "Anne Cavendish. She seemed upset—"

"Anne?" Sarah asked, throwing down the broom. "Why didn't

you say so earlier? Can you not for once understand what's most important?" she accused and bolted out the front door.

Where is she? Where is she?

Sarah ran halfway down the block before she realized she had no idea which direction Anne might have gone. She wanted to curse Daniel Cady for blathering on about Josiah and asking how she was doing before mentioning that he'd seen Anne. He was a stupid man with mixed-up priorities . . .

Where is *she?*

"Sarah!" Lottie called out and rushed up as hastily as her painful ankle permitted. "Sarah, she is long gone."

Sarah slapped a hand against her hip. "He should've said straightaway she was out here. Anne must be in trouble if she came all this way but then decided not to come into the shop. Or maybe Daniel scared her off—"

"Come back to the shop," Lottie interrupted. "You are not going to find her out here. Come back and we can talk about what to do."

Sarah stared down the street, saw the usual assortment of pedestrians and carriages and wagons and someone's misplaced mongrel, and agreed to return. The girls had heard the earlier commotion and were clustered near the doorway. Daniel stood to one side. Sarah frowned. Why didn't he just leave? Everywhere he went, troubles followed.

"What did Anne say to you?" Sarah asked him.

He was crushing that hat of his again. "She didn't say much. But she seemed upset. Scared, actually. She said she had made a mistake to come by and ran off."

Scared? Sarah shuddered.

"I'll bet it's that man of hers." Minnie shook her head dolefully. "He looked awfully angry when she hopped down from the carriage after our trip to the park. I don't doubt he's the one who didn't want her to come to work today."

Lottie shot Sarah an alarmed glance. "When we asked you earlier about Anne, why did you not tell us?"

Minnie shrugged. "He always looks angry, Miss Charlotte. I guess I didn't much think about it, until now."

Sarah knew what she had to do. "I have to go check on her. She needs help. I can just tell."

"She was worried you'd want to do that," said Daniel. "She didn't want you to help."

What was he suggesting? "I'm not going to go back to sweeping and dismiss the fact that one of my girls could be in trouble! They are like daughters to me. Or sisters," she said pointedly.

"You do not think to go to her house, do you, Miss Sarah?" Emma looked appalled at the idea. "She lives in Tar Flat."

"I know where she lives." A rough neighborhood named for the tarry waste the defunct gasworks once dumped into the local waterways, choking the area with the stench. Nowhere anyone with means would choose to live.

Sarah collected her hat and gloves from the counter. "Lottie, I'd ask you to go with me, but your ankle's not up to walking on those streets."

"You cannot go to Tar Flat alone."

"I'll be safe," Sarah maintained, as much to assure herself as Lottie. "It's broad daylight and the area is simply poor, not truly dangerous. I'm not heading to the waterfront or the Barbary Coast, for goodness' sake."

"Mr. Cady, if you want to be useful, go with her before she marches out of here on this harebrained scheme by herself," Lottie commanded.

He glanced at Sarah before answering. "I'd be happy to, Miss Samuelson."

"I will see you later, girls," said Sarah, striding out of the shop without looking back. She knew Daniel would follow; he was becoming about as predictable as a June fog.

"I don't need your company." Sarah stepped into the street and signaled a passing horsecar to halt. "I have been to Tar Flat before."

"So you've said." Without her permission, Daniel took her elbow and helped her climb onto the car's running board and into her seat on an empty bench. "But Miss Samuelson seemed to think there was cause for concern, and I take her worries seriously."

Sarah couldn't mistake the esteem in his tone. He liked Lottie, which gave Sarah an odd feeling she didn't have the time or energy to ponder. She settled against the seat back without comment while Daniel sat next to her, his closeness comforting in spite of her request he not accompany her. Tar Flat was not as safe as she claimed.

"Is it wise to go asking after Anne at her house?" he asked, lifting off his hat and running fingers through his thick hair. "You might anger this man of hers. Plus, she won't thank you."

"I meant what I said earlier about needing to check on her." Sarah realized she'd been staring at the movement of his hands. What a time to be noticing his hair or his strong fingers. "That she doesn't want me to only makes me worry more, and more determined to find out what might be wrong."

"You are very headstrong, Miss Whittier." There was a light in his eyes that, for once, looked curiously like admiration.

"I warned you I was."

"Yes, you did." His eyebrows lifted before he resumed watching the passing scenery. "And I must say, I believe you."

Fourteen

IT TOOK ONLY FIFTEEN MINUTES to arrive at their destination. Every example of a dwelling, shop, or factory could be found in the neighborhoods south of Market and west of the industries packed against the wharves like smoked fish in a tin. Church spires towered over the stone edifices of office buildings and porch-fronted shops. Every example of humanity could be found there as well, thought Sarah as she and Daniel descended from the Third Street horsecar. All except the Chinese, most of whom stayed close in Chinatown, steering clear of the German and Italian factory workers and stevedores, the Irish with their sharp wit and sharper tongues, the Mexican laborers whose families had worked the hills and valleys for generations. After she'd settled into Josiah's house, Sarah had tried to learn German, Italian, and some Gaelic to add to the Spanish she already knew and the smattering of French Edouard had taught her, in order to better communicate with the girls she intended to help. Sarah had abandoned that plan when she realized the time it would take to learn all those languages would detract from the time she had to paint.

"Not exactly Nob Hill," Daniel observed, taking hold of her elbow when they stepped off the planked sidewalk onto the rutted cobbled street thick with horse droppings.

"That would apply to most of San Francisco, Mr. Cady."

Workers, in a rush to return to their jobs after breaking for lunch, crowded the road and walkways. From the doorway of an oyster house, a rumpled fellow in a rough-hewn coat and pants sawed at his gums with a toothpick, eyeing the gent and his lady deigning a visit to the inferior part of town. She would have ended up in a place like Tar Flat if Josiah had not taken her in. Found work in a bakery or a fruit seller's while she hawked the paintings she'd brought with her from Los Angeles and watched her aspirations to become a successful artist diminish year by year.

"Anne's lodgings are past Howard Street," she stated, and dodged a pair of young boys tumbling out of a tin shop onto the sidewalk.

They turned into an alleyway. If Sarah remembered correctly, the rooms Anne lived in were one door down from the corner. Adjacent to the saloon she and Daniel were passing. The smell of stew and frying sausages, sweat and beer wafted through the bar's entrance, doors flung wide in welcome. A thickset man with a scraggly beard, unkempt muddy-blond hair, and a stained neckerchief scowled as he stumbled out of the dark interior, shouldering Daniel aside in his haste to hurry up the alley.

"Here goes." Sarah knocked on the house's front door, its yellow paint rippled and peeling. A flake dislodged and drifted to the ground. "Anne, it's Miss Whittier. Are you there?" she called through the gap between the door and its frame.

She heard the muffled clink of a pot falling against a basin or a sink, but no answer.

"Let me." Daniel stepped around Sarah and pounded firmly. "Miss Cavendish, are you in there?"

A woman across the way flung open her window and poked her head through. "You'd best leave that sort alone, were I you!"

"Thank you, but I'm Anne's employer," Sarah called to her.

"That's a thumper of a lie. You don't own the saloon next door." The woman, her gray hair bundled around her head like a nest of steel wool, scoffed.

Sarah frowned. "Do you have the correct woman? Anne

Cavendish is employed as a seamstress."

The woman cackled. "The Anne Cavendish who lives in that house ain't."

No wonder Anne had been free to attend class any day Sarah requested; she must work nights. "Do you know if Anne is at home?"

The woman shrugged. "Might be. Saw her man not long ago. She's usually nearby when he's around. Wouldn't want to not be, if you know what I'm saying."

Daniel resumed pounding. "Hello!"

The door flung open. Anne, hair straggling around her face, stood on the other side. To Sarah's horror, her left eye was swollen shut.

"What are you doing here?" Anne asked. "You're supposed to be at the shop."

"What in . . ." Daniel released a mild oath and dragged Sarah across the threshold, moving Anne aside, slamming the door behind them.

"I'm not at the shop because I need to be here. Obviously." Sarah's hands were quick to push back the girl's hair. A trickle of dried blood zigzagged, like a red-black lightning bolt, along her temple. "Who did this to you?"

"You need to leave, miss." Her one good eye blinked agitatedly. "It would be a terrible mistake to be here when Frank returns."

"I'm not going anywhere. Daniel, fetch water and a clean cloth. If you can find one. Do you have tincture of arnica to help the bruising, Anne?"

"You have to leave, Miss Whittier. Don't you see? Go back to the shop. You're best off there."

"Don't be ridiculous." She glanced over Anne's head toward Daniel, who was slamming open cabinets in the rear room which served as a kitchen, seeking his support. "I'm not leaving you in this condition. Let me have a neighbor summon a doctor. Or send for the police."

"The police!" Anne jerked away from Sarah's probing fingers. She winced at the suddenness of the motion. "Do not send for them. Either of you. Frank . . . he's just been upset lately. Trouble at work. You know how that goes. This . . ." She gestured at her black eye. "He's never done this before, and he won't again."

"He *has* hit you before, Anne, many times. But he won't any longer because I'm taking you with me. Pack your things. Right now." Sarah looked around, searching for any belongings worth taking among the threadbare furniture, worn rugs, and faded sketches tacked to the stained plaster walls.

"I can't. Frank would come looking for me. Take my advice and go back to the shop and forget you saw this."

Daniel returned, a bowl of water in one hand and a rag in the other. Mutely, he handed them to Sarah. The tin bowl chilled her hands.

"Forget this?" Sarah dipped the cloth into the water, sloshing it against the brim, and began to daub Anne's face. Miraculously, the girl stood still and let her. "I cannot walk away and forget I saw this." She tried to settle her trembling and not jab Anne's bruises.

"You have to forget," Anne persisted. "Trust me, it's for the best."

"I want you to come with me," Sarah repeated slowly and firmly, as if she were addressing a stubborn child. Didn't Anne understand?

"You'd have to drag me from here by force because I won't go. I mean it."

"Then I'll just force you. Mr. Cady will toss you over his shoulder and march out of here."

Anne swallowed, her throat working angrily. "I already have one man who tries to make me do what he wants. I don't need another."

Sarah's hand stopped midstroke. An adamant, cajoling voice

from another time, a different place echoed in her head. "*If you come with me, Sarah, chérie, we can be together. See the world. Go where no person can stand in our way . . .*"

"Miss Whittier." Daniel was at her side, looking down at her. "Do you need help?"

She glanced between him and Anne, forcing herself back to this time, this room. To this young woman whose life was more of a mess than Sarah's had been when Edouard Marchand's charms had overwhelmed her judgment. "Frank will hurt you again, Anne. You know he will."

Her head went up, defiant. "I'll leave him when I can make my own way."

"I can give you money now, if that's what you need, a few dollars left over from the sale of some paintings." The balance of an unspent bribe. "Find you a place to live." Find her someplace safe, where she could start over. Maybe even become a new person. Like Sarah had done. She had to be able to cobble together enough money to do that for Anne, whether or not her budget told her otherwise.

"I don't take charity, Miss Whittier."

"Mr. Cady, tell her to be reasonable," pleaded Sarah.

Daniel slipped the dripping rag from Sarah's grasp, dropped it into the bowl. "She's a grown woman. You can't make her do what she doesn't want to do."

She trembled, the tin bowl rattling against the metal buttons of her cuffs. "She's going to be a dead woman if she doesn't see sense!"

The words hung in the air, suspended like dust motes in a slash of light. Sarah held her breath and wished them back.

"You and Mr. Cady need to leave," Anne whispered, taking the bowl from Sarah. "I thank you, but please, just go. You're not safe."

Daniel reached inside his coat and pulled out a few dollars, stuffed them into the pocket of Anne's skirt. "This is money for a doctor. Not charity. I expect you to repay me."

She nodded. Daniel clasped Sarah's arm and she had no choice but to succumb to Daniel's persistent pressure, pulling her toward the door and the street.

"Anne, I expect you at classes and the studio as soon as possible," she said from the bottom step. "The girls, the shop won't be half as successful without you."

"Cora won't miss me."

"I will," Sarah insisted, wanting to run back up the stairs and shake reason into Anne. A young woman who she'd always thought of as the essence of logic and sensibility. "And if Frank does"—Sarah gestured at Anne's face—"*this* again, you must come to me immediately. Promise me."

"Good-bye, miss," Anne replied, not promising. She watched, solemn-faced, from the dark rectangle of the doorway, the bowl clutched to her chest, a pitiful shield. "And Miss Whittier, be careful, all right?"

Sarah's head rested awkwardly on Daniel's shoulder, and the short tuft of feathers sprouting from her hat tickled his right ear, but he wouldn't move her for the world. Wouldn't accept any amount of money to withdraw his arm from around her shoulders. In fact, he wished he could tuck her nearer, fold her tight against his chest. Protect her.

As he held on, her tears began to subside. And somewhere, deep inside, an emotion stirred.

No, no. Not her. Not now.

"I was a little stupid back there, wasn't I?" Sarah asked, her words muffled by the sleeve of his jacket, sounding weary to the core.

"You want to help Anne. It's not your fault the situation's too thorny to fix." He couldn't protect her from the heartache; he had enough difficulty protecting himself.

She sighed and moved out from beneath his arm, scooting along the bench to lean against the rear wall of the cable car. A draft of chill air replaced her warmth.

"I'm sorry. I shouldn't have been crying on you and now I've ruined your vest." Sarah wiped at the damp spots on his chest with the edge of her cuff. "I hate to cry. It serves no purpose."

"I think it's a situation worth crying about."

"Do you?" She lifted her eyebrows and blew her nose into her handkerchief, stashing it away when she'd finished. "Crying won't solve Anne's problems. Won't solve any of my girls' problems. I just wish I knew what to do for her."

The car shuddered to a halt, Daniel steadying his feet against the floorboards for balance, to deposit two men in frock coats and top hats at the corner. One more block and they would be at Sarah's stop.

"You did the best you could by offering her someplace safe to go," he said.

"The best for Anne would have been to drag her from that hovel, no matter how much she protested, and put her on the earliest train to anywhere several hundred miles distant from that Frank fellow."

"He's the sort who sounds like he'd hunt her down and make her pay for running off. China or India might not be far enough. All you'd gain by sending Miss Cavendish away is trouble for yourself." He hadn't rescued her from drowning to have some vengeful lover of one of her girls decide to wring her neck.

"I don't care about trouble for me."

"That *is* the problem with you, Miss Whittier."

Her eyes narrowed. "We've already discussed this before."

At the pond. He knew. He remembered.

His jaw twitched. "You need to take care of yourself if you want to help anybody. Be more careful."

Sarah scoffed and tossed her head. "Don't make it sound like you care about my health and well-being."

He stared back at her. "You might not believe it, but I do care." More than she could imagine or he liked.

Did she inhale suddenly? Blush a little? Hard to tell in the checkered shadow and light within the cable car.

"Then prove it," she dared, her chin going up, any chance to see if she was flustered by his admission lost in her defiance. "Invest in the shop."

"Maybe I will."

Sarah laughed. "I would like to believe you, but I suspect that'll never happen."

Never say never, Sarah. "We've arrived at your stop." He stood as the cable car glided to a halt.

Sarah scrambled to her feet. "Wait. Did you mean it? Might you invest in the shop?"

Daniel didn't know what he had meant. Any more, his brain didn't think clearly around her. "Let me help you down."

He took Sarah's arm and assisted her down the steps and onto the street. Daniel set a brisk pace but Sarah kept up.

"You weren't serious. I knew it." She frowned at him. "It doesn't matter. We have our backers, so I don't need your money. But what you could give me is Josiah's house."

"Not sure I can help you there."

"Too many promises, Mr. Cady?" she asked, holding tight to her hat as she hurried alongside him.

"In general, I try not to make them, Miss Whittier." *Because promises are too often broken. I learned that lesson from you, Josiah.* "Aside from the promise I made to Lily and Marguerite, that is." And to his mother.

"It's just as well. I rarely believe promises," she responded, laughing lightly to mask what might have been unhappiness in her voice.

They reached the house. Ah Mong, perched on the topmost step, caught sight of them and jumped up. "Miss Sarah, you are home early."

"I left the shop so we could go check on Anne. She didn't come to work today." Sarah turned to Daniel before climbing the steps. "Thank you for going with me to Anne's and showing me home, but I'll be perfectly fine from this point forward."

"Do you want me to check on Miss Cavendish later this afternoon?" he asked. "The Occidental isn't all that far from her house."

"And risk having Frank return and find you, a strange man, in his house?" She looked at him like he was daft. "You're the one who needs to be careful if you're going to do something so foolish."

"Not one of my better ideas, perhaps."

"You've had a few interesting ones today."

He cocked an eyebrow. "Yes, I have."

She smiled. How bright her eyes were, sharp, intelligent, the tears and self-pity in them long gone. Abruptly, she raised up on her toes and kissed him, an innocent, feather-light brush across his cheek. The scent of rose water filled his senses. "Thank you. You didn't need to claim you might invest in my business. More importantly, you didn't need to help with Anne, and I'm grateful that you did. Thank you for being the sort of man Josiah would have been proud of."

Before he could react, she spun about and bounded up the steps, skirts held high, sweeping through the front door without looking back.

Sarah stared up at the ceiling above her bed. Had she never noticed before the faint crack that meandered like the stream back in Ohio, a ragged line advancing from the corner toward the center of the room? Likely not, because tonight there was moonlight to compete with the purpling sky, a rare enough occurrence when usually fog descended like a veil to shroud the houses and trees and yellow hills. It was also a rare occurrence that she was sleepless and staring at the contents of her bedroom, fretting over Anne. Fretting over Daniel.

Her cheeks flared. She had kissed him. Nothing passionate at all. Just a brush against his cheek. A spontaneous act borne from gratitude that he'd been so kind to Anne and to her that afternoon. A kiss that had been nothing like the kisses, the embraces she had once shared—so very foolishly—with Edouard Marchand.

But enough of one to keep her from sleep.

Sarah punched her pillow and flipped onto her side. The wall opposite was no more calming than the ceiling. Her stomach rumbled. With Mrs. McGinnis absent at an opera at the Winter Garden—a treat from Sarah, who'd expected to spend the evening cajoling money out of the Linforths and their guests—Sarah had only managed to scrounge a cold plate of sandwich meats for dinner and now she was paying the price. She'd gone to bed early because she needed to sleep, not lie here staring at walls. Tomorrow, the worktables were set to arrive at the studio, and she would need all her energy. All of her focus to forget what had happened between her and Daniel that afternoon.

Daniel, again. She couldn't keep her thoughts from him for long. He had become a part of her life, as stubbornly attached as a burr to a wool stocking. The look on his face when she'd kissed him . . . Sarah smiled into the moonlight. His look of wide-eyed shock had been the same as if she'd slapped him. Instead of merely brushing her lips against his face, skin softer than it had appeared, warmer than she had anticipated.

A sigh escaped. "Honestly, Sarah. You know better than this." Better than to lose her heart to someone who would not hold it safe.

She shifted to turn onto her other side when a noise downstairs brought her upright in bed. Had Rufus cornered a mouse or gotten into the pantry? But the noise hadn't come from the kitchen. Sarah heard the sound again, the creak of wood, the distant squeak of a hinge. Sounds made by a creature much heavier than either Rufus or a mouse. Maybe Mrs. McGinnis was home early from the Winter Garden opera.

But just in case . . .

Pulse racing, mouth dry, Sarah fumbled for Mrs. Brentwood's nickel-plated derringer, stored in the bedside table. The first time she'd ever handled a gun had been when she was seven, and her neighbor had dared her to shoot the woodchucks burrowing beneath their barn. Never one to let a boy best her, she'd taken his father's pistol—barely able to lift the gun—and shot. The kick had knocked her on her behind. The woodchuck had survived. A corner of the barn's stone foundation hadn't fared as well.

Sarah shimmied into her slippers and pulled on her red silk robe. Striking a match, Sarah lit a lantern. She eased open the bedroom door and stretched the light into the hallway.

"Mrs. McGinnis, is that you?" she called toward the curving flight of stairs across from her bedroom. No answer.

Lantern extended, Sarah started for the staircase. Every few steps, she paused and listened. All she could hear was the sound of her own blood rushing through her ears. Softly, she lowered first one slippered foot onto the entry hall carpet, then the other. She craned her neck to see down the length of the hall and the dining room beyond, then toward the parlor directly across from her. A faint pool of light lit the room's Brussels carpet. She cocked the pistol, praying she wouldn't require more than the two bullets it contained, and tiptoed forward.

Within four steps, she saw him, his silhouette limned by the front bay window and the gas lamp that lit the street out front. He'd pulled the curtain aside to better see. A brute of a man, he was peering behind the secretary, looking ready to shove it aside. He hadn't heard her or noticed the gleam of the lantern. But he would at any moment.

She raised the Remington. Her last thought before she pulled the trigger was that she was grateful he was a lot bigger than a woodchuck.

Fifteen

WOOD SPLINTERED, the gun's retort startling Sarah. The man spun about, his coat pocket catching the knob of the secretary's drawer and yanking it to the ground, spilling stationery and steel pen nibs onto the carpet.

"Stop! I'll shoot again!" she screamed.

He lunged for her and she jumped aside. Her hip smacked against the parlor table, sending the vase of roses in its center crashing. From behind, Sarah heard shouting, the gruff shriek of an angry Scottish woman bursting through the front door. Alarmed, the man bolted through the far archway that led into the dining room. The rear door slammed as he escaped into the garden.

"Miss Sarah!" Mrs. McGinnis sprinted to her side. "Was that a gunshot?"

The room whirled around her like a top skipping across an uneven floor. Sarah gripped the table's edge to steady herself.

"Thank heavens you're here, Mrs. McGinnis." She'd shot the derringer. In her house. At the intruder who had returned for Josiah's treasure. The image of his face, lit by the lantern for a second before she fired, swam in her vision. Where had she seen him before?

Mrs. McGinnis ran her hands over Sarah's arms, inspecting her for damage. "Are you hurt, lass?"

"No. Just a bit shaky." A fresh wave of dizziness surged and

Sarah inhaled. Carefully, she set the gun, still clenched in her hand, and the lantern on the parlor table.

"You need some tea." Tea always fixed everything, to Mrs. McGinnis's way of thinking.

"Thank you for coming home early, by the way."

"Thank the good Lord that not e'en the famed Miss Ethel Lynton could hold my attention tonight! Dornt like opera. Bah." She righted the vase, stuffing the roses back into it. "Let me fetch some towels to clean up this spill."

The housekeeper hastened off, flourishing a string of choice Scottish words like a master craftsman, flinging some of them at Rufus when he scampered beneath her feet. Sarah pulled in another lengthy breath and looked over at the secretary. A ragged hole gaped in the wood. She had missed the intruder but ruined the piece of furniture. She was no better a shot than she'd been at seven, apparently.

"Miss Sarah?" Ah Mong scuttled in from the dining room, his thin-soled black sandals slapping on the floor. "I heard a gun. Are you well?"

"I am unharmed, Ah Mong. And a terrible shot, it appears." She could joke, now that her heart was no longer in her throat. After the threat was gone.

"I saw the man. He ran by me and climbed over the wall." The boy shuffled his feet. "I am sorry. I was asleep and did not stop him."

"It's all right." Although her knees were knocking something fierce.

"There you are, ye daft boy. And it's about time." Mrs. McGinnis thrust towels into his arms. "Here, there's water everywhere. Clean it up so Miss Sarah can rest and have some tea and calm her wee nerves."

A trail of dark spots along the floor caught Sarah's eye. She bent down and swiped one with her finger. Sticky red liquid. Not so bad a shot, after all.

"Blood, Miss Sarah?" the housekeeper asked. She stepped close to peer over Sarah's shoulder. Ah Mong exhaled a murmur of Chinese.

Sarah wiped her finger on one of the towels. "The bullet must have grazed the man."

"Serves him right." Mrs. McGinnis clucked scornfully. "Back at yer chore, Ah Mong." She swiped the towel from Sarah's grasp to blot the drips of blood from the rug.

"I think I've seen him before, Mrs. McGinnis."

"Was he large as a bear and near as hairy?" She dabbed the towel across the floor, tracking the trail of crimson.

Sarah followed her as the path wended its way into the dining room. "You might describe him that way."

Mrs. McGinnis grunted. "That's our intruder then. *Nae* that I thought otherwise. Come back to look again."

"For Josiah's treasure," she whispered. Suddenly cold, Sarah folded her robe around her waist.

Mrs. McGinnis obliterated the final speck of blood and stood. "I thought you agreed there is *nae* treasure, Miss Sarah."

Sarah shivered into the thin silk. "He thinks there is."

In the end, that was all that mattered.

"I have come to speak with you, Mr. Cady, on behalf of the other girls." Minnie, bolt upright on the Occidental's dining room chair and hands folded upon her lap, enunciated each word with the precise clarity of a displeased governess.

"Miss Tobin, you might be more comfortable this morning if you accepted a cup of coffee from the waiter." Daniel inclined his head in the direction of the boy, at his post between two of the dining room's draped windows.

"I don't wish to be more comfortable, Mr. Cady."

"You don't mind if I drink my coffee, do you?" She'd marched through the dining room that morning like an army general, collecting in her wake her fair share of whispered comments, none of them likely complimentary. Not to a girl so clearly a member of the working class and daring to breach the sanctity of the Occidental Hotel, all cut glass and velvet furnishings. "It's at its best when it's still hot."

Her eyes, which were a very nice brown though not as fine as Sarah's, surveyed him scornfully. "If you have the stomach to eat breakfast and drink coffee while plotting to take away all that Miss Sarah has worked so hard for, then I won't stop you."

"I might have figured that's why you'd come." He didn't really have much of an appetite, not while she was so clearly angry with him, but he sipped from the coffee anyway and lifted his fork as though he might eat. Which he doubted he would.

"I am . . . the other girls and me, we are thankful that you went to help Miss Sarah with Anne yesterday." Her glance dipped to his untouched bacon and eggs, a heaping plateful. He suspected she never saw that much food on her plate for breakfast. He would push it over to her side of the table if he thought she wouldn't be insulted. "Anne has it bad with her man. So you can understand how important the shop is to her and to all of us. We can't lose it."

Daniel tapped the fork tines against the edge of the china plate. He didn't need a doe-eyed young woman making him feel guiltier than he already did. "Miss Whittier has told me she has financial backing from various supporters. She seems certain they'll come to her rescue if things . . . don't go as well as she hopes."

"Like you getting the house Mr. Josiah left her and everything else?" She blinked, but her eyes were dry. She was a tough one. Other women might have started to cry by now. Maybe every woman associated with Miss Sarah Whittier was as steely as she was. "I don't know about those folks and if they'll rescue poor Miss Sarah, so you've got to let her have her inheritance. Or at least a goodly portion of it."

"The amount poor Miss Sarah gets isn't up to me, Miss Tobin. It'll be up to the probate judge."

Minnie rapped a fist against the edge of the table. "Mr. Cady!" A matron, severe in dark purple and blue stripes, shot her a disapproving glance. Embarrassed, Minnie lowered her voice. "Mr. Cady, you can always write a check, can't you?"

Daniel set down his fork and sat back. "Miss Tobin, I'm sure Miss Whittier would be gratified to know you're here, speaking up for her. But I have responsibilities back in Chicago and their names are Lily and Marguerite."

Minnie stared at him. "You have daughters?"

"No. I have twin sisters. They're ten. They were born a year before my father . . ." Abandoned them? Decided gold was more important than family? "Before my father came out West. They don't remember him. All they know is life has been hard, especially once we—and everybody else—realized Josiah wouldn't be coming back to provide for us." *Resentment is a cancer, Daniel. Don't let it eat you alive. You have to forgive him. Forgive him.* That was what his mother would have him do, forgiveness coming a whole lot easier for Grace Cady than it ever would for her son.

"What are they like?" Minnie asked.

"They're like two girls." Daniel drank some coffee. It had cooled, and a ground stuck in his teeth. "Why are you interested?"

She smiled wistfully. "I don't have any sisters."

"Well, they're funny at times, serious others. Sweet and pretty, with shining dark hair. Shy." He didn't add that the reason for their shyness was because they were too aware they were gossiped about. The unwanted daughters of a no-good gold miner. The granddaughters of a railroad tycoon who'd prefer to pretend they didn't exist so as not to mar his lustrous status among the Chicago elite.

He smiled briefly at Minnie, in case the cancerous resentment showed too sternly on his face. "They slipped flowers into my bag before I left Chicago. Undoubtedly plundered from the Grays' garden. They're friends of ours who are watching the girls while I've been searching for Josiah. Our mother passed on in October." He inhaled slowly, the pain of her loss still fresh enough to make it hard to breathe. "I didn't find the flowers until about a week later, crushed and desiccated, scattering petals over my spare cotton socks. The girls love flowers. No surprise, I guess, given their names." Which had been his father's idea, he'd always been told. Give them two sweet names and then run off.

"Do they like dolls? My neighbor's little girl likes dolls. I always wanted a doll, but . . ." Minnie shrugged away her disappointment.

"Yes, they do." He could bring Lily and Marguerite any number of dolls, once Josiah's estate had been settled. "They're why I can't return with anything less than I'm owed, Miss Tobin. My two sisters. When my mother died, I decided it was time to get back from Josiah some portion of what he'd taken from us. With the money he had once sworn he'd send us, I intend to start a business venture, something I've been meaning to do for years but couldn't, with my mother seriously ill and the girls to take care of." He'd been dreaming of quitting his poor-paying clerk's job and being his own boss for so long. "So I'm here. For my sisters. Because I promised them they'd never lack for anything. They've lost a mother and a father. It seems the least I can do."

Minnie clenched her working girl's hands atop the snowy white tablecloth. "I'm sorry if you think your promise keeps you from helping Miss Sarah," she said, her voice on the verge of shaking. "But we're her family and all she has. And I think losing the shop might mean losing us, and that could kill her."

Daniel's jaw tensed. Losing that custom art studio wouldn't kill Sarah Whittier. She was too tough. "What about her family in Arizona? She could always go home to them."

Minnie frowned. "She never talks about them. I don't think they want her back." Her hand flew to her mouth when she realized she'd said too much.

Just then, Red hustled up to the table, grinning. "Mornin', Mr. Cady. Here's your paper. Mornin', miss." He doffed an invisible cap at Minnie. "Thought I'd drop by 'cuz there's some interesting news I know you'd like to hear, Mr. Cady, sir. About that house your pa owned up on Nob Hill. Seems someone tried to rob it last night."

Minnie gasped. "What? Is everyone all right? Miss Sarah?"

"Think nobody's been hurt." The waiter looked a little disappointed to admit that. "But I heard there was gunshots."

Gunshots.

Daniel shoved back his chair, threw his napkin onto the table, and stood. "I'd like to talk more, Miss Tobin, but I think I'll go check just how everyone is up at the house."

"I am positive I've seen the man before, Officer Hanson." Sarah folded her hands at her waist while the policeman squatted to examine the chink she'd shot out of the secretary. Rufus, bent tail flicking, was curled atop the piece of furniture, observing the fellow as he bent to his task.

The hem of Officer Hanson's indigo wool frock coat grazed the floor right next to a telltale stain, more visible in the morning light than it had been last evening. He glanced down, rubbed a blunt fingertip over it.

"Blood, Officer," Sarah said in response to the unasked question. "I must have shot him."

"Hm." Officer Hanson sat back on his haunches. He scribbled a note on the topmost sheet of a haphazard stack of papers gripped in his fist. "So, is this the same fellow as was here"—he quickly thumbed through his papers—"three days ago?"

"I ken he is," offered Mrs. McGinnis, pacing between Josiah's stuffed armchair and the walnut table in the center of the room. "The same hairy beast."

The scritch of pen against paper stopped. The policeman

looked over at Mrs. McGinnis, the stubble of his poorly shaven chin rasping against his high white shirt collar. "What does he want, do you think?"

"*Och*, now how would I ken that?" Mrs. McGinnis bristled. "'Tis your job to find out, Mr. Hanson, not mine."

"*Officer* Hanson," he reminded her, straightening to his full, and intimidating, height.

"Officer Hanson," Sarah interrupted before he decided Mrs. McGinnis was obstructing his investigation or some-such charge, "my housekeeper and I suspect that the man erroneously believes there are hidden gold nuggets in this house. He must be looking for them."

The policeman peered at Sarah before making another notation on his paper. "And are there?" he asked, the tone of his voice suggesting she might not be honest in her response.

"No! It's a rumor and nothing else."

"A dangerous rumor for an unmarried woman and her servant, living in this big house alone."

She recognized the admonition in his words. Aunt Eugenie would have implied the same, reminding Sarah that she was a woman just as stubborn, just as imprudent as her mother had been.

"Our neighbor's male servant and his brother will be here tonight to watch over us." If they'd both been at the house last night, they would have scared off the intruder. Sarah was confident of that. "They will be sufficient guard."

The policeman scoffed. "That little China boy I saw skulking on your front porch? He couldn't chase off a squirrel!"

Every nerve bristled. She was tired of the derision, the dismissiveness. Just another Chinese. Just another Irish girl. Just another woman who doesn't know her place. *Ah Mong was told to watch over you, Miss Whittier.* Josiah knew what he was doing when he asked the boy; last night's episode would not be repeated, because Ah Mong would not fall asleep again. She trusted him, even if no one else did.

"If you catch the man who attempted to burgle my house, Officer Hanson," she said, "I will not have to worry about protection, shall I?"

It was his turn to look offended. "Your description of the fellow could fit any number of criminals in this town, Miss Whittier. Unless you can remember where you think you've seen him before."

A memory, faint as a whisper in a crowd, echoed. She had seen him, and not long ago. But where? In a trice, the memory was gone. "I can't recall."

"I'll check the hospitals, but he won't go to a doctor if he's not hurt bad. Too risky that he'd give himself away." The policeman folded his notes and slipped them inside his frock coat, fastening the brass buttons when he'd finished. "I have a hunch I know who he is, though. My men and I have been tracking a fellow in Nob Hill with a similar description for months now."

"Months? Shouldna you have caught him by now?" Mrs. McGinnis accused.

"He's a clever fellow."

"Cleverer than you, it seems!" she retorted, startling Rufus off his perch. The tabby executed an arcing leap to the ground and wandered off, appearing bored with the entire proceeding.

Officer Hanson cleared his throat. "I'll let you know if there's news, Miss Whittier. The man likely won't return, now that he knows he's been seen and also knows you have a weapon, but lock all your doors. Tight."

He tipped his tall domed hat, frowned at Mrs. McGinnis, and clomped out of the house and down the stairs. Near his wagon, a crowd clustered together on the sidewalk, including that newspaper reporter again. Sarah had no idea how someone like that had heard about the housebreaker already. Maybe reporters could spot a crime scene like a vulture knew how to locate carrion. As if he could sense her glaring, he looked up at the house and lifted his hat, revealing a balding head that glistened from a liberal dose of bear's grease pomatum.

"Do not go down, Miss Sarah," murmured Ah Mong, arms folded, back straight, his eyes on the crowd.

"I have no intention of subjecting myself to that bunch." She sincerely hoped they would not linger all day. She needed to go to the shop, and she didn't intend to slip over the rear wall like their burglar had in order to escape.

"Good day to you, Miss Whittier," the police officer called up to the house. He elbowed the reporter aside, causing the man to stumble on a break in the pavement, and hopped into his wagon.

Mrs. Brentwood separated from the crowd, collected her voluminous skirt, and hurried to intercept Sarah before she could retreat to the safety of the house.

"Oh, my dear Miss Whittier, Ah Mong told me everything over breakfast this morning." Her hands flitted like a pair of distraught sparrows, and she wedged her body through the gap between Sarah and the doorframe. "He should have informed me last night of your trauma, of course, as soon as it happened, but . . . how dreadful to encounter an armed man in one's parlor! Though you must be glad you had use of my little Remington." She winked conspiratorially. "You are very brave. I would have swooned away in a dead faint. Fortunately for me, I have the protection of Mr. Brentwood in such times of distress."

"Mrs. Brentwood, I would love to talk with you about my 'trauma,' but not even a failed burglary and all the excitement can keep me from my shop this morning. I have work to do, bills to pay—"

"You are welcome, Miss Whittier," she charged ahead, "to stay with us if you are fearful for your life." Her gaze darted over Sarah's head and into the parlor, possibly hoping to spy some evidence of the "trauma."

"Thank you for the offer, but I'll stay here to protect my possessions."

Mrs. Brentwood tutted. "Ah, yes, the treasure. Mr. Cady should never have burdened you with that. Though I can hardly blame him for not trusting the banks. Look what happened to—"

"There *is* no treasure, Mrs. Brentwood, and I hope you haven't been telling folks, especially that reporter, there is."

The other woman paled. She *had* told the man. "Mr. Malagisi told me he heard the gunshot last night—you know how close his house is to yours, Miss Whittier—and that he would have contacted the police immediately but he was very alarmed—"

"Has he been talking to the reporter too?" Now both her neighbors were gossiping on her.

"These sorts of stories do get out, Miss Whittier," proclaimed Mrs. Brentwood with a complacent shake of her head.

Sarah could not afford stories, because rumors and gossip only fueled the sort of speculation that had surrounded her since the day she had arrived in San Francisco. The nosy questions that might, some day, unearth the unhappy truth of her past.

Oh, Josiah. Now what do I do?

Sixteen

THE ANSWER TO HER QUESTION, Sarah decided, was to go to the shop as she'd planned. No burglar, no inquisitive neighbors could stop her from the one thing she did best—work and work hard.

She hopped down from the cable car at Sansome Street. A burst of rain had left the sidewalks puddled and relatively empty of pedestrians, striped store awnings dripping water onto the pavement below. On the corner, a forlorn newsboy overburdened with unsold papers peddled his wares.

"*Evening Post*! Five cents!" Damp newspapers draped over his shoulder and one suspended from his ink-stained hand, he called out the afternoon's headlines as Sarah hurried by: British steamer sunk, doomed search for arctic explorer described, an assassination in Ireland.

Burglar on the loose in Nob Hill.

Heavens. They'd made the news already. Sarah fumbled for a nickel and purchased a paper. The brief article occupied a corner of the front page where it could be easily seen. There was her name along with a sensational tale from Mrs. Brentwood and a lurid description of the intruder. To read the account, Sarah had blasted the man with a Colt revolver when she'd confronted him as he searched for a rumored stash of Black Hills gold. He'd then staggered off, leaving a trail of blood a mile long marking his path.

"Nob Hill ain't safe no more neither, eh, miss?" the newsboy commented. "Heard that burglar was after more'n gold. Heard there's silver and diamonds too!"

"Have you really?"

Sarah shoved the newspaper beneath her arm and barged into the shop, the bell almost jangling off its mount.

"Miss Sarah!" Cora spun about. "What's wrong?"

"Nothing, Cora." Her hat and gloves and the paper landed in a heap upon the counter. "Nothing for you to worry over, at least. And by the way, I'm glad you're here and look so well."

She lifted her shoulders. "No harm done. The doctor thought another day off work might be better, but my brother wouldn't let me rest for calling me a lazybones, so I had to come in. Minnie wanted me to help her today, anyhow, since none of the other girls could."

"All the more proof you are not a lazybones."

"Tell that to my brother." Cora smirked, then cast a quick look over her shoulder toward the rear workroom doorway. "Anne's here. Been waiting for you."

"You don't have to whisper, Cora." Anne strode into the main room. She clutched at her cloak, shoulders and hem darkened from the afternoon's rain shower. Today Anne's bruises were as purple as ripe plums. Sarah could hardly look at them without wanting to lock the shop door, close the blinds, and whisk Anne away to someplace safe. Safer than the home she shared with that man. "I knew you'd be here today, Miss Whittier. I heard about the break-in, and I wanted to make sure you were all right."

"Break-in?" Cora squealed.

Cora couldn't read well, so she wouldn't have already learned the news; Sarah was surprised that Anne, however, had somehow found the opportunity.

"An attempted burglary, Cora. I chased the man off and the police feel quite certain they'll catch him."

A shadow of unease crossed Anne's face. "You weren't harmed, were you?"

It touched Sarah that Anne was so worried for her. "I'm perfectly fine. But I would feel a lot better if you were here to tell me you'd come to help at the studio today."

"I can't. Frank needs me at the house. I'm sorry." She gathered her cloak around her and headed for the door.

Sarah stopped her as she passed. "As I told you before, I can give you money to leave him. Whatever you need."

Anne's eyes seemed to darken until they were black as beads of jet. "Money won't buy me what I need, Miss Whittier."

Cora laughed aloud. "It works for me!"

Anne's gaze didn't waver. "It can't buy me peace of mind."

"Oh, Anne." Sarah wanted to reach out for the girl, embrace her, but she knew better.

"Who needs peace of mind when you've got cash?" muttered Cora.

"Cora, go help Minnie, will you?" Sarah waited until Cora had gone upstairs before approaching Anne. "This studio won't be half as successful without you. I said so yesterday and I meant it. None of the others can produce a lithograph as beautiful as yours. Besides, we have customers eagerly awaiting your Golden Gate Park prints." Not the complete truth, in that Lottie had yet to convince Mrs. Linforth to order the lithographs, but what was a slight falsification if the telling encouraged Anne to keep working at the shop? And gain her freedom.

A rare smile flitted across Anne's face; she knew Sarah was exaggerating. "It's only for today. Besides, the lithograph equipment is not even here yet."

"The press will arrive tomorrow. I need you to set it up."

"I will try to be here." Anne flipped the hood of her cloak over her head. "Remember to be careful. Truly, be alert and on guard."

Her tone was so earnest it raised goose bumps on Sarah's skin. "I will."

"Good." Brusquely, Anne nodded and rushed off.

"She'll never leave that man," Cora announced from the top step of the shop staircase. "He's nothing but trouble, and he's dragging her down with him."

Sarah rubbed her hands down her arms, chasing off the goose bumps. Her knuckles skimmed the cool ivory of the brooch pinned at her waist—the *Rêve d'Or* roses brooch, the one that called to mind her mother's composure, that brought Sarah courage. She wished she had just one ounce of her mother's pure faith. Any belief that a merciful God was watching out for her and these girls. But faith hadn't saved her mother from the wrath of a summer storm, and bricks had proven to be mightier than the strength of flesh and bones and prayer.

Sighing, Sarah picked her apron off its hook and tied it around her waist. "I wish I understood why she lets him drag her down. I thought she was stronger and wiser than that." *Wiser than I was.*

Cora chuckled. "Miss Sarah, if you'd ever been in love with the wrong man, you'd understand why. Be thankful you never have."

Memories and guilt pricked. Sarah nodded. And said nothing to correct Cora's erroneous notion.

"Good afternoon, Miss Whittier."

The man's voice echoed from Sarah's front porch, startling her, and she dropped the newspaper she had tucked beneath her arm.

"What are you doing here, Mr. Cady?" Her clumsiness made her blush. Or perhaps it was the sight of the face she'd so hastily, unwisely kissed yesterday. She was still making mistakes where it concerned men, and she feared she had more in common with Anne Cavendish than she would care to admit. "Didn't Mrs. McGinnis tell you I was at the shop today?"

Daniel had brought a wicker chair from the garden and situated it on the front porch. Porkpie hat discarded, coat off, and legs stretched out in front of him, he looked prepared to encamp for an extended period of time. Adding to the air of permanence, Rufus lay coiled beneath the chair, a ball of contented ginger fur.

"I am here to check on you." As if sitting on Sarah's porch was an everyday occurrence, he leisurely bent down to scratch Rufus's head. "Have been most of the day. Mrs. McGinnis makes a fine lunch, by the way."

"I *know* Mrs. McGinnis makes a fine lunch. I'm surprised she fed you, though." Sarah collected the paper into an untidy pile, clutching it to her chest along with her reticule. "Where is Ah Mong?"

"Your neighbor needed him. Since I'm here, I told him he could go."

"You told him . . . that was hardly your place, Mr. Cady." Her heart pounded. "And I believe you already checked on me yesterday. No need to put down roots on my front porch to do so again."

He sat up straight in the chair. "Did you think I wouldn't care when I found out someone broke into your house last night?"

"You saw the article in this afternoon's newspaper." All courtesy of that wretched reporter, no doubt. If she ever saw him around the house again, she'd use Mrs. Brentwood's pistol for more than shooting at burglars.

"I didn't have to. I heard enough at the Occidental. No gossip too big or too small for the waiters and bellboys at that hotel." He frowned. "This is the point where you remind me that there are no gold nuggets hidden in the house."

"Or silver or diamonds?" she retorted, gratified by the confusion that wrinkled his forehead. "The gossip has spread far beyond the Occidental. To hear the news on the streets, you'd think I was hiding the whole of the US Treasury in this house."

"Did you recognize the burglar?"

"I felt like I did, but . . ." Sarah shook her head. "I'm not sure. Although the police feel they know who he is and are confident they'll catch him soon."

"I'm mightily reassured."

"The house and its contents are perfectly safe. Ah Mong's brother will be here tonight along with Ah Mong. More than enough protection. Plus, I have a gun."

Frowning, he contemplated her. "I heard about that also."

Her face burned; she must be as red as a Morello cherry. "Listen, Mr. Cady, if you think that you need to stay here as my protector, let me assure you it's unnecessary. As I said, I already have guards. Furthermore, we've hired a locksmith to install more secure locks today. The best I can afford. If you don't mind my spending some of Josiah's money, that is."

"New locks or not, it's unsafe for you with only an incompetent young boy—all right, two young boys—and a middle-aged housekeeper as guards. And though no doubt you're also a crack shot, it might be better if you don't have to prove your ability again." He folded his arms and stretched his legs out farther, his boot heels striking the porch slats to emphasize his point. Rufus blinked at Sarah and turned to grooming his fur, a happy coconspirator to Daniel's occupation of the stoop. "So I insist on staying here."

Had Daniel misunderstood yesterday's impetuous kiss? Perhaps he had decided her ill-considered act of affection meant he had permission to show up at the house and claim a right to be her champion. Daniel Cady, of all people. The man who wanted to take away her inheritance.

Daniel, one eyebrow lifting into a lazy arc just like Josiah's would, seemed to be reading her very thoughts.

"You can't stay here," she insisted, even if newsboys were of the opinion that Nob Hill was becoming dangerous. And even if, deep inside, the idea Daniel might want to protect her gave Sarah a thrill.

"I'm not just protecting you, Miss Whittier. I'm protecting the contents of this house, which are valuable to me."

"Why am I not surprised?" *And why do I keep thinking he might actually have feelings for me?* "Well, my reputation is valuable to me. And you're not doing it any good. Because if this town gets wind of the fact that an unrelated man is at my house, it could do no end of harm to my business."

"I'm just sitting on the porch," he said.

Sarah scooped up Rufus and scowled at Daniel. "No you're not. You're leaving. Right now."

With uncanny timing, Mrs. Brentwood came out of her house. "Miss Whittier! I just had a visit from my sister, who was shocked to hear of your troubles. Terrible—Oh! Mr. Cady! I did not notice you there." She peered at him, her lips compressing. "Looking very comfortable in your shirtsleeves, I might add."

"Do you see?" Sarah muttered to him. "Everyone will hear about this." Sarah turned to Mrs. Brentwood and raised her voice. "Mr. Cady was just leaving, Mrs. Brentwood. He also learned of last night's events and was concerned about my safety."

"Very kind of you, of course," the woman said, tucking her chin to better survey them both. Undoubtedly concocting what she would tell her sister. *Mr. Cady is courting Miss Whittier and in the most inappropriate fashion . . . oh heavens, heavens.*

"You must go," Sarah hissed.

Relenting, Daniel exhaled long and loudly, sliding his feet beneath the chair to stand. He slipped his arms into his coat, his gaze never leaving her face, causing Sarah's cheeks to heat beneath their scrutiny.

"You make me worry for you, Miss Whittier."

"For me? Or for the contents of the house?"

He leaned in, close enough she could smell his lime shaving lotion. She thought for a moment he might reach for her hand.

"You," he answered softly, grabbing his hat, and turned to go.

Daniel rode the cable car for the complete circuit of its line. He should simply go back to the hotel and find some amusement to while away the rest of the day. There was a chanteuse receiving rave reviews over at the Baldwin. Or he could take a carriage to overlook the Golden Gate or visit Seal Rocks. Thinking of them made him think of Sarah's painting. And thinking of her painting made him think of her. Made him remember the softness of her lips on his skin, the scent of roses in her hair, the weight of her body in his arms when he'd pulled her from the lake. Made him afraid that this time her stubborn independence would land her in serious trouble.

So he visited the docks. Bought a sandwich off a street vendor as a quick dinner. Stopped in a coffee shop to read the newspaper and drink some of the shop owner's blackest brew. Took the cable car back again, waiting for the sun to set. He had a plan and it didn't involve letting a scrawny Chinese boy and his undoubtedly equally scrawny brother stand guard over Sarah without him.

The wicker chair was still where he'd left it on the porch. Ah Mong, perched cross-legged at the top of the steps with a yellow-and-red quilt tossed over his shoulders, watched him approach the house. Daniel nodded at the boy, sat down, and stretched his legs.

Ah Mong eyed him, a long, indecipherable contemplation. "Why do you sit here, Mr. Cady?"

"I've come to help guard Miss Whittier, Ah Mong."

The boy's back straightened to a flatness Daniel had only witnessed on young ladies with very stiff corsets. "Miss Whittier has me and my brother. He is out in the garden. And there are new locks on the doors."

"New locks or not, she will do better with three of us. More eyes and ears paying attention."

"That man sneak in the back door last night. Quiet as grass

growing. I did not hear him." His gaze did not falter. "That will not happen again."

"Miss Whittier agrees with you, but I'd like to be certain."

Daniel adjusted the cushion at his back and surveyed the road. A lamplighter with his ladder was beginning to make his way down the street, gas lamps flaring to life in his wake. Across the way, a neighbor alighted from a hired carriage, glanced quizzically in their direction, and climbed the steps into his house.

Daniel settled deeper into the cushions as Mrs. McGinnis—or Sarah—touched a match to a lamp in the front parlor behind him, the light seeping through the closed slats of the blinds, striping the front porch in bands of white. The last breeze of the day rustled the leaves of a palm tree planted at the street, carried the sound of a cable car bell and the shouts of parents calling home their children for the evening. It was far quieter up here than at the Occidental, where the street sounds didn't settle until late in the evening most nights. Much quieter than the tiny, thin-walled apartment he and his sisters shared in the heart of Chicago. Almost as quiet as the treelined boulevards that surrounded Hunt House, where the genteel clatter of landau wheels was the only noise that dared break the hush.

"It will be cold to sit here tonight, Mr. Cady, and you are not needed." Nodding, Ah Mong folded his arms across his chest. "Your father told me to take care of Miss Whittier. I am like a good son and do it."

Daniel turned to stare at Ah Mong. Restlessly, Daniel shifted his feet, planting them firmly beneath the chair. He had been the best of sons once, idolizing his father, the adventurer, the charmer. He had wanted to grow up to be like Josiah, to conquer the world and bring home riches to his adoring family. Up until that vision of his father proved as false as the *trompe l'oeil* wood grain Grandfather Hunt had paid an artist to paint upon his massive kitchen mantel.

Both Sarah and Ah Mong respected—actually, admired—Josiah, though. Were willing to defend his name to his only son, or sleep on a cold and damp porch night after night to protect the woman whom Josiah had come to love like a daughter. The man did not deserve either their loyalty or their admiration. Daniel clung to that conviction, though it grew harder to hold on to. If a woman like Sarah cared about Josiah, an intelligent woman with a compassionate heart, maybe Daniel was wrong about his father.

An old prayer murmured. Daniel couldn't remember the last time he'd heard or said the words, but they had stuck in his head. *For if you forgive men their trespasses, your heavenly Father will also forgive you.*

Daniel's throat constricted and he turned away from Ah Mong's piercing gaze, all-seeing even on the darkened porch. *I am not ready to forgive Josiah. Father in heaven, if You're up there listening, You know I am not ready to forgive the man who broke my mother's heart.*

And who broke mine.

"You are just like a very good son, Ah Mong," Daniel said, his attention fixed on the road, not really seeing it. The fog was boiling over the western hills, and soon the scenery would be shrouded anyway.

"I try, Mr. Cady. I have no father to honor. I do what I can."

"Your father has passed away?"

Ah Mong's eyes shimmered, catching the light from the parlor lamp. "He died in a factory accident. He is with the ancestors now, and I pray to his shrine for courage and strength." Alarm passed across his face. "Do not tell Mrs. Brentwood, please. She would not like to know about my shrine."

"I won't tell her." Daniel considered him. He had to be the same age as Daniel had been when Josiah had strolled out of the Hunt mansion, never to return. "Your father must have been a good man to have a son care like you do." *And I envy you.*

Ah Mong shook his head, his black braid swishing across his

back. "He was not a good man. He beat me often and lost all our money in the fan-tan parlors in Chinatown. But it is a son's duty to respect his parents. Confucius teaches that the father conceals the misconduct of the son, and the son conceals the misconduct of the father. Uprightness is to be found when we do this."

"There is a teaching in our religion that we must honor our mother and our father. It's a commandment, actually. Not quite the same as this Confucius teaches, but you get the idea."

"I know it. Miss Charlotte told me that one day." He blinked, and his eyes freed of their tears. "So we both believe we must honor our fathers, Mr. Cady."

"I would like to, Ah Mong." Daniel stretched his legs again, pulled his coat collar up around his neck, seeking warmth. However, an upturned collar couldn't warm the chill in his heart. "I very much would like to."

Seventeen

"YOU'RE A DAFT LADDIE."

Daniel roused from his fitful sleep, his back stiff and his legs tingling. Hidden in the porch shadows, Mrs. McGinnis's face came into slow focus.

"What time is it?" Daniel asked, rubbing a hand across his face. It had to be early still; the gray fog was heavy on the houses stair-stepped up the street, and the sun was just beginning to tinge the misty sky with orange. Sometime during the night, the quilt he'd seen draped over Ah Mong had ended up on him. He tucked it under his chin and yawned. "It's really early, Mrs. McGinnis."

"It's six in the morn. And afair Miss Sarah has risen, which is the most important thing."

"How was her night?" he asked, glancing upward toward the second floor, though he could only see a sliver of window casing beyond the porch overhang and he had no idea which room Sarah slept in, anyway.

"She is fast asleep in her bedchamber. Which is in the back and canna be seen from here." Mrs. McGinnis extended a steaming cup of coffee. "I slipped a wee drop of laudanum in her evening tea. *Nae* near enough to harm her, mind you, but enough to help her rest. Poor lass. So much to fret about."

Daniel wrapped his fingers around the coffee cup, soaking in the warmth. As he was the cause of much of Sarah's fretting, the housekeeper's generosity surprised him. "Thank you for this. I appreciate the coffee."

She stood back, drawing her crocheted shawl close around her shoulders. "I'm *nae* being kind to you because I've decided you've turned into an angel, Mr. Cady, but if you're willing to brave the San Francisco night air for the sake of Miss Sarah, you canna be all bad."

"I couldn't leave Ah Mong out here without assistance." Propped against the balustrade, the boy snored gently, his head lolling to one side. A meager guard.

Mrs. McGinnis smiled down at him. "He means well, poor laddie. Takes his duty to Miss Sarah seriously."

"And his promises to my father, as well."

Even in the shadowy half-light, Daniel could see her expression soften. "Mr. Josiah was a good man."

How many times could he hear that before he'd stop cringing? Josiah was no more a good man than Daniel was a forgiving son. All those years waiting for a father to return home wouldn't be so easily forgotten.

"Josiah Cady was a man who abandoned his wife and children. Not so good, to me." He stated the words like they were unassailable fact. Which they were, as far as he was concerned.

"And do you think that getting hold of his estate will mend the pain in yer heart?" she asked. "We need to seek the riches of God's grace, Mr. Cady, *nae* the riches of the earth to heal what ails us."

"I doubt I deserve the former, although the latter will do very well to rectify a whole host of wrongs."

The dawning light, rosy-golden, revealed her dismay. Daniel supposed she didn't much care for people who could not understand right from wrong. "You'll need to be gone afair Miss Sarah discovers you out here. She'll *nae* welcome your presence."

"I intend to leave as soon as I finish this coffee."

"Good." She reached for the door handle.

"Wait, Mrs. McGinnis," said Daniel, stopping her. "I want you to know I have decided to invest in the studio." He did want to prove that he understood right from wrong. At least, in one particular instance. He and his sisters would hardly miss a thousand dollars, and the money would mean a world of difference to Sarah. "Not a lot—I have promises to keep—but enough to help for a while."

She stared at him a good long time before replying, likely waiting to see if he'd retract the offer. "*Nae* matter how much she might come to need the money, Mr. Cady, she'll ne'er accept a handout from you. Especially if it's meant to alleviate your guilt."

She'd seemed willing enough the other day. "It wouldn't be a handout. It would be a loan."

Mrs. McGinnis looked skeptical. "She still might prefer you live with your guilt."

"She might at that," he agreed, feeling satisfaction when her lips quirked. Making Mrs. McGinnis smile seemed quite an accomplishment. "Don't tell her. I want it to be a surprise."

"*Och*, it'll be a surprise whether I'm the one who tells her or *nae*."

Sarah yawned and stretched, working out the kinks in her neck. The sun was finally up, and it cast a hazy glow across the study, across the empty armchair where Josiah had liked to sit and smoke cigars, his glass-fronted bookcases stuffed with books she hadn't had the heart to pack away. It lit the mediocre painting of San Francisco Bay he'd bought from an itinerant painter, an impetuous act of generosity that always made him smile. Spilled light over Josiah's desk, fitted with a leather pad, glass paperweight, and silver inkstand topped with a crystal inkwell and blotter as if he might return at any moment. She wished he would return to give her advice, because the sun didn't cast much light on the rows and columns of numbers marching across the account book pages. No matter how often she examined them, the figures added up the same.

She kneaded her neck and examined the numbers one more time. Without Mr. Winston's contribution, which had yet to appear in her bank account even though he'd claimed she would see the money by now, Mr. Samuelson's loan would be stretched thin. It would barely cover the balance she owed on the lithograph press plus the girls' wages and next month's rent. And when she considered she also needed to pay Mrs. McGinnis and the household's daily expenses . . . Sarah sighed and squeezed the kink that tweaked a spot right above her shoulders. Now that she couldn't use any proceeds from the sale of the Placerville property, she was doubly desperate to receive Mr. Winston's donation, or for Mr. Halliday to hand over the money he'd told Lottie he would contribute. The wonders of the Samuelsons' cook's berry tarts must have been quickly and conveniently forgotten.

"You never would have let me sign the lease on the storefront without Mr. Winston's money securely deposited in the bank, would you, Josiah?" she asked of the room, the scent of his cigars clinging to the desk and the bookcases, the armchair and its small round side table. *A bird in the hand is worth two in the bush, Sarah Jane.* She had been so desperate to secure the shop, so perfect in every way, that she had forgotten his best piece of advice. But then, how could either of them have known Daniel would appear and destroy all of her plans like a flood wiping away everything in its path?

She closed the leather-bound book and tried to slide it into the top drawer of the oak desk, but the ledger jammed against an object wedged at the rear. Reaching inside, Sarah pulled out a palm-sized folder of heavy blue paperboard embossed in gold. It was an old tintype of Grace Cady, hidden away. Sarah held it up to the light. Daniel's mother had posed leaning against a chair, opulent curtains and a potted palm at her back, her hair coiled over her shoulder. Even in the severe dress she'd chosen for the portrait, she was beautiful, though her expression was filled with a wistfulness, a melancholy that Sarah had never wanted to recognize before. Not from the wife who had loved a man Sarah had idolized. She couldn't count the number of times she'd caught Josiah staring at the photograph, only to have him stash it away as if ashamed of his sentimentality. Why had he left her? Was the pursuit of gold truly that much more important than being with his wife? And had Daniel inherited not only Josiah's mannerisms but his father's weaknesses, as well?

It's a good thing, Sarah thought as she ran a fingertip down the length of the paperboard folder, *I haven't fallen in love with your son, Grace Cady.* Because if she had, she might come to fully comprehend the unhappy yearning in the woman's eyes. Yet one more time in her life.

"I might not mind if he fell in love with me, however. He might part with enough money to pay some of my bills." Sarah laughed softly, at both her recent compulsion to frequently talk to herself and at the thought Daniel Cady might have actually meant his tossed-off comment to invest in the studio. She may as well believe in fairy tales.

Sarah stowed the photograph in the desk and fitted the ledger into its spot next to Josiah's long, flat mahogany box. It would be wonderful if it contained a stockpile of money and resolved her problems—although, she thought cynically, its contents would probably belong to Daniel Cady too. It didn't matter; Josiah always said the box merely contained old papers he hadn't bothered to keep in his safe. Its key was missing, and she'd never had the heart to break it open. She'd leave that to Daniel too.

Downstairs, Mrs. McGinnis was flicking a feather duster across the parlor room furniture.

"Miss Sarah, I didna ken you were up already!" the housekeeper declared when she spotted her descending the stairs. "The sun's barely over the horizon."

"You didn't put enough laudanum in my tea to get me to sleep that late," Sarah said, smiling. "I wanted to go through the accounts. The money Mr. Winston promised me at Josiah's funeral has yet to put in an appearance. Hopefully Mr. Grant has sold my painting. I could use the cash and soon."

Mrs. McGinnis tutted and glanced over Sarah's shoulder at the front door. "Come into the kitchen and have a bite to eat, then. I'll have some hot coffee for you in a twinkling."

"You can serve it in the dining room. I haven't opened yesterday's mail or finished reading the newspaper. I'm more comfortable at the table."

The housekeeper huffed what sounded like an exasperated sigh. "If you wish."

Sarah watched her rush off. "She's in a strange mood this morning, Rufus."

The tabby, fixated on something beyond the front door, acknowledged Sarah's comment with the merest flick of an ear.

"Do you see Ah Mong out there?" Sarah peered through the cut-glass pane, spotting a patch of blue that had to be the boy's tunic. Shooing Rufus aside, Sarah opened the door. "Did you have a good night, Ah Mong? You should come in and have some breakfast."

"The house is safe, Miss Sarah."

"I see that. Thank you."

He nodded and handed her one of their quilts, the lemon-and-cardinal star-patterned one from the spare bedroom, and a coffee cup.

"I didn't know you'd taken to drinking coffee, Ah Mong."

"I do not drink coffee. Mr. Cady left the quilt and the cup. I need to return them to you."

The cup was still warm, and she could smell the lingering aroma of fresh coffee rising off the china bowl. Sarah stared down at it stupidly, before lifting her head to blink at Ah Mong. "Mr. Cady? What are you talking about?"

The boy buried his arms within the sleeves of his tunic. He looked as though he wished the rest of him could hide there too. "I should not have told you."

"You must tell me, Ah Mong. I insist."

"He stayed here last night. With me. More eyes."

"He did, did he?" After she'd told Daniel not to. The nerve of the man. "Apparently my feelings on this weren't to be consulted." Which would also explain Mrs. McGinnis's earlier peculiar behavior; the cup of coffee hadn't miraculously appeared on its own.

Sarah flounced out onto the porch and scanned the street. There, almost at the corner, trudged a familiar figure barely visible in the morning mist. Daniel, waving a jaunty hello to the milkman trundling down the road in his wagon. If he'd spotted Daniel lolling on the front porch, he would have delivered to Mrs. Brentwood, along with her morning milk, the best gossip yet.

"Why doesn't he listen?" Sarah asked, though Ah Mong had escaped into the house and couldn't hear her question.

She leaned against the porch railing, the cup and blanket held close, and watched the swirl of the fog enclose Daniel, curlicues of white marking his passage.

"You make me worry for you, Miss Whittier."

"For me? Or for the contents of the house?"

"You."

Sarah lifted the quilt to her face, imagining she could breathe in the remnants of Daniel's lime shaving lotion on its soft cotton, and felt a warm thrill move through her. He was the most confusing, most obstinate man she'd ever met. Only slightly more so than his father.

She sighed. Maybe she was falling in love with him.

Maybe she was destined to understand all there was to know about the look in Grace Cady's eyes.

The sign painted on the stone lintel above the Kearny Street shop door simply declared the owner's name—A. H. Grant's. It took a bit of searching to locate all the smaller signs along the doorframe advertising furniture, clocks, and other decorative arts for sale to the "discerning." It wasn't a store Daniel would normally notice, except for what was on display in one of its two windows.

That morning, he'd chosen a different way to his hotel from Sarah's house. There was a restaurant he'd been wanting to try and had stopped in for a lengthy breakfast before strolling back to the Occidental, enjoying the city, feeling rather cheerful. He was whistling what he could recall of Cora's drinking song and almost walked right past Mr. A. H. Grant's establishment without a second glance. Its narrow frontage was tucked among the numerous stores with their unfurled awnings that lined the sidewalk, just about lost beneath the massive bow window-fronted buildings. Daniel hadn't missed the shop, though.

Nor the painting of Seal Rocks.

It was propped on a wood stand between a red table lamp dripping with beaded glass fringe and a gaudy pair of green-and-gold vases painted with scenes of shepherds. Not the sort of place he'd expect her to be offering one of her best works for sale, and a good indication that she *was* in need of money. Those backers must not be coming through for her, after all.

Daniel entered the shop. The proprietor bolted from behind a waist-high counter and waded through a sea of overstuffed furniture and teetering side tables to greet him.

"May I help you?" His narrow shoulders tilted forward as though he wanted to pounce but had to restrain himself.

"I'm interested in that painting on display in the window," Daniel said.

Mr. Grant's gaze darted toward the object in question. "A very fine piece. Done by one of San Francisco's finest artists."

"How much are you asking for it?" He could keep the watercolor for himself or give it back to Sarah, it didn't much matter. Maybe his sisters would like it, a memento of a visit to a place they would possibly never see and certainly never understand what it had come to mean to him. He just didn't want anyone else to own it. Not that painting.

The man peered at Daniel through his glasses, making a quick assessment of the wear in his coat and the possibility Daniel had any ready cash.

"Thirty-five," Mr. Grant said, his voice tight with the anticipation that Daniel would promptly leave without the painting.

It was probably worth more, but as it was, thirty-five dollars would consume most of the money Daniel had set aside for a train ticket back to Chicago. "I'll trade you my pocket watch for the painting."

Mr. Grant recoiled. "This is not a pawnshop, sir."

"Then tell me where there is one." He could pay off the pawnshop loan once Josiah's estate was settled. Buy any number of watches. And paintings. "I have a personal interest in that painting, and I don't want to wait for money to be wired from my bank back home in order to get it."

"There's a pawnshop five doors down." The shopkeeper pointed to his right. "Reputable fellow. He'll give you a fair deal."

Daniel remembered a comment Minnie had made. "What about a good place to buy dolls?" He might have money to spare, if the pawnshop dealer was as fair as Mr. Grant claimed.

The proprietor's brows lifted. "You have very eclectic taste, sir."

"They're for my sisters back in Chicago."

"There's a store on Market Street that has a nice selection."

"Thank you." Daniel headed for the door. "Don't sell that painting before I'm back."

"And here I was expecting Leland Stanford any minute to snatch it up," Mr. Grant replied, snickering over what sounded like a private joke.

Eighteen

"WE'VE CAUGHT THE CULPRIT, Miss Whittier." Officer Hanson hulked by the front door, his domed police hat tucked under one arm, a self-congratulatory grin on his broad face. "I told you we would."

Sarah glanced over at Mrs. McGinnis, whose forehead crinkled with disbelief. "That was very quick, Officer." It was not even ten in the morning yet, barely twenty-four hours since she had made her report to the policeman.

His chest swelled. "Our men are the best in the city, miss."

"You're certain you have the right fellow?" Sarah asked.

"Fits your description to a T." With his empty hand, he located his wad of note papers in his coat pocket and consulted them. "'Hairy brute, tall, disheveled appearance.'"

"It's not a very specific description."

"This man's worked Nob Hill for the past several months, off and on, Miss Whittier." The notes were reinstalled in its pocket. "His *modus operandi* is the same each time—check a residence's locks at odd times of the day, when busy folk might be at work downtown or enjoying an evening's entertainment, return the next night or so with a weapon, and rummage through the first room he comes to. Threaten anyone who discovers him and run off with what he can."

"They just might have him, Miss Sarah," said Mrs. McGinnis.

Officer Hanson peered down the length of his bulbous nose.

"We most certainly do." He nodded, rubbed a hand across his crop of short-trimmed hair and restored his hat to his head. "If you need any further police assistance, you know where to contact us."

With a final crisp wave, he clomped down the steps.

"Thank the good Lord." Mrs. McGinnis smiled after she shut the door behind him. "We can rest soundly now, and you can return that pistol to Mrs. Brentwood."

Out of the corner of her eye, Sarah caught sight of the quilt folded on a chair in the parlor and lifted a knowing eyebrow. "And Mr. Cady will no longer have to secretly sleep on our porch and be served coffee in the morning."

For the first time Sarah could recall, Mrs. McGinnis blushed. "I believe I've soup on the boil in the kitchen."

"They've arrested old Bill Cobb." Frank flopped into the chair and jutted out his legs. The heels of his filthy boots scraped across the rag rug, leaving behind a trail of mud and street muck. He didn't care; she'd be the one to have to clean it up later.

He chuckled and scratched at the bandage patching the wound in his arm. "As if Cobb has the nerve to break into a house with folks inside it. He's too white-livered. If he'd caught sight of that woman with her shiny pistol, he'd have wet his pants and gone running." He twisted in the parlor chair, the horsehair stuffing springing out of its seams, to stare at her. "Ain't that right, Annie? Eh? He's a white-livered coward."

"That's right, Frank," she replied, mustering a smile and a nod.

She was tired—tired, tired, tired—of the strain to pretend she agreed with him. Supported him. Once, she had loved Frank. He had been so strong. Her protector. *Never gonna let anyone touch a hair on your head, Annie girl.* His Annie girl. The only sweet nickname she'd ever been given.

She had been uncharacteristically naive to confuse a tossed-off endearment for real love.

Exhaling, he settled deeper into the chair, the wood frame creaking beneath him. "Not like me. I'm no coward. If she hadn't winged me, I'da demanded she cough up the treasure. I got that cudgel and I'm not afraid to use it."

The hairs stood on Anne's arms, and she folded her shawl close. Thank heavens Miss Whittier had obtained a gun and proved to be a better shot than Anne would have guessed. Not that she wanted Frank hurt, but when presented with a choice between Miss Whittier's safety and a gouge in his tough hide . . . *I would choose Miss Whittier every time*. She hadn't thought she would come to esteem Miss Whittier as much as she did, when Frank had first concocted his plans.

"What are you frowning about? Scared I would've hurt your precious Miss Whittier?" His eyes narrowed to treacherous slits. "Whose side you on, Annie girl, eh?"

Anne swallowed. "Yours, Frank."

"You'd better say that."

She danced on a precipice. Every day. One careless move, and she'd fall into the abyss. "You want lunch? Something to drink? There's fresh ale from the saloon."

He grunted an affirmative. His gaze followed her as she skirted the chair and bent to yank off his boots. He reeked of manure and sweat; the stink no longer made her cringe.

"I'm not done with her, Annie girl," he said, twining around his finger a lock of hair escaped from her bun. He pulled, forcing her to look up at him. "I aim to get Cady's treasure before someone else does, and that's where you come in."

Her neck craning awkwardly, she peered at him. She should never have told Frank about Josiah Cady, Miss Whittier's benefactor, and his Black Hills gold. "Haven't I helped enough already, Frank?"

"Enough?" he mocked, his grip on her hair tightening. "You're in her house all the time, but you still haven't found out where old Cady's hidey-hole is. Time that changes. And when you do find out, you're gonna tell me and we're both gonna break in and take the gold from her."

"I can't do that." She twisted her head, hair ripping from her scalp. "I can't steal from Miss Whittier. Not after everything she's done for me. I was wrong ever to think I could."

"She hasn't done anything for you. *I'm* the one who's done everything for you. Given you shelter. Protected you from your old man. You don't want to go back to him, do you?"

"No." Never. She had nowhere to go. Which was why she had stayed with a man who no longer remembered how to be kind. But she could not hurt Miss Whittier. There were lines even she would not cross. "I don't want to go back to my father, Frank. You're right."

"About time you realized that." Frank flicked the broken strands of her hair off his fingers. "So, you'll help me."

She grabbed his muddy boots and pretended not to hear. "I'll get you lunch, Frank." Clenching her jaw, Anne strode into the kitchen, leaving him to sputter his anger.

Jesus, if You truly exist, show me the way out.

Because she was finished with helping Frank Burke.

It was time to help herself.

"After another incident with this intruder, Sarah, there is only one thing to be done." Lottie paced across the parlor floor, the swish of her bustle threatening to dislodge a potted fern and crystal ashtray from the armchair side table. "You must move to our house for your safety."

Sarah plucked from her mouth the pencil she'd been using to jot notes. "Your mother did not agree to that, I'm sure." Though Mrs. Samuelson supported her art studio, she had always been reserved when it came to Sarah. A woman with a sketchy past might make a nice charity case, but she was not to be boarded in one's guest bedroom.

"Well . . ." Lottie's brows puckered, a momentary concession that the "one thing to be done" was not universally accepted in the Samuelson household. "Papa agreed."

"I can't leave this house unguarded, an open invitation to this burglar and anyone else with a mind to pilfer the contents." Sarah returned to the inventory she'd been conducting before Lottie interrupted. The list of pictures available to sell wasn't long enough. The empty spaces on the parlor wall where the paintings she'd sold to Mr. Grant once hung were as glaring as coffee stains on a white tablecloth. There'd be more spaces soon if Mr. Winston continued to evade his commitment. "Besides, Officer Hanson was very confident this morning that they have caught the culprit. You don't need to worry."

"I have lived in San Francisco most of my life, Sarah. When it comes to the police and their assurances, I need to worry. But I see you insist on being stubborn, so I will relent. For now."

Sarah smiled at her. "You are a dear and I love you."

"I have more news," Lottie said as she peered over Sarah's shoulder, clucking about the itemized tally in Sarah's hands: one watercolor of the conservatory at Golden Gate Park; a charcoal sketch of a schooner in the docks; two small oils of the rose garden. Seagulls at the wharf. A rainy day along Market Street. All of them painted when Sarah had enjoyed more time to pursue her art and, in retrospect, a great deal fewer concerns. "At least you have not included your portrait of Mr. Cady."

"Josiah goes with me wherever I may end up." Sarah glanced at the painting in the corner, overdraped by its black crape. She would never leave him behind. "Back to your news. What is it?"

Lottie's gaze was steady and very serious; there would be no liking the direction this conversation was headed. "We had Mr. Winston for company yesterday. He and his wife came for tea and managed to stay all the way through supper. He wanted to talk to Papa about the studio."

"He hasn't deposited his funds into my account as we'd arranged." Sarah folded shut her notebook. "I take it I won't be happy to find out why."

"Mr. Winston has heard that, in two weeks, a real estate agent intends to put this house up for auction."

"He doesn't even own it yet!" She laughed, but not because she felt an ounce of humor. "He slept on my porch like some guardian angel and all the while intends to sell the house the minute he has possession of it. And it's clear he presumes he's going to get possession of it. Leaving me on the curb."

Lottie screwed up her face. "Are we talking about Daniel Cady sleeping on your porch?"

"I don't want to talk about that. All I'll say is he's a deceiving liar and I bought his pretense of concern." Sarah threw her notebook and pencil onto the nearest table. The pencil rolled off the edge and Rufus shot out from behind the settee to bat it around. At least the cat remained happy and playful. *Drat Daniel Cady. Drat him.* "I suppose your father was forced to explain to Mr. Winston who Daniel Cady is and what he's after?"

Lottie nodded grimly. "Papa tried to assure him that our backers could save us, that you had planned our finances very carefully, but Mr. Winston did not want to listen."

"The lithograph press . . . it's set to arrive in an hour." She frowned at Lottie. "This is ridiculous. Mr. Winston's qualms will *cause* the business to fail, especially if he succeeds in convincing the others to withdraw their offers of support too."

"Papa explained that to him, as well."

"What a mess we're in, Lottie." All because Daniel Cady decided to turn up.

"Perhaps this will help. I have money to pay the balance on the press." As proof, Lottie opened her beaded reticule and withdrew a small roll of bills.

"Don't tell me you sold any of your jewelry to finance our shop."

The dollars returned to the depths of Lottie's purse. "I shall remain quiet, in that case."

"We both can't continue to sell all of our possessions as a solution to our financial problems."

"I have not given up on Mr. Winston, for 'tribulation worketh patience; and patience, experience; and experience, hope'," Lottie responded, quoting the Bible. "He and his wife have been invited to my birthday luncheon, and I have more tricks up my sleeve."

Sarah cocked an eyebrow at Lottie. "Perhaps you could work your tricks upon the despicable Daniel Cady and his equally despicable real estate agent."

"You were supposed to be the one charming him."

Clearly, the impetuous kiss she'd given him hadn't softened his heart.

"I have apparently failed." Sarah untied her apron and threw it after the notebook. The ribbon ties dangled over the table edge, giving Rufus another toy to bat. "Lottie, I need you to attend to the delivery of the lithograph press today. Because I mean to speak to Mr. Cady. He has a few actions to answer for."

"Why didn't you tell me you've set the house up for auction in two weeks, before you even own it?"

Daniel stood at the door to his hotel room, one hand on the knob, the other gripping his straight razor. When he'd heard the knock, he'd anticipated finding one of the chambermaids outside with a fresh pile of towels. Not an indignant Sarah Whittier.

"Miss Whittier, it's not even eleven in the morning. Couldn't this have waited until later?" A dollop of shaving foam dripped off his razor onto the carpet. "And been discussed in a better location than my hotel room?"

Sarah blushed and glanced up and down the empty hallway. The elevator rattled on its ascent from the ground floor, but it glided upward without anyone disembarking on his floor. "I had no way of knowing if—or when—you'd come down to the public lounge, Mr. Cady, and I wanted to talk to you urgently."

"Might I finish shaving while you're talking?"

"I'm not coming in," she said, peeking past his shoulder at the room. As he'd told her, he'd taken one of the smallest in the hotel, so if she'd been expecting a lavish sitting room or a private attached bathroom, she would be disappointed.

"You can stand and query me from the doorway, then," he answered, leaving the door open and stepping over to the small shaving station he'd set up on the dressing table. His sisters stared at him from their tintype alongside the washbasin, somewhat reprovingly, it seemed.

"They have a barber in this hotel, I believe." Sarah's face was reflected in the mirror atop the dressing table, and he could see her fleeting, amused smile.

"I find giving myself a shave relaxing."

"And free."

"No need to spend money on an occupation I enjoy." He'd had to learn frugality, these past years, when doctor's bills and growing girls hadn't come cheap. He wasn't about to change his habits overnight. And after pawning his watch to buy her watercolor of the Seal Rocks, along with some dolls for his sisters, he didn't mind saving the cost.

His gaze flicked to the painting, lying where he'd set it on the bed, the paper partially unwrapped. If she noticed it, she'd have more questions than why he hadn't told her that Sinclair's real estate agent friend had set up a house auction.

"The barber might have asked embarrassing questions, anyway." Sarah was studying him with unconcealed fascination, observing every motion of the blade, even as he swished it through the basin of warm water. She had to have seen Josiah shave, maybe even shaved him herself.

Daniel became acutely aware he was standing there in his shirtsleeves and stockinged feet, collar undone and hair tousled from a hasty comb-through. A domestic scene normally only shared by husband and wife. One far too intimate for the two of them.

He hastily dragged the razor under his jaw, nicking his skin and drawing a bead of blood.

She didn't notice. "For instance, he might have asked why you needed a shave so late in the morning."

Daniel daubed at the blood with the corner of a towel. "Maybe he'd assume I'm a late riser."

"He certainly wouldn't assume it was because you'd spent the evening sleeping on my porch."

Daniel wet the towel and wiped residual shaving foam from his chin. "Ah Mong told you."

"He didn't mean to." Her eyes tracked him as he buttoned up his shirt and threw on his vest. He found her scrutiny unsettling, and if he thought about why he found it unsettling, he would have to admit how much he was attracted to her. "There wasn't any need for you to stand as guard last night, Mr. Cady, and you certainly won't need to repeat the act. The police came by the house this morning to tell me they've caught the culprit and thrown him in jail."

"And you believe them?"

"You sound just like Lottie."

He crossed the room, rejoining her at the door, feeling more comfortable now that he was, minus a pair of shoes, fully dressed. "If you're satisfied with your safety, then I'll have to be too."

"You can't be worried about my safety, Mr. Cady. You were worried about the contents of the house. The house you seem to expect to own." She pulled in a deep breath and clutched her reticule closer to her waist. It had the effect of making her look prim and righteously angry. "The one you've hired a real estate agent to put up for auction in two weeks."

"I didn't hire him. My lawyer did." As if that were a defense.

"You knew, though, didn't you?" she accused. "And didn't warn me. I had to find out through Lottie, who found out from one of our backers. Or I should say, probably former backer. He was alarmed by the news and is dithering on whether or not to advance us the money he promised. If more people decide to withdraw their support, the shop is as good as doomed."

"What if I offered you a thousand dollars to make up for it? I would like to invest in the studio." She hadn't believed his offer last time and he doubted she would now. But he watched her face for her reaction, because his brief experience with her had taught him she hadn't learned to guard her expressions well, and he'd learn as certainly as a finger held aloft which way the wind blew.

Sarah narrowed her gaze. "You're teasing me about wanting to invest. Just like you did the other day when we returned from Tar Flat. I'm not even certain I'd accept money from you if you were sincere, Mr. Cady, because it feels like a bribe."

"You tried to bribe me, as I recall. Only seems fair I return the favor."

She flushed and looked away, finding something interesting to examine on the hotel carpeting.

"If you've decided money from me would be tainted, Miss Whittier," he said, "then we don't have much else to talk about. I'm sorry, I should have told you about the auction. The time never seemed right. But you had to suspect it would happen. That house appears to be the bulk of Josiah's estate. If I don't sell it—"

"You don't get your money," she interjected, saving him from stating the obvious. "You could have had the courtesy to wait to engage a real estate agent until after the probate hearing was concluded, though." Scowling, she stepped back from the doorway. "I'm going to the shop. The lithograph press is being delivered today and I want to be there when it arrives. I'm not giving up on my studio until I can't find two pennies to rub together and my landlord runs me off."

She had set her jaw with its typical stubborn tilt. "I wouldn't expect you to do anything else, Miss Whittier." She was obstinate and strong and he rather liked her that way. *Watch it, Daniel.*

"At least one of us is predictable, Mr. Cady."

He inclined his head in concession to her point. "By the way, if Miss Tobin is at work today, tell her I've bought some dolls."

"Why?"

"She'll understand."

Brow crinkled in confusion, Sarah turned to go. "Good day, Mr. Cady. And I won't ask why you have my painting of Seal Rocks lying on your bed. I don't have the time to try to figure that out too."

Nineteen

THE TWO MEN GRUNTED as they wrestled the hulking iron base of the lithograph press through the side door of the shop, sweat streaming down their faces. With a concerted heave, they cleared the threshold and clomped across the floor, Cora dashing ahead of them to indicate where to place the machine.

Lottie smiled over at Sarah, who had just arrived at the shop. "You should have seen when they unloaded the stones. They were startled by how heavy they were and nearly dropped one."

"Have there been any problems?" Sarah peered into the store. She thought she might see Anne, but only Cora and the two men from the artists' supply company appeared to be inside.

"No, but they are not finished unloading the wagon yet." Lottie considered the wagon parked at the curb, its draft horse nosing the contents of a bag strapped to its head. "Not much left to mishandle, though."

"Thank goodness."

Lottie removed the chunk of broken cobblestone propping the door open and tossed it into the gutter. "Did Mr. Cady defend the planned auction of the house?"

"Not in the least." He hadn't even appeared apologetic. Although maybe she hadn't exactly noticed what he'd been feeling, as distracted as she'd been by the sight of him with his shirt unbuttoned down his chest, his hair damp from an attempt to tame it, a dab of shaving foam clinging to his ear. "He made another joke about investing in the shop and then told me to tell Minnie he'd bought some dolls. The man is confusing and infuriating."

She wouldn't mention that he'd purchased her watercolor of Seal Rocks, the one he'd so admired. Not when just thinking about it left her even more bewildered. And flattered.

"I continue to hold out hope for his ultimate and total reform, nonetheless." Brushing off her hands, Lottie watched Sarah's face. Probably seeing more than Sarah was willing to admit. "Do you want to go inside and see what has been delivered?"

Sarah followed her, setting her reticule on the counter alongside a paperboard box. She lifted one of the flaps. Inside rested a thick cast iron disc about the size of a supper plate. Six holes had been drilled in the top at regularly spaced intervals. A wood handle lay alongside, tucked against the wall of the box. The levigator would be used to polish the lithograph stones: water and fine sand would be placed on the stone's surface and then, with broad circular motions, spun along the stone until any prior etching was removed and the surface properly ground to accept the new work. Any ridges left behind would mar the next print. Careful work requiring a careful hand. Like Anne's.

Sarah let the flap drop into place. "I really thought Anne might change her mind and be here to see the equipment delivered."

"I thought so too." Lottie opened another box and started to lay out the crayon holders and squeegees and palette knives in neat rows across the counter. Elsewhere, Sarah knew she'd find the inks and stacks of tracing paper. Probably on the shelves in the back room.

With a huff, Cora bustled around the half-wall separating the main room from the lithograph area, wiping her hands down a sackcloth apron. "You're going to have to talk to those two, Miss Sarah. They don't seem to know where to put the press, but for the life of me, I can't understand what they're saying! I think they might be gypsies or something."

"They seem to be working very efficiently, Cora," chided Lottie.

The girl cocked a skeptical eyebrow. "Yeah, well, you're not in there with them."

Lottie laughed and went to tend to the press. Sarah went to finish unpacking the box Lottie had opened when the shop bell rang.

Minnie rushed through the door, her brunette curls springing free of her straw bonnet. "Miss Sarah, you have to come. I went to Anne's place to convince her to come to the shop today, but no one answered the door and no one I could find said they'd seen her leave. But there'd been a row between her and that Frank and . . ." Fear was sharp in her eyes. "Oh, miss, I'm just scared to think what's happened to her!"

With Minnie close on her heels, Sarah turned down the alleyway toward Anne's house. She dreaded what they might find. She would break down the door, if required, to find it.

Sarah dashed up the steps and paused to look back at Minnie, standing, pale and trembling, at the street. "I need you not to faint if we find . . ." *Lord, not that.* "If Anne has been hurt and there's blood."

Minnie squared her shoulders, looked defiant. "I don't faint, miss."

Good, because I might. She banged on the door. "Anne? Anne!"

"Are you going to break it down?" Minnie asked.

"I will if I have to." She rattled the knob. The door shook on its hinges. It wouldn't take much to knock it down.

A stout woman, her rough wool skirts hiked above her ankles and tucked into the waist of a filthy apron, strode out of the adjacent tavern and tossed a bucket of slop water onto the roadway. She spotted Sarah. "Hey! What are you doing there? Frank'll thrash you all to pieces if he sees you trying to break in!"

"I'm here for Anne."

The woman looked Sarah up and down. "Don't know why you'd bother."

"Because I think he's hurt her badly this time." Sarah pressed her shoulder to the door and bumped against it as hard as she could, wincing at the responding pain.

"Oh, here, let me. You're as scrawny as a wet cat." The woman set down her bucket and charged up the steps. With one heave of her elbow, she broke the door latch. She grinned at Sarah, revealing a few missing teeth. "After you."

Sarah went inside, Minnie hurrying behind her, skirting the woman from the tavern. "Anne?" Sarah called.

Minnie ran into the tiny back room, returned in a second. "She's not here."

"They'd a dreadful row earlier." From the doorstep, the woman squinted at the dingy front room, the stains on the rag rug, one looking pretty much like the other, any one of which could be blood.

"Do you think she's run away?" Sarah asked her.

"If she had any sense, she would've." The woman scratched at her bare forearm and considered the contents of the room as if she might return after Sarah had left and help herself to some of the items. "I might've seen her running off. Couldn't say for certain, though. Was just a glimpse when I was scrubbing the floors over there. Through the door, I noticed a tall woman rushing down the road. I noticed 'cause she was all bundled up. Sorta strange, given it's a warm day. Might've been Anne."

It might have been. "Any idea where she would have gone? Who would take her in?"

"Can't say. Other than that Miss Whittier and Frank, there's no one she ever talked 'bout at all."

"Thank you for your help," said Sarah.

"Guess I should get back to work." The woman stomped back to the darkness of the tavern.

"We'll never find Anne," said Minnie, stepping around the reddest stain on the rug.

They left, Sarah closing the door as best she could behind them. She couldn't lock it again—the mechanism was ruined.

Out in the street, she glanced up and down the road, hoping—pointlessly—that she might find some clue as to Anne's whereabouts. "Where might you go if you wanted to get help, Minnie? Someplace where your man might not be able to bother you?"

Brow furrowing, Minnie considered the questions. "The streets wouldn't be safe at all. Not if he was looking for her. I don't know if she has enough money for one of the better boardinghouses away from around here. And if she didn't look for a room with me or with Emma, then I'd guess she's gone to one of the charity organizations. Though they're not all as sympathetic as they claim to be. Some of the women who run those places can be awfully harsh to females like Anne and Phoebe and Cora." She lifted a shoulder, her expression more sober than Sarah had ever seen it. "And me."

Sarah hugged her hastily. They must look a sight, two women embracing in the middle of a Tar Flat alleyway, sure to be run over by a trundling delivery wagon or cart at any moment.

"If you think she'd go to one of the benevolent societies, then I have an idea of where to search for her. You don't have to go with me. Go back to the shop and help Lottie. I think she'd appreciate that."

"Good luck," Minnie said, her hand catching Sarah's, her callused fingers rough against Sarah's skin.

"I'll need more than luck." She'd need help from God. Could she rely on Him, though?

Out of the corner of his eye, Daniel spotted an unwelcome figure leaning against a column near the elevator. He wouldn't make it to the dining room for dinner without Jackson spotting him.

He tried, though. Within moments, the reporter trotted over.

"You back again?" Daniel asked him. "Don't they give you an office at the *Chronicle*?"

"Told you I would return. And here I am," he said, grinning as he doffed his derby.

"Yes, here you are. I was heading to dinner—and they don't like reporters in there, I'm certain."

"Not a problem. If you don't wish to speak to me, Mr. Cady, that's of course your business." He nodded. "But I do want to get my story correct. Just tell me you're sure there's no gold up there, if that's the case, because I'd hate to think of more folks trying to break into your father's house—very nice place, by the way—to get to something that doesn't exist. Don't you agree?"

Daniel cocked an eyebrow. "You're here again because you want me to refute the story, or because you want to add fuel to the fire?"

Jackson bobbed his head, the motion beginning to remind Daniel of a high-strung pigeon. "I'll be honest. I want to sell papers. That's what I'm paid to do. Whichever way the story goes doesn't much matter to me." Tucking his hat beneath one arm, he retrieved a notebook, along with a pencil, from an outside pocket of his coat and flipped it open. "I've learned your father came here from . . ."

He paused and squinted at Daniel. He wasn't going to help Jackson by filling in the blank. "You tell me. Seven years ago was the last time he let us know where he was."

"Slippery character, eh?" Jackson winked. "Best as I can tell, he's been all over California—Sacramento, Los Angeles, Placerville, Grass Valley."

His mention of Los Angeles triggered a memory, but it was gone before Daniel could latch on to it. "Is that the sort of information the *Chronicle* is interested in? Your paper can't be that desperate to fill columns."

Daniel's sarcasm did nothing to deter the reporter. "Josiah Cady originally came from Chicago, didn't he? Where he married the daughter of Addison Hunt, railroad tycoon. Big society, I'd wager. Must have been mighty embarrassed to see a daughter of theirs marry a gold mine owner. Even one who hit it big in a placer claim in the Black Hills. Ever wonder where those nuggets went to? Some went to his partner, of course, and the men who worked for them, but there's always a chance a few are hanging around . . ."

Fury was replacing annoyance. As much as he wanted to, Daniel couldn't clout the man in the middle of the hall leading to the dining room. Even if Daniel had once wondered where all that gold had gone to, as well. "Are you finished?"

"Not yet." Back on surer footing, his grin had returned. "What do you know about that woman living up there? The Miss Whittier who inherited your father's estate. Not from around here, is she? Showed up all of a sudden, I hear. Mighty curious doings, all in all."

Daniel leaned into Jackson, catching the pungent smell of the greasy pomade he'd rubbed into his thinning hair. "You leave her alone."

"Taken a liking to her, have you? I've seen her. She's not bad looking."

"I don't like you questioning her character. She came to San Francisco to take care of my father when he was dying, and my father was grateful." It was one thing for Daniel to have doubts about her story; it was quite another to see them splattered all over the pages of some newspaper.

"Extremely grateful, apparently." Chuckling, Jackson scribbled notes in his compact leather-bound book then slipped it into his coat pocket. "I'll let you go for now, Mr. Cady. Here's my card, in case there're any tidbits you'd like to add to your long-lost papa's story. Because dollars to doughnuts, there's more to this story than meets the eye. Yes, siree. Dollars to doughnuts."

"I wish to speak with Mrs. Hill." Sarah leaned toward the narrow gap between the front door and its frame. The door was held ajar by a woman, tall and broad as many a man, who appeared to have been selected for the job of answering the bell because of her size. And the uncompromising glower of her deep-set eyes.

"You need shelter?" she asked.

"It's not for me—"

"In that case, you can come tomorrow. Mrs. Hill has set down for dinner, and I won't disturb her."

The door inched closed. Sarah pressed a hand against the wood. "I want to speak to her about a young woman she might have taken in. Anne Cavendish."

Her eyes conducted a hasty inspection of Sarah. "Is she a servant of yours run off?"

The woman asked the question as though she'd posed it dozens of times before and expected Sarah to fib in her answer, as well. But the fact she asked suggested Anne was here, at the Christian Women's Benevolent House, and gave Sarah hope. She'd searched for hours and her feet and back hurt. Almost as much as her heart.

"Anne is a student of mine. I want to help her." Sarah's hand slipped across the door, closer to the edge. The woman, stern as she appeared, wouldn't slam the door on her fingers. She hoped. "Speak to Mrs. Hill about me. Please. My name is Sarah . . . Thayer." The name Rosamund Hill would remember her by.

Her earnestness must have impressed the woman, because she retreated and beckoned Sarah to enter. "I'll tell her you're in the parlor."

She gestured to her left, to a cramped room crowded with shabby chairs and low padded stools, tables with uneven legs draped with tatted covers to hide the scars in the wood surface below, and hunter-green wallpaper that made the room appear dark even though sun was slanting through the blinds. The faint scent of mold and turpentine cleaning solution drifted into the entry area.

Sarah thanked the woman, who left to fetch the founder of the House. Through the closed connecting door, a whispering arose in the dining room located behind the parlor. The sound of many women's voices, but none recognizable as Anne's.

Within moments, Rosamund Hill arrived. She was tall, her auburn hair a pile atop her head that added to her height, and her hazel eyes soft as a doe's, keen as a hawk's. When she grasped Sarah's hand, her bare fingers were strong. Just as Sarah recalled. All of it. Even the smell of the room.

"Miss Thayer. It has been many years." Her voice was as lush as a mezzo soprano's. A legacy of her time spent on the stage.

"I was hopeful you would remember me. I'm glad you do."

"I never forget any of the women who cross that threshold."

Sarah had been very desperate when she'd crossed that threshold, nowhere else to go and just a few paintings to her name. Before she had found Josiah. "I'm Sarah Whittier now, however. The name I was born with. I've shed that other name and that past."

"Sometimes the past clings to us whether we wish it to or not." Mrs. Hill's tone held no condemnation, only understanding. She indicated that Sarah should sit and took one of the chairs across from her, descending with an elegance that belied the ratty nature of her surroundings. "How can I help you, Miss Whittier?"

"One of my employees has fled . . . a difficult situation." Unaware of what Anne might have revealed, Sarah didn't dare say too much. "I asked at several other charity homes, looking for her. I should have come here first."

"Stella says you are asking after Miss Cavendish."

"She's here then." Sarah started to rise. "Can you take me to see her?"

Mrs. Hill waved at her to sit again. "Miss Cavendish is resting. She was very agitated when she arrived this afternoon. She needs sleep more than anything right now."

"But she's in danger," Sarah explained, reluctantly resuming her spot on the chair.

"She is safe here." Mrs. Hill swept her hand in front of her, a gesture to encompass the house, tucked in a quiet part of the Western Addition, unmarked and unknown except to those who needed it most. "She has explained her situation to me, Miss Whittier. It's one I've heard many times."

"So you understand why I want to help her."

"She needs a chance to have some time to herself and not have someone else prodding her and telling her what to do or where to go."

"I'm only worried for her safety," Sarah said, defending her actions. But she wasn't certain she had been paying attention to what Anne truly wanted and needed. Maybe she'd only been thinking about her own needs.

"Her man won't find her any time soon. But I agree the longer Miss Cavendish stays, the greater the risk." Mrs. Hill reached across the gap between them. "I will send for you in the morning if she wants to speak with you. I expect she will. And then the *two* of you can decide what is best for her."

"You have always known the best path to take, Mrs. Hill."

The woman shrugged off the compliment. "I recall advising you to take that job with your family's friend. Did that work out as you hoped?"

Sarah's breath hitched in her throat. "That remains to be seen."

Twenty

He couldn't believe his eyes, but there she was. Strolling down the road as pretty as you please like it was some fine spring morning, instead of gray and dank and threatening rain, with a sharp wind whistling off the hills to the west of town. Like she had no cares in the world, another woman with her, the hoods of their cloaks pulled tight around their faces against the wind. Or, in her case, against being spotted. Sure as he was standing there, she didn't want to be seen. Not by him. Maybe not by anyone.

"Then you shouldn't have gone out for yer morning stroll, should you have, Annie girl?" he muttered into the wind as a cart rattled past, its driver eyeing him.

Frank clenched his cigar between taut lips and inhaled. It was his last one. He'd miss them. Manuel had gone Jack Tar on him, signing on to a merchant vessel because the "lure of the sea" had finally caught up to him, according to a mutual acquaintance. How sentimental. More than likely he'd run afoul of the cops again. But with Manuel gone, his best source of Havanas had evaporated as quick as fog burning away under a hot sun. If he wanted more, he'd have to buy them. That took money, something he didn't have much of. And for that, he blamed her. She'd run off before she had finished her end of the bargain, and he still didn't have that Cady gold.

"I knew you would." Frank bit down, snipping off a piece of

the cigar end. He spit it onto the ground. But he'd found her. Hadn't been too hard. After a bit of encouragement, the barkeep at the saloon had guessed where she would be, though it had taken most of the night, a few threats, and the ragged edge of a broken beer bottle to get him to speak up.

The two women turned a corner. He'd lose track of them if he didn't follow. Lose his opportunity.

He pushed away from the lamp pole, a bitter smile tugging at the corner of his mouth, and discarded the stub of his cigar. "I knew you'd go soft and want to protect that Whittier woman in the end, Annie girl. You'd better be thinkin' of your own protection now."

It *was* him.

She inhaled, so abruptly, so loudly, that the woman at her side noticed.

"What is it, Anne? Have a stitch?" Hester asked.

"Um . . ." How could she answer? With the truth? Hester should understand, though, like most of the women at Mrs. Hill's. The women who'd suffered from men. But to admit Frank had found her would be to admit just how foolhardy she'd been to suggest to Hester that they go for a stroll, her tiny attic room becoming too much to bear, like a prison cell even if it was a warm and safe prison cell. She'd felt trapped inside that house, anxious and sweaty. Afraid of this very moment.

And she'd gone out, only to walk right into her worst fear.

"It's my man," Anne replied, her pace already so quick that Hester, with her shorter legs, could hardly keep up. "He's behind us."

She wanted to look back, but she sensed that any acknowledgment of his presence would encourage him to chase her down like a coyote on a jackrabbit.

"Then let's run back to the house," Hester suggested, starting to pant. "If we cut through here we can get back quickly. We might even lose him."

She pointed out an alleyway, narrow between a scattering of wood houses, sloppy from an overnight rain.

Anne's heart pounded. What choice did she have? She was a jackrabbit and he, a coyote. The chase was underway whether she liked it or not.

She grabbed Hester's hand. "Go! Now!"

"I believe you do have mail, Mr. Cady." The desk clerk poked around in the wall of cubbyholes, each one marked with a brass room number plate, withdrawing two envelopes, one the distinctive muted yellow of the Western Union Telegraph Company. "Here you go. The telegram was delivered just this morning. I was going to bring it to you over breakfast, if you hadn't stopped by." He beamed over the high standards of customer service extended by the Occidental Hotel and handed the mail to Daniel. "And a Mr. Sinclair was here right before you came downstairs. He said he would meet you in the dining room to discuss important business."

Not the sort of company he wanted to share breakfast with, but the lawyer would be unavoidable. "Thank you. Perhaps you can send someone to tell Mr. Sinclair I'll be with him shortly."

Daniel stepped out of the way, dodging a pair of men headed for the bar at the rear of the ground floor. Not even noon, but there was never a bad time to drink in San Francisco, as far as some folks were concerned.

The first envelope bore the postmark of a Chicago area postal office and one of his sisters' handwriting on the outside. Daniel smiled. He could readily envision Lily or Marguerite—as twins, it was hard to tell the difference in their penmanship—bent over the secretary desktop in the Grays' sunlit front parlor, all seriousness. The girls, mostly Lily, had written often, the letters catching up to him at odd times and in odd places, some never catching up at all. Notes about their studies or the latest happenings at the Grays' house. Sometimes even snippets of gossip about the Hunts, which Lily would manage to wheedle out of Mrs. Gray and never hesitate to share with Daniel. He could hear her voice in his head, soft and certain, trying not to sound worried or hurt that she and Marguerite felt isolated and lonely without him around to cheer them. The trip, though, had been necessary. Even at ten, they both understood that the best future possible was the goal. His driving, unrelenting goal.

Or had it been revenge, plain and simple?

With a faint frown, Daniel tore open the envelope and skimmed the contents. Lily started with news that the Grays' flower gardens were in full bloom and that their King Charles spaniel had born puppies. That she and Marguerite had been invited to a party at a wealthy neighbor's, a thrilling and unexpected treat. Daniel reread the line. Maybe Chicago society had already heard he would be returning with assets sufficient to erase the distasteful memory of Josiah Cady. Money could smooth over even the worse offense.

Frown deepening, Daniel finished reading the letter. Lily closed with a solemn remark about the shock of learning that their father was deceased and that she and Marguerite were praying for his soul, as well as praying for Daniel's safe and speedy return home. There were no further words of grief and no indication how the Hunts felt about the news, if they'd even heard about Josiah's death yet. When they did, they would most likely be pleased and relieved. Archibald Jackson had hazarded a guess that they were embarrassed to have been stuck with Josiah as a son-in-law. *Mortified* would have been a more accurate word.

The tinkle of a piano got underway in the bar as Daniel ran a thumb through the Western Union Telegraph Office envelope. It had come from his grandfather.

D—

Have been contacted by reporter from the Tribune. Wants interview about J, whom Grays have informed me has passed. Apparent rumors about gold. Trust you are taking care of story at that end.

A. *Hunt*

Daniel crumpled the telegram and shoved it into his pocket alongside the neatly folded letter from his sister. Archibald Jackson's tentacles spread far and wide in his goal to dredge a story out of a rumor about a stash of nuggets. Far enough to reach Chicago.

Pulling in a breath, Daniel climbed the stairs leading to the second-floor dining room. He would take care of Jackson later. Right now, he had to deal with Sinclair.

The lawyer had been shown a central table, an honor usually reserved for long-term guests of the hotel. He must have thrown Daniel's name around in order to snag it.

"Cady, over here." Sinclair muscled his rotund frame out of his chair and signaled to him. "Hope you don't mind an early morning intrusion, but I need you to look over some papers for the hearing on Monday."

Daniel took a seat across from Sinclair, prompting one of the many waiters to dash forward with a silver pot of coffee.

Sinclair resumed sitting and snapped open his napkin. "I have news about Josiah Cady's assets you'll want to hear too."

"In that case, Sinclair, I don't mind the intrusion," said Daniel. Sign papers, discuss assets. So simple, like they were finalizing a minor business transaction. And so bitter tasting.

"I thought not." He paused while the waiter—for once, not the red-haired one—poured a stream of black coffee into Daniel's cup and set a menu in front of him. Sinclair didn't wait for Daniel to order, asking for a veal cutlet with a side of toast and some scrambled eggs, enough to satisfy a healthy appetite. Daniel settled on oatmeal; his grandfather's telegram had left him without much interest in food.

Once the waiter had trotted off, Sinclair leaned against the chair back, tenting his fingers over his stomach and the loop of his gleaming gold watch chain.

"I learned that your father's property in Placerville, which Miss Whittier recently put up for sale, has a potentially interested buyer. It should fetch a few thousand dollars. Not bad. No one wants that mining claim in Grass Valley, though." He eyed a stack of papers resting atop the white lace tablecloth. "I also uncovered a small bank account with only a few dollars left in it. My assistants never did find any other accounts or assets."

No gold nuggets either. Wouldn't Jackson be disappointed. "What else do you have?" Daniel asked, impatient to be done.

"I have the copy of your baptismal record, the affidavit of your identity right there with the papers. I just need you to sign it, if one of the waiters"—he looked around—"could bring us a pen."

Pen and ink were requested and arrived with Sinclair's toast. Slathering butter across the perfect brown surface, he indicated with a pointed elbow where Daniel should sign the affidavit.

"Everything is set, Mr. Cady," said Sinclair, pointing out another spot requiring a signature. "We have all we need for next Monday's hearing. I trust you are ready to get this business completed."

Daniel nodded wordlessly and indicated to the hovering waiter that he was finished with the pen and inkstand.

Sinclair peered at Daniel, a worried crease marring his face. He drew a hand down his thick mustache. "Mr. Cady, you look a bit glum. Have you changed your mind about contesting the will?"

"No, Sinclair, I haven't."

Relief smoothed away the crease, pleased that he'd still be receiving his remuneration for presenting Daniel's case. "Good."

The waiter returned with the rest of their food, and Sinclair set to slicing his cutlet. "The real estate agent has contacted me.

He expects the house to fetch close to fifteen thousand. More if the house remains fully furnished. Better than I anticipated, but then real estate in Nob Hill is highly desirable."

"How . . ." Should he say "wonderful"? Grandfather Hunt would. "Sounds fine, Sinclair. This all sounds fine."

"Only 'fine'?" Sinclair stuffed the piece of meat in his mouth and spoke around it. "I hope you weren't expecting more."

"Like you said, I just want to be finished with this business. My sisters are begging me to return home soon, and I'm looking forward to being with them again."

"A noble cause, Cady." Sinclair pointed at him with his fork. "You should be proud that you've gone to this effort to secure their futures. Why, it's only what any decent man should do for his young, orphaned sisters."

Daniel stared at the creamy surface of his oatmeal, speckled with brown sugar. Proud. He should feel proud.

Instead of queasy.

"Miss Lane tells me they were but a block from the House when Miss Cavendish took an unexpected turn." Mrs. Hill was too skilled at concealing her true emotions to twist her hands together in her lap. Sarah swallowed and felt nervous enough for the both of them. "Hester slipped and fell and couldn't keep up with her and lost Miss Cavendish to view. She scrambled to her feet and ran all the way back, fearing an encounter with the man chasing them." She shook her head. "I am sorry, Miss Whittier. I certainly never expected that he would find her. We might have to relocate the House, if it's become common knowledge where we are."

"Is Hester all right?" Sarah asked.

"Very upset but otherwise unharmed." Mrs. Hill shifted on the parlor settee to better face Sarah. "I trust you don't have any idea where Miss Cavendish might be."

If she managed to elude Frank, that was. Words too fearful to say aloud.

"She hasn't come here and she wouldn't go to the shop again, I think. If she didn't find her way back to the Benevolent House . . ." Sarah left the thought unsaid. Anne could be anywhere and in any condition. And Sarah had failed her, one of her girls, though Anne would not care for the label. Had failed her as surely as Minnie's father failed her, and Cora's family let her down. Like Edouard had failed Sarah.

Rosamund Hill's gaze was keen. "You are not to blame for what has happened."

I want to believe that. "I'll go to the police and report this. She was my employee and, as far as I can tell, I'm the only person remotely responsible for her. Anne never spoke of family. For all I know, they're all gone or had washed their hands of her."

In a flash, Sarah was standing in a dusty Los Angeles street, the hot pinks of dead bougainvillea flowers swirling around her feet, the thick front door of her aunt and uncle's house closed tight against her humiliation. After Edouard, after her horrible mistake, she had tried to reconcile with them. They would not have her.

Unaware of Sarah's painful recollection, Mrs. Hill patted Sarah's hand and stood. "Do you want me to go to the police with you?"

Sarah wanted to smile to let Rosamund know how much she appreciated the offer. It wouldn't form on her mouth. "You should probably return to the House, in case Anne shows up."

"Stella and some of the women staying there could tend to her."

Sarah stood as well. "If Anne's anything like me, she'll only want to have you."

Mrs. Hill nodded. "Take care, Miss Whittier, and let me know as soon as there's news. I will keep safe the few possessions she brought with her to the House until she's back among us again."

Mrs. McGinnis showed her out. When she turned back to Sarah, her face was heavy with worry. "*Och*, Miss Sarah, what now?"

"I go to the police. Though I doubt they'll care about an unmarried woman with a dubious background, missing in the warren of San Francisco streets. I just wish Anne had accepted my offer of money when she'd had the chance and fled to somewhere far away."

"*Nae* point in wishing back what canna be undone." The housekeeper's tone brooked no argument. "Besides, Anne would never take what you canna well afford to give."

Money. She was sick to death of brooding over it. "My few pennies mean nothing to me, if they could have bought her safety."

Mrs. McGinnis touched Sarah's arm. "The Lord will protect her."

Like Mother and Jess and Caleb? Sarah's heart ached for all the losses she'd endured, all the unanswered prayers. Would she lose Anne too, who had counted on Sarah? *I tried. I tried to help.*

Sarah's breath was shaky when she drew it in. Brushing past Mrs. McGinnis, she strode into the entry hall and collected her black mantelet from the stand. "I'll be back as soon as possible. Perhaps while you're praying for Anne, you can pray that Officer Hanson is willing to help search for her, though I expect there's not much he can do."

Not much any of us can do.

Twenty-One

OFFICER HANSON YAWNED into his thick-knuckled fist and reached for a second gulp of coffee. He must have had a long day yesterday, and the look he gave Sarah suggested to her he wasn't keen to have another one.

"You must help me find her," she said, leaning forward on the hard-backed chair set at an angle to the officer's desk, her stays jabbing into her ribs. "Anne Cavendish is in danger for her life."

Conversation droned in the airless central office of the North End Police Station like the tired hum of an old steam generator. The room, which smelled of cigarettes and sweaty wool uniforms, stole her breath. Down a hallway, an office door banged and boots stomped across a floor. An alarm bell clanged on the wall opposite where she sat. Officer Hanson glanced at it, wiped his mouth with the back of his hand, and shouted for someone to see to the emergency.

"So you say this woman is in danger for her life," he said, once the commotion died down, and drained his cup.

"She definitely is, and you must help me find her." He looked as disinterested, however, as she had anticipated. What was another woman, a girl from the streets and filthy back alleyways, to him?

"We're pretty busy here, Miss Whittier." He waved one of his fists to encompass the office. "Not a lot of men available to go on a wild-goose chase when there are serious crimes to solve."

"This could be a serious crime if it's not prevented, Officer Hanson."

"Suppose so." He sat back and sucked in a long breath that stretched his blue coat across his barrel chest. "Does she know Bill Cobb, by any chance?"

"What?" Sarah knitted her brow. "Who?"

"The man we arrested for attempting to rob you." He looked at her as though she must be dull-witted to have forgotten.

"What would Anne have to do with him?"

"Well, now, that's what I'm asking you." He peered at her until Sarah started to squirm, sympathizing with the others who'd sat in that hard chair before she had. Officer Hanson made a good interrogator. "Has she run off because she was the one who heard about the treasure rumor and told him? Clued him in about your comings and goings? Maybe she's feeling guilty. What do you say to that?"

She understood why Officer Hanson had asked the question. Somehow, this Cobb fellow had picked the evening Mrs. McGinnis was out and Sarah was supposed to be at the Linforths' for supper.

"She isn't involved with Bill Cobb. Anne has never mentioned his name to any of the girls or to me. She doesn't know him at all. The man she lives with is called Frank. He's the one we believe is responsible for her disappearance. He was spotted stalking her near the Benevolent House where she had been staying." Sarah tightened her fingers around the straps of her reticule resting in her lap. "He's violent and has beaten her before. I've seen the bruises myself." The plum shading to yellow on her pale skin. Sarah was the one who felt guilty. For not doing more, sooner.

"Violent, is he? In that case, she's probably . . . ah, yes, well." He cleared his throat, looked away from Sarah, and fussed with searching for a pencil and pad of paper in the top drawer of his desk. "Tell me more about this Frank fellow."

Sarah did, told him all she knew, which wasn't much. A spare description gleaned from Minnie, who had met him. Where he and Anne lived in Tar Flat.

As she spoke, Officer Hanson nodded. More out of politeness, Sarah thought, than from enthusiasm. "I'll ask my chief to request that one of the men working that district go and question him. Don't think he'll have much to say, if he's even there. Tight-lipped, these sort are."

"And what about searching for Anne?" she pressed.

The policeman scratched a raw patch on his chin where he'd done a bad job shaving. "I can have a notice of a missing woman placed in the papers. Can you supply a description?"

Sarah told him that too. Anne was distinctively tall and lean. She would be easier to spot than most women. "I'm concerned that Frank will see the notice and realize we're searching for her. That might put her in greater danger."

"You think a fellow like him reads the paper, Miss Whittier?"

"I have no idea! I just don't want her hurt."

Officer Hanson snorted, ripped off the piece of paper with his notes, and pocketed it. "If he's gotten hold of Miss Cavendish and is set on hurting her, miss, the harm's already been done."

Sarah clenched her hands. "Is there anything I can do?"

Two thick eyebrows lifted. "Pray?"

"I'm not very good at that."

He looked pityingly at her. A different alarm bell rang and he stood. "Busy day. If you'll excuse me."

He didn't wait for Sarah's answer before he strode off, leaving her to stare after him, the clamor of the office drowning out the sound of his footfalls.

"Miss Sarah isna here, Mr. Cady." Mrs. McGinnis wiped her

hands down her apron and eyed Daniel. "Should be here soon, though. She went to the shop this morn but said she'd be back right after luncheon to hear if there's any news about Anne. *Nae* that I expect much. The police have most certainly been less than useful, if you ask me, and none so kind to her yesterday."

Daniel wasn't surprised. San Francisco wasn't some small town in Arizona, where a missing woman might be more noteworthy.

"I saw the item about Miss Cavendish in the newspaper," Daniel explained. The article had been brief, almost buried beneath the announcements of political galas and a sarcastic commentary on the women's suffrage movement, a lurid article describing a recent spate of murders in Chinatown, and a tongue-in-cheek account of how ladies might best catch suitable husbands. But there, on the second page of the *Daily Alta*, which he'd been reading over lunch, he'd spotted it.

"I want to help find her," he said. Anne Cavendish must have finally suffered more than some bruises at the hands of her man. It was the only explanation for her disappearance that made sense.

The tiny wrinkles crisscrossing the housekeeper's forehead deepened. "*Och*, Mr. Cady, I canna see how you're going to help find that poor girl. But I don't mind telling you that Miss Sarah's half out of her mind with worry. Everyone is. Miss Charlotte was here yesterday evening, wanting to look too. Miss Sarah sent her home, because what else can we do but wait and pray?"

"I can't sit around and do nothing." He had to help, if only to show himself he wasn't the fiend Sarah and her girls believed him to be, even if come Monday at the probate hearing, they'd all be proven right.

The housekeeper nodded her approval of his statement and opened the door wide. "You can come in and wait for Miss Sarah in the parlor, if you'd like."

Beyond her, Daniel noticed the collection of packing crates and boxes assembled in the parlor, and in the hallway, a bright rectangle on the wallpaper where a watercolor of a farm used to hang. Sarah was preparing to leave the house. The sight brought him up short. *Not at all proud, Sinclair.*

Daniel took a step back. "I'll just wait out here on the porch. I don't mind the porch. It's rather comfortable and the weather's good."

A tiny smile tweaked the housekeeper's lips. "As you see, the wicker chair's still sitting where you left it, Mr. Cady. The thought keeps slipping my mind to return it to the garden where it belongs."

"I did notice. Thank you."

"Do you want lemonade? It's fresh made."

"I'll be fine."

"Just mind that Mr. Malagisi next door." She inclined her head to her left. "He's awful curious over what's afoot around here."

Daniel took a seat, the wicker creaking and yielding beneath his weight, removed his hat, and stretched out his legs. The neighbor—Mr. Malagisi—was tending the rosebushes in his terraced front yard. Between snips of his pruning clippers, he shot Daniel surreptitious glances from beneath his broad-brimmed straw hat. Daniel stared straight ahead.

He didn't have to wait long before he caught sight of Sarah coming down the road from the cable car stop. She was clutching a copy of one of the city newspapers and attempting to read it while walking. She made it halfway up the stairs before noticing either Mr. Malagisi's called-out greeting or Daniel sitting on the porch.

Daniel nodded down at her. "Good afternoon, Miss Whittier."

"Mr. Cady!" Her cheeks flared, as they always seemed to do.

He stood. "I hope you don't mind . . ."

"Would you cease showing up at my house if I did?" Sarah folded the newspaper closed, securing it beneath her arm alongside her reticule, securing her composure as well. Already, her color was back to normal. "Wouldn't Mrs. McGinnis let you inside?"

"She said you'd be home soon."

"I suspect you're not here to enjoy the view from my porch, Mr. Cady," Sarah said calmly, climbing the rest of the stairs to join him. There were dark circles beneath her eyes, revealing how little she'd slept. "Especially without Ah Mong to keep you company."

"I read the notice in the paper about Anne Cavendish. What happened?"

She pulled in a long breath and brushed fingers over the brooch pinned at her waist. He'd seen her do that before, caressing the small oval painted with yellow roses like a talisman.

"Anne tried to leave Frank, and she had actually found refuge at a home for women who need that sort of help." She paused for another breath. "He found her, though. Yesterday morning. She took off running, and no one has heard from her since. A policeman was here before breakfast to let me know that they've searched for Frank, but the house in Tar Flat is empty and looks like it has been for a day or so. It seems they're both gone."

"How can I help?"

"You did enough when you went to Tar Flat with me." And she'd surprised him with a hasty kiss afterward. Her gaze danced away for a moment, as if she were remembering too. "I can't ask you to do anything else. Besides, I don't know where she is or even where to start to look. And don't think I didn't try to figure that out. I wasted a lot of time last night poring over an old street map Josiah kept in his office, trying to guess where Anne might be hiding among all the roads. So many choices, so many places, one worse than the next, and all assuming Anne has chosen where to go. If Frank has abducted her, they could be anywhere."

Suddenly, she wobbled, collapsing like a marionette released from its suspending strings onto the porch step before he could grab her.

"Sarah!" He dropped to his knees at her side, her skirts and bustle almost tripping him. Irritated, he swept them aside. "Let me fetch Mrs. McGinnis."

"Please, don't. I'll be fine. I'm just a little tired." She smiled gamely at him. There was pain behind that smile, though. "I'm letting myself think the worst about Anne. I need to hold on to hope. Don't you think?"

She was asking him for reassurance that life might turn out fairly?

"I could hire a cart and search the streets for her," he suggested as he helped her to her feet.

"You and Lottie think an awful lot alike, at times." She was watching him as if judging the sincerity behind the offer. "I appreciate your thoughtfulness, but—"

"Sarah," he interrupted. "There's not much I can do for you and keep my promises to Lily and Marguerite. But I can do this."

"You don't know your way around San Francisco," she protested.

He clasped her hand and looked into her warm brown eyes. "Then come with me."

The cart horse's head hung wearily, dragging on the reins looped around Daniel's fingers. Sarah was just as tired as the animal and her back hurt from bouncing over San Francisco roads—most of them badly paved and a few, in the parts of town where they'd gone, narrow and gloomy and dangerous. She didn't expect better down by the wharves and warehouses.

Daniel caught her contemplating him and smiled briefly as he sat up tall to stretch out the kinks that must be bothering him too. She wanted to return the smile, but what did either of them have to smile about? Anne Cavendish was nowhere to be found.

She gripped the bench seat as they rocked over a set of cable-car rails and sighed, which triggered a yawn. As tired as she was, she could only imagine how tired, how very weary Anne must be. Cold and alone on the streets somewhere.

Dearest Lord . . . she began and stopped, wanting to ask that Anne be alive but unable to. She *should* pray. The words, however, and the rush of faith required to make them genuine would never find her.

Gathering her paisley shawl close around her shoulders, Sarah deeply inhaled the damp evening air. Overhead, the sky was shading from peach along the western sky to lavender to indigo, the first night stars beginning to sparkle between the clouds like pinpricks of candlelight through a pierced tin shade. Along the streets of Nob Hill, gas flames blazed behind their bulbous lamp shades, the stately rows of houses beyond them settling in for the night. How quiet and peaceful it could be up here, as if the worries and miseries of the city at their feet didn't exist. How easy to forget all those people who struggled to make a living, whose hold on a proper existence was as tenuous as the cling of dandelion fluff. One breath and it could blow away. Take someone like Anne Cavendish with it.

Daniel steered the cart onto Jones Street, the wheels clattering over the cobbles. Within seconds, they were at the house.

"We're here," he said, tying off the reins and hopping down to help Sarah descend to the street.

Wordlessly, Sarah let him grasp her around the waist and lift her onto the road. He didn't let go immediately, and she didn't pull back. How warm he was, how reassuringly solid and strong. If only they had met under different circumstances and weren't battling each other over the legacy of a heartbroken old man.

"Will you be all right?" he asked, his voice gentle.

"As all right as I can be." The damp chill of the night air made her shiver.

"No, you're not." He tucked her shawl around her neck, the backs of his fingers brushing against exposed skin, causing a very different shiver. "You're freezing."

"The house will be warm, and what I'm feeling is nothing compared to what Anne must be going through." She studied his face. How could he be so set on revenge, so ready to spoil her plans, and yet so concerned about a woman he barely knew? Who was Daniel Cady, really? "Thank you. You didn't have to search for her tonight."

His hands rubbed down her arms. "I wanted to help you, Sarah. It's the least I could do, given . . ."

He didn't have to say more. Given his goals. Given the hearing on Monday. Given that he'd up and sell her house out from underneath her as soon as it was his to sell. Given that he'd rush back to Chicago and leave her here, the bits of her life shattered around her feet, the makings of a family and a future in ruins.

She didn't hate him, though. She couldn't hate him any longer, and that fact tore at her heart. *Despite everything, you make me want to care for you, Daniel Cady. Despite everything, you make me want to believe in love again.*

His eyes were on her face, on her mouth, and he drew her closer. Was he going to kiss her? Her pulse raced. Would she let him?

Up at the house, the lamp in the parlor flared to life.

"It looks like Mrs. McGinnis is waiting for news," he said with a tiny smile, his clasp easing. Her questions wouldn't be answered tonight.

Sarah moved out of his hold, brushed at her sleeves where his hands had gripped her, a guilty gesture to wipe away any evidence of his touch. "If I hear anything about Anne, I'll let you know." He noticed the motion, and she was sorry he had. "And thank you for buying my painting. I don't know why you did, but if we ever find Anne, I'll use the money to send her to safety."

"That's the best use of my thirty-five dollars I could imagine." He touched fingertips to the rim of his hat. "Good night, Miss Whittier."

He waited at the curb until Sarah reached the safety of the

porch. Mrs. McGinnis threw open the front door and swept her inside, where Rufus curled about her skirts, depositing hairs along the hemline.

"What did you find?" the housekeeper asked.

That I've lost my heart to the wrong man? But Mrs. McGinnis was inquiring after Anne, not the state of Sarah's feelings.

She shook her head, and the housekeeper's face fell. "*Och*, poor lass."

Indeed, thought Sarah. *Poor, poor lass.*

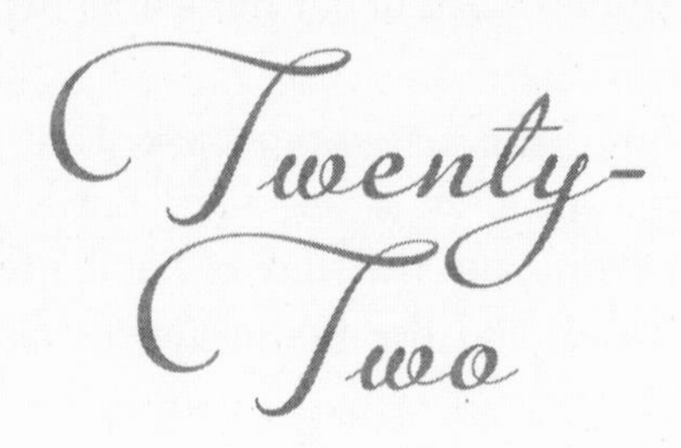

Twenty-Two

SHE COULDN'T REMEMBER. Why could she not remember which place was Emma's?

Anne scanned the road. To her left stood a row of two-story houses, the shadows descending to fill the nooks and crannies between them with ebony. Above and to her right was an uneven line of backyards, empty clotheslines and rickety porch balconies jutting over scraps of gardens and unpainted wood fences, thin flickers of lantern light peeping between gaps in shades and blinds. The houses clung to the side of Telegraph Hill, ascending haphazardly to the summit, better and more solid homes with stone steps and large windows that could catch the first rays of the morning sun up there. A good rainstorm would turn the streets to mud and wash them all down, she thought.

She simply wished she could remember which one was the boardinghouse where Emma lived. It had to be somewhere nearby. She'd been there once, shortly after Miss Whittier had brought Emma to work with them, but long enough ago that she could no longer recall precisely. So much misery and pain between her and clear recollection.

A horse dragging a cart trudged up the incline of the road toward her. Anne's pulse surged and she looked around her for somewhere to hide, someplace to scuttle to like a frightened spider seeking shelter. Her head told her it wouldn't be Frank, but a day spent running and then a night spent huddled in an alleyway between a storehouse and a Chinese laundry, only a begged cup of rice in her stomach, followed by another day of hiding had made her witless and fearful.

The cart passed without incident and Anne's pulse resumed its normal beat. She paused, listened to the noises of evening descending, a mother's raised voice sounding through an open window, the laughter of children in a nearby yard, tussling over a basin of soapy water. Sounds that made her lonely and so weary. She had to find Emma. She had no idea what she'd do if she had to spend another night on the street. She had lost Frank, maybe for good . . . Anne shuddered. She wouldn't think about what had happened. Wouldn't think about the canal, the stench of the water, the sound of the heavy splash, because she couldn't be certain. But if he had drowned, she wasn't sorry. *Heavenly Father, forgive me, but I'm not sorry.*

A break in the sidewalk planks tripped her.

"Anne, pay attention." Looking around to see if anyone noticed and finding the street empty, she pulled in three quick breaths to steady her nerves. "Now remember. Remember."

And there, at last, she noticed a small, discreet sign three doors down. *Rooms to Let.* That had to be the place, the fancy dentil trim beneath the roofline familiar.

It took considerable resolve to keep from dashing up the stairs and pounding on the front door like a hoyden. Mustering what dignity she had remaining, she rang the bell.

An olive-skinned woman dressed in head-to-toe widow's weeds answered, the light from an uncovered gas tap in the hall behind casting her in shadows. Her assessment of Anne was quick and uncomplimentary. There'd been no chance to wash and she was filthy and bruised, her dress torn. She'd fallen more than once, ripping the material that had snagged on her boot heel.

"Good evening," said Anne. "I realize it's late, but I saw your sign."

The woman blinked. "You have the money for a room?"

The few dollars Mr. Cady had given her were stashed with her other meager possessions at Mrs. Hill's. She had nothing but the clothes she wore. "I am actually wondering if a Miss Emma Schulte lives here. I must speak with her."

"Emma Schulte." Her lips flattened into a narrow line.

Was she mistaken? Was this the wrong house? Anne glanced over her shoulder at the street and the hill and the city beyond. Where would she go if it was? She just couldn't be certain about Frank.

Dearest heavenly Father, help me.

The woman exhaled and opened the door wide, a wash of yellow light spilling onto the stoop. "If you're Anne Cavendish, she's been expecting you."

It was a long ride back to the hotel for a man with troubled thoughts and a repentant heart. He'd wanted to kiss her. More than wanted, actually—he'd been set and determined to kiss her. Kiss her until she blushed for a reason other than surprise or embarrassment or whatever it was that always made her blush. Blush until he made her tingle and sigh and never want to leave the circle of his arms. Kiss her until she murmured his name with longing, instead of annoyance or dismay. Give her neighbors more to talk about than just rumors of gold nuggets and stories in the newspaper.

"Well, Daniel Cady, you didn't kiss her, though, did you?" he muttered, flipping up his coat collar against the fog fingering along the roads, chasing him into downtown.

He'd let the parlor light and the briefest hesitation on Sarah's part scare him off. Make him remember that they were on opposite sides of a battle with no possible winner.

"I *am* a coward, Miss Samuelson," he said, his breath puffing clouds into the damp air.

He'd been on one road, the path that led him to retaliation for so long, he couldn't find a way off it, couldn't see a sign that showed him another way to go. He'd give Sarah that thousand dollars whether she wanted it or not, but he didn't feel generous any longer. The amount was a pittance carved out of the estate she'd once claimed, and she would recognize the offer for what it was—an appeasement, a salve to his guilt. So much less than what a woman like her deserved.

"Thank goodness she came to you." The next morning, Sarah stood with Emma in the tiny boardinghouse parlor—not much bigger or brighter than a kitchen pantry—overwhelming relief making her words rushed and her breathing quick. That morning, she and Mrs. McGinnis had almost been too tired to answer the knock on their front door or open it to the scruffy little boy standing on the porch with a note in one grimy fist. "How is she?"

"Scared." Emma's nose wrinkled. "Cleaner than she was last night. Hungry."

"But unhurt . . ."

"*Ja*." The expression on her smooth, broad face suggested "unhurt" could be interpreted many different ways. "I suppose."

"Take me to her, please."

Under the vigilant scrutiny of the landlady, inky-black as a crow in her heavy bombazine, Sarah and Emma ascended the creaking stairs to the second floor. The room Emma rented looked to be one of five and was on the north side of the house, the cheapest side where the rooms would be dismal in the depths of winter. Emma knocked, a series of raps that Sarah presumed was some type of signal. From within, Phoebe in her lilting accent invited her to enter.

The room was as small as Sarah had anticipated and spare of furniture, but clean. Crowding the rag rug–covered floor was an iron-framed bed with a trundle bed tucked beneath. On the opposite wall stood a scarred oak chest of drawers topped by a mirror, the silvering starting to oxidize and darken. Hooks served to hold dresses and capes and hats. Alongside the bed were a modest table and one lone chair, which Phoebe occupied.

She stood when Sarah entered. "Miss Sarah," she whispered and glanced at the bed. Beneath what Sarah had presumed was a rumpled pile of blankets and quilts lay Anne, fast asleep.

"I hate to disturb her . . ." *when she looks so exhausted, her face so thin and bruised.*

"She will not thank us, I think, if we do not wake her to greet you."

Anne stirred, roused by their voices. Her eyes—had they always been that deep-set?—opened. Spotting Sarah, she struggled to sit upright. "Miss Whittier."

"Phoebe," Emma beckoned. "We leave them alone together."

The two girls left, softly closing the door behind them.

Sarah took Phoebe's chair. She stripped off her gloves and clasped Anne's nearest hand. It was so cold. And surprisingly coarse, as if she spent a great deal of time with her hands in soap water, the work she must do at that saloon. She had never held Anne's hand before to realize this. The girl had never let her. But should she have tried?

Sarah stroked her thumb across Anne's skin, hoping to warm it. "I can't tell you how happy I am to see that you're all right."

"I am alive." Anne's voice was weak. "Emma and Phoebe have been good to me."

"Miss Samuelson and the others have all been worried sick. When Mrs. Hill brought me the news that Frank had found you out on the street, might have harmed you—"

"He didn't." Anne's fingers clenched Sarah's. "He didn't catch up to me."

"But where . . . what happened?"

Blanching, she evaded Sarah's gaze. "I would rather not talk about it. Or him. He is best forgotten."

"Of course." Something horrible had occurred. In her head, Sarah ticked off possibilities, all of them awful.

"I just need to leave town," Anne said in a firm voice. "Quickly."

"I have money for you." Sarah reached into her reticule, pulled out ten dollars of the thirty-five she'd earned from Daniel's purchase of the Seal Rocks painting, and tucked the bills beneath the metal candlestick on the bedside table. He would be relieved to know Anne was safe.

"You don't need to give me that much," Anne protested.

"Yes I do. You don't have any money, do you? No. Also, Mrs. McGinnis and I anticipated that you'd want to get out of San Francisco." *Finally*. "And she has come up with a solution. This morning, she's going to telegraph her sister in Seattle, who runs a boardinghouse like this one, about taking you in. Mrs. McGinnis is confident she will. There is a steamer leaving tomorrow. I'll get a ticket for passage as soon as I leave here. Mrs. McGinnis will accompany you on it as far as Portland, where she had plans to visit her niece who is due to have a baby."

Anne sank into the pillows, any argument about not accepting charity spent. Her concession was as sure a sign as any how desperate she'd become. "I have always thought you were generous, Miss Whittier. Thank you."

"I try to do my best for all of you, Anne." Sarah wished she could gather her into her arms, but even now, Anne wouldn't welcome the embrace. Laying Anne's black braid across her shoulder, Sarah rearranged the pillows beneath her head. "I wish you had let me help you leave San Francisco when Mr. Cady and I offered. I also wish you had told me about Frank earlier, about how bad it was with him." Despite her suspicions, Sarah had chosen to not interfere with this proud young woman's life, hoping Anne would come to her. *Like a daughter to me, or a sister.*

"Mr. Cady was right, that day," Anne said, too exhausted to shrink from Sarah's ministrations. "Frank would have only tried to hurt me sooner, if he thought you might take me away from him. I didn't think I could take the risk."

"You deserved better than that man."

"He wasn't always so bad. Not at first." She peered at Sarah through her long eyelashes. For a moment, Sarah thought Anne wanted to tell her something, but the moment passed. "As I said, he is best forgotten."

"And I know you will."

Anne lifted her brows and observed Sarah. "You say that with all the confidence of a woman who has never had to forget her past."

Sarah felt a pressure beneath her ribs, as if the truth was confined in the cage of her chest and trying to break free. *Edouard.* Would she ever forget him? Would Anne really ever forget Frank? "I can imagine."

"You're too good, Miss Whittier, too decent to comprehend the life I've lived."

"I'm simply doing what's right, Anne. Don't confuse my actions for virtue." She stood, eager to be quit of the room and Anne's perceptive regard. "You need rest. I'll see you in the morning. Be prepared to leave early. The ship departs at ten." Sarah headed for the door.

"Thank you again, Miss Whittier." Anne smiled, a sight that was precious and rare, as rare as diamonds or rubies. Or gold nuggets. "I was right to send for you. God answered my prayer." She sounded astonished, but no more than Sarah would be in her place. "Through you."

Impossible. God would never work through her. "You're not completely out of harm's way yet, Anne."

"I'm close enough."

Sarah bit her lip to stop the tears that threatened to fall and fled. By the time she reached the ground floor, her heart was ready to burst.

"I've got the story, Mr. Cady." Archibald Jackson winked and bounced on his toes. "And won't you be interested to hear what I've discovered."

Daniel was acutely aware they had attracted the attention of the usual crowd collected behind the hotel's ground floor windows, men with their feet propped on tables, women in striped day dresses, whispering behind their hands about the parade of humanity one could observe on the sidewalks of San Francisco. The shabby creatures one saw, who poked their fingers into the chests of their betters.

As Jackson was doing to Daniel at that moment.

"I told you I would. More to your pa's story, for certain. And a certain female's." He guffawed, making the Occidental's doorman in his spotless uniform scowl at him. "Might we go inside and discuss it? It'll go down more easily with a glass of whiskey."

"I don't drink," said Daniel. The reporter had rounded the corner of Montgomery and Bush right as Daniel was headed out the hotel's front door, bound for the offices of the *San Francisco Chronicle* and an overdue confrontation. Jackson had saved him the trip, but not the headache. "And even you won't make me start."

The reporter peered at him like he was a new species. "Suit yourself." He leaned against the nearest limestone pilaster, crossing one ankle over the other, making himself comfortable. "Although I'd think you wouldn't want all these people passing by to hear what I have to say."

"Don't you intend to publish your story? They'd all learn it then."

"Well, maybe I won't publish the story." He tipped his derby forward, shading his eyes against the midday sun. "I might be willing to forget all about it for the right amount of money."

Impulsively, Daniel's hands clenched. A passing flock of female tourists, bustles bouncing and feathered hats aquiver, stopped him from applying his fists to Jackson's face. The elderly woman at the rear of the group shook her head at them both then scuttled to regain the rest. "How much?"

Jackson considered. "A hundred ought to be right."

An amount that had to be several months' salary for a reporter. Given Daniel's relation to Addison Hunt, Jackson could have asked for more; Daniel considered himself fortunate Jackson hadn't.

Daniel inhaled deeply, caught a whiff of cigar smoke off a man descending from the cable car recently stopped at the hotel entrance, breathed in the smell of the bay water only a few blocks distant, and glared at Jackson until the shorter man shuffled his feet and his smug grin slipped.

"I have no intention of giving a hundred dollars to you. I don't have that much on hand even if I wanted to." The bulk of his ready cash was tied up in a pair of dolls and a beautiful watercolor of a clutch of rocks sprayed by the sea. Painted by a woman he'd very nearly kissed last night, full on the mouth and long.

"That is a pity." Jackson noticed an attractive young woman hurrying across the road toward them and paused to tip his hat at her. Forehead furrowing, she gave him a wide berth. "But maybe you could telegraph Grandpa Hunt and have him wire you some funds. Today."

Trust you are taking care of story . . . His grandfather would want the story kept quiet, but not at the expense of his bank account. "My grandfather isn't the sort to pay hush money, either."

"He might be. Because when you consider that his son-in-law—and now his grandson too—was involved with a woman who might be a criminal, he might be eager not to let the good folks of Chicago learn the news. Puts a taint on the family name, doesn't it?"

"Miss Whittier's no criminal." He stepped close enough to

Jackson to trod on the man's scuffed shoes. "You're lying, Jackson."

"You don't intimidate me, Mr. Cady, because I believe you're too fine a gentleman—frayed coat aside—to pummel me in public." He squinted at Daniel and blew out a breath, stinking of the oysters he'd had for lunch. "I think my cost has gone up. One hundred twenty-five. And this story is worth every penny."

"I won't pay you." Jackson had to be bluffing.

"Then I guess I'll have to put the story in the paper, get a few extra dollars from my appreciative boss." He shrugged. "Make my reputation. Get better opportunities, maybe. I certainly won't sit on it. Offer it to Miss Whittier, perhaps."

"She doesn't have any spare cash to pay you off, either."

Jackson smirked. "You don't think so?"

"Mr. Cady?"

Daniel turned at the sound of Sarah's voice. She was only a few feet away, coming quickly up the sidewalk, and it was too late to warn her to turn around.

Jackson hopped into Sarah's path to intercept her. "Why, Miss Whittier! We were just discussing you and here you are." Theatrically, he swept off his hat and bowed. "My name is Archibald Jackson. Of the *San Francisco Chronicle*."

"I recognize you, Mr. Jackson," she said without warmth, her gaze sweeping over him and Daniel. Tension corded her throat, tightened the lines of her face. "I didn't realize you two knew each other."

"A recent acquaintance, Miss Whittier." Jackson grinned, interrupting Daniel before he could deny any connection. "And hopefully a profitable one."

"Mr. Cady has always hoped for profits," she replied flatly.

"I sure would like to talk to you about the stash of diggings Mr. Josiah Cady brought back from his little mining operation in the Black Hills," the reporter said. "Lots of gossip about what happened to all that gold, isn't there? Bet his former mining partner might have a theory. Your uncle, right? The one who lives in Los Angeles."

Sarah blanched. "I don't have either the time or the inclination to discuss my uncle or Josiah with you, Mr. Jackson." She shot Daniel a dark look. "I came here to let you know, Mr. Cady, that Anne has been found and will be fine. Thank you so much for your help. It is no longer required. Good day to you both."

"Good day to you, Miss Whittier. Or is it Thayer?" asked Jackson.

"Thayer?" Daniel repeated. What was Jackson talking about? Los Angeles. Josiah's partner. None of it made sense.

Gathering up her skirts, Sarah rushed off before Daniel could stop her, before he could explain that he wanted nothing to do with a slimy reporter. Before he could ask his own questions. She looked back only once before weaving between the carriages and a horsecar trudging along Bush Street, hurrying the rest of the way up Montgomery.

Jackson slapped his hat onto his head. "She's a feisty one. I like her. She won't like the story I'm going to print, though, I can promise you."

"Leave her out of your paper, Jackson."

"Have you discovered a source of money all of a sudden, Mr. Cady?"

"I don't care what story you think you've uncovered. You leave her alone because that's the honorable thing to do."

"Honor?" Jackson guffawed. "I don't bother with honor, Cady. It's too burdensome."

Twenty-Three

"I CAN'T BELIEVE he was with that reporter, Lottie." Sarah gripped the handle of her cup, the sunlight streaming through the greenhouse windows reflecting on the surface of the tea within. Around her, the air was warm and heavy with the perfumed scent of flowers and loam, which on any other day would have made Sarah tranquil and sleepy. Her fingers shook, though, rippling the tea, scattering the reflection. She felt so betrayed, so stupid to have started to trust Daniel. He'd been kind merely to weaken her defenses, probably hoping she'd finally admit to hiding a cache of gold. "They looked like they were conspiring together."

"Surely not conspiring, Sarah," said Lottie. "Mr. Cady would not stoop so low."

After trusting in Aunt Eugenie's love, believing in Edouard's promises, Sarah was not as certain as her friend.

"How else would that reporter have known that my aunt and uncle live in Los Angeles? He called me Thayer, Lottie. My uncle's last name. The one he gave me when I went to live with him and my aunt as their 'adopted daughter.'"

How bitter to remember those days, her aunt and uncle's insistence that she would be Sarah Thayer from the moment she'd come to them. Sarah Whittier was someone to be forgotten, the last name a reminder to Aunt Eugenie of long-standing resentments. She would never forgive Sarah for being the daughter of Caroline Whittier, the younger sister who had married for love, borne children, and found happiness. Instead, Aunt Eugenie's life had been circumscribed by duty and practicality—her marriage to Uncle Henry made for the status it would bring, her girlhood hopes withered on the vine. If they'd ever sprouted at all.

And she punished me in my mother's stead.

"Sarah, I can see you fretting."

"I'm thinking about my aunt and uncle. That always makes me fret." Sarah set down her cup before she splattered tea everywhere. "When we were at Golden Gate Park, Mr. Cady questioned my claim that Josiah had friends in Arizona. That afternoon, I wasn't sure if he was suspicious of my story, but it seems he must have been. He has to be the one who told Mr. Jackson that my uncle lives in Los Angeles and asked him to poke around."

"To what end? What might Mr. Jackson discover?" Lottie's face puckered with impatience. "That you fell in love with a scoundrel? Everyone makes mistakes, Sarah. Such a story makes paltry news in this city."

Sarah glanced toward the archway that connected the half-octagon greenhouse to the parlor at the rear of the Samuelson's house. There was no one to see them, secluded as they were among the maroon gloxinia and amethyst passion flower vines, pots of striped orchids and thick ferns. The small metal table they sat at, tucked against the far wall, was a long way from prying ears. If anyone in the Samuelson household would be so uncouth as to eavesdrop, that was.

"Lottie," she said, lowering her voice nonetheless, "you know what I did was worse than merely falling in love with a scoundrel."

Her friend was undeterred. "You could not have known when you eloped with Edouard Marchand that he had stolen from your uncle."

"I should have known that his promises were lies and that he had no intention of marrying me." Sarah shivered. How could she feel so cold, out in the stultifying warmth of the greenhouse? It was her memories that turned her blood to ice, because she had let Edouard do too much, his kisses and caresses very convincing to a young woman so in need of love. Thank heavens she hadn't made a more serious mistake. "I trusted Edouard and I trusted Mr. Cady, and they have both proven to me that I will never learn."

"Sarah, stop it! I do not know how this reporter found out about your family, but I refuse to believe Mr. Cady was the one who told him," insisted Lottie. "What would it gain him to be in cahoots with such a fellow?"

Fortunate Lottie, who had never had her heart broken or her faith challenged. "A larger black eye on my reputation, which would plainly turn Judge Doran's opinion against my claim on Josiah's estate."

"He would not want to damage your reputation. Sarah Jane Whittier, that man is in love with you."

Was he? Last night, she might have thought so. "Charlotte Samuelson, that man is only in love with revenge."

"It is time to go, Anne." Phoebe's voice was persistent. "Miss Sarah will be here soon to get you, and she will not want you to be late for the boat."

Anne pressed her fingertips against the tiny room's windowsill and stared out at the hills of the city. She shouldn't feel sentimental to be putting them behind her, putting her life with Frank behind her, the life she'd led before behind her too. Did her father ever wonder what had become of his only child? Did he ever regret shoving her to the street when she hadn't . . . when she wouldn't . . . the memories clogged Anne's throat with tears. They'd been poor, dreadfully poor, she and her father, and he had sought the last way he could think of to bring in some money. A pretty young girl was a commodity in San Francisco many men would happily buy.

I can forgive him now, heavenly Father. Anne pinched her eyes closed. *You have shown me mercy and I can forgive.*

I just wish he would miss me and be sorry.

Once she left San Francisco, he'd never know where to find her. If he did have regrets. If he did want to, ever, say he loved her.

"Anne." Phoebe rested her delicate fingers on Anne's shoulder. "It is time to go."

Anne opened her eyes. The hills shimmered out of focus then resolved into their usual shapes, the buildings and roadways distinct and clear. Frank was gone. And for her, her father was gone too.

She gathered up the few possessions Emma had volunteered to retrieve from Mrs. Hill's—a couple of sketches, some underthings, a tiny locket containing a faded photograph of her mother, Mr. Cady's dollars—then looked at Phoebe. "I'm ready."

He'd waited a long time to come to this place, but then he hadn't found the stomach to visit earlier, to stare at a marble headstone and look for answers.

"Thank you for coming with me, Miss Samuelson," Daniel said to the woman at his side. "I didn't know where to look."

She gave Daniel a brief smile. "You could have asked Sarah to accompany you this morning, once she returned from taking Mrs. McGinnis and Anne to the wharf. She comes up to the cemetery often to visit."

"She's upset with me." More than upset. She'd been rigid with righteous indignation. "She saw me with a reporter yesterday, a man who's been asking about Josiah and that nuggets rumor. It didn't look good."

"I did hear," she said, her voice gentle with consideration.

Charlotte Samuelson was always considerate and kind, he decided. "I told her not to think you would willingly have anything to do with a man like that."

"Thank you for defending me."

"I believe in you, Mr. Cady." She lifted her pale brows a fraction. "Do you want me to leave you alone with Josiah?" Miss Samuelson understood. Her insightfulness was rather disconcerting, but today, he appreciated it.

"For a minute or two."

"I shall be right over here. I enjoy reading the headstones. Some folks find that morbid, but I find the practice . . ." She gave a small lift of her thin shoulders. "Comforting."

Miss Samuelson strolled off, her bright pink skirt belling in the wind swirling over the hilltop.

Daniel stared at the headstone. Below the dates of Josiah's birth and death, an inscription had been carved into the lustrous white marble. *Beloved Friend.*

Beloved friend to whom? Not to him.

He skimmed his hat through his fingers, noticed movement far off to his right. A funeral party was proceeding through the cemetery along one of the narrow gravel lanes, a small knot of folks dressed in black following behind a crape-festooned horse-and-cart, a coffin conspicuous in the bed. They were all men, their dark coats tugged by the wind topping the high ground of Laurel Hill Cemetery and bending the tips of the trees. Possibly a brother or a son among the group, relations who might feel the loss of the individual in that spare wood box as keen as an open wound. A different situation for Josiah, who had gone into the sandy soil on the flank of this mountain without a single member of his family to shed a tear over the dirt.

Daniel clenched his hat brim as the funeral party vanished over a small hillock in the distance.

"Grace loved you until the day she died, Josiah," he said, thankful Miss Samuelson had moved far enough away to be out of earshot. Talking to a grave. He'd gone crazy. "She always believed you'd come back. But you didn't."

Grief cramped Daniel's chest. Josiah didn't deserve his heartache. He hadn't when Daniel had been younger, a miserable boy lonely for his father, and certainly did not now. He had spent hours, countless hours, listening for the sound of Josiah's gruff laughter in the hallway, watching for the familiar sight of his handwriting on the mail coming to the house, inhaling air in hopes of breathing the sharp sweetness of his cigar. Feeling disappointment over and over again, so often that he couldn't feel it any longer, numb to the repeated scrapes and stabs to his heart.

I was fourteen, Josiah, a boy on the verge of manhood. And I needed you. Needed a father.

"Beloved Friend." What a lie.

Why had Josiah never returned? Because of gold? Because California had held so much more appeal than life in Chicago? Because he hadn't really loved his wife?

Hadn't loved us?

The carved inscription swam in his vision. Daniel shoved on his hat and drew his gaze off the stone, regarded the ragged lines of tombstones and monoliths climbing the hillsides. There were no answers to his questions, here among the dead.

Miss Samuelson caught his eye and returned. She looked down at the headstone. "He had a small service but he was deeply mourned. Still is deeply mourned by those who were his friends."

"Who suggested the inscription?" he asked resentfully.

"We all thought it appropriate." She studied his face. "I hope you come to understand, one day, how wonderful a man Josiah really was. I hope you learn to forgive him."

She may as well hope he'd suddenly develop amnesia and all those scars on his heart would be forgotten.

"Let me take you home, Miss Samuelson."

"I am sorry to be leaving you, Miss Sarah, at such a time," said Mrs. McGinnis, the wind blowing off the bay ruffling the wisps of hair peeping out from her bonnet. Around them, passengers and their companions rushed along, dodging wagons loaded with cargo headed for the warehouses clustered along the wharf. Coal smoke drifted from the steamer at dock, catching in the breeze and swirling away. Stevedores and dock masters shouted above the din of ship's whistles and the creak of timbers. A cart loaded with mail bags brushed close, forcing Sarah to edge nearer Mrs. McGinnis lest she be swept away in the melee.

"If my eldest sister were still alive, God rest her soul," the housekeeper was saying, one hand outstretched protectively, shielding Sarah, "she'd be with her bairn at such a time. But as it is . . ."

Sarah squeezed her arm. "Your niece needs you during her lying-in. I'll be fine here."

"But the hearing on Monday—"

"Will not be affected by whether or not you're in San Francisco, Mrs. McGinnis. Besides, Anne will appreciate your company until you disembark at Portland and see her off to Seattle."

The housekeeper nodded and hugged Sarah briskly, then stepped back. "Tell me again you'll be fine."

"I shall." She dropped a kiss on Mrs. McGinnis's cheek, causing her to look abashed by the display of affection. "I'll see you in a couple of weeks. And take care of Anne for me. I think she's anxious."

"She'll be well once she reaches my sister. Besides, hope holds up the head, and that's what Anne has again—hope."

"God bless you, Mrs. McGinnis. I don't know what I'd do without you."

"*Wheesht*, lass." Eyes watering, she snatched up her carpetbag. "Tell that girl and Ah Mong to hurry along. The ship'll be gone afair that boy brings her belongings."

"Safe trip."

Sarah waved until Mrs. McGinnis was swallowed up by the

crowd collected beneath the roofed shed covering the dock. She turned and spotted Ah Mong, a satchel in one hand and a wicker basket in the other, hurrying behind Anne. A few more minutes and Anne would be securely boarded onto the steamer and safe from Frank.

"Thank you," Sarah said to the boy, taking the basket from him while Anne took hold of the satchel containing items of clothing Minnie and Sarah had been able to lend, as well as a few of her personal belongings Emma had fetched from the Benevolent House. Which hadn't been much.

Ah Mong inclined his head and returned to the rented trap to wait for Sarah. Sarah found the ticket collector and led Anne along the dock, evading other passengers hurrying for the gangplank.

A sea of ship masts bobbed to their left and their right. Anne eyed the sailing vessels, the seagulls wheeling among the rigging. "I've never been on a boat before."

Sarah rubbed her hand down the coarse sleeve of Anne's thin wool coat, rummaged this morning from a secondhand clothing shop. Beneath was a new dress Sarah had ordered for her weeks ago, intended for opening day of the studio. A day Anne would never see. Or the other girls, either, thought Sarah broodily. "A steamer is perfectly safe."

"It might be, Miss Whittier, but Cora's not the only one who can't swim."

She responded to Anne's slender smile with one of her own. It seemed a million years ago that Cora had fallen into the pond at Golden Gate Park and Daniel had rescued her, ages before Sarah had come to learn that not only was he hard-hearted, he was as false as fool's gold.

"You'll arrive in Portland on Tuesday," said Sarah. "Not too long a journey, and I suspect you'll never be out of sight of land. Plus, you'll have Mrs. McGinnis to distract you. The voyage shouldn't be too difficult, especially for a woman as strong as you are."

"Not as strong as I wanted to be. I stayed with Frank for too long. Let him tell me what to do, even when I knew it was wrong." She swallowed, the lace banding her dress collar quivering with the motion. "At least we're safe from him now."

We're safe? Sarah cocked her head. Had she misunderstood Anne's words, spoken in a whisper, barely audible above the ruckus of the wharf? She decided she had.

"Here, take this." Sarah handed her the wicker basket packed with lunch and a few other items of food. "If you find you can't tolerate the food they serve onboard, Mrs. McGinnis has made certain neither of you will starve. Her sister will collect you when you arrive in Seattle. She sent us a short telegram last night and has agreed to take you on as her housekeeper. I wish the position was a better one, one that could take advantage of your talents. I'm sorry it won't."

"I will make it work, Miss Whittier." Her gaze was steady, her jaw set, refusing to be cowed by the world. No matter how it treated young women alone.

The steamer's whistle tweeted, a signal that departure time had arrived. Sarah and Anne started for the gangplank, a young man jostling them in his haste not to miss his passage.

"I'll write," said Sarah, "after you're settled, to let you know how the shop fares. I'm sure the other girls will want to give you their news and hear how you're doing."

"I'm not as sure as you, but I'll be glad to hear from you and any of them." Anne startled Sarah with an embrace, the basket swinging from her elbow knocking against Sarah's hip. Suddenly, she reached into the deep pocket of her skirt. "Wait! I almost forgot to return the money Mr. Cady loaned me."

"I'll repay him for you. Keep that."

Anne nodded. "Thank you again for everything, Miss Whittier. I will pay you back."

"There's no need." Anne would be better off saving her pennies for her future.

"But I shall. I promise. I have to. You've been my salvation."

"Anne." That was all Sarah could say, her throat tightening around words.

Anne rushed up the short gangplank. When she reached the steamer's deck, she turned and waved. "Trust in God, miss. He rescued me. He'll do right for you," she shouted over another screech of the boat's whistle. Then she was gone, shouldering her way into the cabin spanning the deck.

Sarah waited, hoping to see either Mrs. McGinnis or Anne's face appear at one of the windows, but that was the last she saw of the girl. Tears burned Sarah's throat. Loss . . . she would never get used to the pain of separation, of having to say good-bye. Aunt Eugenie had torn her away from her mother's grave that stormy, humid Ohio afternoon, her arms groping the empty air for the harsh wooden cross scratched with her family's names. One of many good-byes she'd been forced to say. Likely, this would not be the last.

She inhaled and turned her face to the breeze, letting the wind dry her eyes. There was no time for tears, not when she needed strength to face her own trials. *Have faith. Trust in God.* How she wished she could.

Squaring her shoulders, Sarah returned to the trap she'd rented to take Anne and Mrs. McGinnis down to the wharf, parked at the edge of the road that fronted the quay.

Ah Mong, straight-backed on the seat, watched Sarah climb up. "They will have a safe trip, Miss Sarah. It is a good day to travel and start a new life."

The gangplank rattled as it was pulled onto deck, and the ropes tethering the steamer to dock were cast off. "How can you tell that, Ah Mong?"

"My grandfather would say the day is right for such things," he replied solemnly. Sarah grabbed the side of the seat as he flicked the reins across the horse's back, spurring the mare forward. "But I would say I trust in your God."

Thankfully, the remainder of Saturday had passed without hearing either from Daniel or that loathsome reporter. Sarah hid away at the shop, where work could be relied upon to distract her, until it had grown late and she'd had to return home to an empty house. A lonely place without the homey sounds of Mrs. McGinnis clanking pots in the kitchen or humming over the stove, scolding Rufus over some offense. Sarah plucked a hairpin from between her lips. If she lost everything tomorrow, including the house, where would either of them go? Maybe Mrs. McGinnis would return to her niece in Portland or go to her sister's in Seattle. And she herself would . . .

Sarah shoved the hairpin home. It jabbed into her skull, making her wince. She would find a room to rent and continue on. Because she would never return to Los Angeles and beg forgiveness, one more time, from an aunt and uncle so unwilling to give it.

Checking her reflection in her bedroom mirror and noting that her hair was reasonably fixed and her amber twill gown fitted the way it should—an accomplishment without Mrs. McGinnis to help—Sarah went to fetch Lottie's birthday present from her workroom. She was glad for the diversion of a small gathering today; if she sat at home and listened to the clocks tick, she would go mad as a March hare.

Outside, Ah Mong waited patiently in another rented trap. An extravagance, but a better way to arrive at Lottie's house than trudging down the road from the cable-car stop, her nicest pair of shoes dusty and ruined.

Mrs. Brentwood abandoned her post by her parlor window, where she'd been watching the neighborhood's comings and goings, and hurtled onto her front porch. Her face was crimson and she was waving a newspaper like a semaphore flag. "Miss Whittier! Have you seen? How dreadful—"

"I'm sorry, Mrs. Brentwood. I'm in a hurry." Sarah fisted her skirts out of her way and hurried down the stairs to the street. "I'm late for a luncheon and can't talk now. Tell me your news when I've returned."

Despite her ample proportions, Mrs. Brentwood was quick on her feet and managed to arrive at the sidewalk the same time as Sarah. "But you have to see what is in the Sunday paper, Miss Whittier." Her eyes were wide. "It's awful! And it's about you!"

Sarah froze in her spot, one hand on the trap's dash rail, ready to clamber up. "About me?"

She thrust the newspaper at Sarah. It was only a flash, but Sarah noted the masthead: *San Francisco Chronicle*. "Indeed, yes! It has the most dreadful things to say about you and some man in Los Angeles stealing from your uncle there. All lies, of course, since everyone knows you're from Arizona." Mrs. Brentwood squinted at her—checking for guilt, no doubt.

Sarah released her grip on the dash rail. Jackson hadn't waited to hear her version of the story, and now all of San Francisco would learn the truth, or some sensationalized version of the truth. Either way, she was ruined.

I am so sorry, girls. So very, very sorry.

"Ah Mong, I won't be going to the Samuelsons' today." She took the paper from Mrs. Brentwood. "I apologize, but the newspaper is correct. I am from Los Angeles."

"And the rest?"

"I'll have to read the article to let you know."

Mrs. Brentwood turned pale and shrieked.

Twenty-Four

"I GIVE YOU CREDIT for being brave enough to come to my house and face me, Miss Whittier," said Mr. Pomroy.

"I had to," Sarah answered without flinching; she had some pride left. "I need to understand where my business and my girls' futures stand."

"That will depend on how much of this story"—he indicated the open newspaper resting on the parlor table beside him—"is true. Did you steal gold nuggets from your uncle, along with some—excuse my choice of coarse words—some French lover?"

She flinched now. Because of Daniel and Archibald Jackson, she had to stand here, among Mr. Pomroy's brocade curtains and thick-piled rugs and heavy furniture, and relive her greatest foolishness. Her worst offense.

"Unfortunately, much of it is true." Archibald Jackson had found a great resource in Los Angeles. With Daniel's assistance, undoubtedly. "But I did not help Monsieur Marchand steal that gold. All I intended was to run away with him."

Mr. Pomroy cocked his eyebrows. "'All,' Miss Whittier? That is condemning enough behavior for a woman of your upbringing and standing."

"I am aware of my failings, Mr. Pomroy." Aunt Eugenie had

listed them in great detail, the day Sarah had attempted reconciliation, her words brutally unkind. "Which is why I did not want the story known."

"But this Marchand fellow did steal from your uncle?"

She wished she could claim otherwise, but the time for falsehoods and fabrications was past. "My uncle was launching his campaign to run for mayor, and as part of the festivities, he decided to show off some of the gold he'd kept as a souvenir of the mine he and Josiah had run in the Black Hills. He'd shown off the nuggets before; he liked to boast about his success. I told Edouard about the party, that it would be the perfect evening for us to elope. No one would notice me missing. He agreed, but not for the reason I'd thought."

Sarah remembered that night so well, the doors and windows thrown open to catch the cool summer's evening breeze, the clink of glasses and the smell of cigar smoke wafting through the house, the maids in their brightly patterned skirts rushing back and forth from the kitchen to the parlor and the garden beyond where the party had overspilled, her uncle's company enjoying the fountain and the stars overhead. The corner table draped with velvet and the nuggets upon it, winking in the gaslight, guarded closely by one of the male servants. The way her heart had raced as she'd made banal conversation with the guests, all the while anticipating that soon, so soon, she'd be gone from Los Angeles with the man she loved, on her way to starting a new life, creating a new family, one that would love her wholeheartedly. Edouard, though, had other ideas.

Sarah hugged her arms tight around her waist. "I should have suspected what Edouard was up to, but I didn't."

"Your uncle was irresponsible to display his wealth at a party," said Mr. Pomroy, a generous concession.

"He was more irresponsible to drink heavily and fall asleep so soundly that Edouard had no trouble sneaking into my uncle's bedroom that evening and taking the bag containing the nuggets." And she had let him into the house, all as part of their plan to run away together. Utterly unaware of what he really wanted.

"Did Marchand bring you to San Francisco hoping to steal from Josiah too, as the paper claims?"

"He didn't know about Josiah. We came here because we intended to catch a steamer to Victoria, Canada, and go gold hunting in the Cariboo near there. I didn't get on that steamer with him, though." He'd waited until the train had pulled into the station in San Francisco to brag about the gold he'd stolen from Uncle Henry, pulling the newspaper-wrapped bundle from his coat pocket with a wink. How Edouard's eyes had sparkled. How sick she'd felt, realizing she'd run off with a thief. "When I discovered that he had stolen from my uncle, we had a terrible fight, right on the platform. I feel guilty about not getting the nuggets back. I did try, but Edouard knocked me down and fled into the crowd." They'd given the crowd quite a show, a man and a woman brawling like saloon drunks.

"The gold was gone and I was too ashamed and scared to go back to Los Angeles," she continued, a bead of sweat tickling along her collar. "So when I saw Josiah's advertisement for a nurse-companion in the paper, I turned to him for help. I hadn't known he was living here, or else I would have gone to him immediately."

Her landlord nodded to indicate he was following the story. Out in the hallway, Sarah heard the hushed rustle of skirts and wondered if Mrs. Pomroy was listening nearby, preparing to lecture Mr. Pomroy on his choice of tenants.

"Fortunately for me," Sarah said, "the local stories about the event used the name my aunt and uncle had given me, their last name, Thayer. After the news broke, Josiah and I decided it would be best if I called myself by my birth name, Sarah Whittier. A bit of deception, I freely admit, but by doing so, I managed to slip into life here without too many questions about my past. Until now."

"The scandal destroyed your uncle's chances at winning the election."

"No one cares to elect a man whose ward runs off with the family's thieving art tutor." The loss of the election, the reduction of his social standing, had hurt Uncle Henry more than the theft of some nuggets that were a negligible portion of his considerable wealth. "After I'd been in San Francisco a few months, Josiah insisted I go to Los Angeles to speak with my uncle and attempt reconciliation. He refused to forgive me."

"Your uncle could have called the police on you as an accomplice, guilty or not, Miss Whittier, so you should be thankful that was all he did." Mr. Pomroy laid his hand across the newsprint and looked at her long and hard. "So are you wondering if I'm going to throw you out of your shop like my last tenant?"

She held herself as tall and straight as she could. "We signed a lease, Mr. Pomroy, a legal document giving me the right to that storefront for six months."

"It'll be an idle storefront, Miss Whittier, without customers. There isn't a respectable family in this town that'll give you their business after this. Not with so many other art studios and print shops to choose from." He tapped a forefinger on the paper. "The *Chronicle* is doing a good business selling papers, however."

"I can still pay the rent for the next couple of months. Mr. Samuelson's loan and the sale of all my artwork should enable us to survive that long." She'd given up on ever seeing the money from Mr. Winston. And as for the other money promised to her . . . she'd likely never see that either. "And we don't yet know the outcome of the probate trial."

"Do you really think that will fall in your favor, Miss Whittier?" Mr. Pomroy sighed deeply. "I have known you for quite a while and have thought you a headstrong idealist, but I've never thought you a dishonorable woman. I am sorry you have come to this."

She believed him, believed the regretful turn of his mouth,

the way he looked at her like a father might regard a fallen child. "You worried that I or my girls would let you down, and I have."

"I worry about all my clients, Miss Whittier, so don't think yourself exceptional," he answered wryly. "As embarrassing as this news story is, my partners and I will not turn you out of the shop, unless ultimately you can't pay the rent. We would have no choice, in that case; we do have a business to run. However, staying in town means you'll have to weather the storm of gossip."

"My only future is here, Mr. Pomroy. With the young women I still intend to help." *Daniel, how could you do this to them? To Cora and Phoebe and Minnie and Emma? All in the name of revenge against Josiah.*

"You're braver than I would be in your situation, Miss Whittier." Gently, he took her arm. "Go home and rest. Whatever you do, don't answer knocks on your door. You have more to face tomorrow, and I'm afraid the hearing will not go well."

He couldn't possibly be more afraid of that outcome than she was.

Mutely, Sarah let him lead her to his entry hall. Whoever had been out there had gone, and the small rectangle of space, warm in reds and golds and dark wood, was empty.

"Whatever happened to your art tutor, by the way?" Mr. Pomroy asked as she crossed the threshold and stepped onto the porch. "Did he make it to Canada with those nuggets?"

"I don't know, Mr. Pomroy." She'd stopped asking herself that question years ago. "And I really don't care."

If he were a violent man, he'd go to the nearest gun shop, buy a Colt 45 and blow Archibald Jackson's head clean off his shoulders. But Daniel was not a violent man, regrettably, and any rage he felt over the story in the Sunday morning *Chronicle* simply served to make his stomach feel hollow.

Over his shoulder, the dining room waiter let out a low whistle. It was Red, taking too much interest in Daniel's newspaper. "Some story, ain't it? 'A Cautionary Tale of Greed and Immorality.' Catchy."

Daniel slapped the paper shut. "It's a bunch of lies," he snapped, but how much *was* lies, and how much, truth? She'd told him she was from Arizona. She had been able to lie about that, right to his face. Any number of her claims could be false.

Red cleared away Daniel's empty plate. "You think so? I think it makes all sorts of sense." He glanced around him then leaned closer to whisper. "Explains why there's still a story about nuggets up there at the Cady house. Maybe that woman stole 'em from that French fellow and hid them away somewhere. Or maybe she's sitting on a big fat bag of gold your father brought here with him and never told nobody about."

Daniel clenched his fists against his lap.

Red scraped crumbs from the tablecloth and continued to offer his opinions. "Looks like your instinct about her was right. She *was* worth askin' questions over."

"She wasn't ever accused of a crime," he pointed out. Jackson would have uncovered an indictment if there'd ever been one.

"And don't that make her pure as the driven snow!" Red answered, grinning like the reporter might.

Daniel got to his feet; he'd had enough of listening to the Occidental Hotel waiters offer commentary. "Charge the lunch bill to my room."

Sarah's shop was a short block distant, and if he'd come to know her actions at all, she would be there. He had to hear her side of the story, had to get an explanation for how she could have done even a portion of what Jackson had claimed. Needed to square the image the reporter had painted, that of a shameless woman and her thief of a lover, with the one Daniel had come to believe was real.

Daniel crossed the road, barely missing being hit by an oncoming cart. Leaping onto the curb where the worst that could crush him would be a preoccupied pedestrian, he noticed a man on the sidewalk outside of Sarah's shop. He was banging on the door and demanding that she come out and talk to his newspaper.

Daniel ran the rest of the way. "Leave her alone," he demanded, elbowing the reporter aside.

"Who are you?" the man asked, glaring up at Daniel from beneath the brim of his bowler hat. "Trying to get the story too? I was here first—"

He was short and scrawny, and Daniel grabbed his coat collar and easily shoved him toward the curb. "And now you're leaving."

"She won't talk to you, either." Harrumphing, the reporter smoothed his rumpled coat and stalked off.

Not all the blinds on the large plate-glass windows fronting the street were closed, and Daniel peered inside. In the center of the shop stood Sarah, the large oak counter between her and the front of the room acting like a barricade. She was dressed in a striped golden-brown colored dress, the one she'd worn the first day he'd met her, and her arms were clutched around her waist. Her face was colorless and her eyes, unblinking.

He rapped on the glass. "Sarah, please let me in. I want to talk to you."

She heard the noise and her gaze flicked to his face. She frowned. "Go away!" she shouted. The glass muted her voice, but he could read her lips well enough. She rounded the corner of the counter and rushed up to the window, her hand outstretched to tug on the window blind cord.

"I know you blame me for that story in the paper." Could she hear him? He pointed at the door. "Let me in. Let's talk this through." *And tell me I haven't been deceived once more.*

She stared, her expression rigid as granite, mouthed "go away" again. And yanked the cord, the blinds falling to block out her face.

How could he come here? After what he'd done . . .

Sarah eyed the shop door handle as if it might rise up like a snake to bite her. Daniel didn't rattle it again, though. He'd gotten the message and left her in peace, alone in the middle of an empty shop.

Slowly, she spun on the balls of her feet and surveyed the room. The counters, glossy with wax, the glass of the cases so spotless you could hardly tell there was glass in them at all, the walls freshly painted and the floor scrubbed clean. Samples of the girls' work on display on shelves and case-tops. Their whole world, silent and waiting for an opening that was unlikely to arrive. All that next week would bring would be more bills and no customers, unhappiness and disappointment.

Don't let 'em see you blink, Sarah Jane. That's when they know they've got you beat.

"They have beaten me, Josiah," she said in answer to the echo of his voice in her head. "Daniel Cady and his lawyer and Archibald Jackson have all beaten me." But really, she'd beaten herself. She couldn't blame Daniel for the sins of her past.

There was pounding on the door again. Another reporter? Or Daniel again? Sarah ran to the window and peeked around the blinds.

Lottie looked back at her and motioned toward the door.

Sarah hurried to unlock it and usher her inside. "Thank heavens it's you. I thought it was going to be another reporter. I've only had to chase away four so far. A couple dozen papers yet to go."

"Oh, Sarah." Lottie hugged her close. "The story is dreadful. I went up to the house, and when I did not find you there, I came here."

"Thank you." Sarah smiled because it was better than crying all over her friend's aqua-striped *peau de soie* gown, ruining the silk. "With Mrs. McGinnis gone, I need a friend."

"You have me. Always." Lottie hugged her again, hastily. "I

must say that Mama has been in a faint since Papa showed her the newspaper. She sent Bridget around to everyone's house as quick as she could to stop them from coming to my luncheon today. A few arrived anyway. Papa chased them all off without saying a word about you."

"Thank him for me, will you? And tell your mother I'm sorry I ruined your birthday. I have your present in my reticule . . ."

"A present can wait, Sarah." Lottie's brows scrunched tightly. "As for Mama, she will recover."

"She'll never forgive me for causing such gossip."

Lottie didn't deny that. "She did try her best to keep me in the house. She told Bridget to watch me every second, but today is her Sunday afternoon off, and Mama is not so mean as to punish Bridget along with me by canceling her lone free afternoon. I did have to practice some duplicity, however." Faint pink blushed Lottie's cheeks. "After the fuss died down, I told Mama I was going to church to pray, but I neglected to inform her I intended to see you first. To tell you the truth, I cannot believe she let me outside at all."

"Don't get in trouble for my sake."

"I will not go home until I know how you are doing."

"Even though I knew the story was going to come out, I'm stunned. And miserable. I don't know what to do with the shop." Sarah looked around the room. "I saw Mr. Pomroy earlier. So long as we can pay the rent, we still have the lease, but he warned me to expect there won't be a single customer." Sarah eyed her friend, a thought forming. "Perhaps if you ran the studio in my place—"

"No." Lottie shook her head, fluttering turquoise-dyed hat feathers. "I am not an artist. I cannot guide those girls without you."

"There's no one else," said Sarah firmly. "We might hold on to our customers with your name over the shop door. Your reputation is unassailable."

"My parents would never let me take over the studio, Sarah. They are not even permitting me to stay in town." Lottie twisted the ribbon straps of her reticule around her wrist. "At first light, my mother is taking me to stay with my aunt in St. Helena until the gossip blows over."

Sarah's heart sank. "I'm going to lose you too? You won't even be at the hearing tomorrow?"

"I am sorry. Papa will be there to offer any advice, however. You will not be completely alone."

"Why did this happen?" She flung her arms wide in frustration. "Why did Daniel Cady ever have to show up? Why did he have to go so far as to help that awful reporter to print this story? I'd managed to evade my past for so long . . ." But it had caught up.

"We cannot know the reason, Sarah. But if you ask the Lord for guidance, He might answer."

"He never answers me, Lottie." She didn't have to ask God, because she understood the reason. He was punishing her for her sins. Plain and simple.

Frank dragged his fist across the scarred wood bar and glared at the barkeep. "I said I want another."

The barkeep folded his hairy arms over the apron straddling the girth of his fat belly. "And I said you've used up yer credit and won't be gettin' another." He frowned, which made him even uglier than normal. "Go home, Burke. Let that woman of yers take care of you."

Frank slammed his fist onto the surface, rattling the other patrons' glasses. Silence cut across the smoke filling the narrow room, the tense and sweaty silence that preceded a brawl. A fellow at the end of the bar slid off his stool and slunk out of the saloon. Frank shot a glare at his departing back.

"I ain't got a woman anymore." She'd left him to drown.

His Annie, that bit of nothing he'd scraped off the ground in a wharf-front alley, black and blue and swollen from a beating her old man had given her, had left him floundering in a canal. He would've drowned, if some lug of a German hadn't fished him out, sputtering like a beached carp, a twisted ankle paining him worse than his half-healed gunshot wound. And now they were whispering that she'd left Frank Burke for good. He didn't believe she had the nerve. She'd be back. Annie didn't have anyone to run to aside from that Whittier woman. If she were hiding there, he'd flush her out. "So what I need is a drink and a cigar."

"Listen, Burke, I'm not giving you either. Not until you pay up."

"I told you I'll be gettin' the money." Nobody believed him. Well, they'd be sorry. Those nuggets were still stashed in Cady's house and Frank Burke would get his hands on them sure enough.

"You've been telling me you'll get the money for months. Maybe you plan on stealing it from that woman Anne used to work for. She's got gold at that house, doesn't she?" The barkeep chuckled along with a drunk fisting a mug of beer. "Rich as Croesus."

"Those are my nuggets. Mine!" Frank shouted, causing the drunk to slosh beer as he scurried away from the commotion. "I heard about 'em before any of you. That Irishman who worked on that house never could keep his mouth shut, blabbed all about that hidey-hole he'd built for old Cady. I heard first! Understand? And I'm gonna get those nuggets!"

"Right, Burke. Right. But before you do, you should go sleep it off." The barkeep jerked his head toward the open door, a blurry rectangle of light to Frank's left. "Just go on home."

Frank shoved aside his stool, tipping it over. "I'm going but I'll be back, and then I expect to be getting all the whiskey I want."

Twenty-Five

MONDAY MORNING DAWNED unfairly bright and lovely, the breeze gentle, the sky as blue as cornflowers. *The lark's on the wing; the snail's on the thorn; God's in His heaven—all's right with the world!*

Robert Browning was spectacularly wrong today.

Sarah tied her bonnet beneath her chin and inhaled a deep breath, which didn't calm her fluttering nerves or ease her lightheadedness. She glanced around the entry hall and into the parlor, at the bare spots on the walls where paintings had been removed, at the table rug—her rug, purchased on a whim after she'd sold her first painting to a local ship's captain—rolled up in the parlor, Josiah's portrait propped against the wall, the few small crates alongside ready to be shipped to . . . to who knew where. Anywhere but this house, soon to be owned by Daniel Cady and his sisters, of that Sarah had no doubt, and then sold. Judge Doran would have to suddenly become possessed by a fit of sentimentality to settle Josiah's estate in any other fashion. After Jackson's story, she didn't see how that would happen.

Shushing Rufus into the house and locking the door behind her, she took the cable car into town, switching lines until she was finally deposited at the foot of the steps leading to the marble-clad rotunda of the new city hall. Two massive wings extended on either side of the central hall, the sound of masons' hammers clanging off the buildings across Park Avenue. Sarah stared up at the facade, remembering when Josiah had given her a tour of the city like an awestruck sightseer, and had brought her here. Josiah had questioned if they would ever complete construction of the extravagant building before another earthquake came along and took it down. Sarah wished an earthquake would come along right now and save her from having to climb those stairs. But that would only be a temporary reprieve from the inevitable.

Skirts gathered, Sarah climbed the steps. She didn't get far before she caught sight of Daniel. He had paused in the shadow of one of the columns supporting the roof of the curving portico, waiting for a man to join him. Given the stack of folders tucked beneath the fellow's arm, he must be a lawyer. He slapped Daniel on the back, his confident laughter echoing down to where she stood, frozen, indecisive as to whether to move forward or to turn and flee. Just then, Daniel glanced toward the road and spied Sarah's approach.

"Sarah." He started to head down the steps, but his lawyer grabbed Daniel's elbow and tugged him through the large front doors, deep into the vast dimness of the rotunda's entry hall.

Sarah released a pent-up breath and realized she was shaking. If seeing him outside the courtroom made her quiver from nerves, what was going to happen once they were inside?

"Miss Sarah!" Minnie hailed her, hopping down from another cable car arriving at the curb. She bounded up the stairs to join Sarah, her skirts held high, showing plenty of ankle to a passing, appreciative clerk.

"What are you doing here, Minnie? Doesn't your father need you at the grocery?"

"And leave you to face a judge all alone?" She looked offended. "I wouldn't do that, not after I heard Miss Charlotte was gone to St. Helena this morning. I was hoping, though, some of the others would have shown up by now." She glanced around, as if her searching might cause them to appear.

"It's quite all right." Sarah took her arm. "I've got you. That's more than enough support."

Minnie grinned at the compliment. "Let's go up, then, and show them all, shall we? Because if you've taught me anything, Miss Sarah, it's to face the world head-on."

"Oh, Minnie." She smiled back at the girl, so much more confident than when Sarah had first met her. If she lost it all, she had at least achieved some good, which had to be worth something.

Sarah clutched Minnie's arm and faced forward. "Let's go."

Archibald Jackson was the first person Daniel noticed as he entered the courtroom, and the last one he wanted to acknowledge.

He pushed past the reporter, headed for the chair Sinclair was indicating he should take. "I don't have anything to say to you, Jackson."

"Well, now, Mr. Cady, that's awfully unfriendly. Story surprised you, I guess." He looked around with a smug grin. "Bringing in a crowd today. Don't expect it to go well for her. None of these folks do, either."

"Not after those lies you published."

Jackson lifted his hands. "I'm only the messenger, Mr. Cady, and they're not lies. Don't let a pair of fine brown eyes and a trim figure convince you differently."

Daniel glared in response, but he didn't know who he was madder at—the reporter, Sarah, or himself for being gullible.

The bailiff restrained Jackson from following Daniel to his seat, forcing the reporter to stay behind the railing and find a spot on the benches reserved for the public. Daniel glanced behind him as he settled into the hard wood chair set aside for the plaintiff and caught Jackson's smirking wink.

It wasn't long before Sarah entered the courtroom, the crowd's murmurs rising on a swell tide. She had come with one of the girls, Minnie, who hugged Sarah before taking the nearest spot she could to the defendant's chair. Her lawyer met her at her seat, whispered in her ear. She was pale but composed, nodded a few times. She must be missing Miss Samuelson; Daniel had learned from Sinclair, equally as informed as the waitstaff at the Occidental, that she'd left town. Been forced from town was more likely. The scandal of the story had rippled faster than the circling rings of a pond after a stone had been tossed, and it had ensnared Charlotte Samuelson too. Sarah likely never dreamed her actions would harm her closest friend. In that regard, she'd turned out to be just as thoughtless as Josiah. Maybe that's why they had gotten along so well—they were two peas in a pod.

Judge Doran entered from a side door, a robust man with a heavy chin and thick sideburns, and climbed the steps to his bench.

Sinclair leaned into Daniel. "I'm not anticipating any problems. Doran'll sort out the truth and you'll leave this courtroom very well off, Mr. Cady. Very well off, indeed."

"That's what I hired you for, Sinclair," he said, sourly. The money was what he wanted, wasn't it? The reason he'd spent months searching for Josiah. Not just to keep a promise to his mother and the girls, but to return to Chicago with gold in his pocket, finally able to give his sisters the sort of social acceptance and respectability that came with lots of cash in the bank. There was no need to feel bad for Sarah. No need at all.

Daniel sat rigid in his chair, his spine pressed against the wood slats, as the proceedings got underway. Sinclair presented Daniel's affidavits and recounted the circumstances leading up to his challenge of the probate. He submitted that Josiah Cady had left his children out of his will because he believed them to be deceased, a statement Sarah was forced to confirm, which meant they deserved their rightful portion of his estate. Judge Doran nodded and encouraged Sinclair to continue.

"I also submit, Your Honor," Sinclair proclaimed, tucking his thumbs into his waistcoat pockets, "that Miss Whittier's claims upon Mr. Josiah Cady's estate ought to be reviewed. Especially in light of certain aspects of her character that have brought into question her motives behind tending to Mr. Cady in his final days."

The courtroom buzzed as loud as an angry hive. Sarah flushed. Minnie leaned over the railing and rested a reassuring hand on her shoulder.

Judge Doran gaveled the crowd into silence. "Please clarify what you are suggesting, Mr. Sinclair."

Sinclair scowled as if Sarah were the greatest trickster ever to perpetrate a fraud. "I propose that Miss Whittier coerced Mr. Josiah Cady into naming her the primary beneficiary."

"Do you have proof of such an accusation?" the judge asked. If Sinclair did, she'd never see a penny of Josiah's money and probably be required to pay back Daniel everything she'd already spent. "Any witnesses willing to testify?"

"Her association with a thief has been widely reported, Your Honor."

"She's no thief!" Minnie burst out.

"Quiet now!" Judge Doran grunted his dissatisfaction and dismissed Sinclair's accusation.

The rest of the hearing continued without interruption until the testimony was completed. The judge took a short time to consider the petition Daniel had brought.

They stood to hear the verdict. Daniel noticed Sarah sway like her knees had gone weak. Judge Doran cleared his throat and began to read his conclusions.

The result was as ruinous for Sarah as Daniel had figured it would be.

"Look, the others did show up. What did I tell you?" asked Minnie, nodding toward the street, trying to sound chipper.

The girls waited in a huddle at the base of the broad steps—

Cora, radiant as a flame with her red hair; Emma, stern and solid; Phoebe attempting a smile of encouragement, the effort not completely erasing the tension scrunching her shoulders. They were so precious to Sarah. If the judge could simply see the women his ruling impacted, he might have decided upon a different outcome and ignored the story printed—and now reprinted—in the newspapers.

They waited for Sarah and Minnie to descend to the street. Cora was the first to hug her, but the others crowded in until they surrounded Sarah completely, bulwarks against the storms of the world, secure and safe and so much stronger than she felt right at that moment.

"We wanted to come into the courtroom and speak our piece," Cora explained, once they had squeezed Sarah enough, "but some of us were running late, and the deputy in the hall outside the courtroom didn't much like us trying to push our way in, once the hearing was underway."

"You were there for me in spirit."

"Better to have been there in body, Miss Sarah," Cora asserted, the color in her cheeks as high as the brilliance of her hair. "So's we could tell that judge and that Mr. Cady what we thought of him!"

"What did the judge say, Miss Sarah?" asked Emma, always straight to the point. Much like Anne, if she'd been here.

Sarah swept her gaze to take in all the girls, their impatient expressions. "It could have been worse."

"It was bad enough," said Minnie, dropping her false cheerfulness.

"How bad?" asked Cora, scowling.

"The judge awarded me five hundred of the fifteen hundred dollars I had left in the bank, and he let Mrs. McGinnis keep the thousand that Josiah gave her in his will." Sarah rolled her lips between her teeth. "Given that horrible story in the *Chronicle*, Judge Doran said I didn't even deserve what I got, but since

Josiah had made plain that he intended for me to inherit, he felt obligated to let me have some money. None of the property, though. At least the judge didn't require that I refund what I've already spent on rent and supplies for the shop."

"Five hundred dollars is a fortune," said Cora, who couldn't conceive scraping together ten dollars, let alone fifty times that amount. "We'll do just fine."

"It is not enough," corrected Emma, who had been diligent in learning the shop's accounts. "We need over five thousand a year to pay our bills. We owe rent to Mr. Pomroy and his partners. Miss Sarah owes us wages, and there are debts and taxes to pay. And if no customers come . . ."

"You don't have to give me my salary for a while, Miss Sarah," offered Minnie. "I can do without. I'm still working at the grocery. And the others still have their jobs. We can work part-time at the studio like we've been doing. That'll help, won't it? You'll do that, right, Cora? Emma? Phoebe?"

The others nodded vigorously.

"I can't ask you girls to do that," protested Sarah.

"You're not asking," said Cora. "We're volunteering!"

Sarah smiled her gratitude. *I love these girls so much. But can't they see how improbable our future is?*

"What of the house?" asked Phoebe.

"I have to leave within a week," Sarah answered.

Cora fisted her hips. "Quick to throw you out, ain't he? And I thought Mr. Cady was nice. After saving me from my drowning and all."

"You thought he was handsome, Cora," Minnie chided. "Well, handsome is as handsome does, and he's proven to be a perfect snake in the grass."

"*Chut*." With a sharp elbow, Phoebe jabbed Minnie in the side. "There is Mr. Cady now."

"I don't care if he hears me." She raised her voice. "Daniel Cady is a louse!"

"Minnie, that's enough." Sarah cast a glance over her shoulder. Daniel and his lawyer had exited the building on the far left side, staying as far away from Sarah and the girls as possible. He didn't appear to have heard Cora or notice them. They headed for a waiting cab parked at the curb, Daniel's lawyer, Mr. Sinclair, beaming like a cat who'd lapped the richest cream.

Sarah watched them climb into the carriage and pull away. She would never see him again and never get a chance to ask him if his attentions to her, his seeming concern, had been a pretense. She also would never have the chance to explain to him about Edouard. *Not that he would ever really care.*

"I agree with Minnie," said Cora, entwining her arm through Sarah's free one. "He is a louse. Come to San Francisco to get rich like every other man in this godforsaken town. And for him to take everything away from you, Miss Sarah, who has only worked hard and wanted to help us, is the rottenest thing I've ever heard. He's worse than a louse."

She glared at the carriage as it drove Daniel away.

"We'll forget about him, won't we, Miss Sarah?" asked Minnie, pulling Sarah in even closer.

"Indeed, we shall," she answered, forcing her gaze away from the carriage before she did something silly like cry. "We shall forget."

Carve him out of my heart like he never existed.

"A successful day, Mr. Cady." Sinclair adjusted his top hat and smiled at Daniel, his teeth vividly white in the dim confines of the hired carriage. "How about a celebratory lunch? I know of a restaurant nearby that serves excellent steak, and a glass of wine or two might be in order, as well."

"I don't feel like celebrating, Sinclair."

"Wait, now. You're feeling remorse and that is natural, but you and your sisters are the legal heirs and there's no need to feel guilty over the fact."

"It's not every day I've ruined someone."

"You haven't ruined Miss Whittier." Sinclair reclined into the shadows of his seat. "If she landed on her feet before, she will land on them again."

The carriage rolled clear of the curb. Daniel looked out the window, glimpsing Sarah and her girls, huddled together on the sidewalk. He cared for her. But then he'd cared for Josiah, too, and look where loving that heartless good-for-nothing had gotten him.

Sinclair noticed where his attention was directed. "If she had tended to me on my deathbed, I'd probably give her my entire fortune too." The lawyer chuckled. "Well, her wiles have left her with not much more than a pile of bills and a tarnished reputation. If she were smart, she would hop the first train out of town."

"She would never desert her girls." Not Cora, who liked to sing barroom Irish tunes. Not Minnie, with her friendly manner, or Emma, serious and stern. Or Phoebe, petite and pretty. "She'll stay and stick it out."

"We'll see how long that lasts."

Daniel leaned forward, straining for one last glimpse of Sarah, her straight back, her chestnut hair curling around the edge of her hat, her open and honest face, and wondered at how much he hurt when the hired carriage rounded the corner and she was lost to sight.

"She'll stay," he repeated, certain it was true.

"Humph." Sinclair pointed his hat at Daniel. "You really could use some lunch, Cady. You're white as a sheet. Come have a drink and some decent food. Nothing like a good meal to cure what ails you."

Daniel blinked. Outside, the buildings outside passed in a blur, and the clop of the horse's hooves on cobblestone pounded in his brain. No amount of food or drink was going to cure what ailed him. But it might dull the pain.

He couldn't believe his luck. She was alone in the house tonight. He'd been watching for a while and had seen neither hide nor hair of the woman who worked for her, no smoke rising from the kitchen chimney, no lights at all in the rear of the house. Just her alone.

Frank, my boy, this is going to be as easy as rolling off a log.

He stubbed out his cigar—his final one, come to think of it, but there'd be cigars by the crate once he found that stash of nuggets—took a look around and, satisfied everything was quiet, hoisted himself over the rear fence. Wiping his hands, he grinned up at the upstairs bedroom light shining through cracks in the blinds. Downstairs, all was in darkness. Easy pickings.

From his pants pocket, Frank fished out a brand-new lock pick. He'd lost his old pick in his rush to exit the house last time. He could lose this one and it wouldn't matter, because he wasn't planning on coming back. With his empty hand, he patted the gun tucked into his pants. He'd sold his pocket watch to buy himself a new revolver, in case she came armed again. Frank chuckled. Her little pistol was no match for his Smith & Wesson.

A smirk firmly planted on his face and a rapping amount of confidence puffing his chest, he started across the darkening and empty garden.

Twenty-Six

THE HOUSE WAS QUIET; Rufus ensconced at the foot of the bed; the case clock chiming eleven. Sarah tucked her feet beneath her on her bedroom chair, a book on her lap, as the silence descended like a thick blanket of damp wool. She was worn out, wrung dry of the tears she'd shed today, but couldn't sleep. With few days left to enjoy the house, she didn't want to miss a minute spent beneath its roof.

"What a morose creature I've become," she said to Rufus, who flicked an ear but didn't lift an eyelid.

When she'd come home from the courthouse, she had decided to take leave of all the small treasures that would no longer be hers to enjoy, the tabby following her around until he'd grown bored. She'd listened to the sweet chime of the delicate china mantel clock that was so out of character with Josiah's often gruff demeanor. Examined the painting of the bay that hung in the study. Weighed in her palm his glass paperweight with the tiny fleck of gold at its center, a minute sparkle that Josiah had claimed was the first bit of gold he'd panned. Thumbed through his books. Inhaled the scent of his Spanish cedar cigar box.

She had saved the garden for last, waiting until after her dinner of sliced ham sandwiches to say good-bye to the marble cherub, to the *Rêve d'Or* roses. She'd been tempted to take the garden shears to every one of the lilies and lop off their heads. Daniel Cady probably wouldn't even discover Sarah's trivial act of revenge; once Sarah had moved out of the house, she suspected Daniel would be too busy totting up the value of the items Josiah had left behind to stroll around the garden and take notice. Sarah just hoped there would be space in her future lodgings for her oil portrait of Josiah. She wouldn't leave him behind to a son who had no love for his father.

The candle on the bedside table flickered in a sudden draft. It was growing late. She should go to sleep and get some rest.

Setting down her book, she threw back the soft cotton sheet on her bed, disturbing Rufus, who jumped down with a protesting mewl. Sarah pondered if Daniel would miss a set of bed linens. Or two.

She had just removed her robe and stepped out of her slippers when a noise alerted her. "Ah Mong?"

But Ah Mong wouldn't be creeping around, stealthily creaking floorboards in the dining room. Her heart pounded. Through the bedroom doorway, she could see a faint glow of light reflected up the staircase. Whoever was inside had the audacity to light one of the lanterns.

What could she do? If she poked her head out the bedroom window and screamed, who would hear her? No one lived behind her, because the house in back wasn't finished yet, and Mrs. Brentwood, for all her nosiness, wasn't the sort to come to the aid of a shrieking woman. By the time Mr. Malagisi responded, it would be too late.

She wished she hadn't given back Mrs. Brentwood's pistol. Wished that Ah Mong and his brother—and Daniel—were standing guard tonight. But they weren't. And she was alone.

Sarah grabbed her robe off the end of the bed and shrugged it on. The light in the stairwell had disappeared, suggesting the intruder had ventured into the parlor. She tiptoed down the hallway into her work studio, which lay directly above the room.

Crouching down, she pressed an ear to the iron register covering the vent between the floors. She could hear the scraping of furniture across the floor near the front bay window. If he moved closer, she might be able to see him. But who was it? The burglar couldn't be back; Officer Hanson had thrown him in jail.

She straightened. She couldn't continue to hide upstairs. The man would come looking eventually. It was better to go and meet him on her terms.

Dear Lord.

In the parlor, a piece of furniture crashed to the floor, startling her into action. As Sarah retied her robe, she made certain the red silk hem was high off the ground and out from under her feet, in case she needed to run. Rushing back to her room, she snatched up the heaviest thing she could find—a silver-plated candlestick—and headed down the steps, her slippers slapping against the carpet runner, the sound barely audible above the thump of blood in her ears.

Archibald Jackson might not have been able to induce him to drink, but guilt was doing a mighty fine job.

Daniel, slouched in the most secluded chair in the deepest corner of the Occidental Hotel's main public parlor, listened sourly to the happy chatter of guests descending the marble staircase to the ground floor on their way to the theater and other pleasures, and swirled the amber alcohol in his glass. He wished every one of them an amusing evening. His own festivities had extended well past the lunch he'd shared with Sinclair, landed him in the Occidental's parlor where the drinks appeared to be endless and he had decided to partake. Freely. Tomorrow, he would pay the price.

Sober up, Daniel, and go and talk to her. Ask her what she felt for that man. That French fellow. Do what you've wanted to do since she turned you away at her shop. Ask her if she cared for him.

Cared for you.

"Want another, Mr. Cady?" From out of seemingly nowhere, Red had appeared.

Daniel glanced down at his glass, one-quarter full. He didn't want another drop.

"I want to send a telegram," he said, handing Red the glass. He was overdue in informing his sisters of the outcome of the hearing. He'd delayed that as much as he'd delayed talking to Sarah.

"The office is closed for the evening, sir. But I can bring you a form and see that it's sent first thing in the morning."

"Then that's what I want you to do."

Red scurried off, passing Archibald Jackson strolling through the lounge.

"Well, lookie here." Jackson dropped into a chair at Daniel's left. "Having a few drinks to celebrate your success? You should buy me one. Doran would've given her more if my little story hadn't come out."

"Why are you here? You can't be looking for money from me, now that you've published that rot." Daniel's head started to throb. "So go away."

"I'm dismayed you didn't like it, Mr. Cady. 'A Cautionary Tale of Greed and Immorality.' My editor was impressed." He grinned. "Miss Whittier didn't try to defend herself this morning, which makes her guilty as charged in my book. You should be thanking me that I saved you and your inheritance from her thieving clutches."

"Jackson." Daniel sat up straight. "If you don't leave right now I'm going to turn your head into pulp."

Jackson snorted. "That's a good one, Mr. Cady. You're so drunk, you couldn't see a hole in a ladder. You're not about to turn anyone's head into pulp."

"Want to test me?"

"You are feeling sorry for her, aren't you?" He shook his head. "If you think she's been treated unfairly, why not go over there and ask her again about those nuggets? Bet she didn't beg the judge for a larger share of Josiah Cady's estate because she's got them to fall back on. Her little stash of gold."

Daniel stood, the room seesawing for a moment then righting itself. "I'll do that, Jackson, and prove you wrong."

The secretary lay knocked to the ground, its entire contents scattered at the man's feet. He spun around to face her, stepping on the leather-cased calendar Sarah kept in the top drawer and had yet to pack away, bending the cover. The lantern, which he'd set on the center table, lit his face, his expression as wild as his disheveled muddy-blond hair.

Sarah gasped, confused. He spun about at the sound. "You're in jail," she insisted. But he wasn't in jail. He was back.

"Where is it?"

In his search, he'd overturned Josiah's armchair, the horsehair stuffing leaking through a tear in the underside. The settee was pulled away from the wall, its cushions tumbled onto the floor, and sections of wallpaper had been peeled off to look for hidden compartments, she presumed.

"You already know there's nothing in here—you searched the room last time." Sarah didn't move from the doorway where she could see him and both doors out of the house. The possibility of fleeing gave her a measure of comfort all out of proportion to the reality of the situation. She didn't miss how he rubbed his hand against his side where a gun-sized bump bulged his overcoat. Any second now he'd pull it out. She hugged the candlestick against her chest. "So get out of here."

He eyed the candlestick and chuckled. What a feeble weapon it made against a man of his size. "Thinking to scare me off with that?"

"There are no gold nuggets, no cash anywhere in the house."

"And what if I said I don't believe you?" He kicked the books and papers aside and lumbered across the room. He drew close, almost treading on her toes. He stank as though he'd slept in a gutter after dropping a full bottle of liquor on his coat. "Annie always claimed you were decent and I'm disappointed yer lyin' to me."

The pieces fell into place. Anne and her warnings to be careful. Her man who was so dangerous. "You're Frank."

"That I am." He leaned down. His breath smelled as bad as the rest of him. "And I still want to know where that hidey-hole is. And don't tell me there isn't one, because I know the Irishman who put it in."

"There isn't any gold in any 'hidey-hole.'"

"I say there is gold. Even that reporter thinks there is, asking all his questions. So I think you"—he jabbed her in the chest with his fist, grabbed the candlestick from her grasp, and threw it across the room, extinguishing the flame—"need to show me exactly where."

Pain streaked through Sarah's ribs, causing her to gasp for air.

"Search wherever you want. I won't stop you. I don't own the house anymore and don't care what happens to it." She did care about Josiah's beautiful house and all his beautiful possessions, but if Frank believed she wouldn't interfere, maybe he wouldn't hurt her. "Josiah has a safe in his upstairs study. I'll take you to it." She was about to repeat that there wasn't a treasure inside, but figured Frank wouldn't believe her any more now than before.

He thrust his chin toward the staircase and retrieved the lantern. "Lead the way." When she hesitated to turn her back to him, he tapped the bulge in his coat.

Sarah hurried up the stairs as quick as her quivering legs would take her, wanting to keep a safe distance from Frank. His boots thumped on the treads, and he grunted when he reached the landing.

"Maybe I should have a look-see around the other rooms up here too." He peered into the shadows beyond the circle of light cast by the lantern. The door to her room stood ajar, as did the one to her work studio, the crates hulking shapes in the dark. She couldn't bear to think of him breaking them open and possibly destroying the contents within.

"In here," she said, indicating the study. "The safe is in here."

Unlatching the door, Sarah went inside. Frank surged ahead of her.

Setting the lantern on the desk, he issued a low whistle, admiring the fine furnishings, the floor-to-ceiling bookshelves. "Well, ain't this a fancy room? Annie told me it was nice here, but she never said how nice."

Sarah skirted Frank, hulking in the center of the room. "Let me unlock the safe and show you it contains nothing of interest to you. It's mostly insurance policies and property deeds. Some account books too." About a month after Josiah had died, she'd removed the few hundred dollars stored within and taken the money to the bank.

She dialed the combination and turned the handle.

"Here." Frank bumped her aside. "I'll check what's inside on my own."

He scanned the papers, discarding one after another onto the floor, followed by ledger books and a handful of correspondence he'd kept with Uncle Henry in Los Angeles. The longer Frank's hunt came up empty, the angrier he got.

"There's nothing in here!" The last of the papers fluttered to the carpet.

Sarah's heart pounded. She retreated toward the door. She should flee, but how far could she get? "There is no treasure."

His face and neck red with fury, Frank lurched over to the bookshelves and tossed book after book behind him. Sarah jumped out of the way to keep from being struck.

"Nothin'." With a sweep of his arm, Frank sent an entire row of science journals flying. "Nothin'. Nothin'."

"I tried to tell you."

"There has to be somethin'." He turned to the desk and yanked drawers off their runners. "There's always somethin'. Too much talk not to be."

Frank jerked open another drawer, rattling the desk. He swept Grace Cady's photograph onto the floor. Josiah's glass paperweight tumbled off the surface and thudded against the baseboard where it cracked. He was ruining everything.

Sarah rushed across the room and grabbed Frank's arm. "Stop. Stop it!"

He slung her off and reached for the center drawer. It crashed to the floor, the locked box landing atop Grace Cady's photograph. "What's this?"

Frank raised Josiah's leaded crystal inkwell. "No, don't!" Sarah shouted.

He smashed the box's lid. Two bundles of letters, tied with pink ribbons, and a small well-thumbed Bible fell out. Sarah stared. Those were the contents of the locked box?

"This is it?" Frank cursed and glowered at Sarah. She was trembling so much she feared her legs would collapse beneath her.

"That's it."

His gaze narrowed. "Well, I think we just need to keep lookin'."

Grabbing Sarah by the neck of her robe, he hauled her out of the room.

Daniel pitched the fare to the cab driver and scanned the windows of Sarah's house, light visible through chinks in the study blinds. She hadn't gone to bed yet. *Thank heavens*.

"Do you want me to wait, sir?" the driver asked, his coat collar snug against his chin. He didn't look happy about the prospect of waiting in the chilly night air for an intoxicated passenger.

"I don't know how long I'll be. Go ahead and leave."

The driver touched fingertips to hat brim and drove off. Sucking in the cool air to help clear his head, Daniel climbed the steps. A shadow separated itself from the house next door, turned into a slim boy wearing a blue tunic.

He loped across the grass separating the two houses. "I am happy you are here, Mr. Cady, sir."

"Isn't it a tad late to be hanging around on porches, Ah Mong?"

"I heard noise and I think . . . I know that man has come back."

"What man?" Daniel asked, his brain not functioning as well as it ought. *I'll never touch another drop of liquor again*. "What are you talking about?"

"That man who broke into Miss Sarah's house. He is here again."

"He's supposed to be in prison. He can't be here." He wasn't so drunk he'd misunderstood Ah Mong, though. His heart began to race.

Ah Mong shook his head violently enough to set his braid to swinging. "I saw him. I am not wrong."

"But Sarah . . ." He looked up at the house. Were there two shadows in the study? "She's in there. With him."

Daniel rushed the steps two at a time, Ah Mong matching his pace. Daniel pulled off his coat and wrapped it around his fist, preparing to smash in the door glass.

"I have the key, Mr. Cady. You do not need to break the door." From deep within a hidden pocket of his loose trousers, Ah Mong produced a key. "Mrs. McGinnis left it with me before she got on the boat."

They crept inside. "I don't have a lantern," said Daniel, listening for noise. He heard raised voices upstairs and the thud of objects hitting the floor.

Then came Sarah's shouts and he didn't stop to listen for any more. "Get the police, Ah Mong." He reached for the railing and rushed up the stairs.

Frank punched the heel of his boot through the crate filled with her paints, splintering wood.

"This is my studio, my things!" Sarah cried, huddled by the door. "There isn't anything you'd want in here!"

"And I think there is!" he spat, slapping her hard across the face.

She stumbled sideways, dizzy, her cheek burning. *He's going to kill me. I am not ready to die, Lord. Save me. Help me. Please.*

Tears clouded her vision. "There aren't any nuggets—"

She didn't finish the sentence as Daniel charged into the room, launching himself at Frank. Frank screeched, a howl of anger, followed by an explosion, the flash of gunpowder. Searing pain knocking her backward.

And blackness.

Twenty-Seven

THE PISTOL SHOT WAS DEAFENING, stunning Daniel for a moment. The intruder gaped at Sarah as she fell backward, her arm grazing Daniel, her head striking the broken end of a packing crate.

"Sarah!" Daniel screamed, dropping to his knees beside her. He pulled aside her robe. Beneath her rib cage, a stain of red spread across the chemise, but she was still breathing. "Sarah."

The intruder fumbled with his revolver. The cylinder had jammed. Daniel jumped up and lunged for him, knocking him against one of the tables in the room, the pistol flying from his hand. "I'll kill you! I'll kill you!"

Ah Mong ran into the room. "Miss Sarah!"

In the moment Daniel's attention was drawn to the boy, the intruder broke free from his grasp and staggered toward the doorway.

"Ah Mong, stay with her." Daniel gave chase. The man took the stairs two at a time, down through the hallway and the dining room, out the kitchen door into the garden. *If I catch him, I'll kill him. I'll kill him.*

Daniel charged out into the pitch-black garden and spotted the man headed for the rear wall. "Stop!"

He briefly looked back at Daniel and made an astonishing

leap, considering his bulk, his hands grasping the top. If he managed to pull himself over, Daniel would probably lose him.

Daniel grabbed the man's legs and held. He kicked at Daniel, a boot heel striking him in the chest. Next door, lantern light turned the yard golden and the neighbor shouted.

"Get a doctor!" Daniel yelled, not risking a glance toward Mr. Malagisi. He gave a forceful tug, felt the intruder's hold on the wood slip.

"There's one down the street," Mr. Malagisi shouted back.

The lantern light vanished, plunging the garden into darkness. Daniel struggled to hold on to the man's boot. He shouldn't be out here. He should be with Sarah.

Blasted whiskey. He couldn't think straight at all.

The man kicked again, this time catching Daniel full on the chin, shooting pain through his jaw and head. He stumbled and let go.

The man scrambled over the fence, dropping into the empty lot behind. Daniel inhaled, forcing the pain away, and leaped for the top of the wall as well. He missed the first time, but at the second try, he secured a hold. Jerking himself upward, he spotted the man running toward the street just as two police officers, their whistles trilling, brought him to a halt.

Waves of dizziness churned her stomach. She wanted to throw up. She wanted the pain, the burning pain, in her side to go away. She inhaled and it hurt, and her head felt as though it would cleave in half. Where was she? The space around her was dimly lit, shapes casting shadows. Was she dead? Would her side hurt if she was dead?

Running feet pounded somewhere nearby. And then someone was sliding hands over her head, her side, her arms.

"Sarah? Sarah, I'm here. The doctor will be here soon. Rest easy. Don't move." The voice was frantic, the touch, brisk. She wanted him to go away because he was making her head hurt worse, making the nausea rise to choke her throat. "Do you insist on running into trouble all the time? First you try to drown, now you go ahead and get shot." His face came in and out of focus. Dark hair, green eyes. She recognized him, vaguely, but couldn't recall a name. All she felt was pain and dizziness. "Sarah, stay awake. Say something. You have to be all right. For your girls. For all of us. You have to live because I haven't given you that wretched thousand dollars yet!"

"Unh."

There were more footsteps, and lantern light that made her recoil. "Mr. Cady!" a woman screeched. "Miss Whittier! Oh my. Oh my!"

The light wobbled. She wished it would go away too.

"Mrs. Brentwood, bring the doctor here quickly." The man bending over her was insistent, and his hand had found a cloth to press to her side. The pain. It was excruciating.

"He's coming. Oh. Oh."

"Don't faint here. Go out into the hall," he ordered. "Sarah. Dear God."

His voice, his face grew faint. There were more footsteps, more voices. One, commanding and deep, drew near. "Step aside, young man. I have her from here."

Her eyelids fluttered as strong hands prodded. And then she remembered no more.

Daniel paced the length of the hallway outside Sarah's room and yawned into his hand. The doctor had chased him off last night, audibly sniffing at Daniel and scowling over his drunken condition. But the doctor wasn't here to chase him off this morning. Ah Mong had answered the door to a miserable Daniel, glowering over an infernal headache.

I will never *drink again*.

Minnie stepped into the hall, closing the bedroom door behind her. She looked surprised to see him there. "Mr. Cady."

"How is she?"

"Still asleep but less restless, I'd say. Phoebe, who seems to know about these things, says it's good she hasn't been feverish." Minnie glanced back at the door. "But I keep thinking it would be better if she'd just wake up."

"Maybe I can go in and check—"

Minnie put out a hand. "The doc said to keep you out. He said"—a smile flitted over her lips—"that you're just too ornery and loud. You were a bit drunk last night, Mr. Cady."

She didn't have to tell him. A double dose of headache powders had barely dented his suffering. "He did say she was going to be all right, didn't he?"

The smile stuck this time. "Indeed he did. Said the bullet really only grazed her side, didn't even touch bone, and she's mostly bothered by her concussion, which is best cured by rest and time. Thankfully, because I would've hated the thought of her having to go to the hospital."

"That is good to hear." He gazed longingly at the door over her shoulder.

"You can't go in, Mr. Cady. You know, I'd say you need to keep busy. Perhaps you should tidy her workroom and maybe Mr. Josiah's study too," she suggested, nodding toward a room at the opposite end of the hall. "That wretched Frank Burke made a mess of everything."

"You'll let me know as soon as she wakes up," said Daniel.

"Absolutely. And while you're at it, can you look for the cat? I can't find him anywhere! He must have run off in all the ruckus."

"He'll come back. He's got it too good here not to," Daniel assured her, pretty certain he was talking about Rufus. And not himself.

At the end of the hall, Sarah's studio looked like a whirlwind had struck. Daniel picked a half-finished pencil sketch off the floor. A study of roses so finely done it had to be Sarah's work. Daniel set the sketch on the nearest worktable, stacked supplies, those that weren't smashed beyond usefulness, alongside. He shoved bits of shattered packing crates into one corner. At least the revolver was gone, picked up by the police last night.

The doctor had known right away that Sarah's gunshot wound wasn't serious, but when Daniel had seen all that blood, he hadn't been so certain. He'd thought, instead, that he might lose her.

Daniel flung a piece of broken slat onto the pile. Frankly, Sarah Whittier was too stubborn to die. As pigheaded as she was, she would bound out of that bed in no time, gather her girls around her, and try to open that shop. Determined to the end.

And he wouldn't want her to be any different.

Daniel put his back to the worktable and stared out the window at another beautiful San Francisco morning. He couldn't stay here. He didn't want to leave. But back in Chicago a pair of ten-year-old twins were waiting for him to return home, and Sarah was equally committed to her girls and their futures. Duty. They were both willingly chained to it.

Daniel glanced across the hallway to his father's study. Another duty to face in a room that had more to do with Josiah than a carved headstone in a cemetery.

Slowly, he pushed the door open. The sweet scent of cigar smoke rushed like a tide over Daniel, flooding him with memories. How could the space still breathe of Josiah? He went inside, stepping over a handful of magazines blocking the way. Books and papers were scattered everywhere, and writing implements leaked ink onto the rug. The door to a wall safe hung open, its contents tossed to the ground. Daniel picked up an inkwell, righted the reading lamp that had occupied a corner table, straightened a painting that hung at a crooked angle. Even with the mess, Daniel could see what the room had once been—a recreation of the study Josiah had favored at Hunt House, only smaller in scale.

The blasted man had left Chicago but taken part of it with him. Just like the lilies in the garden.

"How dare you?" Daniel asked the space, grabbing up papers by the handful and stacking them on the desk, shoving books randomly onto empty shelves. Josiah couldn't have cared, he couldn't have wanted to remember, when seemingly all he'd ever done was try to forget.

Beneath a pile of correspondence shoved into a corner, a bit of gold winked at him. Daniel picked it up, a lone gold nugget, smaller in size than the tip of his little finger. It must have fallen out of something while the burglar was ransacking the room and gone unnoticed by the man.

Daniel lifted the nugget to the sunlight coming through the slats in the window blinds. "Not much of a treasure, Josiah. Worth all of twenty dollars, I'd guess." But enough gold, apparently, to set off a firestorm of rumors and speculation.

Daniel placed the nugget in the center of the desk. On the floor near the desk's chair, he noticed a long, flat box with a shattered lid. There were letters within, as well as a tidily wrapped set spilled out onto the floor, the pink ribbon enwrapping them as bright as the day it had been tied. Daniel picked them up. He recognized the handwriting.

"Josiah."

He gathered all of the letters together. Some were written in his father's scrawling hand, but many others were covered in the neat, even loops of his mother's penmanship. At the bottom of the box was a faded telegram.

Settling into the chair, Daniel opened the letters and read, one after the other, reliving the most painful year of his life. But once he got to the telegram, that pain was replaced by an even fiercer anger.

Daylight was blinding, squashing any desire Sarah might have to open her eyes and try to figure out what she was doing in bed, her head pounding, her side swathed in bandages.

"Miss Sarah!"

Sarah pried open an eyelid at the sound of Minnie's voice. Minnie sprang from the chair next to the bed and leaned over. Her hair curled messily around her face and her dress was wrinkled as if she'd been sitting there a long time. But her face was wreathed in smiles. "Miss Sarah! Oh, thank goodness, you're awake at last! And never any fever!"

On the other side of the bed, Phoebe smiled. "I told you, Minnie. We keep the wound clean and there will be no cause to worry."

"What am I doing here?" Sarah asked, every word feeling like a blacksmith's strike against an anvil in her head.

"You were shot last night. Don't you remember? By Frank Burke."

"Shot?" That would explain the bandages. "But my head . . ." She probed the back of her skull and found a tender lump. "I can't remember what happened to me."

"When Mr. Cady came to rescue you and that Frank shot you in the tussle, you fell backward and struck your head on the edge of a crate." Minnie exchanged looks with Phoebe, who nodded. "The doc says you were concussed."

"Oh." Sarah tried to scoot higher on the pillows, but the motion set off throbbing in her temples and a rush of dizziness. "I'm afraid I don't understand why Mr. Cady was here to rescue me. And what do you mean about Frank?"

Minnie and Phoebe took turns explaining what they'd learned had happened last night, that Anne's man had come to rob Sarah again and that Mr. Cady, like some avenging angel, had interrupted him, but not before he'd shot Sarah. The police caught Frank when he tried to run off, though, and he was locked away. They'd also heard that Mrs. Brentwood had shrieked and cried yet had managed to help the doctor carry Sarah into her bedroom, right before she collapsed in a dead faint on the parlor settee. The two girls giggled over that.

"Is Mr. Cady here?" asked Sarah. "I'd like to thank him."

"I'll tell him you want to see him," said Minnie. "He's been pacing like a caged animal."

Minnie left the door open as she went to fetch Daniel, and it wasn't long before Sarah heard hurrying footsteps and he burst into the room. Minnie gestured for Phoebe to come with her and leave them alone. Daniel inspected Sarah for injury as if he couldn't believe she was alive and awake.

"Sarah," he said, sitting on the bed, his weight sagging the mattress. He carried a stack of letters, which he deposited on the bedside table, and gathered one of her hands in his. His touch was comforting, whether he meant it to be or not.

I could never carve him out of my heart.

"For a moment last night I thought the worst," he said. "I'm glad to see you're all right."

"The girls told me what happened, because I can't seem to remember much," she said, searching his face for some emotion deeper than anxiety. "And I don't understand how you knew Frank was here."

"I didn't." Daniel's thumb swept across the back of her hand, causing her skin to tingle. "I was busy being stupid at the Occidental when that reporter came along and goaded me into asking you, one last time, about the nuggets."

"Ah." That rumor could have killed her. "Satisfied, Mr. Cady?"

He lifted an eyebrow and she thought of Josiah. "Actually, Miss Whittier, there was some gold."

"There was?"

"A nugget about the size of a cherry pit. It was on the floor in the study," he explained. "Frank Burke missed finding the treasure he was searching for."

"Those stories about gold nuggets weren't completely wrong."

"It seems not." He glanced over at the letters he'd brought

into the room. "But I was completely wrong about other things." His gaze returned to her face, and his expression was somber. "Sarah, I need to go to Chicago."

Her heart contracted. "I know you need to go back to Chicago, Daniel." That had always been his plan. But she'd hoped that his actions last night, how gently he held her hand, meant those plans might have changed.

"I mean I need to leave as soon as I can. If I hurry, I can make this afternoon's three o'clock train." He frowned and took another look at the letters. "There's business I have to attend to. With my grandfather."

She could hear the anger in his voice. The emotion was never far from the surface for him. "Your sisters will be happy to see you."

"It's because of them that I need to go. They've been living with a lie. We've all been living with a lie." He stood, his hand still wrapped around hers. She resisted the temptation to cling. "You have two very capable nurses out there in the hallway. You'll be all right."

Was he saying that to reassure her, or himself? "I'm sure I'll be up and about in no time."

"I never had a doubt, Miss Whittier." Another brief smile that never reached his eyes. "If you want, I'll send you a telegram letting you know I've arrived safely."

"Only if that's what you want to do. You don't owe me anything, Daniel Cady," she said. She wouldn't beg to hear from him or shed tears of longing. Other women might, but not her. He wouldn't expect her to, either.

Daniel slipped his hand from hers, and she felt every finger as it relinquished its hold. *How many times can my heart break, God?*

Many times, it seemed.

"I shall be back, you know."

Did she? Did she know that at all? "Take good care."

"Read those letters." He nodded toward the stack. "They'll explain."

Hesitating, he brushed a hand across her forehead, tucking a strand of hair behind her ear, then turned and strode out of the room.

Minnie rushed in after he was gone. "Have you two worked everything out between you?" She lifted her brows expectantly, as if Sarah might announce they were set to be wed and all their problems taken care of.

Sarah couldn't think about that, think about him if she didn't want to bawl in front of the girl. "Minnie, help me sit up. I need to do some reading. And if you could, bring me some tea."

Her face fell. "Is Mr. Cady leaving, then?"

"He has business to attend in Chicago."

"What? The louse." More roughly than she intended, Minnie hoisted Sarah into a sitting position against the pillows. "And to think I was actually starting to like him."

Sarah fanned Grace Cady's letters across her bedspread. Josiah had kept them secreted away like the treasure he must have felt they were. The item he was guarding someplace that Mrs. McGinnis had told Sarah about. She touched the nearest, like the rest, a missive of love to a distant husband. Grace's affection for Josiah was unmistakable in every note as she described how much she missed him, her arms aching for his embrace, her eyes always searching the road, her ears always listening for his voice, his laughter, her body yearning for the warmth of his in the bed next to her at night. Told him that she read his letters to their children, regaling them with his funny stories about his fellow prospectors, his breathless descriptions of the wide-open West, his excitement at finding gold and knowing his earnings would bring him home one day soon.

Which, in the end, they hadn't done.

On a whim, Sarah lifted the nearest letter from Grace and inhaled. The paper smelled of tuberose, and here and there, the ink was smeared as though teardrops had fallen upon the words. Whether they'd been Grace's tears or Josiah's, Sarah couldn't tell.

The second bundle was smaller, just a few letters that Josiah had written to Grace and her parents, the Addison Hunts, innocuous short missives that detailed travel plans, bank account numbers, and little else. Not the letters Grace would have faithfully read to Daniel and Lily and Marguerite by lamplight. Those had disappeared.

She picked up the telegram that had been at the bottom of the stack, a faded Western Union dated the summer of 1875. It had been sent from Chicago to Josiah in Placerville, eventually finding him at his mining claim in Grass Valley. A yellowing memento of a horrible lie.

Regret to inform you that my daughter and your children have died from the influenza. No need to return. They are buried. A.H.

Died from the influenza. No wonder Josiah had told everyone his family was gone. No wonder Josiah's eyes had always been shadowed with pain and regret.

Sarah reread the telegram again and again, but the words didn't change. What sort of man lied to his son-in-law about such a thing? What sort of man was Addison Hunt that he could be so vile? Forcing Josiah to live with a loss that wasn't real. Forcing Daniel and his sisters and their mother to believe Josiah preferred life without them, when that was utterly untrue. Setting Daniel on a path to revenge that had stripped Sarah of all she'd come to own. Had Addison Hunt despised Josiah, a rough and restless soul, that much?

He must have. And then returned the few letters he'd found in the Hunt mansion along with a terse note from some Chicago solicitor requesting that Mr. Josiah Cady refrain from further contacting the Hunts. The note and the telegram explained why Daniel was rushing to return to Chicago. Why an old anger had found a fresh target.

She tidied the stack of letters, retied the pink ribbon, folded the telegram closed, shutting out the words. So much hurt in that stack of paper resting on the bed, no thicker than a dictionary or a Bible, yet big enough to destroy dreams and fuel revenge. Fuel hatred in a son's heart, hatred that had now turned to a grandfather who had deceived, leaving no space for love.

No room at all for Sarah.

Twenty-Eight

"Mr. Daniel?"

The maid answering the door blinked at him like she was seeing a ghost. Maybe she'd thought he would never come back to Chicago. Maybe everyone at Hunt House was rather wishing he had gone for good. "Good morning, Susan."

"Sir." She retreated to let him enter the foyer.

Daniel lifted his hat from his head and looked around. He hadn't stepped foot inside this house for years, but the entry hall hadn't changed one bit. Beneath the double staircases arcing up to the second floor landing, the parquet floor was waxed as ever to the sheen of a mirror, and the walnut foyer table groaned beneath a massive china vase filled with roses and ferns from the garden. The space smelled of polish and flowers and hollowness. Nothing had changed at all.

Except, perhaps, his own heart.

"I'm here to see my grandfather," he said to the maid, staring at him.

"I will tell him, sir, that you wish to speak to him in the library."

"Thank you, Susan. I remember where it is. You don't need to show me there."

His grandfather's library lay beyond the stairs and down a

short hallway. From the kitchen, angled off to the right at the end, came the smells of luncheon being prepared. He wouldn't be invited to stay.

The double pocket doors stood open, and Daniel went through. The green velvet curtains, fringed in gold, were closed, making the room appear even darker than normal. Daniel strode across the thick carpet, throwing them open with a rattle of curtain rings, letting in the sunlight. Neither the view of the side garden or the morning sunshine did much to brighten the dark paneled walls or the black leather sofas and armchairs arranged around the room, or lessen the oppressive presence of the glass-fronted bookcases towering higher than Daniel. But the sunlight did manage to illuminate the portrait of his mother that hung over the marble fireplace mantel. The only warm spot in a cold room.

Daniel walked over to it. The painting had been completed when Grace was a young woman, before she and Josiah had married. She wore a dress of vivid blue that belled out from a tiny waist, and her blonde hair was arranged into two coils at the side of an unlined and happy face. Grandfather likely wanted to remember her before the taint of a Cady had entered their lives.

He took her from you, Josiah. And, by pursuing a dream in California, you let him.

"You've come back."

Daniel hadn't heard his grandfather's footsteps, and the man caught him by surprise. "I never claimed I wouldn't."

Age hadn't stooped Addison Hunt, and he still carried himself like a man who was used to getting his way. His even-featured face had given Daniel's mother some of her beauty, but the deep lines that bracketed his mouth had not come from a lifetime of smiling, as hers had.

"I suppose I imagined you would stay out in San Francisco with your newfound wealth," his grandfather said, making a wide circuit of the room until his back was to the window, casting his face in shadows.

"Like Josiah?" Daniel asked, aware that was what his grandfather implied.

The other man inclined his head. "The sum was not as much as you anticipated, I take it, and now you're looking for a handout."

"I haven't come back to beg you for a job, Grandfather," he answered, crushing the brim of his hat in his fist.

His grandfather folded his arms. "So what are you here for?"

Daniel strode up to him, standing close enough to see the dark rimming his grandfather's irises. He realized he could look into those gray eyes and no longer be intimidated by the man behind them.

"I found the telegram you sent my father," Daniel said, old anger rising and then, miraculously, dissipating as if it had never been felt. He'd spent a lot of time reflecting during a long train ride east, and his heart was no longer willing to hold on to the pain. "The one that told him we were dead."

His grandfather didn't blink. "You're here hoping for an apology."

"No, not an apology." Daniel knew better than to hope for the impossible. "An explanation."

"It's simple. Josiah Cady was an opportunist who married your mother in order to obtain her money. My money. But she didn't see his ambitions or his weaknesses. All she saw was a handsome fellow who knew how to flatter her. I wanted him out of her life for good."

"Your strategy failed. She never stopped loving Josiah like you hoped she would, did she? And he never stopped loving her, as far as I can tell." Daniel believed it, now. "*Beloved Friend.*" *I wish I'd been there to say good-bye, Father.* "Or stopped loving my sisters and me."

"The only thing Josiah Cady ever cared about was gold," Grandfather scoffed. "That was his first and only mistress. He was a flashy sort who'd been lucky once or twice in the gold fields and thought that meant he was a Midas. Instead of just another overly optimistic dreamer." He regarded Daniel with contempt. "And you were growing up to be exactly like him—headstrong, reckless. I saved you more than once from your own stupidity, Daniel. Fights, unpaid debts, the wrong sort of friends. One worthless job after another."

"Those jobs were the best I could find, given that I had to watch over the girls when Grace got sick."

"Worthless work for a worthless man. Just like your father," he insisted, spitting venom.

"Leave Josiah out of this," Daniel retorted, defending Josiah like his mother might have done. He'd had a *lot* of time to think on that train. "He's gone and doesn't deserve your enmity anymore. Never did."

"Oh, I see. Now Josiah Cady is some sort of saint."

Daniel ignored the provocation. "I almost became what you tried to make me, Grandfather. A man full of hatred, convinced that wealth would make me valuable, consumed with getting what I thought the world owed me . . . rather like you, if you think about it."

His grandfather's look was black. "You are no longer welcome here, Daniel Cady."

"That's quite all right, because I don't intend to ever ask for welcome again." Daniel secured his hat on his head. "I'm sorry we have to part like this, Grandfather. If you hadn't despised my father, things could have been different between us."

His grandfather had no answer, and Daniel turned to leave.

"I shall cut you off without a penny," his grandfather pronounced.

Daniel paused in the doorway. "You've always threatened to do that, and honestly"—he smiled, which turned his grandfather's neck red—"I no longer care."

"*Och*, I'm glad I returned early, I am." Mrs. McGinnis wiped her brow with a handkerchief then stashed it away in a pocket in her skirt. "But what a sad, sad day."

From the level of the street, Sarah gazed at the house, the afternoon breeze cooling her flushed skin. She didn't need to stand there to memorize every angle, every turn of wood, because she would never forget what the house looked like nor what it meant to her. Would it touch the next owners like it had her? Or would they see only its lovely bay windows and elaborate decorations, knowing nothing of the heartbroken man who'd built it, unaware he'd been deceived by his father-in-law? Would they even care to learn about Josiah, or be solely interested in the size of the front parlor or if the dining room could hold enough people for a respectable supper party?

Ah Mong carried her Turkish rug out through the front door and down the stairs to a wagon waiting at the curb. He passed Cora, rushing up the steps to fetch another crate. Minnie fussed over the moving company men, berating them to be careful packing the cargo. Sarah wished she could assist, but the doctor had said a week wouldn't be long enough recuperation from her bullet wound to start lifting boxes and crates. She couldn't wait any longer to move out. Tomorrow, the real estate agent would come and begin the auction.

"Is that all?" one of the moving company men asked Minnie, rearranging Josiah's portrait, wrapped in sheets of paper and a tattered old blanket found in the attic.

"Just about," she answered.

Sarah's entire belongings occupied but a quarter of the wagon bed. She'd be departing the house on Nob Hill with not much more than when she'd first arrived.

"It is a very sad day, Mrs. McGinnis," Sarah said, blinking to stop tears from falling. "I will miss this place."

"We'll find our way. The Lord will guide us and we'll find our way."

"I hope so." Sarah glanced at the sky, clear and blue, as if she might spot Him there, ready to lead her. All she saw was a bird whirling on a current of air.

Mrs. McGinnis patted Sarah's arm. "I'm going to see how they're doing in the kitchen. Don't want anyone packing pots or pans Mr. Cady might claim belong to him." She scanned the street and the yard. "If only that daft cat would show up. Doesna feel right leaving without the wee beastie."

She hustled off just as a man strode up the road. Sarah squinted at him. It wasn't Daniel, who hadn't sent a telegram, even though he'd likely arrived in Chicago by now. Hastily, she reminded herself not to think about him, lest she cry for certain.

The man spotted her staring and he waved his hat, the sunlight reflecting off his balding head.

Sarah frowned. What could he want?

"Miss Tha . . . oh, very sorry, Miss Whittier. Slip of the tongue." The reporter grinned, making an elaborate bow before tapping his hat back on. "An unhappy day for you, I suppose."

"Do you intend to write an article about my grief, Mr. Jackson? I would have thought you'd exhausted any curiosity about me."

"Now, now, can't a man simply be interested in checking that you're recovering from your injuries?" He nudged her arm. "I do wonder what the next occupants would think if they knew about all the gunplay in this charming house. Hope you've cleaned up the blood."

"Thank you, we have." The secretary still bore a chink from a gunshot, though.

"They've set a hearing for Frank Burke in a couple of weeks, by the way. Seems they've composed a lengthy list of crimes, beyond your little burglary and shooting. Receiving stolen goods. A pile of unpaid bills to some rough customers. A fistfight here or there. A theft up on Russian Hill." The reporter contemplated the house as Emma carried what had to be the final box onto the porch. "Don't expect there'll be any trouble convicting him. He'll be locked up for a good while."

"Thank you for letting me know." In the end, there might be justice for Anne.

He flashed a larger grin and bowed again. He was the most ridiculous fellow. "I hear—I have good sources, Miss Whittier—he hasn't stopped ranting about those nuggets, though. Insists that some Irishman he knows wouldn't have lied to him about Mr. Cady wanting to hide some gold. He also claims his woman would have discovered the location from you if she'd had a little more time."

Sarah peered at him. "I don't understand. Do you mean that Anne Cavendish was helping Frank Burke in some way?"

"Seems so, Miss Whittier. She was feeding him all sorts of information, like the fact that your benefactor had been to the Black Hills and struck it rich with his partner. Information Mr. Burke was happy to share with me in exchange for a few silver coins." Jackson puffed out his chest. "Didn't take much looking on my part to find out the name of that partner and where he lived. And that you were connected to him. Which led to a much more interesting tale than the stories about a stash of gold in your house."

"Daniel Cady didn't tell you about my family in Los Angeles."

Jackson guffawed. "That killjoy? He went on about honor and not writing about you." He shrugged. "I ignored him."

She'd been horribly wrong about Daniel and misled by Anne. Sarah had trusted her, never imagining one of her girls might be a potential thief. She'd warned Sarah to be careful, though, more than once. But she'd been too afraid of Frank to confess her role. Poor Anne.

"I should tell you, Mr. Jackson, that there was some hidden gold," she said, noticing how his eyes lit at the possibility of a fresh tidbit of news. "One lone nugget small enough to fit into a thimble. Not much of a treasure to warrant all the gossip it stirred or your interest in Josiah Cady and me."

The reporter pressed a palm to his chest. "You have my deepest regrets for any trouble I might have caused you," he said, failing to sound sincere. "However, it's not too late to tell your side of the story about your escapade in Los Angeles."

"Edouard Marchand stole from my uncle and I didn't help him. That's all of the story you need to know."

"If you ever change your mind—"

"I won't." She was sick to death of gold and the greed it bred in men's hearts, what that greed persuaded them to do. "I won't because I don't want to think about Edouard Marchand or Frank Burke or gold nuggets ever again."

"They're out in the garden." Mirabeth Gray motioned for Daniel to come into the house, shutting the door behind him. As he passed her, he caught a whiff of her rose-oil perfume and recalled another woman whose hair smelled of roses. "They'll be so happy you're home."

"And I'm glad to be back." Even though Chicago no longer felt as much like home as it used to, not when his heart lay elsewhere. "You're looking well, Mirabeth."

She smiled and brushed a hand over the swell of her abdomen hidden by her checked cotton gown. "I'm glad to have an excuse not to wear a corset for a few months." She gestured down the hall toward the kitchen. "Would you like some tea or lemonade? A bite of something to eat?"

"I hate to impose on your hospitality for too long, especially after taking care of the girls for all these months."

"Pooh. They're no bother at all." She shushed him with a flick of her fine-boned hands.

"But it's time they go. As soon as they can pack their things, I'll get them out of here."

"No rushing off, Daniel Cady. I insist you stay for dinner." Mirabeth said, grabbing his wrist as if he might escape right then if she didn't hold on to him. "Michael will be furious with me if I let you leave without feeding you. Besides, we want to hear about your trip." Her warm eyes softened. "I'm sorry about your father, by the way."

"I am too. I didn't get a chance to . . ." Daniel inhaled to loosen the tightness in his throat. "I didn't get a chance to say good-bye to him, and I wish I had."

Her eyebrows lifted. "That's a change."

"It's a long story, Mirabeth." Somewhere between San Francisco and Chicago, he'd forgiven Josiah for being a dreamer. He believed he'd even be able to forgive his grandfather for being a cold, hard man. *Forgive, Daniel. Forgive.* His mother had been right and he, so wrong. The only person he'd hurt with his resentment and anger had been himself.

And Sarah.

He smiled at Mirabeth. "A long and boring story. But I'll stay for a meal and tell you about the Wild West, if you insist, and about a few of the folks I met out there."

She tilted her head, examining him. "I'd love to hear about all of it. And about who it is who's taken the hurt from your eyes."

His smile broadened; they'd known each other a long time. "Mirabeth, you tell that husband of yours that he's a lucky man."

"I do often, Daniel," she teased. "Let me fetch the girls." After affectionately squeezing his hand, she swept off to the back of the house.

He heard the rear door open and her call for his sisters. In seconds, feet pounded up the steps and two twin girls, shrieking happily, hurtled down the hall.

"Daniel! You're home!" they yelled simultaneously, launching themselves into his arms, a pile of ruffled dresses and dark hair. His heart swelled with love.

"I'm home, girls." *Almost all the way home.*

Her belongings relocated to a rented room near the center of town, Sarah went back to the Nob Hill house, tired and aching, to collect her bag and say farewell to the neighbors.

Ah Mong was seated on the porch when she arrived, his arms folded inside his sleeves. Right then, he looked like such a young and lost boy, and she wanted to hug him close, ruffle the blue-black hair always tightly knotted in a braid. But she needed more comforting than her neighbor's Chinese servant did.

"They have taken everything away?" he asked.

"They've taken everything that was mine." She lifted her bustle and plopped onto the porch next to him, her skirts billowing around her. Sarah stared at the street, watched a cart clip-clop up the road, a pair of children giggle as they tossed a ball. "I am going to miss this place desperately."

"I am sorry you must go, Miss Sarah."

"I'm not going far. The room I've rented is just a few blocks from the shop." Its proximity not very important, if customers didn't come and they couldn't pay the rent for long.

"But you will not be *here*," he contended. "For me to protect like Mr. Josiah asked."

"Oh, Ah Mong." She embraced him then, the silk of his tunic whispering against her sleeves. He squirmed when she held on too long. "I'll be safe enough where I'm going. Mr. Josiah would be satisfied that you'd done your duty."

The boy didn't appear convinced.

Sarah stood, brushing down the creases in her skirt, and smiled at him. "I'll send Mrs. McGinnis out with some lemonade, if there's any left and the glasses haven't all been stored away."

Inside the house, the furniture had been covered in sheets, the clocks allowed to wind down, the curtains drawn. Rufus's chair had been cleaned of fur and moved from the second floor landing. She hated to see it gone. She wandered into the parlor, feeling as empty as the echoing space, stripped of the paintings and the rug that had covered the table. Had it been only three weeks ago that the girls had gathered in this room and gossiped over the newly arrived Daniel Cady, blissfully unaware of what lay ahead?

The tears she'd held back all day slid down her cheeks.

"Miss Sarah." At the doorway to the parlor, Mrs. McGinnis's voice was gentle. "I've brought your portmanteau downstairs and thought you might want this."

She held out Josiah's small Bible, the one that had been secured in the box with the letters from his wife.

"It's Mr. Cady's, by right," said Sarah, wiping her face.

"Didna think he would have much use for a Bible. The heartless creature."

"Being heartless," Sarah responded, "I would have thought you'd say he has a greater use for it, not less."

"*Och*." The housekeeper fisted her hips. "He'd need to come back in order to claim the book, now wouldn't he?"

I shall be back, you know . . .

Sarah took it from her. "Maybe he'll surprise us," said Sarah, not permitting melancholy to color her voice.

Mrs. McGinnis looked skeptical. "Mr. Josiah would have preferred you keep it, Miss Sarah. You canna leave here with nothing of his."

"I have his portrait," she pointed out.

"That's *nae* what I mean, lass."

Sarah considered the book in her hands, small enough to fit within the span of her fingers, the tooled-leather cover supple and soft. She rubbed a thumb against the gilt-edged pages.

"A memento, then," she said. A memento of the man who'd loved her as dearly as any father ever loved a daughter. "Is there lemonade left? I promised Ah Mong some."

"Certainly there is, Miss Sarah." Mrs. McGinnis left to fetch a glass for the boy.

Sarah flipped back a corner of the cloth covering the parlor settee and perched on the edge. She started to leaf through the Bible and a scrap of paper fell out. Retrieving it, she saw that it was a pencil sketch she'd done of Josiah smoking a cigar by the garden cherub statue.

She wanted to laugh and cry at the same time. "Josiah, why did you save this? It wasn't even any good!"

He had tucked it inside a chapter of Matthew, using the sketch to keep his place. Some of the verses had been underlined—*No man can serve two masters: for either he will hate the one, and love the other; or else he will hold to the one, and despise the other. Ye cannot serve God and mammon. Therefore I say unto you, take no thought for your life, what ye shall eat, or what ye shall drink; nor yet for your body, what ye shall put on. Is not the life more than meat, and the body than raiment? Behold the fowls of the air: for they sow not, neither do they reap, nor gather into barns; yet your heavenly Father feedeth them. Are ye not much better than they?*

Across time, he was still speaking to her.

Have faith. Trust that God will take care of you.

Sarah firmed her grip on the Bible and gazed out the window, at the shadows lengthening between the houses and the trees rustling in the breeze. She could try again to have faith and trust in God. Her mother would tell her to try again.

God's mercy endures forever, Sarah Jane. It reaches from the highest heights to the deepest depths, and you are not beyond its grasp.

Try again.

She had nothing to lose.

Except hopelessness.

Two months later

"IT WILL TAKE SEVERAL PASSES through the press before the inked stone is ready to give up an image onto the paper, Phoebe," said Sarah. She observed the girl as she cranked the handle that slid the carriage beneath the press head, running the scraper over the leather tympan covering the lithograph stone and the test paper, her mouth fixed in a frown. "The entire process requires patience."

Phoebe blew a strand of hair out of her eyes and looked over. "I try to grab patience, Miss Sarah, but it escapes me."

Sarah smiled. Phoebe had come so far since she'd taken over the work once meant for Anne; she was more talented and far more patient than she gave herself credit for. "You are almost there, and I know Mrs. Linforth will be pleased with the final print."

"She would be more pleased if Anne had done it."

"Anne is too content in Seattle to come back here and save you, Phoebe," Sarah teased.

After more words of encouragement, Sarah stepped around the partition separating the lithograph area from the main shop, looked around her, and felt satisfaction. The first-floor space was much smaller than the shop they'd had on Sansome and not a corner location, but this one was thirty dollars a month cheaper and good enough for Pacific Custom Design Studio. At Sarah's request, Mr. Pomroy had helped them locate a less expensive location and had generously negotiated the favorable lease rate. Also, contrary to his worst fears, the news story about her past in Los Angeles hadn't chased away customers. In fact, Sarah thought, the bad press had had the opposite effect. Folks were either very forgiving or insatiably curious about the "notorious Miss Whittier." And once they were inside the shop, anyone could see the quality of the work on display.

Sweeping fingertips across her *Rêve d'Or* brooch and wishing her mother could be there to share her satisfaction, Sarah strolled through the new shop. She straightened a watercolor of the Seal Rocks she'd recently finished and hung on the wall, buffed away a miniscule smudge on one of the glass cases. Turned her attention to the girls. Cora was touching up a border of flowers on a hand-painted plate. Minnie was helping a customer review possible designs for an advertising poster and Emma, Sarah knew, was working on the accounts in her compact room at the back.

She was blessed. More blessed than she would have dreamed just two months ago. They had trusted in God and managed to find a way. Survival had required that she sell every painting and miniature she could, and she'd also needed to take on a few art students who weren't deterred by the scandal. With the help of Mr. Samuelson's loan and the girls' generous offers of reduced pay—Sarah had insisted they accept some money, and soon she'd be able to increase their salaries to the amount she'd originally promised—they had definitely found a way.

The shop bell rang and Lottie swept through the opening, a sudden wind catching the robin's-egg-blue feathers in her coordinating hat. The color was high in her cheeks and she looked, if possible, even lovelier than she had before she'd been sent to

St. Helena. She'd been allowed to return to San Francisco after the Lawsons had repeatedly asked after her, finally dropping a strong hint that their very eligible son was missing her company. Mrs. Samuelson, informed by Mr. Samuelson via telegram of this development, had put Lottie on the next train home.

"You will never believe what I discovered about the auction, Sarah," she said, making a quick perusal of Cora's artwork and complimenting the girl.

"You didn't leave Gabriel outside, did you?" asked Sarah, searching through the large shop windows for the angular features of Lottie's beau, but two easels displaying watercolors obscured her view of the sidewalk.

"He dropped me off. He had business to attend at the shipping office and could not come in." Her eyes were bright with the thought of him. "I shall see him at supper tonight."

Sarah felt the briefest twinge of envy over Lottie's happiness. She was content with her life as it was, however, and wanted only the best for Daniel. He'd sent a solitary telegram three weeks after he'd left San Francisco saying he was in Chicago with his sisters and that was all. No words of affection. No more promises of return.

"I was hoping to see Gabriel," Sarah said, focusing on matters that were under her control, "in order to thank him for kindly recommending our services to his sister-in-law. She has commissioned a lovely set of invitations—"

"Sarah!" Lottie sounded impatient. "I apologize for interrupting, but do you not want to hear what I learned about the house auction and why it never took place?"

Sarah folded her arms and tilted her head. "What did you learn, Miss Samuelson, that is so urgent for me to know?"

"The auction was not halted because there was some issue with the deed, as we had surmised," she answered, pausing dramatically. "It never occurred because Mr. Cady contacted the real estate agent and told him to cancel it!"

"Why would he do that?"

Lottie's brows perked and her eyes took on the most mischievous gleam. "Perhaps you should go outside and ask him."

Sarah's breath stuttered and she didn't dare move for fear the moment and Lottie's words would prove to be an illusion and the least motion would shatter them. *He is here.*

"Oh!" gasped Cora, exchanging looks with Minnie.

Sarah hadn't realized the girls had been listening. Thank goodness the customer had left and not been witness to Sarah's befuddlement.

Minnie grinned at her. "Hurry up, Miss Sarah, before he gets away!"

Sarah fumbled with the strings of her apron, yanking it off and tossing it aside. "If he's come all the way from Chicago, Minnie, he's not going to get away." He had come all the way from Chicago.

At last.

Lottie winked and held open the shop door. Sarah forced herself to walk at a sedate pace, even though she wanted to run and see for herself that Daniel was really outside and that Lottie wasn't fooling. Fling herself into those arms she'd been dreaming of for two long months.

He was leaning against a telegraph pole, one ankle crossed over the other, a new hat cocked at a tilt upon his head. A small crate sat by his feet, but Sarah didn't waste time pondering what was inside, when all she could do was gaze at him and let joy fill her heart.

"About time, Miss Whittier," he said, with a smile. He was smiling. "I was starting to wonder if Miss Samuelson had forgotten to deliver my message."

"Lottie can always be relied upon." Sarah crossed to where he stood. As ever, he smelled of lime shaving lotion, and his eyes were as impossibly green as she remembered. For the first time she could recall, they were free of the bitterness that had once haunted him. He had changed.

She had changed, as well.

"I must say, Mr. Cady, you continue to have the most interesting tendency to show up when you're least expected." She wanted to embrace him, right then and there. She would probably bring the passing traffic to a shuddering halt if she did.

"Does that mean you're happy to see me, or unhappy?" he asked, reaching out to tuck a loose strand of hair behind her ear, the skim of his fingertips against her temple sending a thrill through her.

"Very happy," she replied simply.

He nodded down at the crate. "And what about this fellow?"

Just then, a protesting mewl sounded and Sarah noticed a flash of orange in the gaps between the slats. "Rufus!" Sarah cried, lifting the hinged lid. The cat jumped free of the box and into her arms. "I'd given up on you."

"We have both returned, Sarah," Daniel said quietly.

"Thank you." She lifted on her toes and brushed a kiss against his cheekbone. A dark-gowned matron exiting a neighboring bank clucked disapprovingly over the display. "Where did you find the silly cat?"

"I decided to show my sisters the house yesterday, after we arrived, and he was sleeping on the porch as if he'd never left."

Sarah twined her fingers through Rufus's fur. "You brought your sisters?"

"Since San Francisco is where they're going to be living from now on, I pretty well needed to."

He'd come back and he'd come to stay. "That's why you didn't sell the house."

"Lily and Marguerite need a roof for them and their substantial doll collection, and I had to find somewhere to hang a watercolor painted by a very talented local artist." He inhaled deeply and dashed his hat from his head in order to curl the brim beneath his fingers. Another hat ruined. "Say you'll live there with us,

Sarah. You love that house and you'll get along with my sisters. I know you will."

Was he asking what she thought he was asking? "I do love that house," she said cautiously.

His fingers paused while his eyes searched her face. "If you still care about that French fellow, let me know right now before I say something stupid."

"Edouard?"

"Do you still care for him?" he asked.

Sarah drew a hand along Rufus's back and off the end of his tail. She'd never seen Daniel so flustered. "No, Daniel, I don't care about Edouard at all."

He gave a small nod, his shoulders relaxing. "Then tell me you'll marry me. I love you. Marry me."

Her breath caught. "Oh, Daniel."

He lifted one eyebrow. Just as his father might. "Was that a yes, Miss Whittier?"

Shifting Rufus out of the way and without a concern about the traffic, she kissed Daniel full on the lips. Behind the shop windows, a cheer went up and Cora broke out singing an Irish tune.

"Yes, Mr. Cady," Sarah said, laughing, and kissed him again.

"*Oui*, I have the money." He woefully contemplated the contents of his wallet. Over the past four years, abundant charm supplemented by nine hundred dollars' worth of gold had not gone quite as far as he had hoped.

Extracting two bills, he handed them over to the waiter standing at the exit. This restaurant hired excessively pugnacious ones, he thought, and there was really no need for the fellow to glower as he was.

"It was a most agreeable luncheon. *Merci*," he offered, together with a smile that did nothing toward improving the waiter's mood. The dollars had vanished into the depths of a vest pocket within seconds of their entering the man's grasp. Edouard desperately wished them back. The meal and the company had not turned out to be worth the expenditure of his very, very precious funds.

His company leaned against his arm as they stepped onto the sidewalk, the strong floral of her perfume washing over him, causing his nose to run. "Monsieur Marchand, thank you ever so much."

She batted her eyelashes in what she must have imagined was coquetry. They had been together for only a few weeks, after her husband had hired Edouard to paint her portrait, but already he was bored of her giggles and flirtations. Once it had become clear which direction the money would flow—and not in his favor, aside from the measly sum he would eventually be paid for an uninspired oil rendering—he had stopped pretending he didn't notice how unattractive she was.

There had been pretty ones, in the years since he'd hopped a steamer in San Francisco. A desperately appreciative widow in Vancouver, a delightful mademoiselle in Quebec. He had even enjoyed the company of an apple-cheeked schoolteacher in Montana whom he'd thought, albeit briefly, of honoring with the last name of Marchand. The last time he'd entertained that notion hadn't lasted long either and had nearly led to disaster. Sweet Sarah. He did wonder what had become of her.

The woman at his side noticed his distraction and tugged, hard, on his arm. "Monsieur Marchand," she said, coquetry dropped, her voice edged like a straight razor. He pitied her husband. "Are you taking me to the art gallery or are we going to stand here like two bumps on a log?"

He lifted a corner of his mouth, a meltingly charming smile that had never failed on a single female he had ever encountered. "*Mon chouchou*, I intend to sweep you off your pretty feet and show this town that I am escorting its loveliest lady."

She dimpled and batted her eyelashes again. "Monsieur, how can I ever thank you?"

He had an idea and it involved an almost empty bank account, but he knew that wasn't what she was thinking. Inside, he quailed.

"Your smiles are thanks enough," he said, pulling her forward, hoping she hadn't observed the despair and misery that had to have flashed across his face.

The weeks flew past, the summer departing with them, until September arrived. The month of their wedding, thought Sarah, and in this very garden, among the last blossoms of the roses, white alyssum, and violet-blue lobelia, by the marble cherub statue that Josiah had so adored.

Lily and Marguerite sat painting in the midday sunshine, their heads close together as they whispered secrets to each other, the coils of their dark hair resting against their identical cheeks. Lily, the most attentive of the twins, looked up when she heard Sarah descending the rear steps from the kitchen.

"Sarah, come and see. Marguerite has painted the strangest rose ever!"

"Lily," her sister complained, "don't be so mean!" But then she giggled, knowing her sister was only joshing. The girls laughed often. When they weren't whispering. "It really is awful, Sarah. Tell me I can stop trying and can go inside to help Mrs. McGinnis make shortbread."

Sarah inspected her painting. Although the girls were almost physically indistinguishable—and Sarah had spent the weeks since they had been in San Francisco making plenty of mistakes when it came to addressing them—they did not have identical personalities or abilities. Lily was quick-witted and more sociable, Marguerite more apt to weigh her thoughts and not as talented as Lily seemed to be at everything. They were loved equally, however, by one doting brother and his future wife.

"Marguerite, it is not awful, but you are thinking too hard

about the underlying pencil work and not letting the lines flow." Sarah bent down to demonstrate, her hand sure as she sketched petals and sepals and stem.

"I will never be that good," said Marguerite, while Lily watched with rapt attention.

"I wasn't always, either." She handed back the pencil and straightened. "I had a very good instructor."

She could mention Edouard without any of the regret or sorrow she'd once felt. With Daniel, she'd come to know real love and had asked God to forgive her foolish heart. She was at peace.

"I think you've both done enough painting today," she announced. "Clean the brushes, scrub your hands, and go help Mrs. McGinnis with that shortbread. Your brother should be here soon and he'll be looking forward to lunch."

They hastened to tidy up and then raced each other to the back door, almost colliding with Daniel as he stepped through.

"Whoa, you wild animals!" he exclaimed, evading both them and Rufus, who had chosen the same moment to dart out of the house and into the garden to chase a sparrow.

"Sorry!" the girls said in unison, ducking by him.

"With my sisters living here, you know we'll never have a moment's quiet," he said, coming up behind Sarah as she folded the girls' painting aprons. Wrapping his arms around her waist, he tucked her close and pressed a kiss to the top of her head. "Good morning, Miss Whittier. Glad you're home. I was afraid you might be at the shop."

"Lottie's managing the studio today." Sarah set down the aprons and leaned against his chest, reveling in the feel of him. Soon, she would have Daniel every morning and every evening, no longer needing to separate at day's end when he returned to the hotel and she shooed two energetic young girls to their bedrooms before collapsing on her own bed, happily worn out by work and the making of wedding plans. Eight more days. That was all. "And I believe it is afternoon, Mr. Cady."

He spun her within the circle of his arms until she faced him. "Sinclair likes to talk almost as much as he likes to eat breakfast, but his real estate agent friend has settled the Placerville property sale. That land is going to bring enough money to let me establish my import business, so the meeting was worthwhile." He smiled and dropped a kiss on her forehead. "Although why I let him ramble on when I could be here with you, doing this . . ." The kiss moved down her face to her lips, and she lost all sense of place or time.

Eventually, she pulled away but not out of his arms, her face warm, her heart filled with love. "Mrs. McGinnis will be waiting lunch for us."

"She can wait a few more minutes." He lifted one of her hands and brushed his lips across the back of her fingers, his gaze never leaving her eyes. "Who would've thought when I came to San Francisco looking for Josiah's money that I would find you instead? I thank God every day, Sarah."

"As do I, Daniel." *Thank You, Lord. Thank You.* Smiling, Sarah slipped her fingers free and tidied his collar, knocked askew by their embrace. "Did you ever hear from the Grays?"

"I did. I got a telegram this morning, in fact. They send their best wishes, but, no surprise with the baby just having been born, they won't be traveling west to visit for some time." He sighed. "I do wish—"

"We agreed to not let your grandparents spoil our happiness," Sarah interrupted, knowing what he was about to say. They had invited the Hunts to their wedding and upon receiving no reply, had both decided to wish them well and try to forget all their cruelties. "So let's not mention them."

"At least your aunt and uncle are coming to our wedding," he said.

It was going to be an uncomfortable reunion, the only possible cloud over the most wonderful day of her life. But they had agreed to attend, surprising Sarah, and she would do her best to heal old wounds. "Tell me again you won't be mad at them for how they once treated me, Daniel."

"I'm too happy to be mad at anyone. Even your aunt and uncle. Even my grandparents." He twined her arm around his and held it against his waist. "I am hungry, Miss Whittier, and would like some of your housekeeper's excellent lunch. Shall you accompany me?"

"My pleasure, Mr. Cady." She smiled her fullest smile. "My dearest one."

He matched her smile with a wicked grin of his own. "Keep talking like that and we might have to skip lunch altogether."

She laughed. "Come on, you incorrigible man."

So together they strolled across the garden toward the house. The house where they would share love. Create a family. Build a future.

"You know," Daniel said, "I wouldn't have minded if more nuggets had turned up. I would've bought you the fanciest diamond ring in town."

"You are the only treasure I need, Daniel," Sarah responded. *The greatest of Josiah's treasures—his son and my beloved. The treasure of my heart.* "The only treasure I will ever want."

He hugged her in tight as they climbed the back steps and chuckled. "Yes, indeed, Miss Whittier, I like the way you talk."

Acknowledgments

Grateful thanks go:

To, as ever, my agent, Natasha Kern – for your tireless support and thoughtful critiques. My work is always better because of you.

To Candace Calvert – you have read everything I've ever written . . . and propped me up more times than I can count. Bless you!

To Donna, Pat, Beth – looking forward to many more afternoons spent talking shop. You guys are the best.

To the folks at Worthy – for your patience and prayers during a difficult year.

To my family – who else would put up with me!

And lastly to my readers – I do this for you. You have all my appreciation.

Nancy Herriman retired from a career as an engineer to chase around two small children and take up the pen. She hasn't looked back. To her delight, her writing has received enthusiastic praise from readers, best-selling authors, and industry insiders alike. When she is not writing, or gabbing over lattes about writing, she is either watching history shows on TV or performing with various choral groups. She lives in Ohio with her husband and sons, and wishes there were more hours in the day. Learn more online at www.nancyherriman.com.

If you enjoyed this book, will you consider sharing the message with others?

- Mention the book in a Facebook post, Twitter update, Pinterest pin, or blog post.
- Recommend this book to those in your small group, book club, workplace, and classes.
- Head over to facebook.com/Author.NancyHerriman, "LIKE" the page and post a comment as to what you enjoyed the most.
- Tweet "I recommend reading #Josiah'sTreasure by @Nancy_Herriman // @worthypub"
- Pick up a copy for someone you know who would be challenged and encouraged by this message.
- Write a review on amazon.com, bn.com or cbd.com.

You can subscribe to Worthy Publishing's newsletter at worthypublishing.com.

Worthy Publishing Facebook Page

Worthy Publishing Website